Mary Mackie has been writing since the age
and has written numerous romances and historicals under
various pseudonyms. She has also written two non-fiction
books, *Cobwebs and Cream Teas* and *Dry Rot and
Daffodils*, about her and her husband's experiences
administering a Norfolk National Trust property. She has
two adult children and currently lives near King's Lynn
with her husband.

Also by Mary Mackie

Sandringham Rose
A Child of Secrets

The Clouded Land

Mary Mackie

HEADLINE

First published in 1994 by
HEADLINE BOOK PUBLISHING

First published in paperback in 1995 by
HEADLINE BOOK PUBLISHING

10 9 8 7 6 5 4 3 2 1

ISBN 0 7472 4684 X

Typeset by Avon Dataset Ltd., Bidford-on-Avon, B50 4JH

Printed and bound in Great Britain by
Cox & Wyman Ltd, Reading, Berks

HEADLINE BOOK PUBLISHING
A division of Hodder Headline PLC
338 Euston Road,
London NW1 3BH

For Mum, who, being born in 1914,
has always said she was probably
the cause of the conflict!

With love and thanks
for support and encouragement
over half a century

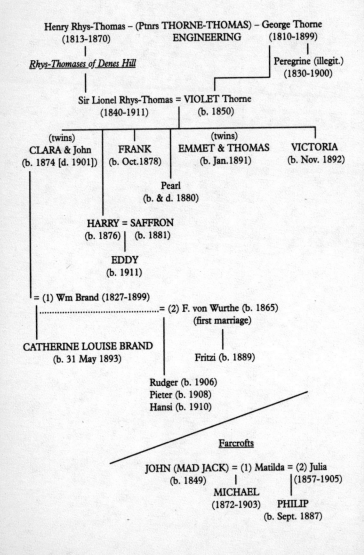

Henry Rhys-Thomas – (Ptnrs THORNE-THOMAS) – George Thorne
(1813-1870)   ENGINEERING   (1810-1899)

Rhys-Thomases of Denes Hill

Peregrine (illegit.)
(1830-1900)

Sir Lionel Rhys-Thomas = VIOLET Thorne
(1840-1911)   (b. 1850)

(twins)   (twins)
CLARA & John   FRANK   EMMET & THOMAS   VICTORIA
(b. 1874 [d. 1901])   (b. Oct.1878)   (b. Jan.1891)   (b. Nov. 1892)

Pearl
(b. & d. 1880)

HARRY = SAFFRON
(b. 1876) | (b. 1881)

EDDY
(b. 1911)

= (1) Wm Brand (1827-1899)
....= (2) F. von Wurthe (b. 1865)
                                     (first marriage)

CATHERINE LOUISE BRAND
(b. 31 May 1893)

Fritzi (b. 1889)

Rudger (b. 1906)
Pieter (b. 1908)
Hansi (b. 1910)

Farcrofts

JOHN (MAD JACK) = (1) Matilda = (2) Julia
(b. 1849) | (1857-1905)
           MICHAEL
           (1872-1903)   PHILIP
                     (b. Sept. 1887)

When my grandmother died recently, the sorting out of her belongings was left to me. I found it a saddening task, but I couldn't help feeling that she herself was happy at last.

I loved to listen to her talk about her life. Such a long, colourful life, stretching all the way from the last years of Queen Victoria. She was a crusading journalist, a great voice in the women's cause, a staunch pacifist, a local councillor and supporter of many charities; she was also a supportive mother, and a fond grandparent. I thought I knew all about her. Now I realize that what she allowed me to share was an edited version, for among her belongings I discovered a manuscript, written some years ago in a clear, firm hand.

The accompanying letter was more recent, addressed to me in writing gone spidery with age. Now at last I understand some of the hints she let drop, with her ice-blue eyes sparkling. She had secrets she was keeping. But she wanted me to know the truth, in the end.

My dear Maggie,
You have often asked me about my life and let me indulge myself in recounting my memories. Bless you for that. An old woman does love to reminisce.

You've also been kind enough to say that my story is worth recording. Be that as it may, some years ago I did put pen to paper – you will remember the time I

1

was convalescing from surgery and had nothing to do but read and scribble. I began this account then, and I found it so absorbing a pastime that I continued it. I've tried to be as honest as I can – that's why I intend to keep it to myself until after I'm gone, to spare my own blushes. It may be a little too frank in places, but I believe you will understand and not be too appalled by the things your ancient grandmother did, and said, and thought, in the days when she and the world were young.

I still vividly remember the spring and summer of 1911, the year I turned eighteen. To be young, then, in Germany, was a magical thing. Youth was the hope, the inspiration, of a nation riding high on arrogance and optimism.

Die wunderschönen Tage! *Those wonderful days! A time of dancing, swimming and boating, horse riding and playing tennis. How we laughed, my three handsome escorts and I, as we motored in Willi's new Benz, noisily weaving through the streets of Berlin, sending horse-drawn carts scattering, tooting the horn to waken wooded suburbs. That's how I learned to drive, zooming at fifteen miles an hour along the lakeside with dust flying in the faces of enraged elder citizens out exercising their dogs. We were rich, youthful, members of the élite, children of the Fatherland. The world was at our feet.*

But even then, in quiet moments when I let myself slow down from the whirl of playing out those merry hours, I could sense the clouds gathering. Changes were coming. How great, I didn't then guess. And for me, personally, the ending of the idyll was to be swift and painful.

ONE

Waking abruptly, from a fitful, dream-filled sleep, I found the cabin airless and my body drenched in sweat. My corset and drawers clung to my skin; even my camisole was damp. Faint moonlight glowed behind the curtain at the porthole. The shuddering throb of the steamer's engine rattled every bone in my body and, from the bunk below, my companion's snores had grown so loud that further sleep was impossible. Moving as quietly as I could, I tossed back the single sheet that covered me and slid my bare feet to the rungs of the ladder.

My stomach felt uneasy, perhaps because it was empty. On the long rail journey that had swallowed yesterday in a haze of unreality, I had only picked at my food. Now I needed air. I could hardly breathe in the close, humid atmosphere of the cabin aboard the SS *Medusa*.

Groping in the darkness for my clothes, I donned them with fumbling slowness, then bent to feel for my shoes. As I did so, my hair let loose a final pin and fell heavily over my shoulder. I shook it back and combed it out with my fingers. Dishevelment hardly mattered. At that small hour of the morning, no one would see me.

The slight snick of the latch caused the snoring behind me to pause. The sleeper turned over, making the mattress rustle, then settled back into a steady rhythm as I slipped out into deep shadow, taking a welcome breath of fresher air, tangy with salt. A few yards away, bright moonlight sliced across the upper deck. Overhead, the stack belched a mixture of smoke and steam that hung in blobs, small clouds dotting our route across a rippled sea so calm it looked more like pond than ocean. And, behind the ship, the wake opened foaming, silvered arms, as if yearning, as I was, for the receding coastline.

But I mustn't look back. Ahead, like pale clouds spread low across a dark horizon, England was waiting.

Slowly, bracing myself against the juddering and swaying of the ship, I made my way down to the lower deck and stood at the rail to let the breeze ruffle my hair. My hand found its way into my pocket, where I felt the edges of the folded paper secreted there. That hateful letter . . .

'You all right, dearie?'

The voice jerked me out of bleak thoughts and I looked round to see beside me one of my fellow passengers from yesterday's train. 'Thank you. Yes,' I replied, and turned my head away, blinking wet lashes.

Until she spoke I hadn't realized I was weeping. My mind had been miles away, back in Berlin.

'Lor', but it's hot!' The young woman made a pantomime of fanning herself with her hands, and gave up with a little grimace that laughed at her own efforts. 'Hot? *Heiss?* Sorry, dear, you probably don't understand a word I'm saying. Only, I could have sworn I'd heard you talking English to that man you're travelling with.'

Of course. Though travelling second class, this fair-haired young woman had, I now recalled, spent the entire journey across Europe parading up and down the first-class corridor, solely for the purpose of making eyes at my escort. I was tempted to prevaricate, to pretend that I didn't understand her, but, 'I *am* English,' I replied.

'Are you? But . . . the conductor on the train reckoned you were German. Fraulein von—'

'You were asking about me?'

She hesitated, confused, then excused herself, 'Only out of interest, dear. You know – being cooped up on the same train and all.'

'Quite.' Deliberately turning my shoulder, I moved a few paces on along the rail, towards the stern, using my fingers to wipe away the remnants of tears beneath my eyes. I wished she would go away. Friendly as she seemed, I was in no mood for conversation; I had come on deck only for some air, and to think. The events of the past two days seemed like a bad dream, but, if I doubted my memory, the letter in my pocket provided tangible proof that all was true.

'Anyway,' the bright voice said at my elbow, 'I said to Elsie – that's my friend, the red-headed one, you may have noticed her. There's seven of us. Call ourselves the Gala Girls – song-and-dance troupe. We've been doing a six-week tour of the old Continong. Paris, Amsterdam, Berlin . . . Anyway, I said to Elsie, I'm sure I heard that young lady talking English. But the conductor said your name was Fraulein von Wurthe.'

Her face, lifted to mine, was alight with friendly curiosity, reminding me of an overeager puppy. Perhaps, at that hour, in mid-Channel, caught between future and past, one world and another, it was good not to be the only one awake and restless.

'That is correct. I am called Katarin von Wurthe.'

'Pleased to make your acquaintance, I'm sure.' She stuck out a hand, giving me a smile so disarming that I found myself shaking hands with her. 'My name's Love,' she told me. 'Judy Love. You don't mind me chatting like this, do

you? Only, we both seem to be in the same boat and—'
Hearing what she had said, she laughed aloud. 'That's good
– "in the same boat". We are, aren't we, without a word of
a lie? No, I meant . . . neither of us can sleep and it's the
middle of the night and all. Stupid to stand on ceremony. I
don't know about you, but I'm glad of someone to talk to. I
was dreading this voyage. Last time I was sick as a pig the
whole time. Mind you, it was rougher then. It's like a
millpond tonight.'

'Yes.' Resigning myself to continuing the acquaintance,
I studied her from a corner of my eye. She held her big-
brimmed hat with its overblown roses in one hand, leaving
her piled butter-blond hair bare, strands falling loose round
her face and neck. Her flounced blouse and tunic-style skirt
were of cheap material, crumpled and soiled from travelling.
From the way she minced when she walked, I guessed she
was wearing a hobble garter under that narrow-hemmed
skirt – the latest Paris fashion, over which Mother and I
had argued bitterly.

At the thought, a wave of homesickness assailed me.
What wouldn't I give to be arguing now about hobble skirts,
and whether it was right for me to wear a revealing
décolletage, or pad my hair to balance a hat draped with a
dozen ostrich feathers . . .

'I hoped I'd be able to sleep tonight,' Judy Love was
saying, 'but it's stifling in that lower-deck saloon. I expect
you've got a cabin, have you? Hot in there, too, was it?'

'I slept for a while,' I conceded, 'but I was having bad
dreams, and the snoring from the other bunk was so loud.
In the end, I decided it might be better out here on deck. At
least it's quiet.'

She was staring at me in a strange way, her mouth half
open. 'You . . . you're *sharing* a cabin?'

'Unfortunately so. We were late in booking. Mrs Joosens was not pleased to be asked to share, but when the problem was explained to her—'

'Mrs Joosens?'

'The fat Dutch lady who joined the train at Oldenzaal yesterday. You must have seen her – mountains of pigskin luggage.'

'Oh – oh, yes, I did, now you mention it. So it's her you're sharing with?'

'Of course.' The relief on her face gave me pause. 'Why, what did you think?'

'I thought you meant . . .' Despite the moonlight, I could see her colour had risen, darkening her plump cheeks. 'No, nothing, dear. Take no notice of me. You're obviously a young lady. I told Elsie she was barking up the wrong tree.'

'*Liebe Zeite!*' I managed. 'Are you suggesting that Mr Wells and I—'

'Oh, not *me*, dear. That's what my friend Elsie said. She makes up stories about people. To while away the time, you know. She reckoned your gentleman friend was probably a playboy. And you travelling incognito as his niece, or something, dressed up like a schoolgirl to make it look innocent. And then when you mentioned snoring, I thought, well . . .'

Part of me was affronted by her suggestion; another part was amused, even flattered. To be taken for Mr Wells's mistress . . . Even Mother had displayed few qualms at allowing me to travel with him. But then, it would not occur to her to imagine anything improper between two such unlikely candidates as her unremarkable daughter and the handsome man who had once been the idol of her own set.

She had kept me young in clothes and manners even after I grew taller than she. Only on my eighteenth birthday, nearly three months ago, had I been allowed to put my hair up for the first time. For this present journey I had been made to dress like a schoolgirl, though I had left the boater, and the navy jacket with its silly sailor collar, back in the sweltering cabin. If Mother could have seen me, out on the open deck in such a state of unladylike undress, with my hair falling loose, she would probably have fainted.

But then – the thought came sneaking like a naughty boy after apples – while I was in England Mother wouldn't be there to adjudicate over every item of my clothing. If I accepted the college place which my uncle Frank had arranged for me, I might stop being the prim young miss just out of the schoolroom and become my own woman. I might even defy all decrees and study journalism, after all.

But the spurt of rebellion died as swiftly as it had risen: I did not want to be in England. I wanted to go home! I wanted to see Carl-Heinz and have him tell me it was all a mistake, that in truth he loved me still. But I couldn't even recall his face. All I could see was Willi, staring with such fierce, cold triumph. It had been he who delivered the letter . . .

'Should've listened to my own head, not Elsie's silly notions,' Judy Love was saying apologetically. 'I mean, your Mr Wells may be a bit of a dandy, but he's probably a real gentleman.' She slid me a sidelong look, adding, 'Married, is he?'

'I've no idea.'

'Is he your guardian?'

'He's more in the way of a postman delivering a special package,' I informed her wryly. 'His responsibilities will end once we reach . . . once we reach our destination.' I had almost said 'home', but Denes Hill was not my home, nor ever would be. 'I hardly know him. He's my grandfather's solicitor. That's where we're going – to my grandfather's house.'

'In London?' she asked hopefully.

'In Norfolk. Though I may go to college in London if . . .'

But it was not *my* movements that interested her. 'Is that where Mr Wells lives, too – in Norfolk?'

'As far as I know.'

'Just my luck.' Wistfully, she added, 'Ever so good-looking, isn't he?'

'Is he?'

'Hadn't you noticed? Lor', dearie, you *are* young.'

'I'm turned eighteen!' I said, stung.

Her smile turned lopsided. 'Quite an old lady, then. Lor', it seems an age since I was eighteen.' She sighed. 'A lot can happen to a girl in five years, you mark my words. Anyway . . . tell me about Norfolk. I've never been there. What's it like?'

'I don't remember much.' Letting out a long breath, I stared out across the moon-glimmering sea. 'We left in the spring of . . . it must have been nineteen-oh-two. I was eight at the time. But we hadn't been there long. Less than two years.'

'So where were you before that?'

It was a long time since I had thought of the years before Berlin. Now the mists stirred and glimpses of the far past appeared, sluggish with disuse – a secure, sunlit childhood, in a big house in a valley by a river, with green mountains soaring all around . . .

'I was born in Cumberland,' I said aloud. 'But Mother took me back to Denes Hill – my grandfather's house in Norfolk – after my father died. It was there that she met my stepfather, Friedrich von Wurthe. He was in the German diplomatic service, attached to the Embassy in London. He

10

used to come and stay at Sandringham, which is quite near Denes Hill.'

'Sandringham – the King's house?' she asked, impressed.

'That's right. King Edward took a fancy to Pa and often invited him to stay at Sandringham, so I understand. Queen Alexandra – I should say the Queen Dowager now, I suppose – she has a small house on the beach where her guests sometimes go. For private visits. Quite informal.'

She was regarding me with open-mouthed awe. 'You mean . . . you're acquainted with the royal family?'

'I played on the beach with the young princes and princesses – King George's children – and their cousins. And I once had tea in the garden at Queen Alexandra's bungalow. That's how Mother met Pa – at the beach. But after they were married we went to live in Berlin. My stepfather is now chairman of the von Wurthe bank.'

'Lor'!' She flapped her eyelashes alarmingly. 'And me and Elsie had the nerve to— If I'd known who you were, I'd never have dared speak to you.'

'Whyever not? I'm no one. I'm no different from you.' At that moment I felt it to be true – she and I were two human females, swept together for a brief hour, like leaves on an eddying stream. With the dawn, fate's current would separate us, probably for ever, but for this moment we were equals. Besides, apart from my background, what did I have to commend me? I was a girlchild, a stepchild, not especially beautiful, nor especially talented, and with few prospects. Indeed, it seemed to me on that night, with my life poised at a crossroads, that I no longer knew who I was or where I belonged. Even my name was borrowed: though for convenience I had been known as Katarin von Wurthe, my real name was Catherine Louise Brand.

Of my own father, William Brand, I knew little – I

remembered him only as a terrifying creature confined to a stifling, malodorous sickroom. Mother had been awfully young when they married, scarcely older than I was now, and widowed after a few years. But that was long ago, of no importance. More sharp in my mind was the immediate past – the last few unhappy days, culminating in the letter I still clutched in my sweating palm. It seemed like a live thing, pulsating there against my flesh.

I found I wanted to talk, to say aloud what was in my mind and discover for myself what I felt about it. Leaning on the rail, watching the silvered wake churn up the sea, forming a curve that stretched far behind us, I said, 'I'm not even sure what I'm doing here, except that my family decided I might be safer in England. Because of the danger.'

'What danger?'

'Why . . .' I looked at her in disbelief. How could she not know? 'The danger of a European war. Surely you've been aware of it?'

'Oh, that's rubbish!' she broke in, dismissing rumours of international unrest with a flip of her hand. 'Everybody said there'd be a war last year, but it never happened, did it? There won't be any war now, you'll see. I said to Elsie, the newspapers love to blow things up out of all proportion. Bang the drum a bit and the men start strutting about, going all patriotic.'

'I think it's a little more serious than that,' I said.

'Oh, it'll blow over. After all, your Kaiser's a first cousin to our King. Your Crown Prince was a guest at the coronation in London only a few weeks ago, wasn't he? I know there's lots of soldiers everywhere in Germany, but they just like to dress up and strut about. It's in the Prussian blood. Very smart and handsome they are, too. I had my share of officers queuing at the stage door, I can tell you. Think about it, dear – if things were as bad as they reckon, would me and my friends have been shown such a good time in Berlin, us being British and all?'

Doubtfully, I answered, 'Even so . . .' The eastern sky began to lighten with dawn over the low contours of England as I thought back on the events which had brought me to this night. All at once I was seeing things with a cold clarity that burned my brain as, for the first time, I began to perceive a pattern I had not recognized before. Was it possible? Had the threat of war been only an excuse? Had my family colluded in sending me into exile solely because I had dared to love the wrong man?

What I knew of politics then was what I heard at the dinner table, what I read in the headlines and what my friends said. But even I knew that, for some years past, a feeling of grievance had been stirring in Germany.

In that summer of 1911, unrest had woven itself deeper into the fabric of our lives. The papers had been full of patriotic bluster concerning a place called Agadir in Morocco, where France had done something that had forced the German government to send a gunboat. In response, Britain's Mr Lloyd George had made an inflammatory speech, issuing a warning which had antagonized all Germans. In the streets of Berlin one had felt anger growing and wherever a group gathered there had been talk of war. Germany would not be threatened. Not for long! Tempers grew short. The Berlin bear was growling, the Prussian eagle testing his wings to defend his eyrie . . .

Understanding few of the deeper ramifications, I was disquieted when Mother and Pa began to talk of sending me away to England because of the danger. How could trouble in far-off Morocco possibly spread to reach us in Berlin?

The unrest disturbed the business community and the resulting uncertainty set my stepfather on edge. He came home late from the bank, looking more and more harassed. He ate his dinner hurriedly, which gave him indigestion, which in turn made him snappish. His moods unsettled the entire household. That was why Mother had become especially nervy and anxious for my safety, I decided. We were all out of sorts, what with the sultry weather, and the worry, and the wild talk ... Being absorbed in my own immediate, private concerns, I dismissed more distant thunders.

Mother and I had never been close. When I was young I always felt that I was a nuisance to her and nothing I did ever pleased her. I was never good enough, or pretty enough, though as I grew up and became useful she tolerated me more. She had, anyway, her new family to think of – at regular intervals, two years apart, she had given Pa three sons, my little half-brothers Rudger, Pieter and Hansi. Pa also had a son from his first marriage – Fritzi, a few years my senior. He had been away, at school and military college, most of the time I was in Berlin. Even so, I had grown fond of him and regarded him as a big brother.

My stepfamily had readily accepted me and been kind, if not openly affectionate – displays of emotion were despised by the Prussian male. But, though Pa had a soft spot for me as the only girl in the family, he believed in discipline and expected unquestioning obedience from all of us. He had insisted that Mother and I should speak German unless we were alone, but that was no problem: I had soon become bilingual. As I grew up, however, I developed a mind of my own and lately I had found myself more and more in conflict with Pa. He didn't like being argued with, especially by a young woman. Nor did he approve of my ambition to study journalism. I suspect he was instrumental in having the University of Berlin turn down my application for a place – a blow which ruined my plans for the future. And when he discovered I had been to hear the socialist campaigner, Clara Zetkin, speak, he forbade me to go out of the house for a whole week; he even burned the piece I had written about it and, for a while, relations between us were openly hostile. Torn between us, Mother sided with Pa. She always did.

The distraction of my eighteenth birthday, and putting my hair up, was followed by my first proper grown-up ball at the officers' mess at the military academy. I wore a gown of palest dove satin, trimmed with pink lace, and my dance card was full all evening. My stepbrother Fritzi escorted me, along with his best friends Carl-Heinz von Siemens and Willi von Sturm, all three of them scions of old, aristocratic families, all officers of the Third Hussars, currently attached to the Crown Prince's guard, tall and fair and fine in their braided uniforms with swords at their sides. The Kaiser loved military accoutrements – parades, uniforms, horses and all the show of Prussian military might – and Berlin was full of fine young soldiers, who went everywhere in uniform, giving a colourful gloss to the crowded streets. But none were finer than my three champions. They called themselves my musketeers, and dubbed me Fraulein D'Artagnan. We were inseparable, the four of us.

Or so I had fondly thought.

At the ball, my beautiful Carl-Heinz kissed me for the first time, in an arbour scented by gardenias. My cup was full. If he loved me then my future was secure. But we kept the secret for ourselves, knowing that our parents would say we were too young – Carl-Heinz was not yet twenty-one.

My stepfather had a fine house in the lakeside suburb of Wannsee, not far from the new palace at Potsdam, so it was convenient for Carl-Heinz to come there after duty. We met secretly on the shores of Lake Havel and walked in the pine forests there, making plans. But recently my sweetheart had once or twice missed our rendezvous, and then one evening – only two days before I found myself recounting it to Judy Love – Willi von Sturm had turned up instead.

I lifted my hand, opening stiff fingers to take out the letter and unfold it for Judy Love to see. 'He brought me this. It's from Carl-Heinz. It says . . . It says he didn't intend that I should take him seriously. It was a flirtation, and I should have known a man of his background could never consider a wife with no name or fortune. It says I was a fool if I thought otherwise, and I should go home to England and never come back . . .'

Her hand was on my arm, offering comfort. 'I'm sorry, dear. I'm truly sorry. Men can be such beasts.'

'But he *did* mean it!' I cried. 'It's this letter that's a lie. Oh . . . why didn't I see it before? It's obvious that Willi made him write it!'

Willi, with his smiling mouth and his cold blue eyes, his waxed blond moustache, his duelling scar, his overweening arrogance . . .

'*That*'s what Fritzi was trying to tell me!' I mourned. 'He said something about . . . I didn't take it in. I suppose I didn't want to listen. But what he meant was that Willi von Sturm had orchestrated it.'

That evening at dinner I had been in a state of shock. All I could think of was the letter – the fact that Carl-Heinz

16

didn't want me. But the presence of an unexpected visitor from England – the solicitor, Mr Wells – had obliged me to compose myself.

'Mr Wells came to tell us that my grandfather is ill and wants to see me again before he dies,' I told my new acquaintance. 'Everyone agreed I should go and I let them persuade me. Before I knew it, I was on the train. And Willi was there, in the crowd, at the station. Making sure I left. Oh . . . you see! It's not Carl-Heinz who has played me false, it's all of *them* – his toffee-nosed family, and my parents, and Willi – plotting to separate us. They can't *do* this.'

The sun had lifted its first bright rim over the horizon, its light ample for me to read the letter. The words still said the same, but I knew he had written them under duress, driven by his family and by his brother officers of the élite guard, the high-born, the blue-blooded, determined to close ranks and make him deny his feelings for a penniless little *Ausländerin*.

'I shan't let them do it!' I cried, thumping my fist on the rail. 'I shall write to him and tell him that I know he didn't mean it. I shall ask him to wait for me. In a few years, when we're of age, they won't be able to stop us.' So saying, I folded the letter again and returned it to my skirt pocket.

Close beside me, Judy Love was peering up at my averted profile, all but bursting with interest. 'That's right, dear,' she soothed. 'Time solves all. You'll probably meet some nice English boy and—'

'There will *never* be anyone else for me.'

'You think that now. But, I mean, if he let himself be bullied into writing a letter like that, maybe he's not the one for you. In a few weeks' time you'll feel differently. After all, you're off to Norfolk, to see your family. That'll be nice.'

'Will it?' I remembered so little about Denes Hill. I didn't *care* about Denes Hill.

'Oh . . . No, sorry. It won't be much fun if your grandfather's dying.'

That was not what I had meant. 'I didn't say he was dying, I said he was ill. At least, that's what I was told.'

'Don't you believe it?'

I forced myself to think of what lay ahead, though I hardly dared put my own doubts into words. 'I don't know *what* to believe. It's all so fearfully convenient. For Mr Wells to arrive at just that moment . . . I expect Mother wrote and asked the family to take me in for a while, to get me away from Carl-Heinz. Why else should Grandfather suddenly want to see me? Even if he *is* ill . . . He's shown no interest before. None of them has. Oh, Grandmother sends cards and small presents at my birthday and Christmas. Tokens, dutifully sent. But they never cared about me.'

'Perhaps they want to make up for it.'

'Perhaps.' I wished I could believe it.

The English coast was near now, gentle hills gilded by the rising sun behind a great estuary full of ships. But what waited further on, at the end of my journey, was unclear.

'Is your mother the only child?' Judy Love asked.

'No, though she's the oldest. The others . . . The only one I really know, because he's been to visit us two or three times in Berlin, is Uncle Frank. He's a darling. But then he's different – he's an artist. Mother says he's much too fond of the ladies ever to be faithful to only one. My oldest uncle, Harry, is married, but he has no children, as far as I know. Why do you ask?'

'I was just thinking. I mean, if your grandfather wants to see you before he dies, well . . . maybe he's left you

18

something in his will.' Her eyes shone at the thought of it. 'Does he have a lot of money?'

The question eased a bitter laugh out of me. 'You've been reading too many bad novels, Miss Love. My grandfather may be a wealthy man, but he has a wife, and four sons, and another daughter apart from my mother. I am *not* about to become a rich heiress.'

Her face fell. 'Oh.'

The ship began to manoeuvre towards the estuary. Around us, other people emerged from cabins and saloons, to watch as we came into harbour. The air was thick with crying gulls, the sun glaring into my aching eyes. Another hot day lay in prospect. And somewhere ahead, hidden by distance hazed in morning brightness, waiting behind more hours of travelling on dusty trains, lay the county of Norfolk, and a house named Denes Hill, where lived my English relatives, the Rhys-Thomases.

I was truly adrift, on currents that swept me ever further from people and places familiar and dear, while driving me inexorably closer to an alien shore. But I had to go on. I couldn't go back. Not yet.

Perhaps never, a voice in my head said clearly and, in sudden panic, I looked back, hoping for a last glimpse of the far, receding shore. But it was lost behind a haze of dawn mist, a swell of ocean, and a roll of sudden thunder.

Disembarking from the ship in the crowded confusion of Parkeston Quay, I felt like an automaton, worked by clockwork. A leaden depression had settled on me, and my head was thick from lack of sleep and from the oppressive weather. I saw Judy Love with her friends, making for a train bound for London. She waved at me, calling, ''Bye, dear. Good luck,' but her main purpose was to draw my

escort's attention, which she succeeded in doing, briefly –
I felt him hesitate and look round as he hustled me towards
the dining car of our own train.

Once we had been conducted to our table, Mr Wells
settled back opposite me to study the breakfast menu. Judy
Love had been right – he *was* good-looking, in a dark, rakish,
mature sort of way, tall and well built, wearing a formal
stiff collar and tie with his tailored summer tweeds. The
black hair round his ears was faintly silvered, and the
moustache he wore made me think of a riverboat gambler I
had seen in a cinematograph. I could imagine him playing
poker, winning or losing fortunes with little outward display
of emotion. What was he thinking behind that calm façade
as he ordered a full English breakfast, with China tea?

My own appetite had deserted me. I drank a cup of coffee
and several glasses of iced water, but my main recollection
of that part of the journey is seeing watchful, khaki-clad
soldiers patrolling beside the line, carrying guns.

A mountainous lady at the table opposite ours exclaimed,
'I never thought I'd live to see the day when British soldiers
were obliged to keep watch on the English coast for fear of
Huns!'

'Not to worry, m'dear,' her bewhiskered husband replied.
'Our lads are exercising, that's all. Nothing for you to worry
your little head about. Didn't you see those naval vessels in
the harbour? Britannia still rules the waves. If Kaiser Bill
dares to try anything, he'll get short shrift. No matter how
many spies he has lurking among us.'

At this, the lady glanced straight at me and, finding me
watching her, did not look away but instead stared into my
eyes with bright challenge, her mouth tightening. It was I
who snapped my head away, feeling my colour rise. Did
she take *me* for a German spy?

'Cold?' Mr Wells's voice made me start. From over the top of that morning's *Times*, a pair of umber eyes regarded me levelly. 'I thought you shivered.'

'Oh, I . . . I wasn't aware of it.' If I had shivered it was not from cold but from a sudden malaise of the soul. I stared again at the view, seeing another file of soldiers walking beside the track. Preparing to defend the coast against invasion by Germany? Dear God . . .

TWO

The Channel crossing, my conversation with Judy Love, and our arrival in England seemed like a part of the nightmare when I surfaced from more troubled dreams. Head heavy, neck cricked, I felt myself being gently rocked, carried along amid an odour of stale smoke and dust. *Clickety-clack, clickety-clack.* After twenty-seven hours we were, at last, on the final stretch of this wearisome journey, aboard the afternoon train from King's Lynn to Hunstanton.

As I forced my eyelids to part, sunlight glared through my lashes, making me squint. I was slumped in a corner of the carriage, with my nose all but pressed against the window and my straw boater askew. Seated opposite me, his back to the engine, the lawyer was perusing a local paper he had bought from a vendor at King's Lynn station. Blinking, I forced my muscles to straighten into a more decorous position as I covertly repositioned my boater, anchoring it securely with its long hatpin.

A glittering expanse of green and blue beyond the window resolved itself into grassland with the sea gleaming beyond it, the horizon meeting a clear summer sky where gulls flashed bright wings. Cows grazed on rich pasture dotted with great yellow buttercups, blue forget-me-nots and dancing scarlet poppies. I had forgotten how beautiful Norfolk could be.

But, ahead of us, storm clouds trailing skirts of rain drove

22

a straight line across the blue sky. Beneath their mud-dark swirling, sunlight still flooded a long wooded hill which dominated the skyline, a double-headed butt of land whose further promontory jutted out almost into the sea.

The sight woke long-forgotten memories, surprising me. Of course . . .

Twisting in his seat, Oliver Wells peered out of the window as if to see what had caught my attention. 'Storm coming,' he observed. 'Thank God for that! Some rain will be welcome to break this heat.'

'Yes, indeed,' I agreed, and saw him lift a wry eyebrow before applying himself to the *Lynn News and Advertiser* again. To him, I surmised, the view held nothing but the familiar and unremarkable. For me, it had stirred a kaleidoscope of impressions both happy and unhappy, all blurred behind nine years of absence.

Before I could fully recapture any of those misted memories, another image intruded. Among tall grasses just beyond the fence that guarded the railway, I saw a young man clad in a dark bathing dress. Dripping wet, hair flattened to his head as if he had just come from the sea, he stood rigid, up to his knees in pasture. He was staring straight at me, as if he had been expecting me.

I must have started, or made some small exclamation, for Mr Wells looked up. 'What is it?'

'There . . .' I gestured out of the window, but now that I looked again there was no man, nor any sign of disturbance in the grasses except the ruffling of a rising breeze. 'For a moment I thought . . .' How foolish! My heart was thudding uncomfortably and I had to force my lungs to expand. I managed a breathy laugh. 'No, nothing.'

Giving me a strange look, he shook his paper and pointedly resumed his reading, as if annoyed to have been disturbed. He considered me more and more a little oddity, with whom he had been saddled much against his will.

Closing my eyes, I tried to relax for the last few minutes before we reached the halt at Eveningham, but I was wide awake now, my heart unsteady, my mind imprinted with the face of the young man I had just seen. Tall, long-limbed and broad-shouldered, with a lithe, athletic body displayed in that wet bathing suit, he had reminded me of Uncle Frank. I had seen the drops of water on his face, even the way his eyelashes stuck together. He *had* been real. Oh . . . he must have lain down, hiding himself, I rationalized. Perhaps he was there with his girl. The grass was probably longer than it appeared.

But I didn't entirely believe it. Instinct told me there had been something odd about the man, standing there so still, so close to the line, watching the train. He had *looked* at me, as if he knew me. As if he were trying to convey some message . . .

We drew in under the wooded rise of the first hill, to pause briefly at Snettisham station, between beach and village, with the storm rolling ever closer. From there, the railway curved round the hill, heading across sandy wastes of gorse and ling, closer to the sea. Half of the water gleamed blue; the rest mimicked black clouds which now hung close above the cutting that drove through the lowest slopes of Denes Hill.

Landward, the curve of the ridge sheltered the horseshoe-shaped valley where lay the village of Eveningham, red and grey roofs among trees, with the squat tower of the church presiding from its place halfway up the ridge. On gentle slopes around the village, harvest was in progress – I could make out a horse-drawn sail reaper sweeping through the crop, and small figures binding sheaves, setting them in stooks with a sense of urgency. Even as I watched, the approaching storm drew a shadow across the harvest field, shutting off the sun, threatening the ungathered acres.

Denes Hill was darkened, too.

For the first time in hours I thought of my grandfather, and was stricken by unease. What if he were really ill? Perhaps dying? What if he really had asked for me? I should be ashamed for coming so grudgingly.

Strange, how memory came back in fragments, sharpening into focus like pictures in a magic lantern show as I drew closer to those scenes of childhood. The house, the people, the dark, secret woods; family picnics on the beach in summer, and looking for birds' eggs and wild flowers; cold winter mornings stuck in the schoolroom with slow Tom and clever, spiteful Vicky . . . The glimpses were all strung together by a ragged thread of unhappiness. I had felt unwanted – even by my own mother.

The newspaper rattled noisily as my companion folded it and tossed it aside. After a moment, he cleared his throat, making me look at him again.

'Before we arrive,' he said, 'I'd like, if I may, to give you some advice. You will probably consider that it's not my place, but since your mother and stepfather gave you into my keeping I am, in effect, *in loco parentis*, and so . . .'

'Yes?' What was he trying to say?

'Katarin . . . Kate . . . Forgive me, but . . . I think you might be wise not to insist on being known as "Miss von Wurthe". As you may have gathered, people of German extraction are somewhat suspect in England at the moment. It will be difficult enough for you to go about and meet people, unless you curb that accent you've developed.'

'Accent?' I was genuinely surprised.

'Are you unaware of it? My dear girl . . . Your English

is good – of course it is – but you have acquired a pronounced guttural inflection which makes you sound like a foreigner. And, if you don't mind my saying so, a more pleasant demeanour wouldn't go amiss. If you're going to treat your family to sullen silences and icy disdain . . .'

I stared at him, hurt and disbelief robbing me of words. Yes, I *did* mind his offering such advice, as if I were a child to be reprimanded. I already felt lost and alone. How could I be 'pleasant' when my whole life was being upturned?

Before I could find a coherent reply, the train sighed into the halt at Eveningham. Mr Wells opened the door to climb down to the platform, offering me his hand.

I refused it, saying, 'I can manage, thank you.'

Descending, unable to look at him, I saw the line ahead disappearing into a cutting, among woods that spread thickly up a slope which, here, was steep, showing outcrops of weathered red carrstone. I was only minutes away from a reunion with my English family.

Lightning and a long, tumbling drum roll of thunder accompanied the banging of the train's door behind us. The light had faded to dull copper-grey and stinging dust swirled up on a wind that brought a scent of rain. In the station yard, a horse and cart waited for us. The driver seemed nervous, anxious to be on his way before the storm broke.

'They din't say nothin' about passengers,' he complained. 'I was given to understand as how somebody else would fetch you, sir. That old cart en't very comfortable for a lady.'

'Well, it'll have to do,' said my escort.

However, just as the man was loading the last trunk, a large open-topped motor car, magnificent with silver paintwork and silver-plate fittings under a film of dust, roared into the yard. Trailing a choking cloud of yet more dust, it slewed round to halt beside me amid a spattering of small stones. As the dust cleared, my uncle, Frank Rhys-Thomas, grinned up at me, doffing his battered Panama as he leapt out of the car. He reminded me of a grasshopper, long legs in ancient cricket trousers worn with a loose, paint-stained shirt.

'Kate!' he cried, enveloping me in a bear hug before holding me at arm's length to look at me critically. He was in his early thirties, an attractive though not handsome man. In a tanned face framed by a tangled mane of dark-gold waves so long they fell over his shapeless collar, slate-blue eyes had narrowed with concern. 'You look terrible,' he informed me bluntly. 'What on earth have they done to you, girl?'

'Oh . . . Uncle Frank, I'm so *glad* to see you!' Feeling like a lost child suddenly finding a friend, I threw my arms around him, leaning my cheek to his strong shoulder. He smelled of linseed, and musk, and fresh sea air.

'You, too,' he muttered in my ear, his arms hardening momentarily as if to tell me he understood.

Recovering, remembering my dignity and my manners, I eased away, asking dutifully, 'How is Grandfather?'

'Holding his own. He seemed a little better when I saw him earlier.'

'Then . . . he *is* ill?'

'A matter of days, they say. But come on, girl, let's get you home. You must be tired.'

He swept open the low door of the tourer and gestured me inside. The car was amply big enough for four or five people, but the wide back seat was littered with painting paraphernalia – canvases and paints, brushes, rags, an easel thrown in at an ungainly angle, the whole roughly covered by a rumpled linen jacket.

'I was down on the beach – a fishing boat went aground and I was trying to draw them refloating her,' my uncle said as he came loping round to the driver's side. 'Quite forgot I'd promised to meet you until I heard the train coming and then I just tossed everything in the jalopy.' As if remembering that I was not alone, he glanced across the car to where Mr Wells was standing, adding, 'Sorry, old man. You won't mind riding with the carter, will you? It will be slower, but just as sure. I'll tell them you're on your way. Must get my niece home before the storm hits.'

He climbed over his door, put the car in gear, and we were off, leaving an irritated Oliver Wells waving his hat at our dust.

'We could have cleared a space for him,' I called above the roar of the motor as we careered through the gate and into the lane. 'He'll get soaked.'

Uncle Frank grinned at me, yelling back, 'Well, he won't melt, he's not made of sugar. Let's see if we can outrun the rain. We'll take the short cut. Bumpy, but much quicker. Hold on to your hat, girl.'

Midway to the village, he turned on to a rutted farm track, iron-hard after weeks of drought. Ahead of us lay the hill, wooded and dark under lowering clouds, branches swept by the strengthening wind. The track forked, the lefthand branch leading past a pond and huge barns to an old farmhouse with low thatched roof and many chimneys, set back among sheltering trees. We took the right fork, between tall thorn hedges, bucketing over ridges that shook the car and rattled my teeth. A plume of dust rose behind us, and huge drops of rain spat down, harbingers of the storm. The clouds had all but covered the sky, turning the day to dusk. As we climbed the hill I could see the surface of the sea churned into choppy waves, the far shore obscured behind a mist of rain.

'Christ!' said my uncle.

A man had stepped out from the hedge ahead, a bulky, bristle-chinned figure in shapeless hat and weatherproof cape, corduroys gartered by string at his knees. He held a shotgun levelled at our windscreen.

I ducked instinctively. The car squealed and swerved to avoid the man, throwing me into the door as we hit the verge with a force that jolted my bones. For a moment I feared we might topple. Level with my ear, I heard a dog barking and when I looked I saw its snarling muzzle and wicked teeth as it raced beside us. *Boom!* The shot half deafened me, but nothing seemed to be hit. We were past the man. Wrestling with the wheel, my uncle regained the track. He was swearing loud and colourfully, his foot on the accelerator making the car leap forward. Behind us, seen through rising dust, our assailant stood straddled, the shotgun aimed over us. *Boom!* The second cartridge exploded.

'He's shooting over our heads!' I shouted.

'I know!' Frank answered in kind. 'Blasted madman!'

The dog was still barking, snapping close by our rear wheel. But we were coming to the edge of open woodland, oak, ash and birch trees growing in copses on the slope, with a few darker pines and shrubby underbrush. The track led between brick gateposts bearing a sign reading '*Private Property. Denes Hill. Trespassers will be prosecuted*'. To my relief, the dog stopped at the gateway as if it knew that it must not come further. Behind it, the figure of its master was lost behind the trees as they closed round us.

The track headed round the hill, through a tunnel of branches that made the light even worse.

'Who *was* that man?' I cried. 'He tried to kill us!'

Frank shook his head, grimly amused. 'Not even Mad Jack would be so stupid. He was trying to scare us, that's all. Lying in wait for me . . . Crazy old buzzard!'

'But who *is* he? Why did he—'

'Why?' His eyes gleamed. 'You may well ask. Who knows why a madman does anything? He's an old enemy, Kate. Farmer Jack Farcroft. An old troll lurking under our hill to play havoc whenever we use this short cut. Take my advice and stay well clear of him.' He took his eyes off the track to afford me a grin, saying, 'Though not even Mad Jack would want to harm a lovely young thing like you.'

Distracted by the compliment, I pulled a face. 'I'm the ugly duckling. Compared to Mother—'

'Compared to your mother's delicate, porcelain prettiness, you *were* an ugly duckling, once,' he said. 'But don't you remember what happens when ugly ducklings grow up?'

'Some of them grow into ugly ducks.'

'Some do,' he agreed with a laugh. 'But take it from me, Kate, you're becoming a swan. With your fine skin against that dark hair, and that willowy slenderness . . . You're tall, but you carry yourself well. Your bone structure is wonderful. And those eyes . . . Such a lovely, luminous ice-blue. Cool, but with the promise of warmth . . . You're not just pretty, girl. You're turning into a beauty.'

'Not in this outfit,' I said, feeling my face burn as I plucked at my sailor collar.

'That's surface trimmings. And whose choice was it? Your mother's – yes, I thought so. Clara never did like competition. Don't be so gauche, Kate. You must learn how to take compliments. If you knew me better, you'd know that I don't say such things unless I mean them. I'd like to paint you. Will you sit for me?'

'Oh . . . Uncle Frank, no! I even hate having my photograph taken. A portrait would be just too much.'

Horribly flattered and embarrassed, I turned away and adjusted my hat in an effort to get more shelter from the rain which by then was falling steadily. It was some minutes before my confusion subsided enough for me to wonder if Frank had deliberately changed the subject to stop me from asking any more about 'Mad Jack' Farcroft.

Emerging from the wood, we approached the rear of the solid Victorian mansion which my grandfather had bought with his profits from industry. It faced several acres of heathland, on the plateau atop the promontory, and was built of the local red carrstone. I remembered great bays at the front framing a broad stone stair which led up to the terrace and the main reception rooms on the first floor, but here at the rear it was plainer, with gardens and yards spreading out behind.

The rain became a deluge, accompanied by thunder and lightning. Just in time, we drove into the shelter of what had once been a stable. There we waited for an easing in the downpour before we ran across the yard and up a flight of narrow steps to a side entrance.

Shadows crowded the narrow hall, among hooks bulging with old coats and macintoshes, hats of all descriptions, with water boots and galoshes scattered on the floor. Shaking wet drops from my skirts and shoulders, I unpinned my boater and patted my piled hair into shape, feeling it loose in places around the pads that lent width. Limp strands fell round my face and neck. I was sure I looked a fright. If I encountered Grandmother while I was in that state . . .

'You look fine!' Uncle Frank assured me, taking my arm to urge me towards the lighter spaces of an inner hallway which connected with the kitchens and service areas. 'Let's go and see who's about. I'm surprised they weren't watching for us. Oh . . . Annie, where is everyone?'

A maidservant of uncertain vintage had appeared on the service stairs, wearing a white lacy cap like a doyly on thin greying hair scraped into a bun. She might have been anything from forty to sixty. Her eyes were red from weeping, one of them turned in, so that she appeared to be looking in two directions at once. Seeing us, she paused, turning her swollen eyes on Frank, screwing her apron with her hands as her mouth worked in distress.

'Oh, Mr Frank!' she got out. 'Where *have* you now been? He's been asking for you. "Where's Frank?" he say. "Fetch him to me right quick." '

My heart seemed to stop as I felt Frank go still. 'Father?' he managed.

More tears bloomed in her eyes and she dried them with her apron. 'He was took sadly about lunchtime. They're all up there with him. And the doctor. Oh, I don't know what your poor mother'll do, that I don't.'

Giving me one swift glance, Frank grabbed my hand and all but dragged me up the stairs into a broad vestibule from which opened three of the reception rooms. Across the grandly furnished saloon, with its chandelier, its Adam fireplace, and its classical bronzes, lay another hallway from which the main staircase angled up to the second floor.

My grandparents' private suite filled the end of the south wing. I did not recall being allowed through that door before, but Frank flung it open and took me with him into a sitting room, where a thin, middle-aged man in butler's dress was in the act of closing a final shutter, as if to bar the storm from a house where death hovered.

Oil lamps with white glass shades sat on side tables, their light fanning up walls hung with watered silk of a pale sea-blue. Mirrors gave an illusion of space, reflecting a collection of watercolours, white porcelain, and spindly furniture. Thunder rattled at windowframes, rain lashed down glass, and the wind found tiny cracks, reaching through to shake long striped drapes in that same delicate blue and white.

'Mr Frank!' the butler greeted. 'Thank goodness! Your father—'

'I know,' Frank said quietly. 'It's all right, Billing. Finish what you're doing. We'll just go quietly in.'

Wishing myself anywhere else, I hung behind as my uncle crossed the room to a door where he paused, took a breath, and slowly, soundlessly, turned the porcelain knob. The opening door revealed a cavelike darkness lit by a score of dancing candle-flames. Some were arranged along the foot of the bed, others on tables, another row above the hearth where a fire burned low. Every time thunder rolled, the candles seemed to quiver in response. I could hear a woman softly weeping and, as my eyes adjusted, I discerned shadowy figures grouped on either side of a carved four-poster hung with tasselled red silk. Candlelight glowed on strained faces, all of them concentrating on the man in the bed. I remember wondering cynically who had staged it all so carefully, for full dramatic effect.

Since I was behind Frank, no one noticed me at first. Several of the people in the room spoke his name, relieved that he had come, and a woman's voice bade him, 'Frank! Come here! Come and speak to him before it's too late.'

Her voice seemed to stir the dying man. He muttered, 'Who? Who's there?'

'It's Frank, my dear,' his wife answered. 'Your son Frank. He's come to say goodbye.'

As my uncle moved to the right of the bed, I saw there

the diminutive figure of my maternal grandmother, holding out her hands to greet him. She looked just as I remembered her – just like a picture Mother had – small, neat and imperious, dressed in black with a touch of white at the neck, with her iron-grey hair dressed in piled waves and around her long throat an Alexandra band of black velvet on which she had pinned a brooch of jet.

A pulse beat in my throat, making it hard to breathe. The room was airless, hot from the fire. A cloying smell of some kind of rubbing oil reminded me of the room where my own father had lain, sick and old, when I was very young. But this was different. I shouldn't be here. My presence was an intrusion. Yet, if Grandfather had asked for me . . .

Uncle Frank knelt by the bed, holding his father's hand and speaking quietly to him. Watching, mesmerized, I wondered if that emaciated being could really be the tall, portly, red-faced Grandfather I remembered. He had been a terrifying figure, who seldom looked down to notice the insignificant child cowering away from his heavy step. This was the man who had fathered a large family, made a fortune by the sweat of his own brow, earned a name in local politics and won a knighthood granted by Queen Victoria in the year of her Diamond Jubilee. Now, this same man lay helpless under neatly folded covers, flat on his back with his eyes closed, so wasted that he already resembled a corpse. His great beak of a nose stuck out like a granite outcrop from a rock face and he was breathing through his mouth, air whistling and gargling in his lungs. Everyone else was silent, hardly breathing, except for the woman who sniffled into a handkerchief.

Squinting past bright light, I discovered the weeper seated in the corner behind Grandmother, with beside her, his hand on her shoulder, a thin man with receding fair hair.

34

Now that I had time to take in detail I counted seven people around the bed – five to my right, two to my left. It looked like a stage setting, with two candelabra on a chest at the end of the bed acting as footlights, and I the only audience. Slowly, I began to identify my relatives. The thin man in the corner must be my oldest uncle, Harry, and the weeping woman seated beside him, his wife, Saffron. She appeared enormously fat, enveloped in shapeless clothes. By the head of the bed, Grandmother stood near the kneeling Frank, while nearer the foot of the bed, leaning on the post and half behind the red drapes so I could not see her face, stood a girl whom I guessed to be the youngest of the family, my mother's only sister, Victoria – only six months older than I. On the opposite side of the bed, the bespectacled doctor leaned to check his patient's pulse against a turnip pocket-watch, while a slender young man, with a pale, beautiful face under sleek golden hair, looked on. That must be Emmet, due to reach his majority the next January.

Just as I was wondering where Tom could be, I heard a muffled sob and saw another figure huddled half on the bed, hidden behind the blaze of candles. The light fell on a golden-fair head, hair curled and tousled, his face bent over hands clasped tightly in prayer. His whole attitude expressed hopeless anguish and I saw Emmet reach a hand to squeeze the heaving shoulder, soothing, 'Hush, Tom. Don't take on.'

'But he's dying!' Tom's wail came hoarse, shocking in that still room, and he stretched out his arm towards his father, sobbing, 'Don't die, Pater. Please don't die!'

'Control yourself, Thomas!' Grandmother snapped. 'Be a man, can't you?'

The sobs diminished – he had buried his face in the counterpane and I saw Emmet again squeeze his shoulder in a gesture of comfort and support.

'Kate?' Uncle Frank had remembered me. He got to his feet, peering past the haze of candlelight. 'Kate, are you there? Dear girl . . . forgive me.' He came towards me, saying, 'Look, everyone. Look who's here at long last. It's Kate. Kate Brand. Clara's girl.'

He drew me forward, into the light at the foot of the bed, where I stood blinking uncertainly at the faces that stared back at me. Before any of them could speak, the sallow skeleton in the bed croaked, 'What's that? Clara? *Clara!*' Like a man pierced by lightning, he sat bolt upright, staring at me with wild eyes. His shaking finger stabbed venom at me. 'What have *you* come for? Damn you, girl! You're not welcome here. You're no daughter of mine. I curse you. A father's dying curse on you! Be damned to hell!' With a groan, he fell back on his pillows, his mouth a gaping hole between sunken cheeks, his thin chest labouring under his nightshirt, each breath drawn ever more painfully. The doctor bent over him again, stethoscope extended.

I find it almost impossible to express my feelings of that moment: disbelief, incomprehension, rejection and bitter hurt – for Mother, too. What had she done to make him revile her so? I felt as if invisible walls had dropped round me, shutting me off from everything. My sight was blurred, and sounds came as if through water. Someone said, 'He doesn't know you, Kate. He's raving.' I think the speaker was Frank. I knew he was beside me, but I couldn't look at him or respond when he laid his hand on my arm.

Then Grandfather opened his eyes again, saying clearly, 'Mother!' and every eye swung back to him.

'I'm here, my dear,' his wife replied.

'No, not you, Vi,' he dismissed her. 'It's *my* mother. And Sadie. Sadie's with her! Hello, Sadie.' He was gazing towards the end of the bed, smiling at someone he apparently saw standing beside me. In my strange state of mind, I too sensed figures there in the shadows, one of them more substantial than the rest . . .

'And who's this?' Grandfather said. 'Why . . . it's John! Violet, it's John! It's our boy! I'll be all right now. I'm going with John. Wait for me, John. Yes, I'm coming.'

Beside me stood a tall young man – the same young man I had seen on the marshes – the young man who so resembled Uncle Frank but was not Uncle Frank. I felt him on my left as real and sure as I could feel Uncle Frank on my right. I saw him, there in the candlelight. Just as I had seen him earlier, except that this time he was fully dressed, though in exactly what garments I couldn't say. All I clearly saw was his face, his wind-blown fair hair and his intent blue eyes, gazing into mine and trying to tell me something.

'Kate! Kate!' Was he speaking my name, or was I only hearing it in my head? Or was it Uncle Frank calling me? I became aware that Frank was shaking my arm, and in the same moment the other presences faded. The room resumed its former appearance. But there was a subtle extra silence about it. I saw the doctor lean to close his patient's eyes, while Tom, lunging across the bed towards his father, howled, 'No-o-o!'

Whatever legends may have arisen later among the family, that is *my* recollection of what happened that night.

THREE

Grandfather had been delirious, not knowing what he was saying – that was what Uncle Frank said, and the rest tacitly agreed. Kind of them, but it seemed to me that the old man had meant every word.

Whatever Grandmother was feeling, she hid it behind a mask of brisk practicality. She welcomed me kindly enough, but, seeming unable to cope with my arrival that sad evening, she left me in the care of my youthful aunt, Victoria.

The bedroom assigned to me had once been used by the governess, Miss Yearling. It lay at the rear of the house, overlooking outhouses, walled yards and gardens; close to the service stairs, it seemed far from the nearest bathroom, but Victoria explained that the more convenient guest rooms would be needed as other relatives arrived for the funeral. What I most remember is the iron bedstead, with big knobs gone dull for want of Brasso, and a delicate Queen Anne writing desk under the window. A fresh scent of lavender polish did not disguise the underlying must of disuse, but, on that first evening, I was grateful for a place where I could close the door and be alone.

My luggage had been dealt with by porters on the journey. Now, faced by an embarrassment of two trunks and five cases, I realized that our housemaid, stupid Marthe, had packed nearly everything I possessed, as if she couldn't decide what I might need for a stay of unknown duration.

How like her! Still, after the scene in that candlelit room in the south wing, it was good to have familiar things around me.

Grandfather's mortal remains had been taken to a funeral parlour, but after a day or two he was brought back, looking like a wax effigy, in a polished oaken, silk-lined coffin which stood, open for viewing, in the library. Large as it was, the room smelled sickly-sweet from lilies and other floral tributes.

Harry and his wife Saffron had gone home to their own house in Lynn; handsome young Emmet tried to lighten the gloom with bad jokes which annoyed his mother; Frank played a supportive role; Vicky was subdued, her face pale under its weight of golden-red hair. I particularly remember poor Tom – he was seldom named without the adjective – sitting by the coffin with helpless tears slipping down his face, or following Emmet around like a puppy. Poor Tom: mentally and physically he was a rough-sketched, unfinished copy of his handsome twin.

One by one other mourners arrived, like black crows round carrion: a grim, elderly great-aunt with a humourless son and a fat daughter-in-law; two fussy spinsters, twin cousins of Grandmother's, from Wales – twins were in the Thorne blood; I met a few people I never clearly placed on the family tree, plus friends and business acquaintances. Some came only to call, others to stay until after the interment. Some were accommodated in the house, while for others Uncle Frank rushed around in his Rolls-Royce, searching for vacant rooms – not easy in late August. The nearby coastal villages were crammed with holidaymakers, as was the new seaside resort of Hunstanton with its colourful cliffs set on the corner of the Wash. A few of our people had to make do with lodgings further inland, at inns set amid gentle hills and rolling farmland generously folded with woods, copses and coverts.

Every time I opened my mouth in that company I was reminded of the 'guttural inflection' upon which Oliver Wells had remarked so crushingly. Blue Rhys-Thomas eyes, sharp and critical, told me that my accent grated upon their sensibilities. So I kept mainly to my room, writing letters and rereading the letter from Carl-Heinz. His photograph smiled from my bedside table, mouth curved under a fair moustache with waxed ends, fair hair brushed flat either side of a central parting. He was in full dress uniform, with his cap elegantly under his arm and his other hand resting lightly on his sword hilt. So straight, so tall, so fine! He *hadn't* meant those cruel words of rejection. He *couldn't* have.

At mealtimes, round a table which grew ever more crowded, conversations dwelled on the deceased and the drama of his last few hours. Among the myths of his passing were the stories of his visions of those who had gone before – his mother, his sister Sadie, and his oldest son, John, who had drowned in the Wash at the age of twenty-seven. Some hearers found the story a confirmation of Christian teachings; others, more sceptical, said that the dying man had been hallucinating.

I did not join in the telling – I had learned at a very early age that to speak of seeing spirits was to invite both anger and ridicule, and often a sharp slap before being sent to bed without supper. 'Little liar!' my nursemaid would call me when I mentioned the elusive playmates who sometimes appeared to me. 'Bad, wicked girl! You know what happens to liars, don't you? They get sent to hell and hung up by their tongues to roast over the fire.' In this case, I was sure, the family would resent my claiming to have shared

Grandfather's clairvoyance. Even some of those who had been there didn't believe he had actually seen anything. I was not about to argue. People must discover these truths for themselves.

It was generally agreed that Grandfather had disowned my mother, Clara, 'For marrying a German!' fussy Cousin Ellen muttered. 'There'll be *nothing* for that trio of foreign brats she's now raising.' Catching my eye on her, she added, 'Kate, my dear, I don't include you in that. What a *good* thing they sent you back. You *belong* in England.'

Out of politeness, I didn't reply.

That night I lay awake working myself into a state of self-pity that became unbearable. Either I must lie and fret, alone in the dark, or I must *do* something to help myself. I threw back the covers, lit my candle, and sat at the little desk in my nightdress writing a passionate letter to Carl-Heinz, along the lines, '*I know you were forced to write those awful things. Oh, please, write and tell me it is not true, my love.*' Not even pausing to read it over, I sealed it into an envelope, addressed it, and propped it up where it could not be missed. Then, feeling calmer, I went to bed and, for the first time in days, slept long and deeply.

When I woke to a brighter morning, the letter had gone, sent by Annie to the post with the other mail when the boy made his usual early trip to the village. So that was done, with no room for second thoughts. All I had to do now was await the reply.

Among shoals of condolence for the family there came a long letter from Mother, full of the trivia of her everyday life, with exhortations that I should, '*stay and complete your education, my dear. After all, your heritage lies in England.*' Evidently Mother did not expect me back for some time. If at all. The advanced education that would have been so

41

infra dig. for a von Wurthe in Berlin had suddenly become desirable for a Catherine Brand who had to make her own way in the world.

Grandmother kept herself occupied, organizing the funeral with help from Vicky and a female person named Anderson, whom I saw flitting about the house. Near sixty, I guessed, thin and dressed in drab, she always politely deferred to me, drawing aside whenever we passed in a corridor, but never actually met my eye or spoke above a mutter.

'Oh, Anderson's been with the Mater for ever,' Emmet informed me. 'Started out as a lady's maid, I suppose, but she's become indispensable in many ways, to both the Mater and Toria.'

I suspected that Emmet had been told to keep an eye on me. He turned up whenever I ventured about exploring my surroundings, and on that day he had found me in the tower room. I had gone to see Uncle Frank, whose spacious bedroom and adjoining studio had been built at attic level, way above the world, with a big window looking out on to slate roofs and catching clear northern light. But Frank wasn't there, so I had opened the final door on the attic landing, which gave on to more stairs.

These stairs climbed directly into the top room of the house, designed as a lookout retreat and now used as a games room. A delicate wooden baluster protected occupants from falling down the stairwell and, as one climbed up, light came from all sides. Windows gave panoramic views of the countryside, and between them hung a gallery of family photographs, taken over many years. Window seats invited one to sit or recline among piled cushions; shelves held picture papers and a selection of the latest novels. All kinds of games – draughts, chess, jigsaws, word games and card games – spilled out of cupboards, and a collection of the latest ragtime recordings waited beside a gramophone.

The place was known as the sanctum, which, as Emmet loftily informed me, was short for '*Sanctum sanctorum* – that's Latin. It means—'

'Holy of holies,' said I.

Emmet stared, blue eyes bright beneath a soft forelock of golden hair. 'You know Latin?'

'A little,' I shrugged. I didn't tell him *how* little.

Emmet was at Cambridge – the only one of the family, apart from John, to have achieved such scholarship. He liked to show off about it and was particularly condescending to me and to his sister 'Toria' – he called her that to annoy his mother. We were, after all, mere girls, and not expected to have brains.

Because I enjoyed seeing his eyes widen with utter amazement, I added, 'I'm hoping to go to college – the London School of Economics. Didn't anyone tell you? That's one reason I came to England.' My parents had held out the chance of that college place like a carrot to a donkey, and it was a tempting prospect – a measure of independence, which might lead to other openings. All depended on Carl-Heinz's reply. 'As a matter of fact, I was offered a place at Berlin University' – *that* made him stare! – 'but Pa – my stepfather – didn't approve. He's old-fashioned. He thinks women should be kept back, with no right to a place in the world as equal beings.' Realizing I was on my high horse, I stopped myself.

'You're a suffragette!' Emmet exclaimed, partly horrified and partly admiring.

'Yes,' said I with a lift of my stubborn chin. 'I believe I am. I can drive, too. *And* I've smoked a cigarette. Fearfully modern of me, what?'

Later, I regretted my moment of hubris. At the dinner table, Emmet informed the company that they had a dangerous subversive in their midst, at which every eye turned balefully on me, as if I were a black beetle that had suddenly crawled on to their food.

'She's a suffragette!' my young uncle gleefully announced. 'And she's going to school in London, to learn how to overturn society.'

'That's not what I said!' I objected, mortified at being the focus of a dozen pairs of disapproving eyes.

Frank came to my rescue, saying, 'Take no notice of Emmet, he likes to make mischief. So, Kate, you've decided to accept that offer, have you?'

'Oh, I . . .' I sent a venomous glance at Emmet, hating him for putting me in this spot. 'I'm not finally decided yet. Not for sure.'

'Why not?' Frank demanded. 'I thought it was your ambition to go to college? Of course you must go, girl. They're holding that place for you. All you have to do is pass the entrance exam next week.' He glanced around the table, saying, 'Our Kate's more than a pretty face, you see. Girl's got brains, too.'

'Brains,' said a pinch-faced Victoria, 'are so unfeminine.'

Grandmother, tiny and neat and calm, put in, 'Not at all, my dear. All women have brains. It's just that most of us don't choose to boast of them. Tom, dear . . . your nose is running, use your handkerchief. Ellen . . . did you manage to unpick those stitches in your knitting?'

I sank back into welcome obscurity, trying not to mind that Grandmother had squashed me as surely as she would have squashed an insect. She did it to all her family, I had noticed – a word, a cutting phrase, a look from those quenching blue eyes . . .

Having rediscovered the sanctum, I found myself drawn to it again the next day, with Frank in his studio beneath, finishing a commission. 'We'll start on that portrait next!' he called as I left him and wandered up to the top room.

Powder-puff clouds floated along in a breezy sky, shapes changing all the time, swathes of sunlight chasing over sea and land, turning the water alternately brown, or slate blue, or brilliant turquoise green. From this height you could see how the house was circled by woods, though in front of it the crown of the hill grew a tonsure of gorse and purpling heather. To the south lay a croquet lawn and tennis courts, with wilder grass areas merging into trees, while behind the house the kitchen garden was divided into three walled sections, beside stables and garage yards. Grandmother kept an old pony named Willow, and a couple of carriage horses, preferring to be driven in old-fashioned style when she went out. She did not like newfangled gadgets, which was why there was no gas or electricity – she said gas smelled and electricity was vulgar.

From the eastern window, you could see the sweep of fields and woods inland, undulating round to the north and the Hunstanton cliffs. From there the eye travelled down past Heacham in its hollow, over Denes Hill woods and on southwards down the coast to the warehouses at Lynn docks some ten miles away, where the Wash merges into the broad Ouse. Ships came and went with the tide, mainly steamers, with the occasional petrol-engined vessel, or a sailing ship might appear, graceful and elegant, and a flurry of smaller fishing smacks with dark blue or red sails sallied out to perch on the sandbanks at low tide, after shellfish. Landward, you could trace the line of the coastal ridge, with Sandringham woods rising above flatlands where the railway's gleaming track snaked between rich meadows. It disappeared behind Ken Hill before emerging to skirt the Eveningham vale. Part of the village was also visible, including the church tower poking up among trees on the slope of the ridge.

I remembered Miss Yearling pointing out landmarks and recounting the area's history – she had had a passion for more ancient days, when woad-dyed warriors roamed these hills under Boadicea's command. She had told us that the Eveningham valley had once been a bay of the sea, with the ridge forming the shoreline – an image that had terrified me. During high winter tides I had been afraid that the sea might rush back and reclaim the valley. The notion had given me nightmares.

But then, my childhood had been laced with nightmares. Photographs crowding on the walls of the sanctum provided endless nostalgia, especially those from the turn of the century, when Mother and I had been among the groups – she the beauty of the young adults and I one of the children, small and plain in my pinafore, with lank dark hair hanging under a floppy sun-bonnet. In summer the house had swarmed with friends of my uncles: cricket matches, croquet parties, tea on the lawn and days at the beach. Happy occasions, recorded for ever by the camera.

Among them, I sought out one particular face – my lost uncle, John. I found him in many of the older group pictures and also photographed on his own – here in mortar board and graduand's robes, there in riding breeches with a horse, and elsewhere dripping wet on a pebble beach, wearing a clinging dark bathing dress, with a big grin on his face. Just as I had seen him on the marshes. Except for the grin. He hadn't been smiling as he waited for my train to pass.

A sceptic would, no doubt, have told me that I had seen the picture when I was young and that I had grafted the

memory on to the view of the marshes as my train
approached Denes Hill. But I knew I hadn't imagined seeing
him. John had been there, waiting for me to come by, though
I had yet to find out his reasons.

There would be reasons. There always are.

John had been the oldest boy, but not the oldest child –
my mother was the oldest, born just seven minutes before
her twin.

Just as I was trying to recall what she had said about
John, Emmet's cheery voice came floating up the stairwell,
calling to Frank, 'Have you seen the elbee?' At least, that's
how it sounded, however nonsensical, but then Emmet was
a great one for making up words and using slang.

Frank answered sharply, to which Emmet replied, 'Oops!
Right, I'll go up and find her,' and he came thumping up
the stairs, two at a time, grinning at me. 'So this is where
you're hiding. Again. You don't strike me as the jigsaw-
puzzle sort. Is it the ripping views that bring you up here?
Or the fact that it's miles away from the rest of us?'

'Don't you ever stop?' I asked with a sigh.

'What?'

'Ragging. Poking fun. You always were a horrible boy –
pulling pigtails and leaving dead mice in girls' beds.'

Emmet laughed and threw himself down on a window
seat. 'I'd forgotten about that.'

'*I* hadn't.'

Attention caught by a chess board where a game was
half played, he reached out and thoughtfully moved an ivory
pawn. 'I wouldn't blame you for hiding away. The house is
hardly fizzing at the moment. Must be a jolly bore. Pater
would have hated it. "Don't mourn over me," he said. "Have
a wake, like the Irish do. Get drunk and tell muddy jokes." '

'Emmet!'

He looked up, blue eyes wide and ingenuous in a face that was beardless and almost girlishly pretty. 'It's true! I heard him say it to Frank. He wouldn't have said it to the Mater, of course – this fearful solemnity is all for her benefit. Mater believes in doing the done thing. But I expect you know that.' With which he frowned down at the chessmen.

Going to stand by him, I took over the ebony pieces, immediately threatening his queen. 'How should I know it?'

'Clara must have told you. She rocked the boat. Did the thing not done.'

'By marrying my stepfather?'

'Um.' But he was more interested in the board, rubbing his chin and pondering his next move.

'Because he's German?'

'Probably.' He looked up again, serious now. 'What *is* that crazy Kaiser of yours up to? What a jackanapes! Strutting about in those fancy uniforms with that silly moustache . . . It'll take more than threat and bluster to beat our chaps, when the time comes.'

'Complacency may be your undoing!' I retorted – it was what Berliners said of England, that she was too sure of herself. 'The German army is the best fighting unit in the world. If we're backed into a corner—'

'*We?*' Emmet's fair brows shot skyward in surprise.

I didn't know how to answer him. If war came, whose side would I be on? 'Oh . . . Let's not talk about it. Please God, it will never happen. Look . . . it's checkmate for black in two more moves. Who were you playing with?'

'Myself. No one else plays. Well, Frank does a bit, but he's not really . . .' He glowered at the board, trying to work it out. 'Two moves? Where?'

So I showed him. Much to his disgust, I was right.

'We must play a proper game some day,' Emmet said, stretching. 'Just look at that gorgeous sunshine. Cricketing weather if ever I saw it. And us under curfew until after the jollities next Monday. No wonder Pater looks so pot-faced, lying there in his box. He loved cricket. Still . . . we must contain ourselves in doleful patience, to please the Mater.'

'Don't you care that your father's dead?' I asked, finding his constant levity distasteful.

As he looked at me, I saw the answer in his eyes – yes, he cared a good deal. 'He's been horribly ill for ages, Kate. Going downhill every day. Losing all his dignity. Isn't he better off where he is?'

'I suppose . . . In heaven, you mean?'

'Zeus, no! I don't believe in any of that old tosh. Do you?'

I hesitated, then said quietly, 'Oh, yes. I know it's true.'

'Oh, do come along, Katie B! Nobody but a fool would claim he knows about all that. I thought you were a modern thinker. When you die, that's an end of it. Dark, blissful nothing. Eternal rest. It's the only logical ending.'

'If you say so,' I replied, knowing it useless to argue with him. 'Now, tell me, since you're here . . . this photograph . . . who is . . .'

Studying the pictures on the walls, we picked out faces and he named them for me, though there were some whom neither of us could identify.

Apart from the group pictures, individual studies showed the seven Rhys-Thomas children in early adulthood. The family resemblance showed clear – the long Rhys-Thomas nose from Grandfather's side, the stubborn chin that was pure Thorne, from Grandmother. The pictures were mostly in sepia tones, of course, but in reality the family all had fair hair, varying shades from Emmet's pure gold to

Victoria's strawberry-blond, with deeply blue eyes, dark like slate or vivid as summer skies. That was another thing that marked me out as different: all I had inherited from Mother, in looks, was the shape of my chin; the rest of me must be Brand, straight dark hair and eyes of a blue so pale they were almost colourless.

'There were eight of us,' Emmet said, 'but baby Pearl, who's here on the Mater's knee, died when she was two. Then John went, of course. We nearly lost Harry, too. He was badly wounded in South Africa, fighting the Boers, you know. That's why he's so thin – only got half a stomach left, poor old chap.'

'Yes, I know.' Now that he mentioned it, I did remember being told about Harry. However, looking at the picture of my uncle John in his student's robe, I was surprised to find no memory of him. 'What happened to John?'

From the corner of his eye, Emmet shot me a guarded look. 'He drowned.'

'Well, yes, I know that. But how, exactly?'

'It happened in the summer of nineteen-oh-one. That long, hot summer. The year the old Queen died. We were on the beach nearly every day. The royal grandchildren all came down to Sandringham. We played beach cricket with them. We had tea at their bungalow. Don't you remember?'

'Of course.' Memories of the two summers I had spent in Norfolk had blended into one long blue and gold blur. Paddling in tiny wavelets over crinkled sand, picking cockles for tea, grey pebbles hard under small soft feet, sand sifting between my toes. And behind me the adults on the dunes, picnic hampers and tartan rugs, blowing ribbons and chiffon skirts, laughing and chatting. My beautiful mother, in her late twenties then, wearing a huge straw hat to protect her complexion, surrounded by

50

adoring men . . . Of course I remembered.

Emmet's blue gaze perused my face with puzzlement. 'John was swimming right out near the deep channel, with some of the other men. And then a sea fret swept up, and John got cramp. No one on the beach realized he was in trouble, because of the mist. Oliver Wells, who was nearest, tried to save him, but . . .' He peered at me disbelievingly. 'Don't you remember *any* of it?'

'Why . . .' I tried, but nothing remained of that day. 'No. Nothing. I can't have been there.'

'Oh, of *course* you were! You were paddling on your own, lost in your usual dream world. You'd wandered quite a long way out – you remember how shallow it is for miles when the tide's low. When the mist came up, it swallowed you and your mother got anxious and went looking for you. You *must* remember!'

Irritated by his insistence – and by the lacuna that had, apparently, blanked part of my memory – I snapped, 'Well, I don't! And neither would you, I dare say, if you hadn't heard your family talk about it a hundred times since. I don't recall Mother ever mentioning it. She hardly ever talks about John. I expect the memories are too painful.'

His face seemed to close up, as if a new thought had darkened the picture. 'Oh,' he said flatly. 'Of course.'

'And what does *that* mean?' I cried. 'I do *wish* you wouldn't all be so unkind about my mother. Are you surprised she wants to forget such an awful tragedy? John was her twin.'

'And she hated him!'

Feeling as if he had slapped me, I stiffened and drew back. What on earth did he mean?

'Emmet . . .' Uncle Frank's low voice came from the

doorway. 'That's enough. Go and find Tom. Tell him it's time to wash for luncheon.'

'Oh. Yes. Right.' Sliding me a shamefaced look, Emmet hurried away as if glad to escape.

'My brilliant little brother talks too much,' Frank said with a wry smile that didn't reach his eyes – his glance was appraising, and concerned. 'He only knows what he's been told. Stories get exaggerated, you know, and with your mother not being here to defend herself . . .'

'I'm beginning to see why she chose to stay away,' I said bitterly. 'They seem to have made her the scapegoat for everything. What did she *do*, Uncle Frank?'

He rubbed his cheek, smearing a spot of bright yellow paint as he came to stand beside me and gaze out to the sea. 'She was young and foolish. Perhaps they expected too much of her. It's not important, Kate. It's all so long ago. Tell you what – why don't you and I get away for a few hours tomorrow? I need to see Harry. You could do some shopping, and get acquainted with your aunt Saffron. She'd probably be glad of some feminine company at present.'

'Oh?'

'The, er, "happy event" is expected soon, I believe.'

'Oh!' Saffron was *pregnant*? I had thought she was merely fat!

'So we'll do that, shall we?' he said. 'Jolly good. Now I'd better go and get some of this paint off before luncheon. See you later, old girl.'

Once again, though I was some while in realizing it, he had adroitly sidestepped an uncomfortable subject. No one was prepared to tell me exactly what sin my mother was supposed to have committed.

FOUR

After breakfast next morning, Grandmother sent Annie to me with a dust coat to go over my mourning and a veil to wrap around my black hat, to protect it and my face, before Frank and I went down to the stable yard where he kept his Silver Ghost. Someone had polished the car, leaving the silver plate and paintwork gleaming. Watched by an envious Emmet and Tom, who had been refused permission to join us, I ran admiring fingers over the high-arched mudguard. 'She really is a beauty.'

'Best car in the world.' Frank allowed me to sit in the driving seat while he cranked the engine into life, and then he climbed over the passenger door and settled beside me, offering me his driving goggles. 'Well, put her in gear, girl!' he answered my look of astonishment. 'You told Emmet you could drive.'

The mechanics were a little different from Willi's Benz, but I managed to set off without entirely making a fool of myself. We took the 'long way' round, avoiding the disputed short cut across Farcroft acres.

After a few days' drying, the road was in good condition. Soon we were taking the fork down into Eveningham village, past a row of shops and cottages and on down the lane towards the station.

Just after we passed the Farcroft farm, ancient and comfortable behind its barns and duck pond, I had to toot the horn to warn a male pedestrian out of our way – I could hardly see in those goggles. Unfortunately, the movement caused me to lose control of the wheel and the car veered to the right. The man leapt aside, on to the overgrown verge, where he stumbled and nearly fell into the hedge. I heard him shout some angry epithet, but I was too busy avoiding a rut to look at him. Beside me, Frank laughed uproariously. 'Nearly got him!'

In the station yard, where we covered the car in case of rain, we heard the train whistle as it entered the far end of the cutting. We had time to buy our tickets and walk on to the platform just as the engine sighed to a halt. Touching his cap, a porter opened the door to an empty first-class carriage. 'Morning, Mr Rhys-Thomas, sir.'

'Morning, Playford,' said my uncle, following me into the carriage. I sat by the door, facing the engine, unwrapping my dust veil and arranging it in elegant folds about my shoulders.

Just as Frank settled beside me, running footsteps brought another passenger to the door – the same young man who had been hurrying in the lane. He had obviously broken into a run after we passed him, for he was gasping for breath, his face red and shiny with perspiration. His tweeds sat on his rangy frame in dishevelled fashion and mud smeared his shiny brown boots. One foot on the high step, he saw us and stopped, every line of him saying that he wished he had chosen another door. But, visibly squaring his shoulders, instead of turning away he stepped up to join us. He took the far corner seat, where he resettled his jacket and ran his fingers through curly nut-brown hair before twisting his cap between work-hardened hands, all the while staring out of the window away from us. I could see a muscle working in his jaw, as if he were grinding his teeth.

A slam of doors, a shrill whistle, a flutter of green flag, and the engine took a deep breath and shook out her couplings before gathering her carriages behind her like so many chicks.

'You should have flagged us down, old chap,' my uncle remarked to our companion as we drew out of the station. 'We could have given you a ride.'

The young man flashed him a cool glance. 'I made it without your help, thanks all the same.' His voice was surprisingly deep and cultured and his eyes slid to me, a swift, assessing look that said he was curious despite himself.

'Let me introduce you,' Frank offered. 'Kate, this is our neighbour, Philip Farcroft. Farcroft, my niece, Miss Catherine Brand.'

'Von Wurthe,' I corrected, nodding at the young man. 'Katarin von Wurthe. How do you do. I must apologize, please, if we startled you on the road. I did not realize the horn was quite so loud.'

His expression didn't lighten in response to the apology, though he said, 'It was probably my fault. I'm sorry if I said anything that—'

'Whatever it was,' Frank put in, 'we didn't hear it, did we, Kate?'

'Just as well,' the man murmured darkly, his eyes still on me. Whoever he was, I didn't care for his manners.

He appeared to be in his early twenties, a tall, lean man, broad of shoulder and long of limb, with big hands and feet and a bony face, deeply tanned. He had a tough, strong look about him, as if he was used to hard work in the open air. Yet he spoke like an educated man. That deep, mellifluous voice . . .

When we reached Lynn, Frank and I alighted first, and, as Philip Farcroft passed us, he touched his cap to me in

55

farewell: 'Miss von Wurthe,' and made off along the platform with a long, loping stride that carried him rapidly out of sight. At least he pronounced my name correctly, I thought.

'He's smitten,' said Frank with a twinkle. 'I bet he's kicking himself for using such muddy language after you tried to run him down.'

'I didn't—' I began hotly, and decided not to rise to his bait. 'Anyway, that's not the impression I had.'

'So why did he sit in our carriage, if not to have a good look at you?'

'Stubborn pride – he wasn't going to give us the satisfaction of actually *seeing* him deliberately avoid us, however much he wanted to.'

Frank was laughing at me. 'You like him too!'

'My heart is safely under lock and key elsewhere,' I informed him loftily. 'Do I assume Philip Farcroft is related to the "troll who lurks under our hill"? What is he – grandson?'

'Son. By a second marriage.' He took my arm, turning me towards the exit. 'Not such a bad chap, when all's said and done. It can't be easy for him, living with Mad Jack.'

He was making allowances, seeing the other man's point of view, as was his wont. But I kept recalling a pair of marsh-green eyes alight with antagonism. It seemed to me that Philip Farcroft disliked us just as much as his father did.

I found King's Lynn a charming town, boasting a wealth of ancient buildings, with modern shops and emporia. In the shelter of a huge church a market bustled busily and the central streets jostled with pedestrians, cyclists, and vehicles both motorized and horse-drawn. Some of the roads were in the process of being metalled, to the stink of tar and the clang and chunter of steamrollers. When the work was complete, it would no doubt bring down the level of noise from clopping hooves and wheels on cobbles.

'By the way,' my uncle said as we mingled among shoppers. 'I was given to understand you'd be using your English name while you were here.'

That set me on the defensive. 'I've been known by my stepfather's name for nearly ten years. I'm not going to change it, Uncle Frank.'

Frank gave me a wide-eyed look, shaking his head. 'As you wish, girl. But on your own head be it. Oh—' He paused in mid-stride to draw my attention to the shop we were passing. 'Look there.'

The window of Lipton's, the tea and grocery store, boasted a display of canned foods marked '*CHEF*' in scarlet letters on a yellow background. '*A boon to the overworked housewife*', declared a banner above the display.

'That's us,' Frank said with a wry grin. 'Chef Canned Foods – Fresh from the Fens.'

My oldest uncle, Harry, I had learned, managed the canning factory, which lay on the outskirts of Lynn. However, the main Rhys-Thomas fortune lay with Thorne-Thomas Engineering, based in Lincoln, which had prospered on steam and was now pioneering petrol-driven machines. Grandfather's heirs would retain a major financial share in that industry.

Frank was saying, 'They say Pater put all our initials into a hat and played Lexicon with them until he'd found his canning trademark – Clara, Harry, Emmet and me. What a way to be immortalized!'

'I'm glad to know he included Mother.'

'You think a tin of green peas is an appropriate epitaph?'

'What would you prefer – one of the new tractors?'

'Maybe,' he said. 'Anyway, better something useful and down-to-earth than a "Land Ironclad", as Wells calls them.'

' "Land Ironclad"?' I queried, puzzled. 'What's that?'

'Oh . . . newfangled machines. Still at the experimental stage.' A gesture dismissed them as unimportant, then, 'Haven't you read any of Wells's books?'

'Books?' I was confused. 'I didn't know he was a writer.'

'Of course he is! Surely, even in Germany, you—'

'I thought he was a lawyer.'

Frank peered at me as if I had turned blue, then a sudden blast of laughter exploded from him. 'Not *Oliver* Wells, dunderhead! *Herbert G.* Wells. One of our greatest living authors – and a prophet of the horrors that science will bring, if we aren't very careful. "The Time Machine", "The Argonauts of the Air", "The Land Ironclads" . . . No?'

'I've never heard of him.'

'Then it's time you did! I have most of his books in my room. Remind me to lend them to you the moment we get home.'

Needing one or two purchases, we found our way to relevant shops, where he introduced me as: 'My niece, Miss von Wurthe,' and when the name caused momentary pause he added hastily, 'My sister's child. Her stepfather's German but she herself is English.'

'Ah!' The polite smiles reappeared. 'Of course, of course. Delighted to make your acquaintance, miss.'

The fourth time this happened, before Frank could add his speech of mitigation, I broke into a torrent of German: '*Guten Tag! Wie geht's? Haben Sie . . .*'

Having left the shop in a hurry, Frank didn't know whether to be exasperated or amused. 'Look here, old girl, you can't go around giving people shocks like that. This is provincial Lynn, where they believe what it says in the papers, and in the papers they're warning about the dangers of the evil Hun who's plotting to descend on our shores, pillaging and plundering, murdering babes in their beds . . .'

'Oh, what nonsense!' I scoffed. 'Surely people don't really believe . . .'

'I'm afraid they do,' he said sombrely, levity draining away. 'And I'm even more afraid they may be right. So, please . . . easy does it, eh? If you go about deliberately antagonizing people it will upset the Mater.'

Grandmother. Of course.

'Especially at this time,' Frank added, appealing to my sympathy.

A sigh escaped me. He was right – despite her apparent composure, Grandmother *had* just lost her husband of forty years. 'Very well, I'll try,' I conceded. 'But I'm beginning to wonder if there's anywhere I can just be myself. In Berlin I was picked on for being English; here I'm not welcome because they think I'm German. Do you know that a woman on the train from Harwich accused me of being a spy?'

'What?' The word exploded out of him on a gust of laughter.

'Well, almost.'

He commiserated, 'My poor old Kate!' but he was hugely amused as he flung an avuncular arm around me. 'What you need is a cup of tea and some of Saffron's lardy cake. Let's find a cab and go and see if she's at home, shall we?'

Harry and his wife lived in the new suburbs that were growing up around the town. Down a broad avenue planted with young trees, Hawthorn House stood detached behind low privet hedges, neatly trimmed, amid tree-shaded gardens laid down to lawns and shrubs. It presented a wide, double bay-fronted aspect behind a gravelled drive, with a half-circle of brick steps leading up to a front door panelled in patterned glass.

A pretty young maid answered the door and, flustered by Frank's smile, went to see whether her mistress was able to entertain us. Returning, she told us to go to the breakfast room. Here, my aunt-by-marriage was sitting in a *chaise-longue* with her feet up, draped in a loose silk robe under a flowing, flouncy tea gown, with slippers on her feet and her long auburn-brown hair held loosely up by combs. Sunlight poured through open french windows and the breeze brought the sound of birds arguing.

'Frank!' Her face lit up and she held out her hand to him, revealing an arm which was not so much plump as puffy. Pregnancy had bloated her. Before it, she must have been quite a beauty, with her olive skin and that soft red-brown hair setting off wide hazel eyes.

'Don't get up.' He bent to kiss her lifted cheek. 'How are you today?'

'Tired. Tired all the time. I shall be glad when the baby comes.' As an afterthought, she added dutifully, 'How's the Mater?'

'Bearing up stoically, as ever,' Frank answered. 'Look, I've brought Kate to see you. She was starting to go crinkled at the edges with being stuck in the house, though we've been out and about locally finding rooms for all the arrivees, haven't we, Kate?'

Saffron was smiling at me, holding out her hand. 'We hardly had a chance to meet the other night. What a rotten introduction to Denes Hill for you. I'm so sorry. Come and sit here by me. Shall we have some tea?'

'Not for me,' Frank demurred. 'I asked the cab to wait. I need to see Harry. Is he at the factory?'

'Isn't he always? Yes, go and find him, Frank. Bring him home for lunch, if you can. Can you stay for lunch, both of you? I shall be glad of some different company.'

Left alone, my aunt and I made a start on polite conversation: she asked about Mother and my family in Berlin, and my journey, and I admired her house, which made her offer to show me round – 'You'll forgive my state of undress at this hour, I hope. I dress for comfort at present.'

The baby was due in three weeks, she told me as she led the way. She would be glad when it was over.

Contrasted with the heavy ornamentation and Victorian gloom of Denes Hill, Hawthorn House was light and airy, almost as large as our house in Berlin, four reception rooms and ample domestic offices downstairs, with the luxury of gas for heat and electricity for light. It was decorated in clear, pale colours with furnishings and ornaments of the latest art nouveau style, printed fabrics and lots of coloured glass. Saffron seemed flattered that I admired her taste. Upstairs there were five large bedrooms, a nursery suite still smelling of fresh paint, ready for the baby, and a bathroom boasting both hot and cold running water, not to mention two lavatories – I sneaked a look round when Saffron sent me up to 'take off your things and be comfortable'. I did so with relief, removing my hat and outer garments, tidying my hair and leaving myself cooler in lacy white blouse and black tunic skirt.

Saffron had returned to the breakfast room where she stood by the french windows enjoying the air. 'That's better,' she approved. 'I want you to feel at home here, Kate. If ever you feel the need to escape from the dragon, you'll be welcome with us. You like the house, then? So do I. I sometimes have to tap wood to make sure I'm really here.' Glancing about her with a smile of pleasure, she slid her arm through mine, partly in affection and partly for support. 'Let's go and sit in the garden, shall we? I've asked Maisie to bring us some gingerade.'

Under an old apple tree where hard green fruit waited to ripen, she sank down on a rustic bench, a Japanese parasol protecting her from dappled sunlight. I sat on the grass nearby, idly plucking daisies as she talked about herself.

'When we were first married,' she said, 'we lived at Denes Hill and Harry came in to the factory by train every day. Not very satisfactory. Well . . . it wasn't so much the travelling as . . .' She let out a little breath as she spread her hands. 'Living with in-laws is not easy, Kate. Especially when you're not quite what your mother-in-law had hoped for, d'you know what I mean?' Letting her smile go lopsided, she touched my arm. 'No woman will ever be good enough for any of Lady Vi's sons. She adores her boys, as you may have gathered. But she doesn't have much opinion of her own sex. Not even her own daughters. Your poor mother must have told you that, and now Vicky's discovering it, too.'

'Actually . . .' I ventured, 'Mother doesn't speak much about the past. I assumed she had her reasons, but now I'm beginning to wonder.'

As I discovered, Saffron loved to talk, especially if she herself was a protagonist in the action. She had been an onlooker at Denes Hill, coming late into the family picture, and she had her own biases – her habit of referring to Grandmother as 'Lady Vi', for instance, was not complimentary.

Like Alice, she had to begin at the beginning, with 'Your mother and John were the oldest of the children – twins, of course.'

'Yes, I know. But she was born first – seven minutes before John.'

'Quite, dear, though John always counted as first, being the boy.'

'Oh?' Mother had never told me that.

After the older twins came Harry; then Frank; then another daughter, Pearl, who had died in infancy.

'Then comes the Great Gap,' Saffron said, hazel eyes sparking with a touch of malice. 'According to Lady Vi, that was caused by her being so upset over losing little Pearl. But I've also heard it said that the old man went astray, for which she banned him from her bed. Whatever the reason, it was ten years before Emmet and Tom were born.'

Sadly, something had gone wrong with the birth of the younger twins: Emmet had arrived normally, but poor Tom emerged feet first, with his cord wrapped round his neck. Thinking of it, Saffron laid a hand protectively on her own bloated stomach. 'I lie awake at night and wonder what I should do if something happened to *my* baby. D'you know what I mean? I think I'd rather it was born dead than . . . Well, Tom's a dear and everyone loves him and he wouldn't hurt a fly, but he's not normal, is he? He'll be twenty-one in January, but he still behaves like a little boy. Sometimes I look at him and Emmet, and I just can't believe . . . What was I saying?'

'You were recounting the family tree. Vicky's the last of them. She's only six months older than I am. So Mother must have married my father before that.' It was Mother's story that interested me.

'That's right. Clara was sent away to stay with relatives in Cumbria. She'd been growing a bit restless, I believe, so—'

'Restless?'

'Growing up. You know what I mean. We all go through it.' But she couldn't meet my eye; she was pleating her tea

63

gown with plump fingers. 'It may have had something to do with her being so jealous of John. I don't know! All this happened before I met John.'

Surely she meant Harry? 'John?'

'Yes, John.' Hazel eyes clouded, she looked down at her distended body, stroking the bulge with a slow, tender hand. 'It was John I knew first. It was John I was going to marry.'

I had been going to pursue my questions about Mother, but this new development had me intrigued. If Saffron had been in love with John, how was she now married to Harry?

'I was terribly young,' she said. 'About your age. Oh, I didn't have any real hope that John would marry me. Not at first. He was so far above me. My mother was widowed young; she had a struggle to manage, so I took work in a shop – a good shop – a hatter's. That's how I met John. He must have bought half a dozen hats he didn't really want. Then we ran into each other on the beach – I'd gone on an excursion with some friends and, well . . . you know what I mean. You somehow know, don't you?'

'Yes.' Chin on knees, I took a deep breath and let it out slowly. Oh, when would Carl-Heinz write? Soon. Please, soon!

'So I found myself being invited over to Denes Hill,' Saffron went on, 'to tea parties and cricket matches. That's when I met your mother, after she was widowed and brought you home. John was the one thing we had in common. When they were children, so she said, he could do no wrong and she could do no right. He got the pony, and the first bicycle, and the chance to escape, to go to school . . .' Misty-eyed, she gazed into the distance, as if seeing pictures projected against the far hedge. 'I'm sure she loved him, really. Everybody did. I mean, he never asked for privileges, he just took them because it was his due, as the boy, d'you know what I mean? That's how he was. Clara didn't understand that. Dear John . . . he would never have hurt anyone. Not intentionally. But Clara . . . she said he caused hurt because he didn't understand that other people had feelings.'

'Some men are like that,' I said, thinking darkly of Willi von Sturm, conniving to separate me from Carl-Heinz.

Saffron misinterpreted my expression. 'Appealing, aren't they?'

'Not to me! I hate arrogance.'

'I thought . . . Forgive me, but I thought . . . Some young man you've had to leave behind? Well, now,' she answered my cautious look, 'it wouldn't be so strange. Do you want to tell me about him?'

'There's nothing to say,' I denied. 'Please, go on – about Uncle John.'

'Well . . . to cut a long story short, we decided to get married. *My* mother was delighted, but *his* mother . . .' She made an eloquent face. 'Lady Vi tried to stop us, said we must wait six months before we could even announce our engagement, and then she said we couldn't be married until John was thirty. Delay, delay . . . But of course he didn't live to be thirty. He was drowned, that very summer.'

Moved by the sadness in her eyes, I blurted, 'It must have been frightful! I don't know what I'd do if anything happened to . . .'

Smiling, she reached to stroke my cheek. 'If you lost him, you'd go on, Kate. I did. Had to. And, for me, there was Harry . . .

'He was away when I met John. Fighting the Boers, you know? He was terribly injured, poor boy. Like a skeleton when he came home. He missed John, and he liked to talk about him. So he came to see me, and we became friends, and then it started to be more than that. But we didn't speak of it until my mother died, quite suddenly. Harry was so sweet to me then. But I was terrified of what Lady Vi would say, so . . . we went away and got married in secret. It caused a bit of a stinko at the time, d'you know what I mean? But I'm not the first to fall in love with two brothers. It happened to the new Queen – when she was Princess May, she was engaged to King George's older brother, but he died before they could be married, so she married the younger boy and they've been as happy as larks. Not that Lady Vi would ever admit it was the same. She thinks I'm a fortune-hunter, nasty-minded old . . .' With another grimace, she stopped herself. 'Thing is, you see, I happen to love old Harry. He's probably better for me than John would have been. He needs me, d'you know what I mean?'

How lucky she was, I thought.

Saffron cocked her head like a bird, bright eyes probing deep. 'Does your chap need you?'

'I . . .' I began and, to my own surprise, couldn't go on for tears.

It was almost a week since I had left Berlin and been carted across Europe in a daze. Only now did reality seem to catch up with me. Why had I agreed, so meekly, to come? How long would it be before I saw my family again? Would I go to college in London, or remain in Norfolk? Would Grandmother forgive me for whatever it was Mother had done? Where was my real home now, here or in Germany? And what if there should be a war – what then, with both Fritzi and Carl-Heinz in the army? And – worst pain of all for a lonely girl of eighteen – why hadn't Carl-Heinz written to me? Why had he let me go with only that cold letter for my heart's ease?

These uncertainties poured out of me, all over poor

Saffron. I found myself with my head against her knee while I wept, telling her my whole story, and she stroked my hair, saying soothing things.

'Of course he cares, you dear goose. Why . . . he probably only meant that you ought to be patient and wait a while. You'll see – he'll write to you soon and beg you to go back to him. I can feel it in my bones.'

When Frank and Harry came in for lunch, we enjoyed a cold collation at a table set in the garden, where a breeze toyed with a green tablecloth and with the big straw hat Saffron had donned to shade her face. Frank kept the party lively. Harry was quieter, suiting his status as the oldest man of the family now. His hair was fair but thinning at the crown and receding from his temples, and his face was hollow-cheeked, with not an ounce of spare flesh on his body. He ate very slowly, small quantities at a time – I presumed because of the injury which had left him with only part of his stomach. But he was friendly enough and joined in the laughter, especially when Saffron explained to me about her name.

'My skin was yellow when I was born and my father . . . well, he had an odd sense of humour. I should be grateful he didn't call me Crocus.'

'Or Sunflower,' said Frank. 'Or how about Turmeric?'

We were still laughing when the maid appeared to inform Harry that he had a visitor. 'He says it's important, sir.'

'Damn it!' Harry muttered. 'Sorry, my dears. I knew I should have stayed at the works. This is probably . . .' Half out of his chair, he stopped as he saw the figure in the doorway, tall and broad, formally dressed in dark suit and stiff collar, carrying a briefcase. 'Oh, it's you, Wells,' he said as he dropped back into his seat.

I sensed a sudden barrier go up around the table, then Saffron was saying brightly, 'Why, Oliver!'

The solicitor strode out to join us, apologizing, 'Forgive me, I had no idea you were still at luncheon. I could come back if—'

'No need for that,' Saffron replied, all gracious hostess. 'We've finished eating, we were just talking. Come and join us. Have a glass of gingerade. Or would you prefer a cup of coffee?'

'Thank you. A glass of something cool would be welcome. I wanted a word with Harry – and you, too, Frank, since you're here. I've been out to the factory, but . . .'

Sliding out of my chair, I suggested, 'Take my seat, Mr Wells.'

After a surprised glance at my face, his gaze leapt with renewed interest over the rest of me, as if he had only just realized who I was.

'Yes, what a good idea,' Saffron agreed. 'Kate and I will have coffee indoors. Then you gentlemen can talk in peace. Kate, dear . . .' She held out a hand and I helped her up, allowing her to lean on me as we made our way back into the breakfast room. 'Take this hat for me, would you? Toss it on that table for now, Maisie will see to it. I think we'll stay in here. It's cool when the sun's gone round, and I'm comfortable on this couch.'

Was it only coincidence that from the *chaise-longue* she had a clear view of the table where the three men were now sitting? She chatted amiably to me, but her mind and her gaze kept sliding away and her eyes were narrowed as she watched the scene in the garden.

We couldn't hear what the men were saying but it was plain that some argument was ensuing. Oliver Wells's overtures were being met with strong resistance. Harry sat stiffly, now and then shaking his head in negation, while Frank lounged in his chair, arms folded and one foot crossed on the opposite knee, his face a mask, his eyes hooded.

'Uncle Frank doesn't like Mr Wells much, does he?' I said.

'None of us does. Lawyers!' She flapped at a hovering fly and reached for a fan lying by her couch, using it to cool her face. 'He behaves as if he were one of the family, and Lady Vi encourages him in it. The trouble is, the old man put a lot of faith in him – too much, Harry says. Harry thinks Oliver has his fingers too deep in the pie. Knows too much, d'you know what I mean?'

'Isn't it part of a lawyer's job to know all his client's business?'

Saffron looked as if she hadn't thought of that. 'I suppose so. But Harry says . . . oh, I'm not sure I understand it myself. They just don't like him and that's all there is to it.'

'But didn't he risk his life, trying to rescue Uncle John?'

'Oh, that!' She flashed me a sidelong look. 'Well, yes, I suppose . . . Oliver *was* quite the hero for a time. I'm not denying his courage, but that doesn't excuse his nasty habit of ruffling feathers.'

Poor Mr Wells. Had I misjudged him, as he had misjudged me? Escorting a strange young woman half across Europe, especially when she was an unwilling traveller, could not have been easy for him. Perhaps he simply had an unfortunate manner, all stiff formality, taking himself too seriously. Perhaps we had both been wrong about each other. I looked at him with new eyes, seeing him as another excludee from the Rhys-Thomas inner circle. Like me, he was close to them, but not close enough.

The sun had gone behind a cloud, leaving the garden less bright. Was that another coincidence? Why did I have the uneasy feeling that Oliver Wells had brought the shadow with him?

FIVE

A mixed procession of carriages and motors accompanied Sir Lionel Rhys-Thomas to his rest. Surrounded by fresh flowers, he himself travelled in a glass-sided hearse pulled by six horses plumed in black, while behind him in the first carriage rode his widow and his younger daughter, with his oldest son and his wife. The other close family – Frank, Emmet, Tom and I – travelled in Frank's car, with Frank at the wheel since no man on the staff was yet capable of acting as chauffeur. Grandmother had wanted to exclude 'noisy contraptions', but when some of the wealthier mourners, including the local MP, had turned up in cars, Frank had decided to defy the decree.

'Father liked my motor,' he had argued. 'Dash it all, Mother, he made a lot of money out of "noisy contraptions". You should be grateful for that. Whether you like it or not, we're in the twentieth century now. Motors are here to stay. Horses are yesterday's story.'

'Then, perhaps, so am I!' she had replied, head tipped back as she glared at him with her Thorne chin set.

On the hill the weather was bright, a clear blue sky letting the sun pour down. But as we made our slow way round by the main drive and the coast road, to reach the Eveningham fork, a mist gathered over the sea, rolling in over shore and marshes in a grey wave perhaps thirty feet high. The top of it shone white in the sunlight. An extraordinary sight.

'Sea fret.' Emmet leaned from behind me to explain. 'It's a kind of condensation – when colder air meets a warm sea. Or is it vice versa?'

'I think she knows that,' Frank replied, sending me a glance from eyes that seemed intensely blue in a tanned face set amid formal mourning.

'Oh,' said Emmet, chastened for some reason. 'Of course.'

In the village, women had come out to stand at their gates and men paused to doff their hats in respect as we passed by. The shops had closed their doors and drawn their blinds temporarily.

Grandfather was to be laid in the crypt beneath the church of St John, set in its yew-circled graveyard on the slopes of the ridge. Large as it was, the church was full, London luminaries, gentry and local dignitaries obliged to sit next to managers and men from the workforce of Thorne-Thomas Engineering and Chef Foods. With the front pew taking only four people, because of the position of a stone pillar, I found myself in the second row, between Vicky and Saffron, with Frank near the aisle. In front of us, Grandmother sat erect, her long black-swathed neck rigidly supporting a huge hat. She was accompanied by Harry and the twins – Tom was in such a state of distress that his sobs punctuated both liturgy and hymns, despite Emmet's efforts to calm him.

Soon after the service began, I became aware that Saffron, swathed in voluminous, concealing black, was in some discomfort. She kept easing her back when we were seated, shifting from foot to foot when we had to stand. Her olive skin had acquired a glistening patina of perspiration in the light pouring through stained-glass windows. Once or twice I saw Vicky glance at her, eyes wide with disapproval.

'I *hope* she's not going to be *ill*!' she hissed.

'It's these hard seats,' Saffron muttered under cover of 'Lead kindly light'. 'My back aches. Frightfully. Oh, dear . . .' She swayed against me, pale to the lips as I turned to support her.

'Sit down,' I suggested. She did so, her head in her hands, while I hovered, not sure whether to join her or remain on my feet. Against the pillar, Vicky ignored us, facing front and resolutely singing the hymn in a reedy, flat voice.

Grandmother looked round. Under the vast black swoop of her hat brim, behind a heavy veil, her face was cold, her eyes like knives. 'For goodness' sake! Take her out, Kate! Frank—'

'Yes, all right, Mother,' he breathed. 'We'll see to it. Come on, Saff. Some air's the thing. Give us a hand, Kate.'

I saw Harry make a move to follow, but Grandmother stopped him. 'She'll be all right. You stay where you are.'

Supporting the swooning Saffron between us, Frank and I made our way down the aisle, our progress followed by a hundred pairs of curious eyes staring from pale, singing faces amid a sea of unrelieved black.

Outside, the sea fret had filled the valley, making the air like warm grey soup hanging under yews along the path. Saffron gulped greedily at it, trying to clear her head. 'I shall be all right,' she kept saying. 'Just give me a minute. Oh, my back! I need to walk. Let me walk.'

We accompanied her down the path. Beyond the lych gate, half hidden in the creeping mist, patient horses waited in harness while bored coachmen stood about in small groups. Interested eyes followed us as we walked past the line of carriages.

'You shouldn't have come, in your condition,' Frank fretted.

'I had to,' Saffron replied bitterly. 'She'd never have

forgiven me if I'd stayed away. She'd have said I was doing it deliberately. Harry said I should stay at home, but I know what she's like. I can't do anything right for her. You'd better go back, Frank, or she'll blame you, too. She's already in a rage because I've made a spectacle of my— Oh!' A new pain made her body spasm. 'Oh, Kate! I want to go home. I must lie down. I can't stand this . . . O-oh!'

Frank and I exchanged a glance. Obviously Saffron wasn't going to be able to return to the church.

'Think you can drive her home?' he asked me.

The prospect alarmed me, but: 'Yes. Yes, of course.'

'Good. I'll find the doctor and we'll follow on. He must be here somewhere. Come on, Saff. Kate'll take you back to the house. The car's just here, look. You can be home in five minutes.' He looked at me over her bent head, adding hurriedly, 'Take the short cut. If the old troll tries to stop you, run him down. All right, Saff, nearly there.'

We eased her into the passenger seat, where she sat clutching her back and grimacing with pain.

'Is it the baby?' I breathed, praying that it was not – if she started in labour while we were alone I wouldn't have a clue what to do.

'It's not due yet – I told you that! It must be those beastly pews, after the bumpy carriage ride. I should have listened to Harry. I should never have come. Oh, Kate . . .!'

Frank bent by the bonnet, swinging the crank handle. After two or three times the engine coughed into life and settled down to a satisfying growl and rattle that I could feel in my bones.

'Go, girl!' Frank shouted, slapping the bonnet as he stepped back. 'Don't stop for anything. I'll be right behind you with the doctor.'

That was a comforting thought.

I had never been completely in charge of a car before, or responsible for someone who was half fainting from pain and fright. But driving wasn't so difficult – so long as the engine didn't stop. That was my worst fear – being forced to stop.

'You'll be all right,' I told Saffron stoutly, as much to reassure myself as her. 'We'll soon be home.'

White-faced, clutching her stomach now, all she seemed able to moan through gritted teeth was, 'Oh, Kate. Oh, Kate! Oh, dear . . .'

Denes Hill seemed a long way away, especially with the mist so thick I couldn't even see the hill. But a baby took longer than a few minutes to be born: Mother had been hours in labour with each of my little half-brothers. I consoled myself that there were women at the house – Annie, Mrs May the cook, and other staff waiting to serve the funeral repast. All I had to do was get there.

Having made it through the village to the station road, I had to slow down in order not to miss the short-cut turning. Worrying about gears and steering, I had all but forgotten about Mad Jack Farcroft. But thanks to the mist he wouldn't see the car, and anyway, with the funeral taking place, he wouldn't be expecting any of us to come this way today. Or so I told myself with gritted teeth.

Aware of Saffron's discomfort, I tried to steer a course between ridges in the track. Not much further. Around the bend, up the slope, and if it weren't for the mist the back gates of Denes Hill would be in sight.

'The pain's easing a bit,' Saffron gasped. 'Perhaps it's indigestion, d'you think so, Kate? It *can't* be the baby, it's not due for three weeks. Oh, Kate! Watch out!'

I had taken my eyes off the road to glance at her. Now, startled back to my driving, I saw a dark bank ahead, right across the lane. I stabbed my foot at the brake before I realized the obstruction was only branches – cuttings from thorn hedges, and long strands of brambles. The solid tyres would go straight over them, or through them, pushing them aside as we went. Just keep going. Keep going . . .

But we had slowed down too much on the rising slope. Even as I stepped on the fuel the engine coughed and died. Oh, no. Oh, no! The car sidled to a stop – and settled with a jarring jolt, its right front wheel in a hole. No, not a hole. As I leaned out, I saw that the car had pushed aside the branches. Beneath them someone had dug a trench, deep enough to have wrecked the car if we had been going at any speed. The thought made me feel sick. That wicked, evil old—

'Are you all right?' I asked Saffron.

'I think so.' Her hat was askew, her bloated face blotched with tears. 'What's happened? Did we hit something?'

Uttering the worst German word I knew, I leapt out of the car to survey the situation, angrily tearing my skirts free of groping briers. Not only was the car stopped, the front offside wheel was jammed in the shallow trench; there was no way I could get it out alone.

'O-ooh,' Saffron groaned. 'That pain's coming again. Let's go, Kate.'

'We can't! That crazy old man . . . He *is* mad! He might have killed us. If we hadn't been going so slowly because of the mist—'

She wasn't listening. The pain had seized her again, convulsing her face and body. Sweat ran down her face. It *was* the baby, I thought frantically. Oh, where was Frank?

I climbed back into the car and jumped up on to the seat, one foot on the back, from where I could see over the hedges. Not that I could see far. About fifteen yards all round, I guessed. Towards the farm, part of a harvested cornfield showed. In the other direction lay a field of green tops – beet, or turnip, or mangolds, perhaps – how did I know? The village was half a mile away, a hopeless distance when I couldn't leave Saffron. She was moaning incoherently, squirming in agony, pulling her knees up to her belly as if to soothe the ache.

'They must be coming soon,' I said. 'They can't be far behind.'

Just as I was about to step down from my perch, a movement in the stubble caught my eye. A rabbit darted there. Then a gun blasted. The rabbit tripped, rolled over twice and lay still. Out of the mist raced a black, shaggy dog, to pick up the still-twitching body in its mouth. A whistle summoned it back to its master.

Was it the old man? Was he coming this way?

Even Mad Jack Farcroft would be better than no one. He couldn't refuse to help two women in distress, especially when one of them was about to have a baby.

Desperate, I cupped my hands to my mouth, calling, 'Hello! . . . Over here! . . . Help us, please! Please! Over here.'

After a moment of total silence when my ears sang, a faint male voice answered. 'Where?'

'Here! In the lane! Oh, come quickly, please! Please!'

'Who is it?' Saffron managed. 'Is it Frank?'

'No. It's . . .' The dog appeared first, dashing into the circle left by the mist. A moment later its master strode into sight. Not Mad Jack, thank heaven, but a younger, lankier man – a farmhand, from the looks of him. Collarless twill shirt with sleeves rolled up, waistcoat hanging open, corduroys and heavy boots, peaked cap, shotgun safely broken over his arm, a couple of rabbits dangling from his belt . . .

My heart quirked with dismay as I realized, 'It's Philip Farcroft.'

'Who?' But she didn't really care who. 'Oh . . . O-oh! Kate! It's coming again. It's getting worse. I can't have my baby here. Not in the car! Not in the open air. Lady Vi'll never forgive me!'

Philip Farcroft had paused, as if surprised to see me peering over the hedge.

'Well, don't just stand there gaping!' I scolded, frantic with worry. 'We need help. My aunt's ill, and we're stuck here! All because of your wicked old . . . *Come back!*' He had run off, out of my sight. He wasn't going to help! In my agitation, I lost my balance and toppled over, to land in an ungainly heap in the back seat, half winded and wholly distracted. By the time I righted myself, the dog was running up, barking loudly. Saffron screamed, though whether because of the dog or because of her pain I didn't know.

'Oh, be quiet!' I yelled at the dog, clambering out of the car, going to open the passenger door. 'Aunt Saffron! It's all right.'

She huddled on the seat, her hat battered, her hair dishevelled round a blotched face running with sweat and tears. 'It's not,' she whispered. 'I think I'm dying, Kate. I've lost the baby. I'm losing so much blood . . .'

'That's not blood,' Philip Farcroft's brisk deep voice said from behind me. 'Your waters have broken, that's all. Let's get you out of that car.'

Shouldering me aside, he laid his gun down in the grass and bent over the car. He lifted Saffron as easily as if she were a child, taking her to the thick grass of the verge where he laid her down, kneeling beside her.

'I need to take a look at what's happening,' he told her, quietly but firmly. 'I'm no doctor, but I've played midwife

to a lot of animals in my time and I don't see why this
should—'

Outrage made me catch my breath. 'You can't—'

He threw back his head to spit me on brilliant green spears
of anger. 'Then you do it, if you prefer. No? No, that's as I
thought. Then keep your mouth shut and let me handle this.
Mrs Rhys-Thomas . . . if your waters have broken that means
the baby may be here any minute. When the pain comes,
do you feel the need to push?'

Saffron bit her lip, nodding. 'Yes.'

'Then may I . . .'

Tears spilled over, trickling down her bloated cheeks. 'I
suppose . . . Oh, yes. Yes, anything. Just help me! Oh, dear.
Oh, dear!'

As she doubled up with another spasm, Philip Farcroft
looked up at me. 'You hold the dog. Stay near.'

'I certainly shan't leave her alone with *you*!' Scandalized
by the impropriety of what he was doing, I turned my back
and walked away, calling to the dog, 'Here, boy.'

'She's a girl, not a boy,' the young farmer said flatly.
'Her name's Bess. All right, Mrs Rhys-Thomas. I'm sorry
about this, but . . .'

I managed to catch the dog and take hold of her collar,
talking to keep her calm – or was it to calm myself? My
heart beat unsteadily in my throat. The mist pressed round.
Like one of my nightmares. Behind me, Philip Farcroft's
deep voice murmured reassurance to my aunt. I couldn't
hear what he was saying, but I was grateful that he seemed
to have taken charge. Grateful, embarrassed, angry . . .

'This would never have happened if it hadn't been for
your father!' I raged. 'He could have killed us! He should
be locked up for a madman!' And similar remarks, because
I felt so helpless.

Philip ignored me.

I heard Saffron moaning, muttering my name, 'Kate . . . Kate . . .'

Then: 'Kate!' Philip bellowed with an urgency that made me spin round. What I saw made me pause in horror – Saffron with her knees in the air and . . .

And then there was no time for thought, for embarrassment, or formal niceties. There was only practical action. The child was being born.

I did as I was bidden, soothing Saffron, encouraging her to hang on and push. I was dazed, but I remember it in detail, the three of us sharing those moments of unreal time, cut off from the world by walls of grey mist. Saffron's nails bit into my hand, my other hand held the dog's collar tightly. My frantic, pain-riven aunt watched my face, as if trying to disassociate herself from indignities elsewhere. But I was mesmerized by the glistening, black-streaked pate that was pushing its way out of her. I had had no idea it happened like this. No idea at all. The head slid out, already yelling lustily. Tiny, with a red, wrinkled face, slimed with blood, long black hair matted to its head . . . Horrible. Beautiful. Philip wiped mucus from the screaming mouth, cradled the small head, guided the shoulders out. 'No!' Saffron gasped. 'Oh, I can't! *No!*' But her body convulsed again. The child slithered out in a mess of water and blood, straight into Philip Farcroft's big, gentle hands.

A child was born. A new life. A new Rhys-Thomas. Still attached to his mother by a pulsing blue cord . . .

'Something to wrap him in,' Philip snapped. 'Quickly!'

All I had was the jacket of my black two-piece. I stripped it off and spread it on the grass, and watched as he laid the yelling baby down. 'Is he all right?' Saffron croaked.

'Perfect,' I assured her, my throat thick.

'I need some twine,' came the next command, making me look at Philip in astonishment.

'Whatever for?'

'I need to— Just get it. It's in my left pocket. Bess! Down! Stay!'

Finding the twine was a horribly intimate performance, so close to him I could feel the thick stuff of his shirt and smell the sweat on him, and hay, and dead rabbits. He had a knife in a sheath at his belt – he told me to get that out, too.

While I watched in appalled fascination, he cut two lengths of twine with which he secured two places on the cord attached to the baby's navel. Using his wicked-looking knife, he severed the cord, and swaddled the now-silent baby in my jacket. It made an unsatisfactory covering. Seeing that, Philip stripped off his shirt and used it as extra wrapping before placing the precious bundle in Saffron's arms. I swiftly pulled her skirts to cover her, my glance unwillingly drawn to the young man's naked white torso as he bent beside her – broad shoulders and muscled back, every vertebra in his spine visible, curving down to where a thick leather belt held his corduroys. It was a relief when he straightened to his feet and moved aside, allowing me to kneel closer to my aunt.

Her clothes were ruined, her hair a bird's-nest, her face puffed and discoloured. But her eyes lit with glory as she gazed at her tiny son.

'I knew it!' she breathed. 'I've been praying for a boy. "Please God, let me do something right, for once." D'you know what I mean? Maybe she'll like me better now – now that I've given her her first proper grandchild.'

First proper . . . The words shook me into silence. Before I could think how to react, our helper said, 'We ought to get them to the house.'

I got to my feet, trying to keep my eyes on his face though his bare chest held a terrible fascination for me – I had never seen a man stripped to the waist before. 'How? The car's stuck. She can't possibly walk—'

'I'll carry her.'

'All that way?'

'Not to Denes Hill! We'll go to the farm. It's nearer.'

'We can't—' I stopped myself, realizing there was little choice. 'Is your father there?'

His mouth twisted into an unhumorous smile as he bent to take the baby from Saffron and hand him to me. 'No. He went to Wells on the early train. He won't be back until this evening. Here, you take the baby. Just make sure you support his head. Like this, look.'

'I've held a baby before!' I snapped.

A glittering glance, full of undisguised disgust, pierced me for a second. Then he crouched again and set Saffron's arms round his neck before bracing himself and gathering her up against his chest, using his long legs as levers. I remember thinking grudgingly that, whatever his feelings towards my family, he was a good man to have on hand in a crisis.

'Home, Bess.' Responding to his soft command, the dog bounded ahead.

Not far away, a gate led into the field of stubble. While I closed it behind us, holding the baby in the crook of my arm, Philip strode on, strong boots and corduroys armouring him against jabbing stubble. My own light shoes and long skirts were scant protection. Forced to pick my way step by step, I trailed behind, scratching my legs, snagging my stockings and skirts, sinking deep in soft loam, all the time protecting the small warm weight in my arms. He was wide awake, but quiet, as if testing all his senses trying to make out what was happening. Great dark-blue eyes stared at me from his wizened red face. Though I had been told that a newborn baby couldn't focus properly, this one seemed to be watching me with intelligence and interest.

I found myself talking to him. Talking nonsense. 'Hallo, *Kleinschen*. I'm your aunt Katie. Hallo, then, *Bengel*.'

Eventually, the clear patch that moved with us through the mist parted to reveal a hedge. A gap in it led to a plank over a dry ditch, and then along a path worn in deep grass, beneath gnarled old pear trees hung with long green fruit. The farm appeared piece by piece as we approached, yards at the rear behind head-high walls, the end wall with a single leaded window gleaming like a watchful eye under a dipping sweep of roof. Purple and pink clematis sprawled up a trellis and round a wooden porch that protected a side door.

'Through here,' Philip instructed with a nod that bade me open the door, and, 'Stay, Bess,' to the dog, in much the same tone. He was sweating profusely, face and neck red from the effort of carrying Saffron, the muscles in his back visibly knotted. My aunt seemed to be asleep, but I guessed she had simply closed her eyes, resting and trying not to think about what was happening. She was right – the past fifteen minutes were hardly comfortable for a decent woman's recollection.

Through a dark passageway floored with quarry tiles, we came to a low doorway where Philip had to duck his head as he kicked the door further open. Beyond lay a large room with a low ceiling striped with old dark beams. All I gained at first was an impression of comfort, solid old furniture, functional rather than fashionable, and a great inglenook fireplace, its hearth cold but still holding the ashes of its last fire. A dark wooden stairway climbed up against the far wall.

'Cupboard under the stairs,' he threw at me. 'A blanket. Quickly!'

Beneath the stairs, a wedge-shaped door opened on to shelves crammed with linen, where warmth came out and met me. One-handed, I grabbed the first blanket I could see and swathed it over a big horsehair sofa, where he laid Saffron gently down with a sigh of relief.

'All right? Rest now.' Straightening, he eased his aching body, sending muscle rippling under pale skin that contrasted oddly with his sun-browned face, neck and forearms as he turned to me. 'There's no one here to help, I'm afraid. We fend for ourselves on Mondays. Mrs Gaywood stays at home and does the washing.'

'I can manage.' I hoped he couldn't read my confusion: the nearness of his naked body both appalled me and aroused me. His skin looked as though it would be soft to the touch. Vulnerable. Appealing ...

'Right, then.' He took off his cap, raked his fingers through tousled curls. 'Just stay with her. Keep her calm. Let her hold the baby.'

'I know what to do!'

The answer was a mutter which didn't sound complimentary; he turned away, making for a door at the foot of the stairs. Glad of his absence, I bent over the couch and gave up my sweet burden, laying the baby in his mother's waiting arms.

'He ought to be washed,' she fretted. 'Kate ... Where are we?'

'The Farcroft farm.'

'Mad Jack's place?' Her eyes filled with tears, but she was laughing, too, biting her lip. 'She'll be beside herself. Spitting fire. Won't she?'

'Probably,' I agreed with a sigh. We didn't need to

identify the 'she' – both of us knew who the female dragon was. 'But there's not much we can do about it. At least the baby's all right. And you, too. Aren't you?'

She pulled a face. 'I'm in a horrible mess, down below, but don't—' She stopped, glancing beyond me as our unlikely knight reappeared. He had found a shirt from somewhere, buttoned it to the throat and was now rolling back the sleeves. Though more grey than white, and with a large patch at the shoulder, at least it covered him decently.

'Will the others be coming this way?' he asked.

'Uncle Frank was going to find the doctor and bring him after us,' I told him. 'I presume he'll take the short cut.'

'Then I'll go and wait for them. I'll see what I can do about that motor, meanwhile. Can you manage alone, till someone gets here?'

'Of course I can.'

His look said he doubted that, but he started for the door.

'Mr Farcroft . . .' Saffron was gazing down into the blood-streaked face of her sleeping child. One tiny hand peeped from its wrappings and curled round her forefinger. 'I'm going to call him Edward, after the late King. Little Eddy, that's who you are, my sweetie. And Henry, for your Daddy. And . . .' She looked up at the young man looming behind the couch. 'And Philip. That's your name, isn't it? Would you mind? Edward Henry Philip Rhys-Thomas. That's a lovely name.'

'It's longer than he is,' the young farmer said, gruff but not displeased, a stain of red creeping up his lean brown face. 'No, I don't mind. I can't say about your family, though. Well . . . Help yourself to anything you need. You'll find the kitchen through there.'

And he was gone.

'I shall call him what I choose!' Saffron muttered, kissing

the tiny fingers. 'You're Edward Henry Philip, my darling, aren't you? Besides, the old witch will be so pleased to have a grandchild at last . . .' She stopped herself, glancing up to add hastily, 'A grand*son*, I mean. The first boy.'

Though my mind and heart were racing, I heard myself argue, 'You've forgotten my half-brothers. Rudger, Pieter, Hansi . . .'

'Oh, yes, but they don't count. Not really. They're von Wurthes. This little man is the first Rhys-Thomas. And he does need a wash, Kate. D'you think you could . . .'

Beyond the door at the foot of the stairs, I discovered a short passageway which led to a kitchen. Ancient oak beams spanned the ceiling, supporting muslin slings bearing great hams and marrows, above a scrubbed table still laid with the remains of breakfast – dirty cups; a fat teapot; milk and sugar with muslin covers weighted by blue beads; plates showing evidence of egg and fat ham; and a bread knife lying among crumbs on a battered board. A fire burned in a big kitchen range, with a kettle on a chain hanging near it, faintly steaming, and on top of the side oven a great iron stockpot sent out a savoury aroma. A pump supplied cold water to a stone sink, where I used the carbolic soap and scrubbing brush which lay, still wet, on the wooden drainer. The lace curtain at the window was splattered and stained, with dead flies scattered on the windowsill around pots containing vigorous flowering plants.

I found what I needed – hot water in the kettle hanging over the fire, an enamel bowl under the sink, clean cloths, towels and other linen from under the stairs. The linen cupboard backed on to the kitchen range, that was why it was so warm; some of the things at the back had been there so long they had gone yellow. I found a voluminous apron and wrapped it over my skirt and blouse somewhat belatedly.

Only then, catching sight of myself in a mirror in the hall, did I fully realize what a dishevelled state I was in, from head to foot.

Saffron, though, was in even worse case, as I discovered after we had gently dabbed the blood from the baby and wrapped him in a clean sheet. We laid him in a nest of blankets on the floor while I tended to his mother, learning a great deal that my sheltered upbringing had kept from me. The lesson was a messy one. I managed to pad her thoroughly and make her more comfortable. Then I settled her to rest, and went to make a pot of tea.

With a battered old tea caddy in my hands, I stared past the stained net curtain at the yard outside. Outbuildings with patched roofs and green-painted doors surrounded it, a few leggy weeds grew in cracks, an old tin tub hung against the wall, a couple of chickens scratched . . .

An old, old house, with a personality of its own, it seemed almost to be breathing. I was conscious of the quietness, another sheltering layer around me. From a corner alcove, a grandfather clock ticked off the seconds, emphasizing the stillness. Strangely, though, I felt safe there, all alone with Saffron and the baby, especially when Mad Jack was far away. The world seemed distant, shut out by thick walls and leaded windows beyond which the mist still pressed.

But even in this brief Eden a worm stirred in my mind. Twice, Saffron had called her baby 'the first grandchild'. Oh, she had spoken unthinkingly, too full of her own distress to consider the effect her words might have. But I had no doubt she had voiced the feelings of the family – Harry's child was to be the favourite. Clara's children didn't count. The *Menschen* were little German half-breeds, beneath notice, and I . . . was female.

For myself I didn't care: I had never hoped for anything

from the Rhys-Thomases, so another rejection couldn't hurt me. And my little half-brothers, with their father to provide for them, could laugh at indifference from this side of the Channel. It was my mother I felt sorry for. How could I stay here? Oh, I had to go home! Soon . . .

SIX

As I set the tea tray down on a table near the window in the living room, I heard the sound of wheels, and through the mist a carriage appeared. Frank leapt out, followed by Harry, and then the doctor. Thank goodness!

The doctor had not been at the funeral: he had been called away to attend an injured man and Frank had commandeered a carriage to go after him. When eventually they returned, they had encountered the funeral procession forming up at the church, where the anxious Harry had joined them. They had met Philip Farcroft at the entry to the back lane.

He had not told them the whole truth: they believed he had taken Saffron to the house and left us alone to cope with the birth. If they had thought about it, they would surely have known that I couldn't have managed alone, but I suppose they preferred not to think about it. So another myth was born – that I was the one who had played midwife. Saffron seemed to feel it was simpler that way.

Less commendably, our gallant knight Philip had implied that the car had stopped of its own accord. When Frank discovered what had really happened, he was so furious that he sent the police to have a look at the lane, and told Oliver Wells to sue Mad Jack for damages.

Grandmother was furious over the whole affair, though she hid her anger behind tight lips until the funeral guests had departed. Then, she summoned Frank and me to her pretty blue and white sitting room in the south wing, and blamed him for 'leaving a young girl to cope. That's so typical of you – you're irresponsible. When are you going to grow up?'

'I'm in no mood for post-mortems, Mother,' Frank said stoutly. 'In my opinion, the "young girl" coped admirably. Now, if you'll excuse me, I have to get the men together and see about rescuing my car.'

'This was all because you defied me,' she threw after him. 'If you had used a carriage like normal people, none of this would have happened!'

The slamming of the door was the only reply.

Drawing a breath, she lifted her neck to its full extent and looked along her nose at me, blue eyes sharp as gimlets. 'You did manage well,' she grudged, and for a moment I thought she was praising me, but, 'I do wonder at the kind of education they allow young girls in Prussia. At your age, Catherine, I knew *nothing* about childbirth. Nor did I wish to. I suppose your mother spoke freely to you when she was engaged in breeding those three boys. Clara always did have a strange sense of propriety.'

'I wish you wouldn't say such things!' I exclaimed. 'I don't intend to be impertinent, Grandmother, but . . . Everyone seems to be against her, and it's not fair.'

She watched me in silence for a moment and I could almost see her brain working, cold as clockwork. 'She brought it upon herself, Catherine. She was headstrong. It's a trait you appear to have inherited.' (She prounced it 'tray', the French way, which was typical of her.) 'But I shall say no more. No good ever came from opening old wounds.'

'I'm not a child any more. If I'm to be asked to take sides—'

'No one is asking that. Nor do I expect you to think badly

of your mother. But what happened, happened. Your grandfather . . .' Pain veiled her eyes for an instant, then was gone, put aside as sternly as she put aside most human emotions. 'He was a very sick man. He didn't know what he was saying. For that reason, it should be let alone, Catherine. We shall put aside past mistakes, whether your mother's, or yours, or mine. We must go on, not look back. Now that you're here, I should like to get to know you. You're my granddaughter, after all. And, until you're of age, you are my responsibility.'

'No!' I found myself on my feet, trembling. Until I was of age? Three whole years? 'No, you needn't worry about that. Thank you for the offer, but I think I shall go back to Berlin on the first boat.'

'No, Catherine. You will not.'

'But I want to be with my family! I'll go into town tomorrow and buy a ticket. Uncle Frank—'

'Frank won't help you,' she cut in, her voice hardening. 'Neither will anyone else here. If you ask, you will be disappointed. The decision has been made. You will not go back, Catherine.'

I couldn't believe my ears. 'You can't *hold* me here! If I decide to leave—'

'The decision is not yours to make!' Realizing she was losing her temper, she took hold of herself, drew herself up and compressed her lips, letting her breath slowly out through her nostrils. I almost expected to see flames ignited by the blue fire in her eyes. 'I don't intend to argue,' she said, then, 'My dear child . . . I don't blame *you*, entirely. Your mother has obviously allowed you too much latitude.'

What? I felt as if I had run into a sudden bank of mist that hid every familiar landmark. 'I don't understand.'

Her eyebrow arched with fresh impatience. 'Of course

you do, Catherine! You understand me very well. Let us have done with this pretence! Your mother has written and told me the whole sorry story.'

'You mean . . . about Carl-Heinz?'

'What else?' Her lips formed a slit in her face as she got to her feet, smoothing down her black silk bodice with thin, gnarled hands. 'You will not leave. You will stay, here in England, for the foreseeable future.'

A knock on the door interrupted my incoherent protests and through a fog of exasperation I heard the butler inform Grandmother that Mr Wells had asked to see her.

'Ask him to come up, Billing,' she replied, and glanced at me. 'You may go, Catherine. Let us hear no more of this.' Her mind was already on more important matters as she turned away.

I made for the door, inwardly seething, but stopped to look round and say hoarsely, 'My name is Kate. Not Catherine – Kate. Kate von Wurthe. And I'm proud of it!' I, too, let the door slam behind me.

In my room, I stood staring out as the sun set behind the thick carpet of mist that was slowly dispersing as the air cooled. I watched it ebb like a tide, washed pink by afterglow. Red sky at night . . . Yet again, I turned for answers to Carl-Heinz's letter of rejection, but it only said what it had said before – lies and untruths. He loved me, I knew he did. But Willi, and the others, had made him write and say . . .

Of course! *That* was why I had to stay away – because Carl-Heinz *did* love me, and if I were in Berlin they feared what might happen. We might elope, or kill ourselves, like the tragic royal lovers at Mayerling . . .

Sitting at the little desk, I wrote again to Carl-Heinz, pleading with him to reply. I told him I was being forced to stay away from him, that I would love him for ever. But *please* would he write and let me know for sure what he felt? Until I heard from him my life was not worth living.

The morning brought a steady, depressing rain, and letters for me, but nothing of import. My friends' lives were going on; Mother and Pa and the little men were well and sent their love – she told me nothing new. She was part of the conspiracy of silence, it seemed.

For a day or two the house was busy with the aftermath of the funeral. Extra men came in to heft luggage down the stairs and ferry people to the station, while women stripped the beds and cleaned the guest rooms. When the last guest had gone, Grandmother and Vicky spent a day in Lynn with Saffron and the baby. I would have gone with them, but Grandmother said that I might better spend my time doing some reading in preparation for the college entrance exam which I was to sit that Friday. She felt sure I would find something of use among the collection in the library.

She was wrong – I did glance along the library shelves but none of the titles struck me as particularly useful. Anyway, I wasn't interested in the entrance exam. I didn't care whether I passed or not.

Tempted out by the fairer weather, I changed into clothes suitable for outdoor activity and, wondering if I might find a bicycle to borrow, I went down to the yards. Bed linen billowed in the breeze, festooned from long lines held up by props. With the same breeze tugging at my well-anchored boater, I petted the carriage horses in their stable, and saw that Frank's car was gone.

'Hello, Kate!'

'Oh – Tom, hello. I didn't see you there.' He had appeared from behind a corner of the stables, carrying a kitten which seemed contented under his stroking fingers. In his smiling face, blue eyes gazed incuriously under a mop of tousled fair hair.

'They've gone into Huns'ton,' he said.

'Who have?'

'Emmet and Frank. Gone to Huns'ton to see if they can get the mudguard fixed. It was bent.'

'It's lucky nothing else was damaged,' said I. 'I thought for a while I might have wrecked the car.'

But since Tom hadn't been there when the 'accident' happened his memory didn't stretch that far, so he couldn't follow my logic.

'Do you want to come and see the kittens?' was his reply.

The kittens and their mother were installed in a nest of hay at the back of one of the old carriage houses. Above them, swallows flitted in and out and sparrows chirped from the rafters, scavenging for seed. An old dog lay on guard in the sunlight by the door, somnolent and grey.

Tom took me to see his aviary, where in separate cages he had a parrot and a mynah bird. The latter kept saying, 'Where's Tom, then?' in an uncanny imitation of Emmet's voice, and answering himself, 'I'm here! I'm here!' in Tom's excited chuckle. Not far away another cage held canaries and budgerigars, flitting their bright wings from perch to perch. Tom kept rabbits, too, some chinchillas and one huge white fellow with pink ears and red eyes. 'I call him Ghost – because he's white and scary. But,' Tom solemnly assured me, 'he wouldn't hurt you.'

Wondering if he shared my ability to see glimpses of the other side, I said, 'Are ghosts white and scary?'

'Only in stories,' said Tom, eyes steady as a child's. 'There's no such thing as ghosts, not really. And this is my newest one – Frank found her hurt in a field. She's a wild rabbit.' He slid me a sly look, adding, 'Don't tell, but I call her Toria. She scratches.'

We shared a conspiratorial smile as I guessed that poor Tom was still suffering his sister's impatience. 'I won't tell,' I promised.

Despite the birth-trauma that had left him so sadly damaged, Tom was the gentlest of creatures, and cared well for his animals. He had built their pens and cages himself, with help from one of the gardeners, and his brothers brought gifts for the pets – mirrors for the budgies, water bowls for the rabbits. 'Emmet bought the cat's bell, to warn the birds when she's coming. She's very bad. She kills birds if she can.'

'Well, yes, cats do kill things.'

'Well, they shouldn't!' His face went red. 'Things didn't ought to die. I don't like it when they die. I didn't want Pater to die!'

'I know, Tom.' But as I reached to touch him in comfort he jerked away, scrubbing at a tear.

'Well . . .' I sighed, not knowing what else to say. 'I came out hoping to go for a bicycle ride. Is there a bicycle I could borrow?'

That distracted him. 'I'll show you.'

Another outhouse stored half a dozen bicycles of various shapes and sizes. Tom helped me choose one suitable for myself, and pumped up the tyres for me, then decided, 'I've got to go. I promised to groom the horses. Goodbye, Kate,' and he was gone as quickly as he had appeared.

Making down the drive on the cycle, I soon came to the main road and turned north, an invigorating ride in a gusty breeze, freewheeling at speed into the hollow, then riding up the next hill until my protesting legs obliged me to dismount and walk. Fields lay all around, some of them still busy with harvest, men with scythes sweeping at the grain, other folk behind tying it and stacking it in stooks; gulls wheeled, trees rustled, and away to the left the sea lay blue in sunlight. Carts and wagons carried goods from village to village or farm to farm, and I passed a rumbling, hissing steam wagon laden with barrels of beer.

Another young woman cyclist seemed pleased of company as we walked up a long incline, but when she said, 'Where you now from, then? You don't wholly sound English,' my reply made her stop and stare at me in fright. She pretended that something had gone wrong with her wheel. 'No, that's all right, go you on. I can fix that myself, thank you.'

In Hunstanton, I found summer visitors strolling round the shops and enjoying the promenade, the pier and the views from the cliffs – a merry scene with flags flying, skirts and ribbons fluttering, and children dashing about. On one of the sloping side streets above the broad green that fronts the sea, I spied a butcher's shop with the name 'Ehrenfried' over it. There, I asked for some offal, intending it for Tom's cats.

The butcher had a strong south German accent and was pleased when I asked him in his own language where he came from. Frankfurt, he said. And I? Since he had no other customers at the time, we fell into conversation and I told him of my encounter with the girl who had been so worried to learn that I came from Berlin.

'It's a problem,' Mr Ehrenfried agreed. Local people were suspicious of him and his family, though he'd lived in Hunstanton for twenty years. It was ludicrous! His neighbours knew he was a decent, God-fearing man, but anti-German comments in newspapers, cartoons, advertisements, plays and even jokes all worked on underlying fears. He had heard one mother threaten her child that, if he didn't behave, 'Butcher Ehrenfried'll come and chop off your head. That's what Germans do!' His business was beginning to suffer. He was thinking of changing his name.

'Harald!' his wife admonished, appearing from the back and drawing our attention to two or three customers who had come in. So we switched to English, I paid him for the meat and withdrew, smiling and greeting the other customers, 'Good morning, ladies, what a lovely day!' but not one of them replied and I was aware of hard stares following me.

Just as I was deciding that I didn't much care for Hunstanton, I met Frank and Emmet, who teased me out of my irritable mood. We all had lunch at the Sandringham Hotel, and later they tied my cycle to the back of Frank's motor and we went home in style.

That evening I sat down to write an article about the anti-German feeling which pervaded even sleepy Norfolk. I wrote it in German, and packed it off to my schoolfriend Gudrun Thunissen, for submission to a magazine in Berlin, which had published pieces of my writing before. It seemed to me that Berliners ought to know that malicious rumour was making life difficult for their countrymen in England. Yet the ordinary German man had no more desire for war than had the ordinary Englishman.

I settled down in bed that night, trying to distract myself with an old copy of *Strand Magazine* which Uncle Frank had given me. It contained the H. G. Wells story, 'The Land Ironclads', and within a page or two I was engrossed by the tale of armoured battle machines that could cross any terrain and surmount any obstruction, dealing out death as they went. The graphic description of trench warfare bothered

me: I couldn't help but imagine Carl-Heinz and Fritzi –
and other young officers of my acquaintance – engaged in
such a struggle. Could it be true, as Frank had implied, that
the Thorne-Thomas factory was experimenting with battle
machines like these?

Next morning, my uncle and I made an early start, catching
the train before eight o'clock, bound for London, where I
was to sit the entrance exam for a course at the School of
Economics. Frank proposed that we should stay at the
family's Mayfair apartment until the Monday, when he had
an appointment to see someone who had commissioned a
picture from him. Grandmother didn't entirely approve, but
I suppose she knew Frank would take care of me.

The local train was quite full, but we found two seats
together. Tired after a restless night, I told Frank that I had
read the beastly story: 'It gave me nightmares.'

'It was intended to. Wells is trying to warn us what
science can do if we don't keep it in check.'

'So it's not true? Thorne-Thomas Engineering isn't really
making some dreadful battle machine that wi—'

The look on his face stopped me – a look of alarm with
wide, warning eyes that made me aware of other ears in the
carriage. Our fellow travellers were carefully not looking
at us, but they were all listening.

Next second, Frank's laugh was scorching me with
mockery. 'Of course not! It's a story, silly goose! Good
heavens . . . you'll be asking me next if there's really such
a thing as a time machine! Mr Wells is a genius at imagining
such things. Maybe you're not old enough to appreciate
him yet. Stick to *Alice in Wonderland*.'

Mortified, I turned my burning face away and didn't
speak to him again until we arrived at Lynn. Indeed,

conversation between us was spasmodic all the way to London on the crowded express.

Under a pall of smoke that greyed the sky and caught at the back of one's throat, pedestrians crowded city pavements, news vendors cried the latest headlines, and roads ran thick with motor omnibuses and trucks, horse-drawn traffic, steam wagons, a few private cars, delivery vans . . . Frank hailed a one-horse hansom and directed its driver to Mayfair.

'We'll get settled in and then have a quiet lunch. The exam isn't until two o'clock. You need to be relaxed for that.'

'Oh, it doesn't matter,' I sighed, watching the traffic and the dirty grey buildings go by.

'Of course it matters! It's your whole future.'

The doorman in the foyer of Mayfair Mansions greeted him warmly by name – apparently Frank often used the apartment when he was in town. The block contained half a dozen serviced flats, with the doorman to check all callers, and valets and maids on duty night and day. Our apartment lay on the top floor, reached via a lift, the rooms large, airy, panelled in oak and newly decorated art deco style. I didn't have time to study the place in detail; Frank was hungry, eager to be out in the city, and rattled by the tension that still lingered between us.

As we rode down again in the lift, he demanded, 'What's wrong with you, Kate? Would you rather be studying here in London, with some degree of freedom, or stuck at Denes Hill, at Mother's beck and call, like Vicky?'

'I'd rather go home!'

'Well, that's out of the question, isn't it?' His glance said he knew the whole story and, flushing with annoyance, I turned away as he added, 'I don't believe you'd be happy squandering your talents. You're an intelligent girl.'

'I thought I was only fit for *Alice in Wonderland*!'

He made an impatient sound, grasping my arm. 'Look at me, Kate. You know why I said that, surely? We weren't alone on that train. You don't seem to realize . . . I was fearfully indiscreet ever to mention the subject to you. It's secret. Top secret.'

My heart seemed to contract. 'You mean, there really are horrible machines like that? Being made by Thorne-Thomas?'

He watched me intently, a deep furrow biting between his brows. 'I shouldn't tell you this. But since I respect your intelligence I also trust you to understand . . . No, there aren't any such machines, as yet. But prototypes are being tested. Even the men who're working on the frames don't know exactly what those great metal boxes are for. Tanks, they're being told. Storage tanks, for water and such like. If the truth got out and the Germans got hold of it . . . God knows, even as we speak, Berlin is probably working on something similar. They're not fools. H. G. Wells isn't the only one who can foresee where mechanization is heading.'

'But that's frightful!' I breathed.

'I agree. I can't imagine anything more horrible than men in machines cold-bloodedly killing each other. Land ironclads. Aeroplanes. The next war, when it comes – and it *will* come, sooner or later – is going to be the bloodiest, beastliest yet. You and I should take no part in it. Let's not play their game.'

A shiver ran through me. 'No, we won't.'

'I'm glad to hear it. Parliament's just passed an Official Secrets Act, you know. If you breathe one word of this . . . If you write it in a letter . . .' The lift stopped, the door rattled open and the doorman emerged from his little office to touch his peaked cap and usher us out.

But I understood well enough. If I wrote about this, even to Mother, Frank would be in trouble. I had half been planning to write another article to send to Gudrun. Indeed, if I had read the story before I wrote the first piece I might have . . . *Mensch!* If I did that, I really would be a German spy. But wasn't that what I *should* be, out of loyalty to my stepfather and my friends in Berlin?

Only a few of us took the special late-entrance exam for the course beginning that autumn at the London School of Economics. We sat at desks spread wide apart in a large room with high windows, while a female invigilator paced up and down, her heels heavy on bare floorboards and a ruler tapping against her skirts. I don't remember what questions the paper posed. I kept my head down, writing and writing, part of my mind far away. Dear God, let there not be a war!

Frank and I were out in the streets again by three thirty, with amity restored between us. He took me to an art gallery where one of his paintings hung alongside works by more famous artists. I was impressed.

'Shall you let me do your portrait now?' he laughed.

We had tea at the Ritz, and later he took me to a box he had reserved in a music hall on whose bill both Little Titch and Marie Lloyd appeared. I loved the colour and gaiety, the dancing, bright costumes, and the catchy songs in which the audience joined. Neither Mother nor Grandmother would have approved of the innuendo, but it made Frank laugh. I laughed, too – even at the jokes against the Kaiser. Absurd to believe that anything could harm this jolly world of warmth and togetherness.

The master of ceremonies announced 'The Gala Girls',

but it was not until the dance troupe came on to tap their shoes to the 'Maple Leaf Rag' that I recalled where I had heard the name. There, among the beauties in their frothy short skirts and long ringlets, was my acquaintance from the Channel steamer, Judy Love, and next to her a vivid redhead who could be none other than her friend Elsie.

'You know her? Which one?' Frank lifted his opera glasses to examine the girls more closely, and what he saw made him whistle. 'The blond one? Quite a corker, isn't she? We'll go round after the show and say hello.'

'There's no need for—'

'Of course there is, Kate. You can't spot an old friend and just go away without saying hello.'

We did more than say hello: we took Judy and Elsie out to supper. They had a riotous time, bowled over by Frank's charm, wit and artistic looks, by his long hair, his soft shirt with its cravat and baggy jacket, by the big-brimmed hat he affected, by the waiters who greeted him as an old friend, the well-dressed people who paused to speak to him and, not least, by the money he spent. His behaviour scandalized me, but after an unaccustomed glass or two of champagne I found myself joining in the laughter. Thoughts of war retreated, gladly put aside for happier things.

'Lovely to see you again, dear!' Judy Love cried as we delivered her and Elsie to their lodgings. 'Didn't I tell you that German boy wasn't worth your tears? I knew you'd soon forget him.' Giving Frank an arch look, she laughed. 'But you should have told me more about your family. Wish *I'd* got a gorgeous uncle like this to take me about.'

'Oh, so do I!' Elsie shrieked. 'Night, night, Uncle Frank! Going to give us a goodnight kiss, then?'

He was only too happy to oblige both of them with kisses,

after which they stumbled up the steps to their front door, giggling and waving.

In the morning, I had only the slightest headache to remind me of a few hours which, by daylight, appeared scorchingly decadent.

Frank and I spent the next two days seeing the sights and visiting museums and galleries. On Saturday we attended a performance of *The Cherry Orchard*, which, said Frank, would convince his mother we had been serious in our pursuit of culture and, er-um, we needn't mention the music hall, need we? He was incorrigible and I adored him.

On Sunday we walked in the parks and listened to the opinions at Speakers' Corner. Frank heckled some of them, and raised laughter from the audience. Watching him, I knew I could never take the risk of having him hanged as a traitor. No one in Berlin would hear about armour-plated 'water tanks', not from me.

On our final day in London, Frank gave me some money to go shopping while he kept his appointment with his client. I bought a silver-plated lapel pin, with a tiny biplane on it, to send to Carl-Heinz as a memento; I knew he dreamed of being a flier some day. He could wear the pin, and think of me whenever he touched it.

After lunch, we took a boat trip on the river and, like any tourist, I goggled at landmarks I had only heard of before. If my uncle was trying to persuade me that a sojourn in London, as a student, was a desirable thing, he succeeded very well. The city would provide ample material and opportunity for me to practise my journalism. I almost began to hope that I might pass that wretched exam. Almost. In my heart I still prayed that a letter from Carl-Heinz might be waiting for me.

We dined in the restaurant car on the train that evening,

arriving home after nine o'clock. I was able to plead extreme weariness and retreat to my room to think over all that had happened. Where did my future lie? Where my loyalties?

My heart leapt as I saw two letters waiting for me. Both of them were from Berlin – one from Gudrun, the other from my stepbrother. Sighing, I laid them aside, thinking that reading them would serve to send me off to sleep, but first I took my time about preparing for bed, put on a clean nightdress, gave my hair a good brushing, took a sip of the hot cocoa Annie had brought me and, already yawning, opened Fritzi's letter.

Some phrases remain etched for ever in my mind, written in an erratic hand that revealed my stepbrother's distress. I can't think of it without the whole scene coming back in detail: pillows yielding against my back, feather mattress hugging me, fresh sheets harsh against my bare feet, smelling of air and starch – the beds were always changed on a Saturday. Lamplight laid a soft arc across the bed with its thick cream blankets and heavy white cotton spread, throwing patterns up the wall from the brass-knobbed bedstead. Shadows crouched in corners, water gurgled in pipes, and in the darkness outside drawn curtains a wind in the woods shushed and sighed . . .

And Fritzi's letter in my hand silently cut me to pieces. They had not wished me to know the truth, he said. Indeed, he himself had not believed it, at first. Now, since I persisted in my folly, he felt it was time I knew, even if it hurt me, which it would, and he was sorry about that, but it had to be, my own behaviour obliged him to be brutal in order to save me and my family from further shame and humiliation, to which end he had to tell me that I *must not* write again to Carl-Heinz. Carl-Heinz was using my letters to make mock of me – using them as proof that his stories of my immodest devotion to him had not been exaggerated.

Stories of . . . *what*?

Feeling as if an iced draught were stirring my scalp, I learned the truth about Carl-Heinz von Siemens, the honourable, blue-blooded, nobly born young officer of the Crown Prince's élite guard. He had courted me as an amusement, regaling his friends with every detail of his pursuit of the silly young *Ausländerin* who had worn her heart high on her sleeve. He had recounted, amid laughter, the words he had used to turn my head, and the way I had responded, adding a little more, and a little more, until his audience gasped for each new instalment in the story of the sexual seduction of Katarin von Wurthe.

Seduction, total and complete – that was what he had claimed – my becoming his mistress, willingly surrendering to his frequent demands . . .

No . . . My brain refused to take it in. I sat without moving, hardly breathing, staring at the letter, reading it over and over. The words danced in front of me, mocking me.

Fritzi's meaning came over more in what he hinted than what he said directly – he couldn't write such things to me in plain words. Being my stepbrother, he had been the last to hear the rumours, but as soon as he got wind of what was being whispered he had told Pa, and Pa had sent word to Carl-Heinz that the association must finish. So the joke had ended and the rejection letter had been written, delivered by Willi. My parents had decided to ship me off without saying a word to me of what had happened. '*We wanted no unpleasant scenes. Your mother is distressed enough.*' Anger made his penstrokes jagged. '*The more I think of it, the more I thank God you are not my sister in blood. If you*

were, *the shame would have killed my father, and forced
me to resign my commission. You must never come back.
You are no longer welcome here. You have disgraced us
all.*'

I had been branded an immoral woman without the
chance to defend myself. *That* was what hurt me most.
Rather than ask me, they had believed Carl-Heinz's lies.
'*We knew you would not admit to it,*' Fritzi had written.
Even if I had denied it, I would not have been believed.
Did none of them know me at all? Did none of them trust
me? Not even Mother?

I threw back the covers and went to the desk, to write an
impassioned letter assuring her that the rumours were wrong.
Wrong! A few kisses, a close embrace . . . That was all. I
had trusted him. Loved him.

Throwing down the pen, I ran to snatch his picture from
beside my bed and stare at his smiling, lying face. The truth
hit me with a force like talons clawing inside me. They had
let me be part of their playtime, let me laugh and dance and
drive with them, and then they had used my name, destroyed
my reputation . . . Oh, I knew the way they talked about
women! But that was *other* women, loose women, light
women. Not the sisters of brother-officers! Except, of
course, that I wasn't Fritzi's sister. I was low-born English,
not Prussian aristocracy. I didn't count.

Feeling as if my heart were dead inside me, I removed
the photograph from its frame and tore it across and across,
then laid the pieces in the fireplace and set a match to them
and watched them burn, and used the flame to light a corner
of Fritzi's letter, and let it curl and blacken in my fingers
until the final corner floated to charred ashes in the grate.
After it I burned my last letter from Carl-Heinz, severing
every tie.

It's not true, Mother! I wrote again, in despair, the ink blotched by tears of both pain and fury. *I swear it's not true!*

SEVEN

My appearance in the kitchen at six thirty the next morning startled a sleepy Annie. As we shared a pot of tea I told her I hadn't slept well, that I was going out for some fresh air and if I did not return in time for breakfast would she make excuses for me, please? Annie's good eye regarded me worriedly while the other fretted beyond my shoulder.

'All right, miss, if you say so. Only . . . I'm not telling any lies. If anybody asks, I'll tell the truth.'

'That's fine, Annie,' I agreed levelly, not caring. 'We should all tell the truth, as often as we can.'

On that misty, golden morning the trees all wore the same dark-green uniform, some turning brown at the cuffs, and in hedgerows blackberries hung in thick clusters. As I turned my trusty sit-up-and-beg cycle into the vale, laughter sounded from a field where women gleaned among corn stubble, while on the opposite side of the road a horse-drawn reaper chopped down bean stalks. The summer had done her work of ripening grain and fruit. Now she was withdrawing, shyly and sadly, leaving the stage for her sister, autumn, waiting in the wings.

Something of my life was ending, too. The last of childhood, perhaps. Despite the brightness of the lifting sun, the breeze brought a warning of colder days. My heart matched it, cold as the heart of the boy Kay, stolen by the Snow Queen. I would never care for anyone or anything, ever again. My pride in being German by adoption looked like stupidity now. Ten seemingly happy years in Berlin had been based on illusion.

A need for solace drew me up the rise to the church, lying quiet behind walls of dark yew. The click of the latch sounded like a shot, ricocheting through the stillness, and as I stepped over the high threshold the smell of old stone, dusty sunlight and damp hymn books enfolded me.

The church seemed even bigger now that it was empty, filled with the calm of long ages of listening for the still, small voice. Shafts of sunlight slanted through stained glass while great wooden trusses in the roof, soaring above like the inside of an upturned Ark, took and echoed every sound. I found myself walking on the balls of my feet, trying not to disturb the tranquillity as I waded through pools of coloured light, going softly up the central aisle and through the rood screen with its defaced paintings of saints. Like one seeking sanctuary, I sank down at the back of the choir stalls, my back to the great organ whose pipes lifted in stately symmetry. It almost seemed alive. Vibrations in the air still strummed to the memory of its music. Oh, yes, there were presences. Kindly ones, breathing a peace that failed to reach my shuttered heart.

Tears came stinging, making me pull a handkerchief from the soft purse at my belt, and as I did so something clinked to the floor – the lapel pin which I had bought in London for Carl-Heinz. I bent and picked it up, turning it between my fingers to watch the tiny silver biplane glint in the light, delicate as a dragonfly, a frame with wings, to be ridden by daredevils. I had bought it with such love, such hope . . . No, I mustn't think like that. Blinded by more tears, I wiped them away, took a deep breath and lifted my head.

Opposite, on the wall between two tall stained-glass

windows, a black marble plaque had been carved with words
that leapt at me:

In Memory of John George Rhys-Thomas
a beloved son and brother
Drowned, August 4th, 1901, aged 27
'When our tears of grief are dried,
we shall remember your laughter.'

John . . . I closed my aching eyes, reaching out with my
senses to call him, as once I had called my secret playmates.
But John wasn't there. The church couldn't contain him.
He belonged outside, with the wind and the sun, part of the
elements, in the woods, on the marshes, along the shore. It
was there he would find me, when the time came . . .

A sharp bang jerked me back to reality. As it echoed
through the empty spaces of the church I heard a male voice
curse softly, then the measured tread of heavy boots on stone,
and a curious swishing sound. Through gaps in the rood
screen I saw a great sheaf of ripe wheat bound with twine,
being carried on someone's shoulder; the wheat was making
a sibilant noise, ears and straw brushing together as they
bounced up and down, whispering memories of sunlight
and promises of crusty loaves.

I sat still, hoping I wouldn't be seen. I couldn't see the
man's face, only his faded blue shirt and brown corduroys,
but there was something about the long legs and thick leather
belt at his waist, the muscular brown arm embracing the
sheaf . . . He came into the chancel, manoeuvring his burden
through the screen, and went to drop it in a corner by the
altar rail. He had taken off his cap, so I could see the curly
hazelnut hair, newly cropped, and the angle of a hard brown
cheek and jaw . . .

Philip Farcroft stood a moment gazing at the jewelled crucifix on the altar, taking his rolled cap from where he had stuck it in his belt. Then, turning to leave, he straightened with a visible start as he saw me.

'Miss von Wurthe!' He spoke softly, his deep voice hardly stirring the echoes. 'I didn't see you there! Good morning.'

I don't think I replied.

'I, er . . .' He gestured at the wheat. 'I'm just bringing the sheaves for the harvest service next Sunday. Got some more on the wagon outside.'

'Don't let me delay you.'

The flicker in his eyes said he had noted the rebuff. 'Yes. Right,' he said, and strode loudly away.

He brought six sheaves in all, two framing the altar, another four along the bottom of the rood screen. Each time, his boots made a rude intrusion in that quiet place. I could have left while he was doing his job, but I stayed where I was, my head bent, my handkerchief balled in one hand, the lapel pin in the other. I reasoned that I was waiting for the place to be quiet again, after the farmer had gone, but perhaps I was lying to myself. Something about Philip Farcroft had intrigued me from the moment I saw him standing in the doorway of the railway carriage.

At last a silence fell. I could sense Philip hesitating, then I heard hobnails clink on stone as he came to the chancel steps and said with a heavy attempt at humour, 'Well, that's my bit done. "Bringing in the sheaves", eh?'

I nodded, murmuring something.

Another pause ensued. When I didn't look up, he came slowly up the steps. 'Is something wrong?'

I lifted my head, knowing my face informed on me. 'No.'

Green eyes regarded me steadily as he said, 'Our

111

harvest's nearly in, so long as this weather holds. We plan our barn supper for Saturday night, and then the thanksgiving on Sunday . . . Will you be coming to the service?'

'I'm not sure.' Wishing he would go away, I stared at my hands. How could I think with this great clumsy farmhand hovering over me?

But, instead of leaving, Philip slid into the pew a few feet from me, leaning on his knees, fiddling with his tweed cap. 'It's peaceful here.'

'Yes.' After all, I was glad that he had stayed.

He turned his head to slant a look along his shoulder. 'Am I intruding?'

'The church is open for anyone, I suppose.'

The silence gathered round us, but, given my intense awareness of him, and the confusion of my feelings, it was hardly peaceful.

'How's the little 'un?' he asked. 'The baby. Edward Henry Rhys-Thomas.'

'Edward Henry Philip,' I reminded him.

After a moment, he rumbled, 'She'll forget about that.'

'I don't think *any* of us will ever . . .' I stopped myself. 'I suppose you know that everyone believes it was I who . . .' I couldn't put it into words, not to him. I was remembering the baby cradled in the big, calloused, gentle hands that were toying with his cap. I was remembering his body, half naked . . .

'It seemed best to let them believe what they wanted to believe,' he said. 'I didn't tell any lies, but when they made assumptions I didn't argue. Easier that way. For everyone. It might be better if *we* forget about it, too. Miss von Wurthe—'

'It's Brand,' I interrupted. 'Catherine Brand.' The edge in my voice made him send me another puzzled glance, but he was too polite to ask about it directly.

'If you're niece to Frank Rhys-Thomas,' he said, 'then you must be Clara's daughter. You were here before, when you were a little girl.'

'Yes. But I don't remember—'

'Oh, we didn't meet. I was away at school a lot of the time. But everyone in Even'm knows the Rhys-Thomases. Your mother was very beautiful, so they say.'

'All the men seemed to think so,' I sighed, folding my handkerchief around the little silver aeroplane on its long pin. 'Well, it was true. Still is. I don't take after her – not in that way.'

After a long moment, Philip said slowly, 'If any other girl said a thing like that, I might think she was fishing for compliments.'

That made me look at him. 'I'm not.'

'I know.' His eyes held mine – clear, green and suddenly inimical. 'You don't care spit what I think of you, anyway.'

It hadn't occurred to me that he thought of me at all, not in that way. 'Please?'

He shrugged and looked at the cap he was twisting in his hands, the jumping muscle in his jaw revealing his annoyance. 'I know what you think of *me*, though.'

'I don't think anything of you!'

'Yes, you do.' Now his eyes sparked anger at me. 'You think I'm beneath your notice. You, and all your blessed family. Well,' he got to his feet, towering over me, 'that'll teach me to try playing Good Samaritan. I only stayed because I thought you might need some company. I should've known *my* help wouldn't be wanted. I'll bid you good day, Miss von Wurthe – Brand – whatever the heck you call yourself.' And he turned to march away.

Until now my acquaintance with young men had been

confined to the likes of Carl-Heinz and Willi von Sturm, neither of whom had ever been asked to do a serious day's work in his life. Philip Farcroft was different, far more than the simple farm labourer I had originally taken him for. I didn't quite know what to make of him, but I knew I didn't want us to part as enemies.

'It's Kate,' I said heavily.

He paused, not answering, his back rigid under the faded shirt.

'You might as well call me Kate,' I added. 'May I call you Philip? Philip . . . you're right, I am feeling . . . badly. I had a letter. A hateful letter. From Germany. That's why I came out. I couldn't face them at the house. I don't belong there. I don't belong *any*—' My voice broke on the last word and I bit my lip, choking back my distress. What on earth was wrong with me? Why did I feel I could say such things to him?

Slowly, almost reluctantly, he let himself relax. He sat down again, turned towards me with his arm along the back of the pew between us.

'Do you want to tell me the rest?'

I shook my head. 'I can't. It . . . oh, it's long and complicated and tedious. You must have work to do.'

'I have. But there's no hurry if . . .' His voice turned rueful as he added, 'History repeating itself.' Blinking back the threat of tears, I saw his mouth lift at one corner. 'My brother used to get into trouble for neglecting his chores on your mother's account. If he knew she was about, he'd drop everything trying to catch a glimpse of her.'

'He would?' I was puzzled. 'Where is he now?'

The faint smile in his eyes faded. 'Dead. Eight years ago. A plough toppled over on him. He bled to death.'

I was too appalled to know what to say.

114

'Dad swears *that* was all on account of Clara Rhys-Thomas, too,' Philip added. 'He believes that, after Clara married that German fellow, Michael lost heart. Got careless. Stopped caring.'

'I had no idea. I . . . I'm sorry.'

'Why? Another Farcroft less . . .'

Aware that fresh hostility was hovering between us, I said earnestly, 'I'm not a part of that feud, Philip. We aren't *obliged* to be enemies, you and I, just because you're a Farcroft and I'm from Denes Hill. Are we?'

He didn't answer, but I could see he was thinking about it.

'What did your father say when he found out the new heir had been sheltered under his roof?' I asked.

'I didn't tell him.'

'So the whole truth is our secret – yours, and mine, and Saffron's.' The thought of sharing a secret with him was delicious, somehow. 'You know . . . you were splendid.'

Mouth wry, he shook his head. 'No . . .'

'You were! And I'm enormously grateful for it. I couldn't have managed alone.'

'I'm sure you could,' he argued, a stain of blood creeping up his lean cheek. 'It was the least I could do, anyway. If it hadn't been for Dad . . . I, er, suppose they told you they sent the police to see us.'

'I didn't hear what happened.'

'Dad told them there'd been an accident with a plough and that was how the trench was made.'

'Did they believe him?'

'To tell you the truth, by the time they got there I'd cleared away the evidence, so there wasn't much for them to see. They warned us to be careful in future, but they didn't press charges.'

'Perhaps they should have done! I'm sorry, I know he's your father, but . . . it was a dangerous thing he did. Someone might have been badly hurt. We do have a right to use that lane, don't we?'

'There's been a right of way there for ages past,' he admitted. 'The thing is . . . it goes right on up through the woods, over the hill and down into Heacham Hollow. There used to be some good rough shooting. But when your grandfather came he put his gate across it, and a notice claiming it was all private property, and he got his men to chase the local people away. He got a court order stopping all public access – he knew the magistrate. So Dad says if the villagers can't use the path going up to Denes Hill, then he'll stop the Rhys-Thomases using *his* bit of the lane.'

'I see,' I sighed. 'I didn't know.'

'He knows he went too far this time, though,' Philip added. 'We had a threatening letter from your lawyer. But I wrote offering to pay for any damage to the car and yesterday we heard that your uncle Frank was willing to settle for that. Maybe Dad'll cool down now the old man's dead and gone. But . . . you were going to say – about that letter you had.'

'Oh . . . no, it's nothing.' I couldn't explain my problem, not to him. 'I mustn't keep you from your work.'

'Then I'd better go and show my face or Dad'll think I'm slacking. You, er . . . do you need a ride back?'

'Thank you, but I have my cycle. Besides, what if your father saw us together?'

'What if he did? He's not a monster, you know. He's got a quick temper, that's all. Anyway, I was only offering you a ride, not asking you to start walking out with me.'

Stung, I gazed at the lapel pin in my hand, reminded of Carl-Heinz. 'Just as well. You'd have received a dusty answer.'

'That's what I thought.'

The disgust in his voice made me look up and see that he had taken my answer as a personal slight. 'Oh, Philip! Don't be so testy. I didn't mean . . . What I meant was I have no wish to become involved in that way. Not for a long time, if ever. I'm not going to college to get an education just to waste it on becoming some man's chattel.' Somehow, the decision had formed without conscious effort.

'You're going to college?' Philip asked in surprise.

'To the London School of Economics. That's why I came to England.' If I said it firmly enough, maybe I would in time believe it.

'You mean . . . you're staying? I assumed you'd be going back to Germany now that—'

'No. No, I— Ouch!' In my agitation, I had stuck the sharp end of the lapel pin into my thumb. As I sucked the pain, tasting blood, the pin again went spinning to the floor and Philip reached to retrieve it for me, holding it between his fingers. The little aeroplane seemed to fascinate him.

'It's a Farman, isn't it?'

'Is it?'

'I think so. You can tell by the shape of the wing, though they've modified it since this was made. They're experimenting with . . .' He stopped himself, giving me a rueful glance. 'Sorry, I expect it's all Greek to a girl, but I find the whole idea of aviation exciting.'

'And so do I! Being a girl has nothing to do with it. I can drive a motor, too, which I bet you can't.'

'I could soon learn, given the chance,' he responded at once. 'But I'd much rather fly. I'd have liked to go to that air meeting they had in France a couple of years ago, but Dad said we couldn't afford to throw good money away on that sort of jaunt.'

'The meeting at Rheims?' I asked. 'I'll tell you about that some time.'

His face lit with boyish envy. 'You were *there*?'

'No. But my stepbrother and . . . and some of his friends went.' Carl-Heinz had gone on that trip. And Willi von Sturm.

'Lord! Wish I'd seen it. Being a Territorial is all right, but if—'

'A Territorial?'

He paused to collect his thoughts. 'A part-time soldier. We train at weekends, and summer camp. But if I could do just as I wanted I'd go off and join the RNAS tomorrow – that's the Royal Naval Air Service. They've established a naval air battalion down south, you know. A place called Farnborough. With them, I could learn to fly.'

How strange, I thought with a curious lump in my throat. Who would have thought that Philip Farcroft and Carl-Heinz von Siemens had anything in common? I felt that I had been allowed a glimpse of his deepest secrets. 'You may as well keep that pin,' I said.

'What?' He looked at me in startlement. 'No, I couldn't.'

'Of course you could. *I* don't want it. I bought it . . . I bought it on impulse, as a souvenir. Keep it. Call it a thank you for being so kind. No, don't argue with me. You have been kind. Again. I seem to be falling deeper and deeper into your debt.'

Philip shook his head, his eyes steady on mine. 'You don't owe me a thing,' he said quietly, and added, as if testing the sound of it, 'Kate.'

Without warning, the atmosphere around us became charged. I had been aware of him as a personable male creature ever since he had stepped aboard the Lynn-bound train, but there in the quiet church the feeling swamped me and instinct told me, with stunning clarity, that he was equally aware of me. My face grew hot, my head tight. I caught myself picturing his sturdy torso, naked beneath the rough clothing, and . . . My thoughts shocked me, for I had never reacted to a man, not even Carl-Heinz, in quite that physical way. Surely it wasn't decent!

Needing to escape from a danger I didn't fully comprehend, I leapt to my feet. 'Is that the school bell? *Mensch!* I must go.' I edged away from him, out of the pew.

'No, don't . . .' he began anxiously, rising as if to stop me. 'Have I upset you, going on about soldiering and such? I mean, with you being raised over there in Germany . . .'

'I hadn't thought of it.'

'Nor had I, until that minute,' he confessed. 'But, if enemies try landing on the Norfolk coast, whoever they are, I'll be there to meet them. A man has to stand ready to defend his own.'

The thought made my head feel tight with panic. 'It won't come to that. It *can't*! Oh . . . why must everyone keep talking about war? I don't even want to think about it. Philip . . . do I *really* sound like a foreigner?'

'Not so much as you did when we first met.'

'Good. Good. Well . . . I must get back, or I shall be in trouble.'

As I made for the chancel steps, he said, 'If you felt like taking a walk Saturday night, I might be out getting some air myself.'

'Oh?' What was he suggesting – that I should meet him?

'I'm hoping to slide out from the barn supper. The dogs'll need a run. And if I have to sing "To be a Farmer's Boy" once more, I'll go batty.'

'Oh. Yes, I see.'

A wry twist to his lips said he took that for a 'no'. 'Thanks for the pin, anyway. So long, Kate.'

At Denes Hill, Annie informed me that she had 'had to tell Lady Rhys-Thomas as how you'd gone out, miss. She asked me straight out. She say I was to tell you, soon's you came in, that she want to see you in the study. Right quick, miss.'

Though I was hot and dishevelled from cycling, I went upstairs to find Grandmother, pausing only to remove my hat and straighten my hair. Somehow I had found the beginnings of my future path. It resembled a way through tangled woods, fraught with weeds and brambles, but I could fight my way through if I were strong and resolute. The first obstacle was about to be removed: I was going to tell Grandmother the truth.

The study had been Grandfather's room, but his widow had taken it over and spent her days busy with paperwork – business affairs and personal letters – assisted by her maid-cum-secretary, Anderson, and by her daughter Vicky. As I turned into the upper hallway, I saw these last two outside the study door, talking in lowered voices. I detected a smirk in Vicky's voice as she said what sounded like, ' . . . rid of the elbee for a while. She can't—' The sentence snapped off as she saw me and turned to say, with a lightness so studied that it told her discomfort, 'Oh, there you are at last, Kate. Where have you been? We've all been worrying ourselves awfully over you, and Mother's waiting.'

What was she feeling guilty about? And then I realized . . . I had misheard 'the elbee' – it wasn't a slang phrase, it was initials: C.L.B. Emmet had used the same expression, I recalled, and Frank had shut him up. C.L.B. – it stood, of course, for Catherine Louise Brand. And it was *not* a term of endearment.

120

Grandmother sat behind a businesslike desk, dressed in her accustomed black and writing on an envelope. 'Close the door. Wait.' Having completed the address, she took a stamp from a small box and placed it carefully on the envelope, which she added to a few others in a tray. 'Now . . .' She turned to give me her full critical attention.

Anticipating an inquisition about my absence, I said, 'I've been to the village. To church.'

That took her by surprise. 'To church?'

'I needed to think.'

'I see.' She toyed with the cameo brooch at her throat, obviously disconcerted. 'Well . . . if you've decided to mend your ways, of course I can only approve. A sinner brought to repentance . . .'

'It wasn't forgiveness I was seeking, Grandmother,' said I sententiously. 'It was enlightenment. I wanted to understand why my entire family had painted my character in the most vivid shade of scarlet without even giving me the chance to defend myself. Even a murderer is allowed his day in court. *I* wasn't given a hearing of any kind.' The story of the misunderstanding poured out in an incoherent jumble, ending: ' . . . and now, because Carl-Heinz lied about me, everybody thinks the worst – Mother, and you, Uncle Frank, Emmet, Vicky . . . Do all of them know the sorry tale?'

Grandmother sat with a hand to her throat, her face pale and still, only her eyes moving, searching my face. When at last I ran out of words, she got to her feet. 'I'm distressed that you take me for a common gossip, Catherine. I told the family only that your parents felt you should spend some time here in order to forget an unsuitable attachment. To be frank, I've had rather more on my mind than your sordid infatuation with some callow youth. I do not see what profit there is in discussing it further. It's over. Whatever happened, you must learn from it, and go on.'

'But nothing happened! That's what I've been trying to tell you. Don't you believe me?'

'Whether I do or not is not the issue. Your own conscience must be your judge.'

'You *don't* believe me! *Why* don't you believe me? How can I prove . . .'

'You can prove yourself by your behaviour from now on,' she said with a dismissive gesture. 'Now, please . . . I have other things to do. The reason I asked Annie to send you up here was . . .' She took an envelope from her desk. 'This came for you. I wanted to be with you when you opened it. It's from the School of Economics.'

I tore the envelope open with shaking hands, taking a deep breath before unfolding the letter. Its few brief sentences offered me a place in college, beginning that October.

'Your uncle Frank was afraid you might have failed the exam for lack of trying,' Grandmother said. 'I'm glad he was wrong. This is a splendid opportunity for you.'

'And it means I shan't be imposing on your hospitality much longer,' I answered unsteadily. 'I'm sure that will be another relief for you.'

She drew a sharp breath, arching her neck as she strained to her full five feet four. 'How *dare* you speak to me like that?'

'Because it's true,' I said, and walked out.

Vicky was still outside, thin and sly with her reddish-fair hair in a style so widely padded that it looked too heavy for her swanlike neck. Having heard most of what had passed between Grandmother and me, she smirked as she slid by me, murmuring, 'See you at luncheon, Kate.'

Oh . . . I couldn't wait to get away, to make a new life for myself. In London.

Uncle Frank had the addresses of three prospective lodging places in the city – all of them eminently respectable, he assured me. When I told him of my quarrel with Grandmother, and explained what lay behind it, to my relief he believed my word.

'Of course I believe you, Kate. Damn it – excuse me, I mean, dash it all – I shall write to Clara myself. If only they had given you the chance to speak up, they couldn't have failed to see that you're telling the truth. Don't worry, girl. I'll set them straight. The Mater, too. Though don't think too harshly of her. She's been lied to and had her trust shaken before now.'

'Not by me!'

'No, that's true. Leave it with me, eh?'

Whatever he said to Grandmother, I did detect a slight lessening in the frost from then on, though she never forgave my plain speaking.

I kept myself busy, reviewing my wardrobe, making repairs and putting items out to be laundered. I had been annoyed to find that Marthe had packed nearly all of my belongings. Now, I guessed she had been instructed to do just that: I was not expected to go home – not for a very long time.

A small allowance was being paid into the bank for me, but I determined to augment it by my own efforts – by my pen, if I could. There would be much to write about in London, especially the suffragette movement – my friends in Berlin would be interested to hear how the women's cause progressed in England.

In spare hours I resorted to physical activity, playing

tennis with Emmet, or cycling, or walking, often taking a book or a magazine to read in some quiet corner. So long as I said where I was going, and when I expected to be back, no one objected to my doing as I pleased: Grandmother was trying to show me she trusted me. All too often, my way took me past the Farcroft farm, alert for glimpses of Philip.

One evening, on my way back for dinner, I walked up through the woods with a bag of books hanging from my shoulder. The day had grown cloudy and the light was deceptive – I kept flinching away from clawing branches only to find they were actually some distance away. Then I glimpsed a figure among the trees ahead. It looked like Tom. Whatever was he up to, skulking along from tree to tree as if he were stalking something? His attention was turned away from me, to a place where the woods thinned into a clearing. Was that another man walking there?

Before I could decide whether the second figure was real or illusion, Tom suddenly yelled aloud, leaping up and waving his arms, then went crashing through the undergrowth of brambles and bracken, hollering like a Red Indian. Wildlife fled ahead of him, birds rising, calling, a flurry of startled wings, pheasant, blackbirds, jays, all darting away from the uproar. There was a shot . . .

I stood still, appalled. Who was shooting in Denes Wood? Where? A hare came loping along the path towards me, saw me, and veered out of sight. Somewhere a dog was barking. I couldn't see it, but I heard a distant shout that silenced it.

Tom had stopped too. He was poised, listening.

'Tom!' I called. 'Tom, what's happening?'

He didn't answer. He was watching something I couldn't see. Was that someone hurrying away, crashing through the wood? Catching up my skirts, I forded through browning bracken, the books banging on my back. 'Tom . . . ?'

When he turned towards me he was laughing, a wicked grin splitting his ingenuous face. 'That stopped him. Did you see, Kate? He was after pheasant and I stopped him.'

'Who? Who was it?'

'That old man. Mad Jack, they call him. He comes up here poaching. I watch for him. I stop him when I can.'

'Stop him? *Liebe Zeite!* You mustn't take such risks, Tom. You might have been shot.'

'No, not me.' He shook his tousled blond head, eyes sparkling. 'I creep quietly, and then I run fast. Like the wind. It's all right, Kate. He never sees me coming.'

'But if he doesn't see you, he might accidentally . . .' No, he wouldn't understand. 'Tom . . . promise me you won't do this again.'

'I've got to,' he insisted. 'I'm the guardian of the wood. Pater said so. I found that wounded fox and took it home. But it died and that made me sad. And Pater said, "No more shooting in my woods. I won't have my boy upset." So I have to make sure the animals don't get hurt. That's my job.'

It was hardly my place to interfere, but it worried me. Tom was a Rhys-Thomas, and if that crazy old farmer was out with a shotgun, in the twilight . . . It didn't bear thinking about.

EIGHT

Uncle Frank promised to have a word with Tom about the dangers of leaping out on a man with a loaded gun, though he was angry, too, about Mad Jack's poaching. 'I shall have to get Wells to write another letter,' he said. 'The man can't be allowed to go around indiscriminately letting off guns on other people's property.'

'Perhaps he thinks he has good reasons for feeling aggrieved.'

Frank frowned at me. 'Think so? Dash it, Kate . . . What is this? Are you defending him?'

'No, of course not! I'm trying to be fair – the way you usually are.'

'I gave up being fair to Mad Jack a long time ago. He's used up his right to be given the benefit of the doubt.' Narrowed blue eyes perused me closely. 'Who've you been talking to?'

I had forgotten that the other side of the story had been given to me by Philip. 'No one! I just thought . . .'

'Well, don't think. That old madman's dangerous. You stay away from him. In fact, steer clear of the farm altogether. Don't go near that short cut. I'll tell Tom the same. I don't want either of you getting hurt.'

This decree irritated me: I didn't see why I should be forbidden to go anywhere. That was partly why, on Saturday night after dinner, I found myself creeping out of the house like a thief. The other part of my reasoning had to do with Philip Farcroft.

During that week I had occasionally glimpsed the curly-haired young farmer going about his work on the land – I had been watching for him, feeling curious, intrigued and, for no reason, unsettled by him. He had hinted at an interest in me strong enough to distract him from his work, as his brother Michael had been distracted by Mother. And he had, after all, asked me to meet him that Saturday night. I assured myself I wasn't interested in him personally – how could I be, with my heart dead? – but I caught myself thinking about him more often than was comfortable.

I hardly needed my trusty little refill torch: the sky was clear and the moon two-thirds full. Among the growth on either side, wildlife stirred amid thick black shadow. I wasn't afraid. For me, the dark was always full of friendly spirits breathing and whispering around me.

Before I reached the edge of the wood I heard the harvest party and, as I went down the track, the noise grew louder – music from a piano, a fiddle and an accordion, voices raised in song, and shrieks of laughter, with rhythmic clapping as if to encourage a dancer. The shouts grew louder, a storm of applause and whistling, banging on tables . . .

The barns lay off to the side of the farm lane, closer to the main road than the house itself, a sprawl of buildings flanking yards where haystacks flung great shadows. From one particular barn, with a swaybacked thatch roof, lamplight shafted mistily out from high windows. Beyond a half-open door large enough to take a laden wagon, I saw men, women and children seated at a trestle table strewn with the debris of a feast.

As I paused in the shadow of a hedge, I saw other people in the yard, a young couple taking the opportunity to do a little sparking. The girl giggled softly, the sound all but swamped in another burst of table-banging and boot-stomping before a silence fell and voices called out for a song: 'Come on, bor. Your turn. Get you up.' A piano struck up a brief introductory phrase; then a male voice began to sing, ' "The sun had set behind the hill, Across the dreary moor..." ' I recalled Philip saying he'd go batty if he had to sing that song again. Did that richly resonant baritone belong to him?

The courting couple moved away, heading behind the haystack as the whole company joined with gusto in the chorus: ' "To be a farmer's bo-o-o-o-oy..." ' Listening to the sound fill the barn, the words telling a romantic story, I remembered the look that had passed between Philip and me in the church, charged with lightning force, and I felt the hairs on my nape lift with awe and, perhaps, presentiment.

I wished I could be in the barn with him, joining in the age-old celebration of a harvest secured. Unseen presences, jostling now around me, had swung scythe and sickle, tossed sheaves, threshed grain, sung the same songs, danced to the same tunes... Strangely, my soul felt more at home here than ever it had at Denes Hill. Some old, old ties were reaching out to reclaim me.

And then two dogs came hurtling out of the darkness, breaking the mystic spell. Behind them, the huge door opened wider, and against the glow of light I saw the burly figure of Mad Jack, bellowing, 'Come you back here, you blamed beggaring dogs! Come here, I say! Boss! Bess! Heel!'

I had ducked back behind the hedge, terrified the dogs might sense me hiding there. But they must have obeyed their master for I heard him talking to them in a growl whose words I couldn't catch. When I looked again, he was heading for the house, with the dogs at heel, their shadows long in the moonlight.

' "He left the lad the farm he had, and his daughter for a bride . . ." ' Philip sang.

He was among his own people. He probably didn't even remember hinting that I should meet him. And why had I come? Because I wanted to see him again? Or from sheer perversity, because he was forbidden fruit? It would be wrong of me to lead him on when nothing could ever come of any relationship between us. Oh, I had been a fool, yet again.

As I hurried back up the hill, glad that no one had seen me, I told myself that I would forget about romantic entanglements and concentrate on the future. But only my intellect heard me. The rest – heart, soul, blood, sinew and instinct – sang songs of ties that could never be unbound.

When next I wrote to Mother, I put in a line or two asking why she had never mentioned the Farcrofts. In reply, she said she hadn't spoken of them because they weren't important: they were not the sort of people she, or I, would wish to cultivate. But baby Hansi was teething, Rudger had fallen and cut his knee, and guess what Pieter had said . . .

Staying in King's Lynn for a few days, as a guest of my uncle Harry and his wife, I found their genuine welcome a relief after the constant undercurrents of Denes Hill. One evening, much to my surprise and pleasure, they asked me to stand godmother to their son, my new cousin.

'Well, you did bring the little chap into the world,' Harry said.

'Oh – yes.' Too late now to deny it.

'We're going to ask the twins, too,' Saffron added.

'Emmet will make a gorgeous godfather, and it will please Tom to be included, even though he probably won't understand. But three godparents is enough, we think.'

'Ample,' said Harry heartily. 'Vicky can be godmother to the next one.'

Ah, so that was the cause of their defensiveness – Grandmother had thought her own daughter ought to be first choice. 'I'm immensely flattered,' I told them. 'Have you finally decided what names you're going to give him?'

Saffron's smile went a little askew, but Harry's thin face was bright with pride as he answered, 'Yes, we have. Edward Henry John.'

John, not Philip. I flicked a glance at Saffron, who said hastily, 'Harry was very close to his brother John.'

'You were fond of him, too,' Harry reminded her. 'They were engaged once, Kate, did you know? Like Queen Mary and Prince Albert Victor.'

I enjoyed my stay at Hawthorn House. Saffron was still recovering from childbirth and confined to the house, but she belonged to a women's suffrage group, some of whose members came calling on her; so I widened my acquaintance and enjoyed stimulating conversations. After her visitors had gone, Saffron made me laugh as she confided all their personal secrets. Harry, for his part, took me to the Chef Foods factory and introduced me to the staff in the offices, food preparation areas and the noisy room where canning machines operated. And then there was my godson-to-be, tiny Eddy; the nursemaid let me hold him, help her bath him, and take him for walks in his big perambulator. At other times, free to please myself, I was drawn by the delights of the town museum, the library, the historic buildings, the shops . . .

Inevitably, I found myself thinking of Carl-Heinz. I talked

130

to Saffron about him and, to my relief, she was appalled that no one had had enough faith in me to question the lies he had told.

'The trouble with Lady Vi,' she told me over lunch, 'is she doesn't think any young woman is capable of staying on the straight and narrow. A girl wouldn't need to do more than smile at a man for Lady Vi to scream "shame", d'you know what I mean? I often wonder what she got up to herself, to have such a low opinion of other women. Though don't tell Harry I said so.' Sharing gossip with Saffron was a wicked delight. No one else dared speak of Grandmother so irreverently. 'Clara was a beauty, so she was shipped off into the wilds of Cumberland. Next it was me in front of the spotlight, and I was labelled a fortune-hunter. And now there's you – and poor Vicky, who may end up married to Oliver Wells out of sheer desperation. He's just about the only man who ever gets near her.'

Poor Vicky, indeed. Not yet nineteen, she was being turned into a vinegary old maid.

Trying to bring the conversation round to Philip Farcroft, I asked if the same restrictions had applied to Mother when she and I came back to Denes Hill for those two years, after my father died.

'Oh, it was different then,' Saffron said. 'She'd been married, after all. She had men crowding round like butterflies on buddleia.'

'Was one of them Michael Farcroft?'

Saffron's almond eyes widened in a face beginning to fine down now that she had had the baby. 'Farcroft? What, the man who was killed a few years back? My dear girl . . . certainly not!'

'I heard he was keen on her.'

'Well he may have been. But Clara would never have

associated with a man like that. They're a strange bunch, that family.'

'Even Philip?' I asked pointedly.

Worried eyes met mine and she blushed crimson as she looked away. 'I don't even like to *think* about that. How could I have let him . . . He didn't even wash his hands! Harry would be furious if he knew. I couldn't ask him to call the baby Philip – it's not a family name. You don't think Philip Farcroft will hold it over me, do you?'

How little she knew of Philip. And how easily she had forgotten the extent of her need of help when he came along. 'Of course he won't!'

'How can you be sure?'

'I just know!'

'What – sixth sense?'

'No. No, I . . .' It was my turn to feel uncomfortable. 'I ran into him in the village. We agreed it was "least said soonest mended", for everyone's sake. You're wrong about him, Aunt Saffron. I don't know about his father, or his brother, but Philip is . . .' I had no words to explain my opinion of Philip.

She surveyed me with narrowed eyes. 'Philip Farcroft is a fine upstanding young man, and you, my dear, are on the rebound from a rotter. Been flattering you, has he? You should be careful, Kate. He's a Farcroft. He might enjoy leading you astray, just to get back at the family.'

Early in October, Emmet returned to Cambridge and I began my life as a student in London, at the School of Economics in Clare Market, a gaunt maze of lecture halls, common rooms and crowded passages. I had never known a place like it. Wherever one went, earnest discussions on the Great Realities, or the latest political Cause, were in progress. I found it exhilarating.

My lodgings were in Lincoln Square, within walking distance of both the college and the British Museum. The tall house had once been a family home, but Mrs Armes now found herself alone, and so she took in 'gentlewomen students'. Her taste ran to plants and draperies, the main rooms being laden with heavy curtains, bobbled pelmets and velvet table covers, several aspidistras and in the front room bay a monstrous prickly cactus which she referred to fondly as 'Giorgio'.

My room was on the second floor at the back, a light and airy retreat with sprigged wallpaper and delicate Georgian furniture. The window looked out on back-to-back gardens festooned with laundry and haunted by cats, very different from Denes Hill, and from the von Wurthe house in the pineclad lakeside resort of Wannsee in Berlin. I found the strangeness challenging, exhilarating and, I must admit, a little daunting, too. I was truly 'on my own feet', for the first time in my life.

I was also more alone than I had ever been, both physically and emotionally. Mother had written that *of course* she believed my innocence: that wicked Carl-Heinz! But we must not even think of my returning to Berlin. She and I would keep in close touch – of course we would, always! – but, she hinted between the lines, I was no longer to consider myself part of the von Wurthe family.

Some detached part of me pitied her. Trapped by circumstance, she had been forced to make difficult choices – Pa, the *Menschen*, and a secure family life; or standing up for me. The choice had been no choice. Poor Mother. Damned by her parents for some youthful indiscretion, married in desperation to an elderly man who left her widowed with a small child, coming back to the strict watch of her parents, escaping into a new life abroad with a wealthy husband . . . she was still a prisoner. But that, as I was soon being told by new friends, was the lot of women. That was why we demanded the right to vote, to secure a better life for ourselves.

My fellow lodgers at Lincoln Square both proved to be ardent feminists, though in different ways. Hermione Harmistead – 'Miss H' to all who knew her – was a devotee of the more militant wing of the suffrage movement, a stringy woman in her thirties, a research fellow and occasional lecturer, who strode everywhere in a rush. When preoccupied she was brusque to the point of rudeness, and she carried about with her a strong odour of tobacco – she loved Turkish cigarettes, and belonged to some peculiar club in whose rooms she was wont to smoke a hookah, so it was said.

The other gentlewoman student, Winifred Leeming, with mouse-brown hair, mouse-brown eyes and a penchant for mouse-brown clothes, had, she said, been a bookworm since she was a child – which accounted for the extreme short sight which caused her to peer at the world through gold-rimmed spectacles perched on a *retroussée* nose. Brought up by a maiden aunt, Win had attended a strict convent school, and now was compiling a thesis which she anticipated would take her years to complete. To me that seemed a dreadful prospect, but to her it meant order for the foreseeable future. She too was a suffragette, but not of the active kind – the thought of window-breaking and fire-raising filled dear Win with horror. She preferred attending meetings, armed with facts and figures. She was always analysing and coming to wise conclusions – often hopelessly impractical conclusions since her experience of life had been so narrow.

But she did have one passion – a sailor cousin, an officer with the White Star cruise line, whose picture she kept with her at all times. 'My cousin Stanton,' she would say with a soft look to her mouse-brown eyes, taking out the picture and caressing it with thin fingers with long thin nails like claws. 'Isn't he handsome?'

As shown by the picture, her cousin looked boyish in his naval uniform; so I was somewhat disappointed to discover that the photo was several years old. In the interim, Stanton Leeming had put on weight and lost most of his hair. But he was still considerate, charming and attentive to plain little Win.

When Stanton heard that Win and I had planned to go and see Frank's exhibition, he insisted on escorting us to the gallery. He talked to Frank while Win and I toured the gallery, I standing back to see the pictures while she peered closely at detail through her oval specs. I loved the energy my uncle portrayed in scenes full of vigorous activity, men at harvest, fishermen at sea, factory workers bathed in sweat and the glare of furnaces. Stanton admired the figure work, too, so he said.

Later, the four of us had supper, and the next day Stanton went back to sea. His visit left a glow on Win for days. She was mad about him, but she hoped for nothing from him, was simply glad to be in the same world, to have a postcard from him now and then, and an occasional visit.

'Cousins have been known to marry,' I reminded her.

'Marry?' The word seemed to horrify her. 'Oh, Kate, it's not like that. Goodness . . . I've always known no one would ever want to marry *me*. I don't think I'd like it, anyway. I prefer my books.'

The end of the exhibition coincided with the weekend of Eddy's christening, so Frank and I travelled to Norfolk together. He went on to Denes Hill with the few of his paintings which had not been sold, while I happily made for Hawthorn House, where I was to stay for a few days. Harry and Saffron had decided that their son should be christened at St Margaret's, the massive and beautiful church in Lynn, where their many town friends could easily attend.

As godmother, I had the privilege of holding the baby throughout the ceremony. Emmet had confessed himself 'absolutely stiffened' by the responsibility of becoming a godfather, but Tom stood with bright eyes, hopping from foot to foot and clutching at his twin's arm as the three of us repeated the promises. Around us undercurrents of disapproval swirled: mean lines bracketed Vicky's mouth, while Grandmother was long-suffering – she had wanted Eddy to be christened at Eveningham. Ignoring them, I watched my little godson blink and scowl at the vicar as the cold water touched his brow. He didn't cry, though. Not Edward Henry John, youngest of the Rhys-Thomas clan. 'The only grandson', I thought, hurting for Rudger, Pieter and Hansi. Much as I loved baby Eddy, the little men in Germany were just as sweet, and as worthy of love, for all their father's name was von Wurthe. How I missed them. I thought of Philip Farcroft, too. He should have been here, given due credit for this baby's safe delivery.

Two days later I walked into town to return some library books for Saffron. In the Tuesday market place, laden stalls stood under awnings, itinerant peddlars next to vociferous street traders, farmers' wives with carts full of their own vegetables, eggs, butter, jams and pickles. The streets clamoured with farmers' traps and the occasional rattling, oil-smelling motor jalopy with a loud and arrogant horn barping at pedestrians who risked their necks sidestepping goods stacked outside shops; and in the cattle market red-faced men in bowler hats struck deals over pens full of sheep and cows and turkeys.

Enjoying the bustle, I failed to see rain clouds gathering and was forced to make an undignified dash to the library to avoid a soaking as the heavens opened. A man in a brown tweed suit and cap was coming from the other direction, also bound for the library entrance, where a knot of people sheltered from the downpour. We nearly collided on the step, both drew back, apologizing . . . and only then did I realize who he was.

'Mr Farcroft!' I couldn't decide which was uppermost – pleasure or confusion.

Philip wrenched off his hat, nodding at me warily. 'Miss Brand. Shall we go inside?'

The shelterers parted to allow us by. Philip held the door and we both stepped into the dim-lit lobby, brushing at our clothes.

'I never expected to see you here,' I said. 'Have you come to choose some books?'

'No, I thought I might buy a yearling bull.' His voice dripped sarcasm and as I blinked at him he added belligerently, 'I *can* read, surprisingly enough!'

'Well! . . .' was my sparkling reply as, tipping my chin, I dismissed him with a look and marched into the hushed atmosphere of the main library. The door swung heavily behind me. Philip didn't follow. Perhaps, after all, he had come in only to shelter from the rain. That suited me well enough, I told myself. What an uncouth oaf he was!

Determined to stay inside until he had gone, I moved between tall bookcases looking at titles. Which might Saffron like – a new play from Mr Shaw, or a political treatise by Mrs Pankhurst? A novel by Mr Conan Doyle, or by Uncle Frank's prophet of the future, Mr Herbert G.

Wells? I couldn't decide. I was still twitching from Philip Farcroft's rudeness.

Flipping through a slim volume of Shakespeare's sonnets, in a quiet corner of the library, I became aware of Philip's approach. He was sidling nearer, pretending to look along the rows of massed titles. I went on staring at the book in my hand, doing my own pretending.

Pausing behind me, he murmured over my shoulder, 'Forgive me. I didn't intend to be unmannerly.'

'Yes, you did,' said I sweetly through my teeth.

'I thought you were ragging me.'

'You shouldn't be so touchy. If you—'

'Ssssh!' someone hissed, and a lady in a tall purple hat looked briefly round a bookcase to glower at us over a pair of pince-nez.

Irritated, I muttered, 'This is a fine place to pick another quarrel.'

'I didn't pick it – you did!' he whispered furiously. 'I was trying to apologize. Anyway, you started it.'

'How?'

'By calling me "Mr Farcroft"!'

'I was being polite.'

'You have a gorgeous way of putting me in my place without trying.'

'I don't have to try!' I retorted. 'You're ready to misunderstand before I even open my mouth.'

The purple hat appeared again, the face beneath it pinched with disapproval. 'Sssssssssh!'

Philip's green glare might have sizzled her if she hadn't ducked away in time. 'Did you see that?' he said under his breath. 'It must have been a snake. It came out, hissing, from under a hideous purple plant pot.'

He kept his face straight, but as our eyes met a bubble of

mirth burst out of me and I had to clap my hand over my mouth to prevent myself from exploding.

'Please!' The librarian appeared, an anxious little man in black coat and striped trousers, wringing his hands and speaking through lips that hardly moved. 'If you wish to hold a conversation, go outside. People are complaining. Or do I have to eject you?'

I couldn't help myself – the thought of his trying to manhandle Philip, who was twice his size, struck me as so funny that I all but collapsed in helpless mirth. Philip took hold of my arm and, apologizing under his breath to everyone we passed, 'Sorry. Sorry! She's not well,' he propelled me past the frowning assistant behind the desk and out through heavy swing doors back into the half-light of the lobby. There, he let me lean on the wall until the giggles diminished. I was wiping my eyes, holding my aching ribs, gasping for breath, when the swing doors bellied again and another man joined us, saying anxiously, 'Kate? Is that you, Kate? What's wrong?'

What a moment for Oliver Wells to appear! Suddenly I wasn't laughing any more, I was choking with dismay while Philip solicitously pounded on my back.

'Are you ill?' Oliver asked, peering at me in the gloom. 'What are you doing here? Are you alone?'

'She was choosing a book,' Philip answered laconically. 'I think she breathed some dust. She was choking, and people started shushing her, so I thought she needed some air.'

'Did you, indeed?' Oliver Wells looked him up and down, his mouth a disdainful curve under the dark moustache. To my relief, he didn't appear to recognize Philip. 'Well, you can leave her to me now, young fellow. If she needs escorting anywhere, *I'll* see to it. Now, Kate . . .'

Beyond his burly shoulder I saw Philip open his mouth

to argue, but he must have caught my silent plea for discretion for his mouth compressed as he turned away without a word and went out. I caught a glimpse of heavy skies, huddled bodies and black umbrellas, and then the door was slammed shut with a thud. Oh, Philip . . .

'Are you here on your own?' Oliver Wells enquired. 'I heard you were spending a few days with Harry and Saffron. Good heavens, what are they thinking of, letting you wander in the town alone?'

'I'm not wandering,' I objected. 'I came to choose some books. Now, if you don't mind, I'm going back to Hawthorn House. I don't need escorting, thank you. I'm not a schoolgirl. Goodbye, Mr Wells.'

I too went out into the rain, squeezing through the clutch of people in the doorway, hurrying out to the edge of the pavement to look up and down the busy umbrella-sprouting street. Which way had Philip gone? There was no sign of him.

The downpour had settled into a steady drizzle. Finding myself in an area of public garden, I trudged the pathway towards a ruined tower, planning to shelter beneath its arched openings until the rain passed. But before I reached it swift footsteps sounded behind me and as I looked round Philip again grasped my arm.

'Are you trying to catch your death?' he demanded. 'Get under shelter, quick.'

We ran the rest of the way, arriving breathless under the tower. It stood open to the elements through two high archways, with a plain stone sarcophagus set centrally under a curved roof. Around it pathways wound among flowerbeds and shrubberies which muted the clop and rumble of the traffic in cobbled streets.

As we huddled in separate corners, with ten feet of damp

draught between us, Philip said, 'That was Wells, wasn't it? The solicitor?'

'Yes. I was afraid he'd know you, but he didn't seem to—'

'I'm beneath his notice – except to write threatening letters to. But I've seen him about. I felt sure he'd appropriate you.'

'He tried. I escaped.'

The gleam in his eyes appreciated that. He said, 'Funny how we keep meeting in churches.'

Shivering, I looked round the ruined walls and soaring archways, blackened by time, limed with birds' droppings. 'Hardly a church.'

'It used to be. It's all that's left of an old Franciscan friary.'

'Really?' I reviewed the place with deeper interest, touching the ancient bricks.

'Lynn's a historic town,' Philip said, stuffing his hands into his pockets as he leaned on the wall behind him. 'It's had two markets since the Middle Ages. It was Bishop's Lynn once, then it became Lynn Regis. You can still see lots of the old buildings.'

With the odd question from me, he went on to expound on the history of the town and the delights still to be found, making me ever more eager to go out and explore further for myself. But after a while he stopped in mid-sentence. 'Sorry. I'm boring you.'

'You're not,' I denied. 'Not at all.'

I could have listened to his caressing baritone all day, watching his face change as he talked, eyes flashing with enthusiasm, hands gesturing to emphasize points. I didn't know why I had ever thought him uncouth or ungainly or ill-bred; he was a big man, but he had natural grace and, when he smiled, that lean, angular face came alight. And his green, green eyes were so expressive . . .

Words can't tell the reasons. The simple fact was that I was immensely attracted to Philip Farcroft. Because he was he and I was I . . .

'I'm glad we met,' I said. 'I've been wanting to talk to you.'

'About what?'

'Your father was poaching on the hill. Tom was in the wood. There could have been a nasty accident.'

Mouth set, he looked at the floor, kicking a stone. 'He told me. I'm not going to make excuses for him. He was wrong. I told him so. He said I was soft.'

'He'd probably say you were softer still if he knew you were here talking to me,' I observed.

A corner of his mouth went wry. 'Probably so. But . . . Dad isn't an ogre, you know. You should come and meet him for yourself and then you'll see. Anyway . . .' The light in his eyes turned baleful as he remembered: 'If you had wanted to talk to me you knew where I was. You could have come that night we had our harvest supper.'

'I—'

'No, don't make excuses,' he interrupted moodily. 'It was my own fault. I knew you wouldn't come. But I still walked up to the gate and stood there waiting for nearly two hours. What a fool!' Levering himself away from the wall, he trudged to the further corner, diagonally across from me with the stone sarcophagus between us, and stood there scuffing his boots, grinding his teeth to make his jaw muscle jump in a way I was beginning to recognize as a sign of tension.

'Is that why you were so pot-faced in church the next

day?' I demanded. 'Oh, honestly, Philip! Do you always take offence so easily?'

His head came up. 'Then why weren't you there? Couldn't get away, I suppose. What do they do, lock their doors at sunset, so none of their skeletons can get out and terrorize the countryside?'

'It so happens I did come! But you were among your friends so I went away again.' He opened his mouth to reply, but I rushed on, 'Oh . . . what's the point? Perhaps it will be best if I go.'

He started towards me instantly, anxiously. 'No, don't. Not yet. Kate . . . You said once that you aren't part of the feud. Well, I'm not, either. I don't want to be. Perhaps it's up to us to make a start on ending it. It's stupid for us to be enemies. I feel . . . Don't laugh, but . . . I feel I've known you for ever.'

My brain seemed to go blank with shock. I couldn't speak for the sudden tightness in my throat. That he should feel it, too, and say so . . .

'Maybe it's with Michael having that thing about your mother,' he added, trying to explain away feelings that were inexplicable. 'They were friends, you know. When they were children.'

This astounded me. '*Were* they?'

'Michael used to talk about her a lot. Mother was always telling him to forget her. I don't remember her visiting. Michael was a lot older than me – fifteen years or so. He was my half-brother.'

'I see,' I said faintly, trying to take in this new information. 'I had no idea. She never mentioned . . . Oh, I *wish* I knew the truth about her! When Grandfather was dying . . . he cursed her. On his deathbed. He sat bolt upright, pointing at me, saying . . .' The scene came back in throat-catching detail – candlelight flickering, the awful smell, the shadowy figures of the family . . . I hadn't intended to let it all pour out, but I found myself recounting the scene, and how it had made me feel.

Philip was staunchly on my side. Endearingly so. 'That's appalling, Kate! That's so cruel. Whatever your mother may have done, it's not *your* fault. How could your own family be so unkind?'

Like one awaking from deep dreams, I realized he was standing close to me, enfolding one of my hands in his big, warm ones as he looked down at me. Did he guess the thoughts that had been in my mind as I talked to him? Intimate thoughts, buried beneath the flow of words – how beautiful his eyes, his voice, the shape of his mouth, the touch of his hands on mine, the rough caress of his coat, the warmth emanating from his body . . .

I'm not sure which of us moved first to break that tingling contact. Did I twist my hand or did his grasp loosen? All at once we both remembered the world not far away, and our place in it. The rain had stopped and people walked freely again, hurrying about their business. A spear of sunlight touched a million sparkles among the leaves in the garden, making the pathways shine, reflecting light into our dank sanctuary. We stepped apart, and I found myself chattering nervously about nothing.

He reached inside his waistcoat pocket, where a silver chain looped across, and took out a turnip watch, flipping the lid open. 'Oh, Lord,' he sighed with a rueful smile. 'I was going to catch the three o'clock train. It's now five minutes past.'

'I'm sorry.'

Philip looked at me, about to make some light comment, but as our eyes met his glance altered, softening into intimacy as it flickered across my face and settled on my mouth. 'I'm not,' he said softly, his voice so deep and low that it sent an answering jolt through me and I felt my lips tingle in involuntary response to that look in his eyes.

Even in the privacy of my head, my thoughts darted around like trapped birds in a cage. The power of what lay between us sent tremors through my flesh, twisting my stomach, drying my throat, sending my heart into erratic pounding. Frightening me. I didn't want to feel that way, about Philip Farcroft or anyone. It was too shattering. Too soon.

'May I walk you home?' he asked.

'No!' But the moment it was out I was sorry. 'I mean . . .' I bit my singing lips, trying to make them behave and stop wanting to be kissed. I dared not look at him. 'It's a long way, out in the suburbs, and you'd have to come all the way back to the station.'

'I've plenty of time.' The rueful note was back. 'The next train leaves just before five. I'd be honoured if you'd allow me to—'

I wished he wouldn't smile like that. It made my insides feel molten. All I wanted to do was escape from him and get myself back under control. 'No, you can't.' My head shook convulsively. 'It's best that you don't. I must go. I'm sorry. Forgive me, I . . . Goodbye, Philip.'

I all but ran from him, blindly going in the opposite direction to that I had intended. And then I saw Oliver Wells, coming along the path from the library. I stopped, and he stopped, and glanced beyond me to where Philip stood in the archway under the tower. He must have guessed we had been together.

Knowing only that I had to get away, I darted aside on to a path that took me to the London Road, where I kept walking at a rate that soon put the Greyfriars Tower, and Philip, and Oliver, way behind me. The force of my feelings disturbed me. Everything I had felt for Carl-Heinz now seemed superficial. He had been a fairy-tale prince, a game to be played for fun. But Philip . . . Philip was no fantasy to be dreamed on with girlish glee, safely alone in my bed. Philip was a threat.

NINE

Back in London, I applied myself to my studies and soon had my own space – seat J14 – in the Reading Room at the British Museum, where I spent hours poring over dusty tomes compiling tables of statistics. For instance, in 1850, how many hours did a man in Northumbria need to work to provide adequately for his family, compared with, say, a man in Streatham? The work taught me how to use resources, how to marshal facts, and how to concentrate. But the details of it were deadly dull.

To enliven my spare time, I joined several societies, including the local federation for women's suffrage; for exercise I chose the cycling club and the tennis club, and I became an avid visitor to theatres and cinematographs – moving pictures never failed to excite me. Thinking of my future, I took typewriting lessons, and wrote articles for our student magazine. Visits to the East End, to observe the condition of the poorest people of the city, provided more material. I frequently translated the pieces into German to send to Gudrun. Gradually, I discovered myself to be a socialist, and a pacifist.

In lectures and during social activities, men and women mingled freely, with an innocence hard to credit in retrospect. But most of my friends, of either sex, were intent on intellectual pursuits and Great Causes that left no room for romantic nonsense. Which suited me, too.

My foreign upbringing gave me an exotic appeal and friends would seek my opinion on the latest news about German stances as tension waxed and waned. In the background of life, like a wind blowing through distant trees, expectation of war remained a constant refrain. It was summed up in the words of a song, written for earlier troubles but still as relevant and widely sung: 'We don't want to fight, but, by Jingo! if we do, We've got the ships, we've got the men, we've got the money, too.' Odd, for that had also been the refrain in Germany – 'We don't want to fight, but if you push us, watch out!' Like a loaded blunderbuss, waiting only for the flint to be struck. But who would be the first to strike it? And on which side would my heart lie?

That first term passed in a whirl. Hardly had I settled in than it was time to think about Christmas. Win Leeming planned to continue her research as long as the museum stayed open – she had no other home to go to. Miss H had demonstrations to attend and meetings to organize – she, like Scrooge, thought Christmas was humbug.

Imagine my surprise when Grandmother wrote to say that she would be pleased if I brought my new friend Miss Leeming home with me for the holiday. When I imparted this invitation, Win's mild brown eyes widened behind her specs. 'Why, your grandmother doesn't know anything about me. How very kind . . .'

'I imagine Uncle Frank has told her what a lovely person you are,' I said. 'She probably thinks you'll keep my wilder excesses in check.'

Win blinked at me, never sure how to take such remarks. 'I don't know what you mean, Kate. Why, there's not a more sober and industrious student in the school.'

Innocent Win didn't guess what a reputation I had at home, nor imagine the turmoil going on beneath my 'sober' exterior. Even as we spoke, I was wondering if I might see Philip Farcroft, and what I should say, and what he might do, and whether that fearful, turbulent lightning would flare between us again. I wanted it, but I feared it, too.

Though snow and sleet kept us indoors most of the time, Win Leeming seemed to enjoy herself at Denes Hill. She showed a kindly interest in Tom and, up in the sanctum over games of chess, she and Emmet had sparking arguments on emancipation and socialism. Her presence made us all more polite with each other, but I was aware of walking on shifting sand, with my behaviour under scrutiny.

I attended church with most of the family – except Frank, who was a professed atheist – and found the Christmas devotions evocative and moving, just like the services in Berlin, with candles flickering in the darkness, even the same hymns sung to the same tunes. Philip's rich dark voice, from somewhere behind me, added depth to the carols he evidently loved. When I glanced round, our eyes met, shooting a lightning bolt through me. I hoped to steal a word with him as we left the church, but couldn't get close enough without drawing attention to myself. Anyway I had the distinct impression that Philip was avoiding me. Maybe he too had thought better of his impulse to make friends with a girl from Denes Hill.

It being only four months since Grandfather died, the New Year's Eve party was less gay than it might have been. The entire family, with a few intimate friends – including the solicitor, Mr Wells – dined at eight thirty. Afterwards, the younger element were planning to go on to gatherings at other houses where first-footing and other 'gorgeous japes', to use Emmet's phrase, might be had. Only a small party of us remained to see out the year.

Vicky installed herself at the piano, inviting Mr Wells to stand beside her and turn the pages of her music while she favoured us with more carols and her latest piece, 'The Mysterious Rag'. Grandmother excused herself and went to bed, while Win and I made for the library, to find a book we had been discussing earlier.

It was cold in that big room, despite barred shutters, thick curtains and the fire which had been burning all day. I was glad of my blue shawl – a Christmas gift made by Mother, who loved to do fancy crochet work. 'I'm sure it was somewhere here,' I said as I climbed the library steps to search a particular shelf.

'Actually, Kate . . .' Win blinked up at me, lamplight making golden ovals of her glasses as she huddled in her own brown wrap. 'Would you mind awfully if we left it for tonight? I have a slight headache. And I want to write to Stanton – I always write on New Year's Eve, it's a sort of tradition with us, swapping resolutions. I didn't want to say anything in front of everybody, but . . . Would you mind awfully?'

'Not at all.' I was not sorry to climb down from the steps. I too was tired, and depressed. Somehow I had hoped to manage a meeting with Philip – stupid, I knew. 'What are your resolutions this year?'

'To persuade Miss H to give up her militancy, and . . . to stop chewing the ends of my pens. Good night, Kate. Happy New Year.'

Dear Win, she left me smiling over her innocence.

Enjoying the respite from crowding company, I went to curl up in the leather armchair by the fire, letting its wings enfold me along with the shawl which still retained a faint scent of Mother's perfume. What was she doing tonight?

Were dancing candles glowing in the windows of Berlin, as always at New Year? I stared into the warm heart of the fire, letting the silence seep into me as I wondered what resolutions to make. To forget Philip Farcroft, the answer came at once, making me sigh ruefully.

Katie! Be careful!

Inside my head the warning sounded as loud as a shout, jerking me erect with wide-open eyes. No one at Denes Hill ever called me Katie. I looked round, half expecting to see someone there, but the library was empty – empty of tangible presences, that is. *Unseen* presences swirled about me, making my nerves sizzle and my hair lift. As clearly as if someone had spoken, I knew my invisible friends had sent a warning. About what? Was I, perhaps, being warned not to become involved with Philip Farcroft?

'So there you are!' The male voice was not loud, but it sent the spirits scattering as Oliver Wells, darkly handsome in black tie and tails, closed the door and came across the polished parquet and the Turkey rugs, moving lightly for all his size, like a dancer in patent leather shoes. 'No, don't move, please. I didn't intend to disturb you. What are you doing here all alone? Has Miss Leeming gone to bed?'

'She was tired.'

'It has been a long day,' he agreed. 'Do you mind if I join you? Would you mind if I smoked a cigar?'

I indicated the chair opposite mine. 'Please . . .'

He settled in the chair, making a performance of clipping the cigar and lighting it with a spill from the fire, every movement graceful and elegant. Blowing out a stream of aromatic smoke, he squinted at me through it, smiling. 'Are you making any New Year resolutions tonight?'

'Only to apply myself more assiduously to my work.'

'How frightfully worthy! All work and no play, you

know. I would have thought a pretty girl might have more personal matters on her mind.'

'Such as?' I enquired cautiously.

'That's up to you to decide. How are you getting along in London? I expect you miss your Berlin friends a good deal.'

'Yes, I do, at times.'

'But you're managing to find others?' The cigar wrote a writhing figure in the air. 'Apart from the estimable Mouse Leeming, I mean.'

I sat up, frowning. 'Miss Leeming is a good friend. I won't have her mocked. She's a deal brighter than most people I know.'

'I don't doubt she's a fine intellect – she was tying elaborate knots in young Emmet's arguments at dinner – but she's a little . . . lacklustre, don't you think?'

'We can't all be scintillating company like Vicky.'

The wry gleam in his eye appreciated the irony in that, but he didn't rise to it. 'There must be other acquaintances you've made. More after your own style.'

Was he making idle conversation, or had Grandmother sent him to spy on me? I said evenly, 'My style? Coldly disdainful and given to sullen silences, you mean?'

Mr Wells blinked, removing a speck of tobacco from his tongue with well-manicured fingers as he narrowed his eyes at me. 'I beg your pardon?'

'Isn't that how you characterized me after our journey from Berlin?'

'Is it?' A frown creased between straight dark brows as he sighed. 'Yes, perhaps it is. And I apologize. That journey . . .' He sat forward, leaning on his knees as he gazed at the fire. 'That journey was a sore trial to me – as it must have been for you. It was beastly hot, and I was disconcerted to be asked to play escort to a strange young woman – an extremely attractive young woman, if I may say so.'

'I'd much rather you didn't. Flattery isn't necessary.'

'It's not flattery, it's plain truth.' The bark-brown eyes met mine, deep and direct, startling me with the realization that he was, after all, a man, with normal human thoughts and feelings. 'If I was stiff and awkward with you, that was the reason. Sheer embarrassment.'

I said nothing, mainly because I didn't know what to say. My assessment of him was undergoing another adjustment. He was not much older than Uncle Frank, whom I considered almost a contemporary. But Frank was fun, lively and joking; Mr Wells was all formality, with a *gravitas* that made him seem older. Perhaps his profession was to blame for that – plus the fact that, like me, he never felt quite at ease at Denes Hill.

'But you were saying,' he went on, relaxing in his chair and crossing his legs comfortably, 'about the new friends you've made. You must have met some young men, too.'

'One or two,' I answered cautiously.

'But no one in particular? Or, er, perhaps your affections are still engaged elsewhere?'

Suddenly aware of the chill of the room, I gathered my new shawl more closely round me and said stiffly, 'If you mean Herr Leutnant Carl-Heinz von Siemens, you can tell my grandmother I've forgotten him. Completely.'

A corner of his mouth twisted wryly. 'So had I, as a matter of fact. I was thinking of someone closer to home. The young man in the library in Lynn, for instance. The young man with whom you sheltered under the Greyfriars Tower.'

A finger touched my spine, freezing, or was it boiling? Even my face tingled and I knew my flush betrayed me.

'He's no one. A stranger. I only met him that day. He told you how I started to choke and . . .'

Deep, dark eyes perused me with a gleam. He said softly, 'You're a very bad liar, Kate. Remember that, if you're ever called to give evidence in court. The whole truth, and nothing but the truth . . .'

No use prevaricating, then. 'Did you tell Grandmother?'

An eyebrow twitched in hurt surprise. 'What do you take me for? Why . . . would she object to this acquaintance?'

She would if she knew who he was, I thought. Thank God Mr Wells hadn't recognized him. 'She might. Though . . . I shan't be seeing him again.'

The gleam deepened, as if he understood. Then, one long finger against his lips, he ruminated, 'I was thinking . . . I have to go up to London on occasion. May I call on you there? We might go out for a meal, or to a theatre. I gather you do that with Frank when he's in town. I know I'm not your uncle, but I am an old friend of the family and as such, perhaps . . .'

The ensuing silence sang with all kinds of nuances. Was he hinting that if I refused he might tell Grandmother about the young man in Lynn?

Before I could decide, the door crashed back and Vicky erupted into the room, crying, 'Oliver, are you— Oh!' She was startled to find me with him, but: 'Come quickly. Quickly! It's almost midnight. We must all be together when it strikes. You too, Kate. Hurry!'

But as we started for the door we heard a faint cheer from the distant salon, and the first '*bong*' of midnight from a longcase clock in the hallway. 'Too late!' Vicky mourned. 'Oh, dash it, we'll just have to . . .' She came to peck the air near my ear. 'Happy New Year, Kate. And you, too, Oliver.' To him she lifted her cheek, her pale skin flushed along the cheekbone where he brushed his lips.

From the salon the others were laughing, crying excited greetings. Harry called for Vicky and she hurriedly ducked away from Oliver, as if discomposed by that daring moment of intimacy.

'Well . . .' I offered him my hand, keeping my distance. 'Happy New Year, Mr Wells.'

'It's Oliver,' he said in an undertone, his warm hand folding firmly round mine. 'Goodness, you're cold!' His other hand came to complete the wrapping as he moved closer, his dark gaze on my mouth. 'And a Happy New Year to you, too, Kate Brand.'

Aware of disturbing vibrations between us, I tried to pull away, but he held me, and might have drawn me closer except that a clatter of heels on parquet made him let go. Saffron came dashing to bring us back to the party, where we exchanged more New Year greetings and all joined hands to sing 'Auld Lang Syne'. Vicky contrived to have the solicitor next to her, well away from me. I couldn't meet his eye. I was too jittery, startled by my own equivocal reaction to him. Part of me was disgracefully flattered that Oliver Wells found me attractive.

On the train going back to London, Win and I relived the holiday. 'Such *nice* people,' she had found them. 'So very kind. Tom's a dear. And Emmet, so very bright. He needs a few misconceptions knocking out of him, but that will come in time. He's awfully young yet.'

I couldn't help asking, 'What did you think of Oliver Wells?'

'Very handsome. Very charming. A respectable, professional gentleman, comfortably off and with all the social graces.' Her reply was typical of her, logical and analytical. 'He'll make a very good husband. The wonder is he isn't married already.'

'Perhaps he and Vicky will make a pair.'

'Oh, no,' said Win at once. 'If Vicky has her heart set in that direction she'll probably end up an old maid, like me. Anybody with eyes could see. Mr Wells was only paying her attention out of politeness. The one he really wanted to be with was *you*, Kate.'

This assertion made me fidget. 'Oh, really . . .'

'I know he's a little older than you, but an older man is more stable. He'd be a good catch. And he's sympathetic to the prime tenets of the Cause. As a lawyer, he'd be an asset to the suffrage movement.'

'That's all very cerebral,' I argued. 'But logic is not a good reason for marriage. Not on its own.'

'I suppose it's not enough when your heart's yearning for more. There's someone else on *your* mind, isn't there?'

I stared at her. 'What makes you think that?'

'I watch, and I listen. Often it's the things people *don't* say that tell you most. Gracious . . . I don't envy any of you. What a whirligig! I think I'll stick to my books.'

Thick winter fogs hung about the London streets, getting into one's throat and eyes. They reminded me of Philip and the day Eddy was born, when the cool grey sea fret had cloaked us from the world, affording a kind of privacy for things best kept untold. I even imagined I saw Philip in London, looming out of the fog, but always on second glance the man proved to be a stranger.

The fog had other echoes in my mind. Strange hidden stirrings, as in mud at the bottom of a cloudy pond. Something about fog that I should remember. Something vitally important. Maddeningly, the meaning of such hints and portents remained elusive.

Continuing my studies and my social activities, I exchanged letters with Mother, Saffron and, dutifully, with Grandmother. Correspondence with friends in Berlin began to dwindle, inevitably, though I kept in touch with Gudrun. In my head I composed letters to Philip, too, but it was probably best to leave that door closed. As time passed my memory of him blurred, partially erased by common sense: I didn't really know him; he had been kind when I was vulnerable and my response had been natural, but not necessarily lasting; we were both young, of a mind to fall in love with any likely member of the opposite sex, especially someone forbidden. Besides, could I really visualize myself as a farmer's wife?

Time was what I needed. Work should be my main preoccupation from now on. But I was eighteen years old, and oh! with the cold, the fog, the short, dank days and the long, dull nights, work became unutterably *tedious* at times.

One evening, after a particularly enervating day in the museum, I came out on to the steps, eyes sore and shoulders aching, and stood viewing the choking brown swirl that, dimly penetrated by streetlights, filled the museum courtyard. I was feeling miserable, recovering from a head cold, my studies seeming futile, when a dark figure striding vigorously up the steps resolved itself into . . . Oliver Wells. I felt my heart skip – with surprise, mostly – as his harassed expression broke into a broad smile of pleasure. 'Kate! Thank goodness I caught you. I was afraid we might pass each other unseen in this fog. What a peasouper! May I see you back to your lodgings?'

He had come to London on business and, he said, with only his own company to look forward to he had decided to chance calling to see if I would do him the honour of having dinner with him. I had intimated that he might call on me, had I not?

I couldn't remember exactly what I had said, but the prospect of an outing was welcome.

I don't recall what we did that evening, but Oliver proved a charming and attentive companion. As the winter progressed, he came up to town every two weeks or so, always with some excuse about business in the city, always happy to treat me to a meal, or a show. We talked about my life in Berlin (skirting round the subject of Carl-Heinz), and about his work. I told myself he was just being kind to the daughter of an old friend, that it was no different from spending time with Uncle Frank. And I almost believed it. Almost.

I still vividly remember one particular Friday evening in March: the dining room of a plush hotel – possibly the Ritz – all pink tablecloths and napkins, tall pink candles in silver holders, with light glinting amber in the brandy Oliver had ordered to go with his coffee. A small orchestra played 'Oh, you beautiful doll' and other jolly tunes that everyone was humming, while Oliver and I had fun drawing up family trees, on pages torn from his notebook, and speculating over the Great Gap between the older and the younger Rhys-Thomas offspring. I remember the gold-topped fountain pen he used, and the slanting, neat but almost illegible scrawl in which he jotted down the names.

This exercise had started when Oliver had remarked that Grandmother had been feeling rather low lately, grieving afresh because of the approach of that day's date, the eighth of March: exactly forty years before, also on a Friday, Miss Violet Thorne had married Lionel Rhys-Thomas, son of her father's partner, thus combining the two fortunes.

'In fact,' Oliver confided, 'I'm reliably informed that it was because of that wedding that my own parents met.'

'Really?' I was intrigued. He seldom talked about himself.

'My mother, Hannah, was a seamstress who made clothes for the Thorne ladies – in Lincoln, that was. She happened to be at the house one day, measuring Miss Violet for her bridal gown, when the family solicitor, Mr Joseph Wells, called. They left at the same time, shared a hansom, and the rest is history.'

Oliver had been born in Lincoln, but before long his parents had moved to Hunstanton in Norfolk, where Joseph Wells had become legal adviser to Lionel Rhys-Thomas. Since Hannah Wells had died young, her son had been raised by a succession of nursemaids before being sent to boarding school at the age of seven. 'It was the same school your uncle John attended, though he was a year ahead of me.' His smile turned wry, teeth white and even under the attractive line of his moustache. 'The Rhys-Thomases were sorry for me, poor motherless urchin that I was. In the holidays I was frequently invited to take part in their activities. I virtually grew up with John, and Harry and Frank – and Clara, of course. Beautiful Clara.'

His eyes held a wistful light as he glanced at his brandy balloon, turning it between long, elegant fingers. Lifting it to the light to admire its tawny clarity, he took an appreciative sip of it before looking once more at me. 'You shouldn't let me go on so. You're too good a listener, Kate.'

'I'm interested.'

'You're polite. Rewarding the old bore with your full attention, in return for your supper. If the truth were known, you probably think I'm stuffy, and dull, and old . . .'

'No!'

159

He pulled a wry face, making the dark moustache twist. 'Perhaps not so old as your father, when he married your mother. But I'm certainly old enough to have been bitterly jealous of him. Do you mind if I smoke?'

I watched him perform the ritual of the cigar, rolling it between pale fingers, listening to it crackle near his ear, clipping its end with a gold cigar cutter and then applying the match, letting the smoke curl out of his nostrils, squinting against it reflectively. His mind remained on Mother, I surmised.

I heard myself say, 'Every man Mother met seems to have been in love with her.'

'She did have a very special quality,' Oliver agreed. 'I wasn't the only one who adored her. I doubt she noticed me among the crowd.'

'Oh, she must have done!'

His quizzical look teased me: was that a compliment? Feeling my face burn, I had to qualify, 'I mean, well, you were something of a hero, I understand – you risked your life trying to save my uncle John.'

'Oh, that!' His gaze slid away, as if the memory troubled him. 'I'd rather not talk about that, Kate. It's painful. John was my best friend. And I didn't save him. He died, in spite of my efforts.'

I fiddled with my cutlery, adjusting the set of it across the empty dessert plate. 'I'm sorry.'

'So am I. If it hadn't happened, I might have had the courage to declare myself to Clara, but, as it was, I felt I should let a decent interval pass before I bothered her, and in the meantime Freddie von Wurthe stepped in. Oh . . . I don't suppose she would have accepted me even if I had asked her. But I've never forgotten her. Why do you think I've never married?'

I hadn't given it much thought, but, 'Because of Mother?'

'I've never found anyone to compare with her,' he said. 'That is, until . . .' He left the sentence unfinished, but the implication hung between us, his meaning written plainly in a pair of clear dark eyes.

I felt stricken, knowing what he was trying to say but wishing he hadn't said anything. He had pushed me to the edge of an emotional precipice for which I was not prepared.

My feelings must have shown; Oliver's face twisted and he reached for the brandy glass, draining it in one gulp before thumping it down. 'Forgive me. Too much wine. Too much brandy. But I've always regretted not speaking to Clara. If I lose my chance now . . .'

'But I'm *not* my mother,' I managed. 'I'm not like her at all.'

He leaned towards me, umber eyes intent as he reached a hand to cover mine. 'That's true. In many ways you're a nicer, kinder person than Clara ever was. But you have something of that same rare quality. A stillness. A quietness. I find it immensely appealing. My own life has been a turmoil. No mother, a father too busy to care, farmed out to boarding schools, passed to other people in the holidays, never with a settled base. And now . . . I dash about between clients, the courts, the office . . . I work too hard, to hide the gap at the centre of my life. I never found anyone to share that centre with me. No woman who . . .' He stopped himself, taking his hand away from me and sweeping it through his hair. 'I'm sorry. It's the brandy. I won't embarrass you further. Waiter . . .'

While he paid the bill I went to get my coat, pausing to stare at my flushed face in the powder-room mirror. I hadn't expected him to start being so intense, so suddenly. How did a woman handle such a situation?

He summoned a passing motor taxi and, as we moved through electric-lit streets, he sat silent beside me. Groups of men hung about doorways and corners, thrown out of work by the miners' strike whose ebbs and flows filled the newspapers. But I noticed them only vaguely. Their presence was a mere backdrop to what sang in the shadowed silence between Oliver Wells and me.

'Kate . . .' He took my gloved hand, pressing it between his own. 'At least think about it, won't you?'

I said nothing, did nothing, only sat still, staring ahead as if the hand he held was not attached to me. My pulses jumped as he lifted my wrist, parting glove and sleeve to find an area of bare flesh against which he pressed warm lips. His moustache felt surprisingly soft, and his breath stirred the tiny hairs on my arm, sending darts of dismay – or was it delight? – shooting through me.

To judge by the palpitations of my heart, even the one glass of wine I had taken with dinner had been too much. I knew I should stop him, but didn't know how. I heard myself say, 'Vicky's fond of you, you know.'

'I know.' His voice was dry. 'And Lady Rhys-Thomas would not be displeased if I were to press my suit in that direction. It would keep both Vicky and me safely chained to her yoke.' His hand came under my chin, making me look at him in the flicker of light and shadow as he murmured, 'Unfortunately, my heart seems to have hitched itself to another star,' and in one smooth motion he slid his hand behind my head, pulled me closer, and kissed me full on the lips. I remember the scent of cigar smoke, a hint of brandy, the steady, confident pressure of his mouth, both pleasurable and shocking . . .

A commotion outside the taxi interrupted the moment. Shouts and screams sounded, and breaking glass. As we rounded a corner, the cab swerved to a halt, jerking me away from Oliver. I clutched for a handhold, seeing a knot of struggling men and women spilling across the pavement and into the road. Another shop window shattered into a thousand glittering shards. Behind it, flames leapt up, licking round a display of silk fabrics. 'Votes for women!' a shrill voice screamed. 'Down with capitalist male scavengers!'

'Drive on, man!' Oliver ordered, but the crowd in front of us barred our way. Handbags and umbrellas flailed and skirts tossed as the women aimed kicks and blows at the men who had run up to stop them. More men were coming, shouting, boots loud on the paving. Some of the women began to scatter, dodging past the taxi on either side.

Recognizing one of them, I opened the taxi door and called to her: 'Miss H! Hermione! In here!'

She stopped, breathless, started towards me. 'Kate! Thank God you—'

'No!' Oliver pulled me back, sending me sprawling into the seat as he leaned across me and reached for the door handle, saying furiously, 'Stay away from us, woman! You asked for trouble, now stand and face it!'

'But we can say she was with us!' I cried, grasping his arm. 'She's a friend, Oliver!'

'She's a criminal!' he answered.

'Please—'

Hermione Harmistead drew herself up, her face tortured into hatred. 'Thanks all the same, Kate, but I wouldn't accept help from a man of *his* kind. I'd sooner rot in prison.' The words were lost in a rush of boots as policemen converged to grab her. But before they reached her, and wrenched her away, she spat full into Oliver's face.

He snapped back into his seat, taking out a handkerchief, muttering, 'Filthy bitch!'

'It wouldn't have hurt us to—'

'It would have hurt me!' he broke in roughly, glowering at me through the darkness as, outside, policemen joined the fray and the protesters were hauled away, much to the delight of the onlooking men, who catcalled and whistled after them. 'I have a professional reputation to protect.'

One of the policemen bent by the driver's open window, shining a torch on us. 'Everything all right, sir?' The beam of light examined my evening wrap and jewellery as I threw up a hand to guard my eyes. If Miss H had been in the taxi, her clothes would have revealed that she had not been with us all evening: we would have been branded as accomplices.

But that didn't make me feel any more charitable towards Oliver. When the cab moved on, the atmosphere inside it had chilled.

'I can't afford to be found shielding criminals,' Oliver said. 'And neither can you, if you're wise. I sympathize with their cause, but I can't condone their methods. If that woman *is* a friend, I'd advise you not to become involved in her political activities. Prison is not a pleasant place for a young woman, Kate.'

'Thank you for the legal advice,' I muttered, and turned my head away, not speaking again until we drew up in Lincoln Square when, as he reached for the door handle to precede me, I said, 'No, don't bother to get out, I can see myself to the door. Thank you for the dinner, Mr Wells. Thank you for all the attention you've been paying me. But—'

His hand came on my arm. 'Kate. Please . . .'

Shaking free, I turned my head to look him in the eye, feeling cold and angry. 'I hadn't quite understood your intentions. You should have made it more plain. You said it would be as an old friend of the family, not . . . I'm flattered by your interest, but I'm afraid I can't return it. I'm sorry, but I'm not prepared to be a substitute for my mother.'

TEN

Some of that evening's window-breakers went to prison but, this being the first time she had been apprehended, Miss H herself was bound over, much to her disgust. Over dinners at Lincoln Square, she and Win and I had long talks about the injustices done to women by men. I remember quoting Lytton, ' "The pen is mightier than the sword",' to which Miss H replied that ladylike reason was a hopeless weapon; the thing to do was to make a row and *force* people to listen.

Lighter mornings tempted me out early, to walk in Temple Gardens, or by the river, before smoke from city chimneys laid its pall across the sky, but it was not the same as being in the country. Something in me needed to be close to green things, breathing open air. Even so, at Easter I did not go back to Norfolk, largely for fear of bumping into Oliver Wells. I was horribly afraid that, before we had been interrupted, I had started to respond to his embrace. Yet I was not in love with him. That was partly why I had been so angry – because my own feelings troubled me. Better to avoid him until I felt more secure.

Similar reasoning applied to Philip Farcroft, whose presence filled me with an instinctive longing that ran devastatingly deep and disquieting. Philip felt it, too, in his own way. Had we met before, in another life? Were we bound to each other across time? The thought was too much – I didn't want to face it. It was better – more comfortable

166

– to deny the existence of any psychic bond between us.

In April, Win and I made a trip down to Southampton to say farewell to her cousin Stanton, who was sailing on the White Star liner *Titanic*, bound on her maiden voyage. Crowds of people waved her on her way, bands played, flowers and streamers flew ... As she edged away from the quayside I wished I, too, could be afloat, bound for the Hook of Holland, and home.

'Never mind, Kate,' Win consoled. 'I'm sure you *will* go back some day. Oh, isn't *Titanic* splendid? And totally safe, they say. It has always worried me that Stanton doesn't swim.'

Only days later, the nation reeled under the shock of the sinking of the unsinkable liner. Win's beloved cousin Stanton went down with her – a hero, we later learned. Hero or not, he was no less drowned.

The news brought Uncle Frank hurrying to express his sympathy for Win. But Win was inconsolable; neither comforting friends nor her own logic could help her solve this problem. She wept for days, keeping to her room, barely eating.

'I wish now I'd been kinder to the chap,' Frank said to me as we walked in Hyde Park among the daffodils. 'He wrote and asked me to go down and see him off, you know, but ...'

'I didn't know you had kept in touch,' I said.

'I didn't. *He* did. The thing is ...' His slate-blue eyes flicked to my face and away again. 'Stanton seemed to have the mistaken impression that I shared his, um, leaning toward the Oscar Wilde affliction.'

Only when I questioned my friends about the mystery did I realize the shocking thing Frank had been implying. I hadn't known such men existed. And I certainly wouldn't mention it to Win – she was hurt enough.

Though Grandmother had not objected to my staying in London for Easter, her letters made it clear that she expected me to spend Whitsun at Denes Hill. Emmet was having friends to stay – lively young people, whose company I would enjoy, she wrote. Miss Leeming would again be welcome, if she cared to accompany me.

This time, Win couldn't be persuaded. She planned to visit her old convent school. Though she had no particular religious faith, her grief for Stanton was so insupportable that she, the most rational of people, began to seek answers in strange byways.

After a dismal wet spring, the weather cleared and the Whit weekend brought a foretaste of summer. Not without a few misgivings, I took the Friday evening train to Norfolk and found Emmet and a few of his university friends already installed at Denes Hill. Together with local friends, both men and girls, they made a merry party. But, though I was with them, included in their games and pleasures, I was not quite one of them. Because of my German connection? Because of old stories about Mother? I couldn't fathom the cause, but the barrier was there.

To my disappointment, Uncle Frank was away that weekend.

'I seldom know what he's doing from week to week,' said Grandmother, a slender figure in black silk frills, seated under a large parasol. We had taken tea on the lawn, at a table now littered with the debris of our repast. Most of the party had gone back to their tennis and croquet, leaving Tom collecting crumbs in a saucer, for his birds, and Vicky slumped in a garden chair frowning moodily into space. 'Frank never plans anything,' Grandmother added. 'He goes as the mood takes him. I had hoped he would be back for the dinner party tonight, but . . .'

'Dinner party?' I broke in, dismayed. Did that mean Oliver was coming?

She dabbed her mouth with a napkin. 'I thought you might enjoy having a few extra young people in. I know your birthday doesn't officially fall until next Friday, but you'll be back in London by then.'

'Why . . .' I was taken aback by such kindly forethought.

'You see, I'm not quite the wicked old witch that you thought me,' she said, tossing her napkin across the table as she dipped out from the parasol's shade. 'Now, if you will excuse me, I shall go up and rest for an hour. Vicky, wake me at six.'

Across the table, I met Vicky's narrowed eyes. As her mother moved out of hearing range, she said, 'I hope you're sorry now for the muddy things you said to her. You don't deserve her consideration. If it were me, I'd let your birthday pass without even a card.'

'C.L.B.!' Tom sniggered to himself, squinting on a level with the table top as he brushed a last few crumbs from the cloth. 'That's her, isn't it, Toria? C.L.B.!'

Her eyes slithered briefly, unwilling to meet mine. 'Don't call me Toria, Tom. You know I hate it.'

'C.L.B.?' I enquired.

'Why not?' she shrugged. 'It was a silly habit Emmet got into, calling us all by initials.' Jamming her straw hat further down her forehead, she got up abruptly. 'This sun is giving me a headache. If I don't come down for dinner tonight, that will be why. *And* the fact that Emmet's friends are so juvenile. It will be *all* children tonight. Apart from Mother – and Harry and Saffron. But with Frank away, and Oliver . . .'

I looked up at that. Oliver?

Vicky let her lip curl, her eyes darting blue daggers. 'I *thought* so. I knew at Christmas you were dangling after him. Well, you're out of luck. He won't be here. Mother did invite him, but at the last minute he had to go away to Lincoln. Something to do with Thorne-Thomas.' If my relief showed, jealousy blinded her to it. 'It does seem to prove that he hasn't the slightest interest in a little—' She bit the sentence off, turning away. 'Come, Tom, let's go back to the house.'

'A little what?' I demanded, but she was stalking away, her back stiff.

It was Tom who answered, eyes bright with mischief as he cupped his hand over another snigger: 'C.L.B.'

'Tom!' Vicky snapped, and he went slyly loping after her, cradling his saucer of crumbs, leaving me feeling cold.

Poor Tom only repeated what he heard others say, but obviously Vicky used my initials as a form of abuse, and to Emmet they were a joke. I was reluctant to ask any of the older members of the family about it because it would look as if I were telling tales, complaining of a silly nickname coined because Vicky was jealous of me. But thank goodness Oliver had elected to be away on business that weekend. Perhaps he was as reluctant to see me as I to see him.

For my birthday dinner party Cook had made a cake, with candles; every guest brought a small gift for me and they sang 'Happy Birthday', which made my eyes sting. Even Vicky was there, evidently under orders to be sociable. Everyone tried to make me feel at home. Which, perversely, had the opposite effect – if they had really accepted me, they wouldn't have needed to try quite so hard.

Near midnight, after Grandmother had gone to her room, when Vicky had also retired and Harry, the oldest of the company, began to consult his watch, Emmet suggested we should all go for a walk to 'clear the cobwebs'. Most of us were ready for an adventure, what with wine at dinner, youth in the blood and spring in the air. Harry and Saffron declined to go with us, but didn't stop us, begging only that we be quiet and not alert 'the Mater'. So out we went, a dozen of us on a heady May night with the waxing moon riding among flying wisps of cloud.

Some had found torches, which was just as well since Emmet elected to take us along the spine of Denes Hill, heading for the sea on a path that wound tortuously through the woods. Brambles tugged at skirts, girls giggled and whispered, boys seized the chance to hold a soft hand or slide an arm round a slender waist. I found myself attended by a young man named James Lacey, whom Emmet characterized as 'short, but sweet' – James stood about five feet six. The way dipped down a steep slope into the railway cutting, where the company had built a gate in the fence either side, to allow walkers through, with notices warning them to beware of trains. 'Choo-choo!' someone wailed ahead of me. The sound disturbed an owl that came floating ghost-pale across the moon.

Up through the trees and over the last of the wooded rise, the path sloped down to open marshes, along the edge of a drainage dyke and through low sand dunes. By the time we arrived on the beach, where a stretch of rounded pebbles hemmed acres of flat sand, it was past one in the morning. The tide was coming in, rapidly surging over the sand.

'Anyone for a swim?' Emmet suggested.

'What, starkers?' came the reply.

'Well, I'm not ruining my best drawers,' Emmet quipped. If the young men had been alone they might have done it; as it was, with four girls along, they let discretion decide. The wind was cold, anyway. One of the girls protested at the thought of going back the 'rough way' and so we set off down the road to the village, past the station, making for the short cut past the Farcroft farm.

The farmhouse itself lay in darkness: the Farcrofts must have been abed hours before. We planned to creep past and not disturb them, but, shushing each other, whispering and giggling over the adventure, we had hardly passed the fork that led by the barns and down to the house when one of the dogs started to bark. Then another one gave tongue.

Some wag decided to return the greeting, imitating the dogs. Someone else began to howl like a wolf. Stifled giggles egged them on and though, thinking of Philip, I pleaded, 'Oh, don't!' my protest was half-hearted. The joke carried us on until a light flared in one of the bedrooms, the window scraped up and a head came out, bellowing obscenities. Laughing, we fled away from Mad Jack's wrath, some of the men still howling and barking, speeded by the impotent blast of a shotgun behind us. Breathless and dishevelled, we reached the safety of the gate, but as we trailed home through the woods I regretted my own part in the foolery. Had we disturbed Philip's sorely needed rest?

I had anticipated seeing him in church, but by the time I woke in the morning it was too late to go to service. The weather had changed, bringing another grey sea fret to muffle all the lower slopes, leaving us on a sunlit island with our tennis and our croquet and our swing roped to a tree. Dutifully, we attended evensong – Philip wasn't there – and ended the day with a singsong and dancing round the piano. Even Vicky enjoyed herself – her talent for ragtime won approval and, James Lacey's brother, David, having taken a shine to her, she became quite skittish.

When Whit Monday dawned hot, with blue skies promising a fair day, the entire crowd of us walked down to what the family regarded as their special area of the shore, midway between Eveningham and Heacham, where few trippers ever penetrated. Among the sand dunes, a large wooden beach hut provided a place, for those who wished, to change into swimming costume. We spread our rugs and had lunch, then some of the group walked out to meet the tide, some tossed a large ball on the sand, some sat idly, doing what everyone does beside the sea.

I remembered similar picnics around the turn of the century: Mother, John, Frank and their friends – Oliver must have been there, too, just one of the adults. They had had their own circle, leaving the twins and Vicky to play with me, or ignore me, as the mood took them. Even then, I had often been alone in the crowd, wandering off by myself.

'Dreaming!' Grandmother had sighed. 'That child is always dreaming.'

'We all need dreams,' someone had said. Who? Why . . . Uncle John, of course. Infuriatingly, that snippet was all my memory yielded.

At eight I had been a solitary child. Now, a few days away from my nineteenth birthday, I was still alone, walking barefoot along the edge of the sea, warm ripples round my ankles, my toes relishing the feel of ridged sand as my mind drifted back in time. My long hair fell loose about my face and shoulders, brown-black strands fluttering in a warm breeze from under an old straw hat. I had on a loose dress whose hem could get wet if it wished – I didn't care. I was too busy looking for cockles, picking up shells, collecting stones and fronds of seaweed, aware of the small, plain, lonely girl who still existed inside me. Would she ever find her place?

Lost in reverie, I wandered to where other people were enjoying the beach as the tide rose, covering the dangerous deep channel that awaited the unwary paddler two hundred yards or so from the high-tide line. Waves surged in over sloping sand, green ripples edged with foam, growing deeper by the minute. Not far from me, two young women and a man sported, all in knitted navy bathing suits. Only the man was thoroughly wet; the girls stood in shallows up to their knees, squealing and ducking aside as their companion kicked up gouts of glittering water.

Cutting through the waves directly towards the two girls and their playful tormentor, a swimmer made powerful strokes. He moved purposefully, the sight sweeping me suddenly back to another day on this beach, long ago . . . mist seemed to gather, denying me the full picture, yet it was important that I remember. I stood half in the present, half in the past, watching the lithe, athletic arms that brought the man closer, until he was in the shallows. With a surge of motion, framed by glittering drops in the sunlight, he rose up from the sea, lifting his arms to sweep water from his face and flick it at the girl who had turned to welcome him. It was John. Surely, it was my uncle John!

The girl flung out her hands as if to ward off the cold shower and, shrieking with laughter, spun and fled towards me as the man started after her. She darted past me, fleeing him and yet wanting him to catch her. She didn't know I was there. Was I invisible? Were they the ghosts, or was I? The young man was near now, his fine body, strong shoulders and long limbs displayed by the clinging bathing suit. He stopped, only feet away, and the mist swirled in my mind. John . . .

His face seemed to shimmer and the illusion faded, no longer my lost uncle but more familiar, frowning features, lean and brown, gleaming wet in the light. The hostility in his green eyes softened to puzzlement as he studied my face, clearly wondering at my pallor. I probably looked as if I had seen a ghost.

'Kate?' he said.

I had to swallow and lick my dry lips before I could utter, 'Philip! I . . . I didn't see you.'

The frown deepened, knotting the muscle between his brows. 'What's wrong?'

'Nothing!' Trying to gather the scattered shreds of my composure, I said the first words that came to me. 'How are you?'

'I'm well, thank you. You?'

'Yes.' My voice was too light, too breathy. 'Home for the weekend. Emmet's home, too, with some friends.'

He glanced beyond me, his cheek twitching. 'We saw them. That's why we didn't go any further. I didn't realize you were with them.'

'No, you wouldn't.' What were we doing making this ridiculous small talk? I felt weak and dazed, realizing how much I had longed to see him. How I ached to be in his arms! But what I said, bitterly, was, 'I suppose if you'd known I was there you'd have given us an even wider berth!'

I expected him to take offence, but instead he moved closer, responding to the message in my eyes rather than to my words. He lifted a hand as if to touch me and I'm sure I swayed towards him, but—

'Philip?' The girl's shrill voice came from my left. 'Philip!' She was short, curvy, her pretty face shaded by a straw hat, mouth pursed and eyes snapping a warning at me. 'I want some ice cream. Are you now coming?'

He hesitated, glancing from her to me and back again before making his decision. 'Yes. Yes, I'm coming.' About to move off, he paused again and looked me up and down, the frown creased again on his brow. 'Was it you came rowdying past the farm in the small hours yesterday morning?'

'Yes,' I admitted. 'I'm sorry. We'd been having a party. For my birthday. I'll be nineteen on Friday.'

'Then it's time you grew up a bit and stopped behaving like a spoiled brat. You – and the rest of your blessed family. Come on, Lou.' And he turned on his heel, grabbing the girl's hand as he dragged her away.

'Nice seeing you,' I called stupidly after him, but if he heard he made no response. The girl named Lou was saying, 'Kate who? Who is she, Philip? She gave me the shudders. She's got witch's eyes.'

Her complaints faded as they moved away, leaving me feeling more alone than ever. Until I saw him in front of me, I hadn't realized how strong my feelings for him still were.

Win Leeming had not found any answers at her old convent school, but she was about to embark on another path: she wanted me to accompany her to a spiritualist meeting. 'There's no one else I can ask, Kate,' she said, her eyes huge and limpid behind her glasses. 'The others would only laugh at me. I know it's not logical. But Mrs Bly, the medium, is going to try to contact her mentor, W. T. Stead. Twenty years ago, he wrote a story exactly predicting the *Titanic* disaster, but . . .' She shivered a little, glancing round as if fearing listeners. 'He didn't heed his own warning. He was on board, too – he died with Stanton. Oh, Kate, I wouldn't ask if it weren't important to me, you know that. But I have to try. If I could just be sure that Stanton is happy . . . I keep dreaming about him, lying at the bottom of the sea, trapped and alone.'

I would have liked to refuse: for me, clairvoyance was
more burden than blessing, an intensely private thing about
which I seldom spoke. My unseen friends came when *they*
chose, not to any summons of mine, nor with dimmed
lighting, dancing trumpets or rapping tables. I suspected
those who used their powers to make money, or for notoriety.
From all I had heard, Mrs Bly was an attention-seeker.

But I said, 'Of course I'll come,' and laid my arm about
my friend's bent shoulders, hoping to stop her thinking such
awful thoughts.

The meeting was to be held that Friday – on the last day
of May, my birthday. When the day came, Win didn't appear
at breakfast so she missed seeing the flurry of cards that
came for me; I asked the others not to trouble her by
mentioning the significance of the day. Among the cards
was one with a poignant picture of a man sitting by a lily-
pond, gazing at a reflection of a dark-haired girl. The verse
was a paean to regret and lost chances and, for a moment, I
let myself imagine it might be from Philip. It wasn't, of
course. It was signed simply '*O.G.W.*' in a neat, slanting
hand I recognized: Oliver Wells, who else?

The simple, subtle appeal of the card touched me more
deeply than impassioned speeches might have done. In
calmer mood, I understood why Oliver had acted as he had
over Miss H, and my own behaviour seemed brattish,
deliberately rude to someone who did not deserve it. Would
I ever learn how to handle men?

That evening I was on my way downstairs when Mrs
Armes intercepted me. 'Your friend Mr Wells is here. He's
in the front room with Miss Leeming.'

Oh, Lord! Not knowing how to interpret the leap of
response inside me, I went into the parlour, where Win was
in tears.

Oliver snapped to his elegant feet at sight of me, looking perturbed. 'You can't be serious, Kate! I came to invite you out to dinner to celebrate your birthday and— What is this nonsense about a seance?'

'You should have reminded me it was your birthday,' Win sniffed. 'I'd forgotten all about it.'

'It's not important,' I assured her. 'I promised I would go with you and so I shall. I've already had my birthday dinner, at Denes Hill.'

'If you insist on going to this meeting,' Oliver said, 'then I equally insist on accompanying you. Any kind of undesirable might be there. Who knows what may occur?'

'He's probably right, Kate,' Win agreed.

Before I could muster argument, Oliver swept up a bouquet of hothouse roses from a chair and presented them to me. 'Please,' he murmured, his eyes expressing much that could not be said in front of a third party. 'Please allow me to escort you. I shall not be happy unless you do.'

When he looked like that, so handsome and sorrowful, with his hands full of expensive flowers whose perfume spread a scented aura round us, I was unable to refuse.

Mrs Bly, the famous medium, had booked a public hall in the Brompton area. Though she made no entry charge, collection plates lay ostentatiously on a table by the door. The hall was half full when we arrived, with more people gathering. I managed to have Win sitting between Oliver and me – my nerves were on edge without the added turmoil of having him too close.

On a stage framed by black felt curtains, a venerable gentleman in a clerical collar began the meeting with a prayer and a minute's silence to remember souls 'recently passed over'. At this, Win groped for my hand and held it tightly, a handkerchief pressed to her face, while I heartily wished myself elsewhere. Next, the white-haired cleric introduced Mrs Bly, who came slowly from behind the curtain leaning on a stick, an elephantine figure with dyed black hair, dressed in voluminous black. Against that darkness her face was pale as she spoke in a surprisingly soft voice, warning us that she could guarantee nothing: the spirits would decide if the evening was propitious. All she could do was seek to become an instrument, through her spirit guide, the Red Indian Chief, Black Hawk.

'Tommyrot!' Oliver muttered, and someone shushed him.

Seating herself in a thronelike chair, Mrs Bly folded her hands in her sleeves as the lights dimmed, leaving only her moon face floating in limpid darkness. Then her head drooped; a silence spread; the hall held its collective breath. In the darkness my eyes played tricks, forming vague moving shapes and flying sparks on the edge of vision. But if my flesh crawled it was more from distaste than the presence of ghosts.

Win's sharp nails bit into my hand as Mrs Bly's head snapped up with a jerk that made the audience gasp. The medium was apparently wide awake, but the voice that now emerged from her was loud and sonorous, totally unlike the meek tone she had employed in her introduction.

I had to admire her talent for picking up clues from her audience, fishing around with hints until someone rose for the bait, and was hooked. There was a moment when I felt Win stiffen in response to, 'I'm getting an S – a name beginning with S. Someone recently passed over, I think. Simon? Stephen? Stan—'

'Stanley!' a woman across the hall cried. 'It's my Stanley. Stan, love, it's me, Esme!'

The show went on, sometimes crude, sometimes clever,

but never quite convincing enough, not for me. The writer W. T. Stead 'came through', much to the joy of his sister, who was in the front row – probably an old friend of Mrs Bly's, if Mr Stead had been the medium's mentor. But what he had to say from the beyond was no more illuminating than any of the more personal messages we heard that evening. Gradually, Win's hold on my hand became less desperate and I guessed she too had seen through the trickery.

Then, just as Mrs Bly seemed to have exhausted her repertoire, there came a finale that shocked even me. She appeared to be jolted out of her chair, jerked to her feet like a marionette on strings, and a different voice came from her throat, a lighter male voice, saying urgently, 'Katie. Be careful, Katie! Don't—'

A woman not far from us shrieked and leapt up, sending her chair clattering to the floor. 'It's me. It's me! I'm Katie! Oh, God . . . it was our Bert. It was!' As she began to sob loudly, the medium's huge bulk shuddered. She slumped, and people rushed from the wings to support her as she apparently came out of her trance and looked about her in a daze. In the darkness around us, voices began to speculate: at least one other woman claimed to be the intended recipient of the message, while others remembered Katies they knew, who were in possible danger.

I felt cocooned, surrounded by invisible walls, for I too had been convinced the message was for me. The voice had been so different from the laboured tones of 'Black Hawk', vibrant with anxiety, saying *my* name. But, as far as I remembered, only Mother in rare fits of tenderness, when I was very young, had ever called me by the diminutive, 'Katie'.

As Mrs Bly was helped from the stage, the lights went

up. The furore diminished as the reverend gentleman came out to thank us all and bid us good night and God speed – and to remind us of the collection plates.

'She might as well have said "Mabel",' Oliver said with a glance that spoke of his concern for me. 'Or "Fred". Any name common enough for there to be someone in the audience who—'

'I know,' I cut him off. 'Win . . . are you all right?'

She had a calm, almost beatific look on her face as she returned from whatever dream world she had been lost in. 'Yes. Yes, thank you, I'm well. She was wonderful, wasn't she? I felt so . . . reassured. But I knew Stanton wouldn't come through tonight. Something told me so. As if he whispered in my ear. But I shall come again. It's such a comfort, don't you think, to *know* there's something beyond.'

Over her head, Oliver and I exchanged a look. Win had been taken in – the last person one would have expected to succumb to such arrant trickery – or *was* it all trickery? Had there been an element of truth?

We were leaving the hall, emerging into a misty spring evening pooled by the gaslight that still illumined that part of the city, when a bright voice cried my name and I turned to see Judy Love and her friend, the red-headed Elsie, pushing through the crowd towards us.

'It's lovely to see you, Kate,' the dancer cried, her butter-blond ringlets bobbing under an impossible yellow hat. 'Were you in the hall? Mrs Bly's amazing, don't you think? Oh . . .' She had just recognized the man who stood next to me. Her eyes popped, and then her eyelashes went mad. 'Why . . . it's Mr Wells, isn't it? You were on the train with Kate. Coming back from Berlin. Kate . . . do the honours, won't you?'

So I introduced them to each other – Oliver Wells, Win Leeming, Judy Love and Elsie . . .

'Pratt,' the redhead supplied, preening under Oliver's cool dark gaze. 'Elsie Pratt.'

In a few breathless sentences, she and Judy managed to tell him a good deal about themselves and where he might find them appearing, but he hardly bothered to hide his impatience as he broke away to hail a passing horse-drawn cab.

As we were taking our leave, Judy grasped my arm, saying in an undertone, 'How's Frank? Is he—'

'He's very well,' I said.

'Is he? Really?' She surveyed me worriedly.

'When I saw him last, he was fighting fit. Why do you ask?'

'Oh – no particular reason. Give him my kind regards, won't you?'

'I'll do that,' I replied, guessing that she just wanted, through me, to remind Frank of her existence. Hastened by the impatient Oliver, I followed Win into the cab, while behind me Oliver tipped his hat to the two Gala Girls, and climbed in opposite us.

'Friends of Frank's?' he asked as the cab moved off.

'We met them once,' I replied. 'Last summer. Frank treated them to supper – you know how gregarious he is. Judy Love appears to be susceptible to every eligible man she meets. On the steamer that night, she was asking me all about *you.*'

'Can't say I noticed her,' he said. 'But then, I did have other preoccupations.'

I couldn't see his face clearly, but the air was suddenly electric between us. Win had lapsed into a reverie, gazing out of the far window at the passing streets.

'I hope you both realize that what we saw this evening was trumpery,' Oliver said. 'I could have done better myself. Red Indian guides, my hat! What's wrong with people that they turn to such nonsense?'

'What's wrong with people who refuse to accept?' Win responded. 'Tonight, for the first time, I truly believe there is something beyond this life. Couldn't you feel it, in the hall? A vibrance? The presence of unseen forces?'

'No. I certainly could not.'

'But it was so clear! Surely you couldn't fail to observe it. Why do you resist it, Mr Wells? What is it you're afraid of?'

'I'm afraid for both of *you*.'

'Then don't be. We are both quite capable of making up our own minds. Aren't we, Kate?'

'Yes, we are,' I replied, and took the hand she reached for mine.

Arriving at Lincoln Square, we all alighted and Win insisted on paying the cabbie before quietly taking her leave, moving up the steps. The cab clopped away, leaving Oliver and me alone in a damp night smelling of smoke, with light falling through blue and white glass in Mrs Armes's front door. I turned my shoulder to him, my foot on the first step.

'This was not the way I had planned to spend the evening,' he said with chagrin. 'I had booked a table, for a special birthday dinner . . . I know I was taking too much for granted, but I did so want to see you, Kate. I wanted to see you alone. Not at Denes Hill. That's why I cried off the party last weekend – too many people. But I've booked into a hotel in the West End for this weekend. I thought we might—'

'I'm sorry,' I broke in and, when he was silent, turned to look at him across my shoulder. 'I *am* sorry, Oliver, but . . .

I'm sorry.' I didn't know what else to say.

He watched me for a moment, his eyes scanning my face as if he hoped to find signs of uncertainty. But I had no doubts. I felt calm, clear, sure of myself. At length, he let out a long sigh. 'I see. I had hoped . . . No. My own fault. Charging in too soon. Bull in a china shop, as always. Perhaps one day . . .'

'No.' Feeling sorry for him, I added, 'I can't let you go on hoping. I'm flattered, Oliver. Terribly flattered. But, you see, I have too much else to do before I think of . . .'

His dark gaze fixed passionately on my mouth as he said, 'Yes. I do see. Very well, Kate.'

'There's Vicky,' I reminded him.

'Indeed.' His mouth twisted bitterly. 'But it's a wife I want, not a clinging vine still attached to her mother's apron strings. I'm obviously destined to die a bachelor. I'm sorry to have . . . Good night.'

Tipping his hat, he turned and walked unhurriedly away, not looking back. I almost called after him, but what I had told him was the truth: I wasn't ready to commit myself to him, or ask him to wait – that wouldn't have been fair. At that moment I wasn't sure I should ever want to commit myself to anyone.

Except, perhaps, Philip Farcroft. Oh, yes, I thought with a passion that made my head spin, if Philip had been with me tonight, the evening might have ended very differently.

Later, in my room, I lay awake listening to the sounds of the city – a late train hooting, the clop of hooves on fresh tarmacadam, the noise of motors and the squalling of cats. Only then, alone with my thoughts, did I allow myself to remember the spiritualist meeting. I relived the scene, the fat woman on stage, leaping to her feet with black draperies flowing round her, her round pale face a void as the voice came out of her mouth: '*Katie! Be careful, Katie!*' Not *her* voice. No. Not even a voice she had summoned up for herself. For behind her, in the darkness, there had been another figure – the same man I had seen twice before, tall, fair and slender, and intent on reaching me . . .

I hadn't imagined him. I was sure of it. My uncle John, drowned eleven years before in the Wash, had this time spoken directly to me through Mrs Bly. Warning me. But warning me of what?

ELEVEN

After sitting exams, I returned again to Norfolk in early July, the time of haying, with gorse blazing yellow above purpling heather on the hilltop in front of the house. Denes Hill was quiet, Uncle Frank in Scotland and Emmet off cruising the Aegean with chums whose people had a yacht. Missing his twin, a glum Tom sought the company of his birds and animals, both those he kept caged and his wilder creatures in the woods. Grandmother and Vicky, assisted by the unobtrusive but ever-present Anderson, had their own round of charitable committee work and social engagements.

Since I always felt an object of curiosity, when company came I made excuses about studying, or took a walk to the beach, or a cycle ride to Hunstanton. There, I often stopped for a chat with Butcher Ehrenfried, who seemed to enjoy speaking his own language for a while.

Too often, I found myself near the Farcroft farm, on foot or on my cycle. A steam engine hissed and chuntered in the yard, driving a saw, or cutting chaff for feed, while men thatched hayricks against inclement weather. In the fields, hoers moved among root crops and blue-flowered beans, while boys with clappers scared crows from ripening corn. Mad Jack, astride a heavy horse, supervised these activities, a big old man with an iron-grey growth of beard, which he seemed to shave only once a week, and angry eyes glaring under a brown bowler hat. I also saw Philip – working in the fields, or astride a fine bay hunter. Though we exchanged only the occasional nod and time-of-day greeting, my pulses beat faster at sight of him and his eyes told me he shared my awareness. Circumstances separated us, but given the right moment, perhaps . . .

One evening, Tom came to supper in a rage against Mad Jack. 'He's been shooting my pigeons! Blast him! Blast him! Look!' And on to the table he threw three limp bodies, bloody from pellets, pale feathers drifting.

Vicky, with a shriek, leapt up, sending her chair crashing, and Grandmother's face went grey. 'Thomas! Take them away at once!' At his shrinking look, her voice softened. 'You mustn't get sentimental over pigeons, my dear. Give them to Cook. You like pigeon pie.'

'No,' he said. 'Not any more.' But he took the pigeons away and, as ever after such episodes, we pretended nothing had happened.

In Lynn, spending a few days with Uncle Harry and his family, I renewed my acquaintance with young Eddy, who at ten months old was a fat, lively baby, already trying to walk. Saffron had by that time lost most of her excess weight, but she would never be slender again. The roundness suited her – she was the earth-mother kind, already talking of having more children. Three or four would be ideal, she said; she agreed with Dr Marie Stopes that control should be practised.

I endorsed this view, though I hadn't much idea what it meant. For all my imagined sophistication, the 'facts of life' remained obscure.

Grandmother and Vicky also stayed at Hawthorn House over a weekend when we attended an outdoor meeting of the National Union of Women's Suffrage Societies, whose local president was Mrs Holcombe Ingleby, wife of the Lynn

MP. Uncle Harry came along to show his support. Indeed, a good third of those present, both in the gathering and on the platform, were male.

Under trees in the gardens of one of Lynn's grand houses, the platform was draped with bunting fluttering red, white and green in the sunlight. Rousing songs, and speeches in support of women's right to vote, preceded a tea, served to the accompaniment of music from the town band. Mingling across the lawns, I encountered several ladies I had met before when staying with Saffron, including the Hon. Mrs Lacey, a doll-like figure who lived in the Manor at Lenhoe, inland from Eveningham. Her sons, David and James, had been at my birthday dinner, their mother reminded me. I had not forgotten; the Lacey boys were charming, though, like their mother, somewhat lacking in physical stature.

Mrs Lacey was wondering if she might recruit my services during the summer, for the distribution of leaflets and to do some house-to-house calling to explain the Cause. As we chatted, Grandmother hove to beside us, with Vicky behind her and – to my discomfort – Oliver Wells as escort. He gave me a polite smile to which I made no outward response, though my pulses jumped.

'Kate will be delighted to help, won't you, Kate?' Grandmother answered Mrs Lacey, adding to me, 'It will give you something to do with your time.' Taking Mrs Lacey's arm, she drew her away, adding, 'I'd offer Vicky's help, too, but she has enough to do keeping track of all my commitments. Now, my dear Elfreda . . .'

In their wake, Vicky flared her nostrils at me. 'I'd be no good at it, anyway. I don't mind addressing envelopes, but doorstep politics are *so* unfeminine. Don't you think so, Oliver?'

'Not so unfeminine as some of the antics the militant

section indulge in on occasion,' he answered with a sidelong glance at me that recalled a misty March evening and a kiss in the darkness of a taxi cab, interrupted by breaking glass and flames.

'Some of them feel that physical action is the only way of getting noticed,' I said.

He glowered at me. 'All they've achieved lately is to make parliament vote down the Conciliation Bill.'

'Well, *that* was only a token gesture!' I flared. '*All* women should have the vote, not merely unmarried ladies of some means.'

'And where did you hear that argument? From your friend Miss H? I trust, for your sake, you're not intending to emulate her, Kate. Stick to leaflet-delivering. It's safer.'

Vicky had been listening like a spectator at tennis, understanding only half of it but growing more annoyed with every word. 'And *who* is Miss H?'

A swift look passed between Oliver and me and I saw his eyes narrow and his mouth twist. 'Kate has acquired some strange friends while she's been in London,' he said bitterly, and laid his hand under her elbow, steering her away.

'How do *you* know that?' she demanded.

'Frank told me,' the lie came smoothly, and over his shoulder he cast me a bleak look. 'But we don't want your mother to find out, do we?'

Was that a threat? I wondered. Might he also tell Grandmother about other friends I had made, nearer to home?

Having acquired the habit of early rising, I frequently went out before breakfast, when everything seemed fresh and new. Tom evidently agreed: at dawn he'd be down with his animals, or carrying out his 'job' of guarding the woods. Whenever I roamed close to home, Tom was wont to appear without warning, wanting to talk, drawn to me because he was lonely. I grew fond of him, but his habit of appearing out of nowhere made me cautious about being seen too often near the Farcroft farm. Not that it stopped me – nothing could have stopped me. Something stronger than myself was at work, drawing me to seek meetings with Philip.

One day I encountered the girl who had been with Philip on the beach at Whitsun. She was coming from the farmhouse carrying a basket of food and a stone bottle of drink and she didn't recognize me as I rode past on my cycle – I was better dressed than I had been on the shore, with my hair neatly up. Covertly following, I saw her taking the snap to where Philip and the others gathered in the shelter of a hedge for elevenses. She stayed with them, sitting close to Philip, sharing his food. She even drank from the same bottle.

Knowing I was making myself ridiculous, I went home feeling depressed and vowing not to go near the farm again.

A letter posted in Lynn awaited me, the address typewritten.

'Who can that be from?' said Grandmother, who took an intrusive interest in all post at the house.

'I've no idea.' In front of her, standing in the overfurnished grand saloon, I opened the envelope and read the letter. It was from Oliver, apologizing with nice humility for losing his temper at the garden party: '*I was in a bad mood, I fear. Nothing to do with you. I beg you to forgive any offence. Please believe that I am concerned for your welfare and your happiness. If we can only be friends, that will be enough.*'

Grandmother was watching me. 'Well?'

'It's from a friend of Aunt Saffron's,' I lied, returning the letter to its envelope. 'About the Cause. They want me to help, but . . . I think, if you don't mind, I'm going to take up Win's invitation and go to Devon.'

'All that way? Alone? My dear girl . . . I shall ask Frank to meet you and see you safely on the train for the West Country.'

'I thought he was in Scotland,' I said.

'So he was. Now he's at the Mayfair apartment. I told you his movements are erratic. You would be met the other end, I assume?'

'Of course. I'll go up straight away and write to Win.'

I didn't reply to Oliver's letter: I burned it in the grate in my bedroom, and stirred up the ashes, which was a measure of my insecurity – I always felt under observation at Denes Hill. I needed to get away for a while – away from Grandmother and Vicky, away from reach of Oliver, and especially away from the proximity of Philip Farcroft. Evidently I had been mistaken in imagining the attraction between us to be mutual. By pursuing him so openly, I felt, I was demeaning myself.

A day or two later, I was on my way to London.

A beaming Uncle Frank met me at Liverpool Street and swept me off my feet in a bear hug. I was so delighted to see him again that we were having tea in Lyons Corner House before I had a chance to say, 'You're thinner, aren't you? Are you all right?'

'Couldn't be better,' he assured me. 'Been working too hard, I expect. I don't eat properly when the muse is at the wheel.'

'I wondered.' Shadows under those slate-blue eyes worried me. 'I saw Judy Love some time ago. She was asking after you rather anxiously.'

'Sweet girl, Judy,' he said. 'And so are you, to worry about me. Just for that, I shall take you out this evening. And tomorrow . . . I've decided to come down to the West Country with you.'

That pleased me even more. Round-eyed, I said, 'To Westward Ho!?'

Frank laughed at my expression. 'I'm flattered, but Miss Leeming won't want your old uncle as an extra. No, I'll see you safely as far as Exeter and then you take the high road and I'll take the low road. I've friends in Torquay. I plan to do a spot of painting and feed myself up again. Speaking of which, take a look at those cream cakes over there! Which one would you like? Decisions, decisions. Or shall we have the whole plateful? I feel like spoiling my favourite niece.'

I started to be coy over the compliment, but, 'I'm your *only* niece.'

'I know,' said Frank, and we both laughed immoderately, making other customers stare. Oh, it was good to be with him again. He always made me feel better. I determined to forget everything and enjoy this holiday.

Glorious Devon . . . everything the railway posters promised, with Westward Ho! a gem by the sea, full of holiday-makers. The Leeming cottage lay on the outskirts of the village, by a stream in a verdant valley where nightingales sang in the wood nearby.

Win and I enjoyed going about together, walking off the huge meals her aunt provided. The widowed Mrs Sidney Leeming was a quiet person, doing her chores with single-minded determination, as if keeping her house clean and her table laden with good food was her reason for existing. Perhaps it was, now that her son Stanton was gone. Win obviously felt familial duty towards her, though Mrs

Leeming had never shown much interest in her. Now, she complained about everything, making Win feel guilty. Within a few days I knew it was not healthy and I urged my friend to come back with me to Norfolk. But she refused.

'I'm all she has now, Kate. I shall stay with her, as I promised, until the end of September. I'll see you back in Lincoln Square.'

On Exeter station, changing trains, I noticed a poster advertising the summer show at one of the theatres in Torquay. One of the acts was the Gala Girls. Ah-ha! Was *that* what had drawn Frank to the south coast?

I sent him a card, telling him I was going home and adding as a PS, '*If you happen to see Judy Love, give her my regards.*' After I returned to Denes Hill I received a card from him, saying only, '*Judy who?*'

Vicky saw the card, and demanded to know what it meant. When I told her it was a joke, too complicated to explain, she scorned, 'Oh, really! Frank is such a fool!' Vicky was born middle aged.

It was a year since I had left Berlin. A whole year. Since Carl-Heinz's betrayal. Since Grandfather's death. Soon it would be Eddy's first birthday. Saffron and Harry were giving a birthday tea for him at Hawthorn House, to which I had been invited.

A few days before the celebration, waking early to find bright clouds breezing across a sunlit sky, I went down to the kitchen and shared an early pot of tea with Annie. Then I took my bike and pointed it inland, with the wind at my back, intending to ride the six miles to Lenhoe Manor; Mrs Lacey had sent to say she had another set of leaflets to distribute.

Toiling up the inclines and freewheeling down again,

aided by a rising wind, I didn't even see the clouds that came driving from the north. A rumble of thunder alerted me and when I glanced round I was horrified to see the sky coloured like mud, a menacing swirl shot through by flickers of lightning, trailing black skirts of rain that hid the Wash from sight.

I was four miles from Lenhoe, on an open track between dusty-gold cornfields, with no cottages nearby. Eveningham lay a mile or so behind me, Denes Hill a little further. I turned back, but the battering head wind made pedalling difficult.

Before long a curtain of rain hit me with drenching force, making me gasp and blink as I tucked my head well down. If any shelter had presented itself I might have stopped, but thorn hedges provided scant protection in a downpour that soon soaked my light summer clothes. The lane beneath my wheels turned to mud, running with rivulets of chalky reddish water. The tyres sent up a stream of wet mud to splatter my skirts and shoes. I wished I had never set out, but the rain wasn't cold and since I was already soaked through there seemed no point in worrying. Just forge on.

I came to a place where the lane forked. The main branch headed up a rise, the other angled downhill. I had walked that way once and knew that, half a mile on, it ran past the rear gate into Eveningham churchyard. If I could get that far I might shelter in the church.

I started off pedalling, but soon momentum carried me, rattling and jolting, down an ever steeper slope. My brakes were too wet to work properly. Gritting my teeth, I hung on. High banks channelled the water, turning the lane into a stream. It grew deeper, up to the wheel-hubs, dragging at the spokes, spraying up . . .

Lightning stood white against slaty clouds. Thunder

broke overhead. Was that a voice, a shout? I couldn't tell. I could barely see. Twilight enfolded me, the rain still driving. All my strength went into holding the cycle upright in what was now a stream with a stony, uneven bed hidden from sight beneath a spate of watery mud. More lightning cracked, sizzling at a tree in a field nearby. Too close! Its light blinded me. The cycle bucked under me, hitting an obstruction . . .

The bank came up and thumped me breathless.

I found myself clinging to the hedge, a torrent tearing at my lower body, trying to drag me away with it. My hands were slipping, torn by thorns. If I let go, the rush of water would sweep me away. I felt it take my right shoe. I couldn't hold on. I hadn't the strength. Dear God—

Then something fastened strongly round my wrist. A hand. A man's hand. He was beside me, shouting incoherently. I couldn't see him for the rain battering at my eyes, but he hauled me to my feet, clamped me to his side with a brawny arm about me, and forcibly dragged me with him, slithering and sliding as he forded through the spate, to where a smaller stream rushed down the bank through a gap in the hedge. Digging toeholds with his iron-shod boots, he clambered up out of the lane, leaning back to lend me his hand and pull me up after him. My left foot, still in its shoe, slipped in the mud. I would have tumbled back had my rescuer not held me firmly, saying hoarsely, 'Come on, Kate!'

Looking up through blinding rain, my senses jerked as I recognized Philip Farcroft, hatless, hair flattened to his head and his face dripping. 'Come *on*!' he repeated impatiently. A final tug on my arm wrenched me to safety beside him and as my legs sagged weakly he caught me in his arms. I leaned on him, clinging to him, aware of sodden clothing plastered to his body. Hot tears joined the cool rain in my eyes. My heart was thumping from both fright and exertion, my blood pulsing a song of gratitude and love: Philip, Philip, Philip . . .

'Oh, Philip!' I croaked, lifting my head. 'Philip . . .'

His face was dark, his expression fierce. But I saw it for only a split second before his mouth plunged for mine, shocking me with its savagery. A jolt of emotion shook me, and then something in me rose with answering ferocity and I struggled to get my arms free and wrap them about his neck, clasping him to me, lips, teeth and tongue melding with his in bruising kisses. His arms hardened about me, pulling me in closer until I could feel every sweet, strong contour of his ribs and belly. A rage of response flared like fire inside me, liquid heat rising to engulf me. I wanted to pull him down to lie with me. I wanted to wrench at his clothes and feel his nakedness against me. I wanted—

As my knees gave under me, he bent and swept me up into his arms and began to stride steadily across the squelching field. Over his shoulder, through misting rain, I saw we were in a cornfield, half of it harvested and gathered into stooks now sagging and sodden, the rest battered down. I could see the church tower on the next rise, and knew that behind me Denes Hill rose a dark mound on the horizon. But we might as well have been a million miles away from normality.

'Philip—'

He didn't look at me, though I saw the muscle jump in his jaw as he clenched his teeth. 'I'm taking you home,' he said.

'My cycle . . .'

'I'll fetch it later.'

He had a wagon waiting at the far side of the field, with between its shafts a great shire horse securely tethered to the gatepost. Its coat was dark with water, its ears flattened under the relentless rain as it tossed its head and stamped uneasily, frightened by more lightning and thunder that battered the sky from horizon to horizon. 'All right, girl.' The reassurance was for the horse as Philip tossed me up to the wagon's seat and went to unhitch the tether.

I was shivering uncontrollably, not so much from cold as from reaction. If he hadn't come, I would have drowned. As it was I was scared half to death, and shattered by the force of feelings that had flared so suddenly, mindlessly, inside me. Shocking, immoral feelings that horrified me now. What would he think of me if he knew? All the things of which Carl-Heinz had accused me . . . But I had never felt like that with Carl-Heinz. The embraces I had shared with him had been childishly innocent beside what had flamed in me when Philip touched me.

Soaked through, with water dripping from him, he moved as calmly and easily as if the sun were shining. He came round the wagon and, after an instant of uncertainty, our glances faltered and slid away. He swung up to the seat beside me, saying something that was lost in the tumult of teeming rain.

I wiped my face yet again. 'Sorry?'

'I said,' he shouted across his shoulder, 'you should have stayed on this top road. The back lane always floods when . . .' More thunder cut him off and, shaking his head as if to say talking was impossible, he slapped the reins. 'Walk on!'

The huge horse took up the strain, leaning all its weight into the harness. Slowly, the wagon oozed free of sinking mud and began to move out of the gate, on to the top road. The rain continued. But what did it matter? Once you're soaked to the skin you can't get wetter. I tore off my ruined hat and lifted my face to the downpour, hoping it might clear my head. It didn't. My senses were still reeling. All I could think of was the reality of Philip beside me. So close after all this time, and so much I wanted to say to him. *I'm not like that. Really, I'm not. I've never . . . I don't . . .* But I couldn't speak. I was too mortified. I should never dare look him in the eye again.

Reaching the main coast road, he pointed the wagon straight across, heading down into the village.

'I thought you were taking me home,' I said.

'I am,' he answered with an unreadable look from green eyes fringed by wet lashes, rivulets writhing down his face. 'It's all right, Mrs Gaywood will be there today.' *His* home, he meant, not mine. So we would be together a little longer. A chirrup of joy quirked inside me, quenched at once by dismay: what if his father were there? What if my family found out? I ought not to go to the farm. I tried to find words to say so, but they wouldn't come. Fate had taken over.

By then the storm centre had passed, thunder moving away behind us, rain settling to a steady stream. The lane rippled with water, around jagged stones dislodged by the flood, leaving holes and hazards. But the wagon trundled sturdily behind the horse as she plodded on, head down, feathered hooves bedraggled and sploshing. In the village centre, the green was flooded, the pond twice its normal size with families of duck and moorhen enjoying the unaccustomed space. People peered from cottage windows at the teeming rain, or watched anxiously from open doorways as the tide rose towards their thresholds.

We went on, down the drowned lane to the farm.

Halting the wagon at the gate of the rear walled yard, Philip leapt down and came to offer me his hand. I accepted it, burned by his touch but avoiding his eyes, and trailed after him to the kitchen door, which was flung open by a plump woman wearing an apron.

'Bless us all!' she exclaimed. 'Now what's to do, Master Philip?' And to me, 'Come you in, my beauty. Come you on in by the fire. Why, poor soul, you're all a-shiver! Master Philip—'

'Take care of her, will you?' he said. 'I have to see to Plum.' With which, he returned to the horse.

To my relief, Mad Jack was not there. The kitchen was empty but for a cat stretching on a peg rug by the big hearth where a fire burned bright and blessedly warm. From the oven came a delicious aroma of baking bread.

'Come you along o' me.' Mrs Gaywood led the way to the big beamed parlour, up the stairs in the corner to a passageway all dark panelling and brown paint, creaking boards and enfolding shadows. She showed me into an unused bedroom – bare mattress, surfaces thick with dust, faded lavender flowers piled in a bowl on a bow-fronted chest of drawers. A low window, festooned with cobwebs, peered out under jutting eaves.

'Get you out of those clothes, my dare,' Mrs Gaywood enjoined. 'Here's some towels. Get you dry while I find something for you to wear. That'll have to be whatsomever I can find, mind. There hen't been no young ladies in *this* here house, not for many a long year.'

Left alone, I stripped off my clothes with numb, fumbling fingers and wrapped my shivering self in towels, rubbing at my limbs and body in an effort to restore some warmth before taking all the pins and pads from my hair and towelling that, too, as dry as I could. My flesh felt clammy, blotched and goose-pimpled, and uncontrollable shivers shook me. Bruises were flowering, too, red scratches and scrapes, my hands torn by thorns . . .

'You'll soon feel better,' Mrs Gaywood assured me, returning with an armful of clothing which she tossed across the mattress, along with some slippers. 'There, see if them'll fit you. That's some of Mrs Farcroft's things. Mr Jack hen't had the heart to clear that all out, though that's seven year since she went to her reward, dare soul. They're aired, mind. But listen to me a-runnin' on, and you standing there quaking. Get you dressed, my beauty, and come you on down by the fire. I'll now go and put the kettle on. A nice cup of tea'll soon set you right.'

She took my wet clothes with her.

With my hair turbanned in a damp towel, I climbed into a voluminous pair of drawers and a camisole with pretty broderie anglaise trim. The blouse she had brought was sprigged blue, the skirt black. Both fitted only where they touched, made for a woman three times my width. The well-worn, shapeless slippers would serve to protect my feet from bare boards and cold flagstones. I found some safety pins in a pot on the dressing table under the window and managed to make myself decent after a fashion, though it was far from *haute couture*.

Beyond the window, the tree-clad hill brooded behind veils of weather, as it must have brooded for centuries, sheltering the farm from the north wind. The farm had been here long before the house on the hill. It knew its place and was content with it, the rhythm of changing seasons, seed time and harvest. So it had been. So it would be. To belong in such a place was to be one with the earth. To belong . . . But that was wishful fantasy: all my saner instincts clamoured to be gone. My family would not be pleased if they knew I had been here. And what if Mad Jack came home?

As I shook my hair free of the towel, combing the damp

strands with my fingers, I caught sight of my face in a mirror set in a swivel stand. A long bruise spread round a red lump on my cheekbone. My skin was pale, tinged blue under eyes which, in that grey light, looked luminously pale against the darkness of my tumbled hair – eyes that saw the unseen, windows to a mind that dreamed impossible dreams. Witch's eyes, Philip's girl Lou had said with unthinking cruelty. Philip . . .

Though my shivering had stopped, I was still cold, beginning to feel stiff and sore. The thought of the fire in the kitchen tempted me out into a passageway lit only by grey rain-light filtering up the stairs. Another thought – of coming face to face with Philip again, and maybe encountering his father – slowed my steps, making me pause to examine the pictures on the walls: sentimental prints; a couple of remarkably bad oils that Frank would have scoffed at; and old sepia photographs, stiff studio shots and a few blurred snaps . . .

This was Michael, surely, a gangling youth in his first suit with long trousers. This must be Philip, angelic in tumbled curls and sailor dress, aged about four. And here was Michael again, sitting on a bale of hay with, behind him, peeping from the barn doorway, a girl with long fair hair. She looked familiar.

Then a board creaked and, as I turned towards the sound, all thought of photographs faded to insignificance beside the living reality of the adult Philip, watching me from beyond a mist of light that flowed up the stairs. He had changed into dry working clothes, but his hair was still damp, curling crisply to the shape of his head.

Self-conscious, not knowing what to say, I felt my hand creep to my throat, where a pulse leapt against my fingertips. 'I was just . . .'

'I saw.' Moving without haste, hands in his pockets, he ambled along the passage towards me, making the boards creak. 'Are you feeling better?'

'Yes, thank you.' The closer he came, the more unsteady my heartbeat. Unable to look at him, I looked again at the photographs. 'Is this . . .'

'Clara Rhys-Thomas,' he confirmed, pausing beside me. 'I told you she was a friend of Michael's.'

'Yes.' I touched the glass, removing a faint film of dust so that the girl's face came clearer. Incredible though it seemed, here was proof that my mother had been wont to visit the farm. 'And is this you? You were a beautiful little boy.'

'I keep telling Dad he ought to get rid of some of these wretched old pictures,' Philip said, embarrassed, 'but he won't have them touched. He likes to keep everything as Mother left it.'

Why did we always talk about such irrelevant things? 'Philip . . .' I ventured, and cleared a frog from my throat. 'Up there on the hill, in the storm, I—'

'You don't have to explain.'

'I do! I want you to know, I'm not the sort of girl who . . .'

'Neither am I – that sort, I mean.' He was as much in knots as I was.

Unwisely, I turned to look at him, startled to find him very close, his gaze intent as he searched my face, saying things that spoke directly to my heart. If he had been a beautiful boy he was even more beautiful now he was grown. So male. So strong. So gentle. Remembering the way he had kissed me, I felt my heart plummet and then soar. Maybe I *was* 'that sort'. Or could be, with him, if he wanted it. 'You saved my life.'

'I saved you from a ducking, that's all.'

'You mean, if you hadn't been there, I might have got wet?' I tried to laugh, but he wasn't listening: he was watching my mouth, which had begun to tingle. I couldn't help myself. I wanted him to kiss me again. I wanted him to touch me, hold me . . .

Scanning the way my hair fell round my face, he lifted a hand to touch one of the damp strands that fell across my breast. 'You look different with your hair down. That day on the beach, I hardly recognized you.'

Did he have to remind me? I had been trying not to remember how he looked in a wet bathing suit. Waves of helpless longing lightened my head. 'Was that your girl you were with? Lou? She's pretty.'

His voice a vibrant undertone, he said, 'Those clothes fitted Mother a good deal better than they fit you. She'd have said you were skinny. I could probably span your waist with my two hands.'

How I wished he would! But I found myself backing away, drawing his attention back to my face, where he must have read my uncertainty.

'I won't, though,' he said.

'No. Better not.' I could hardly breathe. My body seemed to be one vast pulse, beating in response to his nearness, and when he looked into my eyes I felt I was drowning. We both knew we were flirting with danger; neither of us could resist the lure.

'You've bruised your face.' He touched the place with gentle fingers, light as a butterfly's wing, tracing the side of my cheek. His hand trembled as he let his thumb brush my prickling lips. All I could see was his strong brown face, dark lashes veiling his eyes, his mouth slightly parted as he tilted his head . . .

'Master Philip!' Mrs Gaywood's voice shrilled up the

stairs, making us leap apart as if stung. 'Master Philip, are you ready yet?'

Three feet of air lay suddenly between us. Three feet of air pulsating with guilt and shock. 'Just coming!' he replied.

'Tell the young lady breakfast's now ready,' the housekeeper called. 'Come you both down right quick.' And a door banged as she went away.

Letting out a long breath, Philip looked at me, straight-faced. 'Breakfast's ready.'

I bit my lip against a bubble of dizzy laughter, watching a slow answering smile light his eyes before he turned and led the way along the passage, down the creaking stairs to where there was more daylight. Reaching the bottom, he looked back at me, holding out his hand, and after a moment's hesitation I took it, feeling his fingers twine fiercely with mine. When I responded with pressure of my own, he said in a low voice, 'I've been praying something would happen, so that I could see you.'

Emotion misted my sight. 'Please, Philip . . .'

'From the moment we met.'

Our eyes held, confirming mutual feelings too strong to be denied. Though I knew it was wrong, I heard myself confess, 'So have I. But you do know that we mustn't . . .'

He nodded. 'Yes, I know.'

'Master Philip!' Mrs Gaywood bawled.

Pulling a wry, rueful face at me, Philip answered, 'We heard you!' and opened the door into the kitchen passage, gesturing me to go ahead.

Standing by the laden table, Mrs Gaywood was sawing at a soft fresh loaf, holding it upright so that what came off were uneven wedges. The savoury smell of warm bread and frying ham filled the room, drifting up to time-darkened beams, from which hung marrows and bunches of herbs.

Above the hearth on its pulley, the drying rack held Philip's clothes and mine, steaming intimately next to each other.

'Sit you down, then.' The housekeeper nodded at a chair nearest the fire. 'You sit there, my dare, where it's warm. Master Philip, you—'

But whatever she was going to say stopped as the outer door came open and, with a blast of damp wind that swept away the friendly warmth in the room, the huge bulk of Mad Jack Farcroft, clad in bowler hat and all-enveloping cape, with boots and buckled buskins, stood framed in the gap.

TWELVE

When Mad Jack appeared, time itself paused, unbreathing. Or was that only in my mind?

The burly, grizzled farmer slammed the door behind him, shutting out the rain, roaring, 'Blast! That's all we need. That'll *ruin* the blessed harvest.' Wrenching off his bowler hat, he slapped it in the air, sending an arc of spray across the room to sizzle in the fire. It just missed me, and as I flinched away he seemed to register my presence for the first time. He froze, peering at me through narrowed eyes.

I felt the tension in Philip as he moved to stand protectively beside me, a hand lightly behind my waist. 'Kate got caught in a flood up on Back Lane.'

'Did she, though?' said Mad Jack. Rasping at the grey stubble on his jaw, he continued to peer at me, noticing the fact that I was wearing his late wife's clothes. Beneath a thatch of unkempt grey hair, his face was inscrutable. 'Well, bor, are you now going to introduce us?'

'Yes, of course. Kate, this is my father, John Farcroft. Dad, this is Miss Catherine Brand.'

He came forward warily, holding out a huge horny hand. 'Pleased to meet you, Miss Brand. Well, sit you down. You look like you could do with some good food inside you. Let's eat before that get cold.'

Philip drew out the chair for me and saw me settled, then sat beside me, helping me to the food, while his father went through to the hall and returned without his cape. In brown corduroys, with a fustian waistcoat over a collarless shirt, he sat opposite us, piling his plate with fried ham, eggs, tomatoes and potatoes, which he ate with slabs of Mrs Gaywood's wonderful bread.

I should like to say that I wasn't hungry, that the accident, the excess of emotion, and the guilty excitement of being at the farm had quenched my appetite, but the fact is I was ravenous and tucked away my share of the tasty fare, while Philip recounted my misadventure. His father didn't say much, but kept surveying me narrowly, suspiciously, trying to weigh me up. I could hardly believe I was there, in the lair of the enemy. Tension heightened my senses and adrenalin made my heartbeat swift and strong, my whole body preparing for flight. Yet, because of Philip, I wanted to stay, too.

After a while, the first pangs of hunger diminished, the farmer afforded me another of his looks, under beetling grey brows, ruminating, 'So you're Clara's girl, then? Not much like her, are you?'

'I'm more like my father, so they say.'

'She used to sit there – right there where you're now sitting.'

A piece of bread and butter dripped honey into my hand. 'Yes, I . . . Philip did mention . . .'

'She was no more'n a sprat,' he told me. 'But I reckon she felt more at home here than she ever did up at the big house. Lady Muck up there on the hill was only interested in her boys, and then not much. That's why Clara came here. Poor little mawther needed a bit of attention.'

'Please, Dad!' Philip objected.

'Well, she did.'

As Philip turned to me, to apologize for his father's

tactlessness, I said, 'It's all right, Philip. I've heard the same from other people.'

There was a moment's silence, then: 'Blast!' the old man roared. 'D'you know what you're saying, agreeing with me? D'you know who I *am*? Mad Jack Farcroft – bane of all Rhys-Thomases! Hen't they told you about me?'

'I prefer to find out for myself,' I said, beginning to suspect that he relished and played up the role of 'Mad Jack'.

Eyes narrowed behind those shaggy brows, he pulled at his lips and scratched in his stubble with work-hard fingers. 'Independent miss, eh? Hah! Times are changing. *Women* are changing. Wouldn't've caught neither of *my* old mawthers daring to go against their folks. What's it all coming to? Votes for women, by God! What d'you need the vote for, heh? Your husband'll do the voting for you. It's him as pays the piper. If my Julia'd've been here, she—'

'She'd have said you don't talk politics at her table,' Philip put in lightly. 'And you'd have listened to her. She had you right where she wanted you, Dad. She was the boss in this house.'

The old man glared at him, but couldn't keep up the pretence for long. His face softened as he watched his son. 'That's true, bor,' he conceded. 'Your mother was a fine woman. A motherly woman. She was fond of the girl.' Turning to me, he added, 'Then *they* found out. Put a stop to it. Next thing we knew, Clara was sent right away, up north somewhere. Wasn't the same when she came back. Didn't want to know any of us Farcrofts then. Too good for us, she was.' He stared into space, bleak memories darkening his brow. 'Still, that's all long gone by.' With a glance at his watch, he scraped his chair back and eased himself to his feet, cocking his head at Philip. 'We've work to do, bor. Rain or no rain. Can't sit here a-jorin'.'

They both went into the hall, the old man returning in his cape, Philip swirling a macintosh round him. We exchanged a look, regretting the parting but acknowledging its inevitability. He said, 'Shall I see you before you go?'

'It depends,' I replied with a glance at the rack where our clothes steamed merrily. 'I mustn't be too long. Mr Farcroft . . . There's just one thing – about Tom. You know about Tom?'

'The feeble-minded one?' the farmer asked, frowning defensively. 'I know him.'

'He's not feeble-minded,' I objected. 'He just doesn't understand things in the ordinary way. And I'm concerned for him. He thinks it's his job to guard the birds and animals in Denes Wood, and when you go up there shooting . . .' His eyes narrowed, glimmering with warning, but I plunged on, 'It upsets him. If you could see the state he gets into . . . I'm worried what he might do.'

'To *me*?' A harsh laugh broke out of him. 'No imbecile scares me, bor.'

'It's *him* I'm worried about,' I said. 'We never know quite how he's going to take things. If you push him too far . . . I don't know what he might do. I thought you should know. I don't believe you'd want to cause any real harm – especially not to someone like poor Tom.'

He grabbed his bowler hat from where he had left it on the wooden drainer by the sink, jamming it on to his head. Until then, his temper had been half playful; now he was coldly angry. His voice had lost much of the Norfolk richness he affected as he said flatly, 'I'm a landowner – my own man – not some tenant farmer you can order around. My pedigree's longer than yours, I reckon. I've been shooting those woods since I was a boy, and my father before me, and *his* father. Way back. That's unwritten law we have rights to shoot there. Squires always allowed it. So did the chap who bought the hill and built the house, before Rhys-Thomases ever dreamed of coming here. I won't let some lack-brained halfwit prevent me from exercising my rights. No, nor a chit of a thing like you, whoever you are. I've been polite since my son brought you under our roof, but—' His arm shot out, a thick finger pointing damnation at me. 'Once your clothes are dry, take 'em and go. And don't come to my house again. None of your blood's welcome here.'

He snatched the door open and stormed out into the rain that was still steadily falling. Behind him, Philip surveyed me unhappily.

'I didn't mean to upset him,' I croaked. 'I'm sorry, Philip, but I do worry about Tom. I just thought he ought to know . . .'

He nodded. 'I'll talk to him. Don't worry.'

As he strode across the yard, boots splashing through the puddles, I leaned on the sink and watched him through the stained net at the window. He paused at the gate to look back and wave, and I replied in kind, but when he had gone I felt bereft, aware that I had no place here. What had I hoped to do – persuade the old man to call a truce? His hatred ran too deep. I should never have come, never have stayed.

Suddenly anxious to be gone, I said, 'Are my clothes dry yet? My family will be worried about me.'

Mrs Gaywood let down the drying rack, so it was nearer the fire, and we turned the clothes, shaking them out. They were still too damp to wear and I couldn't possibly go home in Mrs Farcroft's cast-offs.

While I waited, I found myself helping the housekeeper to clear the table (something I wouldn't have dreamed of doing at Denes Hill) and then I dried the dishes for her as we talked. The Farcrofts were a close lot, she said. Kept their affairs to themselves. Quick-tempered, Mr Jack was. Got wholly riled and in a puckaterry over nothing, 'times. But Master Philip was a nice old bor. She had a real soft spot for Master Philip, who, she would have me know, had a young lady he'd been walking out with since spring. Lou Roughton was a fine strong mawther without any fancy notions. She'd make a fine wife for Master Philip.

Well aware that she was warning me off, I said, 'Does Master Philip think so, too?'

'He will if he know what's good for him,' said Mrs Gaywood darkly.

By constant turning she soon had my clothes dry enough to wear, mud-spattered and creased as they were. I returned to the empty bedroom to change, pausing in the passage to look again at the picture which had caught my eye earlier. Mother must have been about thirteen when it was taken. Michael looked older – thin, dark, intense. Had he loved her even then? When she came back as an adult, had he hoped she would return his affection? But by then the enmity between his family and hers had hardened, and she herself had changed, grown away from him.

But at least I now knew why she had been sent away – to prevent her from becoming any more entangled with the Farcrofts. What a bold, wilful child she must have been, to come here at all. She had known it was wrong.

I, too, knew it was wrong, yet I had let myself be brought here. Was I more like Mother than I knew? But *her* disobedience had been that of a naughty child trying to draw attention to herself: my own motives were more questionable. My intelligence told me that the more I saw of Philip the more pain I invited, for both of us; but instinctively I longed for him, felt incomplete without him. Heart and soul, we were inexorably bound.

Dressed again in my own clothes, I put my hair up as best I could and went downstairs, carrying my left shoe – the right one had gone in the flood.

'That's now stopped rainin',' the housekeeper observed, glancing out at the yard. Where sunlight caught the roof of a shed, it was steaming.

'Yes, I know. I'd be on my way, except . . .'

We were discussing the problem of what I should wear on my feet when Philip solved it by arriving with the lost shoe. He had been up to Back Lane and found both my cycle and the shoe, but he brushed aside my thanks. The cycle was damaged, he said, not looking at me; he'd left it with the blacksmith to be mended. The shoe I put on, though it was wet and shrunken: it would suffice until I got home.

'Well, if you're ready . . .' Philip ran a hand through his hazelnut curls and fitted his cap over them. 'Shall I hitch up the trap, or—'

'No, don't trouble, please. I can walk now the rain's stopped. I'll go by the short cut – if your father won't mind too much.'

He opened the door. 'I'd better come with you. I'm not sure what state that lane might be in. Don't want you getting stuck in the mud.'

'No . . . No, really – you've gone to enough trouble on my account. I'm capable of finding my own way.' Fixing my eyes on the top button of his macintosh, I held out my hand. 'Thank you. I . . . I'm most grateful.'

I felt his hand envelop mine, hard and warm: though he had been out in the wet it was I who was cold. Our flesh seemed to blend in more than physical contact, awareness leaping between us. I wanted to cling, never to let go. I daren't look at his face.

'You're welcome,' he said.

Knowing that if I delayed I might never find the courage to leave, I turned to Mrs Gaywood, thanking her, shaking hands, making for the door. We all said the required politenesses, and then I was away, part of me relieved to be escaping, part of me forever left behind with Philip. I would, no doubt, go on, make a life, maybe even find a measure of happiness. But nothing could ever equal what Philip and I might have had, if circumstances had been different.

At Denes Hill, I encountered Grandmother, who expressed dismay at the state I was in. But she accepted my explanation that I had fallen from my bicycle and that 'some people' had taken me in and dried me off. To my relief, she hadn't time to delve too deeply: she was on her way to discuss menus for the special buffet ball she had been planning for weeks.

Little I cared about parties. I went about in a daze, assailed by memories of Philip. Most of my energies went into staying well away from the farm when all my instincts howled for me to go back, to see him again. It would be so easy – just a walk down the hill, to a casual, accidental meeting. Despairingly, I resisted the temptation. But, waking and sleeping, I dreamed of our passionate embrace in the storm and longed to repeat it.

When I wrote to Mother, I told her I had actually met the Farcrofts. Why hadn't she told me she had known them as a girl? Her reply, when it came, was brief, repeating her assertion that the Farcrofts were of no importance. To cultivate their acquaintance would be as foolish for me as it had been for her, especially when I was beginning to win the family's approval; both Frank and Grandmother had written and told her how well I was doing, studying so hard and making the right sort of friends.

She was right, of course. Philip was not for me. I should forget him. But knowing it and doing it were two different things.

The arrival of little Eddy's birthday gave me an excuse to escape for a while, if only as far as Lynn.

The floods had been bad in the town, streets filled with mud and some riverside properties inundated – everyone was talking about it. The *Lynn News* reported devastation all across the county, houses hit by lightning, crops ruined, roads damaged and impassable, and a postman drowned when the flood water caught him. I had been lucky.

I wished I could tell someone how Philip had saved me. He was so much on my mind that I needed to talk about him. However, I daren't mention him, even to Saffron, though she knew there was something wrong. When she asked me to stay a few days I happily accepted. It gave us a chance to visit the dressmaker and have fittings for our gowns for 'the bash', as she irreverently called it.

'You'll stun them all,' she said, eyeing me with some surprise as I stood in a creation of jewel-green silk – a colour which reminded me of Philip's eyes. 'My dear girl, I hadn't realized how quickly you're growing up. We shall have to watch the young men, I can see, or they'll all be proposing.'

The mirror told me the gown did look well, setting off my pale skin and dark hair as I turned for the girl to pin the hem. But since the only man I cared about wouldn't see me wearing it, what point was there in it?

'It's time you forgot about that young man,' Saffron said, and, when I turned my startled head to look at her, she wagged a finger at me. 'He's a bounder, Kate, d'you know what I mean? Didn't he prove it, with all the lies he told about you?'

She was talking about Carl-Heinz. 'A little, perhaps,' I conceded.

'Then it's time you stopped. You should fall in love, Kate. With some nice young Englishman. Maybe you'll meet him at the ball. Or maybe you already know him.'

How right she was. 'Someone like whom?'

'Lady Vi mentioned James Lacey.'

'*Did* she?' I almost laughed. I had seen James once or twice when I visited his mother at Lenhoe Manor. A charming, diffident, thoroughly pleasant young man, his only apparent defect was his lack of height. I liked him a lot – as I did his brother, David – but it had never occurred to me to imagine anything beyond friendship with either of them. How could it, when for months now my heart had been set on Philip Farcroft?

But perhaps there *were* other possibilities. Perhaps I should let myself enjoy the company of other men and see what happened. How could I be sure Philip was my one true love? Wasn't that schoolgirlish fantasy? I had, after all, been dismally deluded about Carl-Heinz.

So my head decided. My heart and soul remained sick with loneliness, thoughts of Philip a constant pain inside me, memories burned into my being. A part of me knew, even then, that no one else would ever touch me quite as deeply as Philip had.

Uncle Frank called in at Hawthorn House, restored to health by his sojourn in the south and on his way home for the ball. He fobbed me off when I asked him about Judy Love, though I gathered he had seen her.

A day or so later, Emmet arrived back from the Aegean.

He too looked bronzed and fit, impossibly handsome with his hair turned almost white by the sun, and bursting with stories of adventures concerning renewed conflict in the Balkans. It could turn to full-scale war, I heard him telling Harry with enthusiasm, and that would bring the French in, with us not far behind. And *then* we'd show the damned Hun a thing or two!

'Hush, Emmet,' said Harry with a glance out to the garden where I was reading, and they moved out of earshot.

Emmet and I travelled back to Denes Hill together, he full of nonsense that made me laugh despite myself. I was the envy of every girl who saw us: none of them would have believed he was my uncle.

But the cheer afforded by his witty company was only temporary, for next to my bed in the small room which had once been inhabited by the governess, I found a letter waiting. Not recognizing the writing, I tore it open and looked for the signature. It was from Philip.

I scanned it eagerly, devastated to find it a rather stiff, formal communication, which spoke of his regret for his father's brusqueness: he hoped it had not upset me too much. He understood why I had felt it best to hurry away, though he had been sorry for it. '*I should like to see you again so I know you understand,*' he ended. '*Can you come to the gate on Friday night at nine o'clock? If this is not convenient, perhaps you would consider sending me yr address in London, so that I might write to you.*' He signed it, '*Yrs, Philip F.*' What he meant, my heart decided, was that he wanted to see me as much as I wanted to see him, in spite of all the barriers between us. Oh, Philip . . .

I made excuses to go early to my room and sneaked out just before nine by the side door, making my way through the yards and gardens to the woods, and thence to the gate.

I was a minute or two late, but Philip wasn't there. I waited, but he didn't come. I even walked down the lane to where I could see the farm, but the hollow was all darkness, faint starlight slanting along the sway-backed thatch of the roof. Not even the dogs stirred that night.

Disconsolate, calling myself all kinds of a fool, I trailed home again and reread the letter, wondering if I had misunderstood him. Only as I tucked the paper back into the envelope did I notice the postmark: 18 September, 1912. Nine days ago. It was *last* Friday he had meant.

Next morning I felt listless, unable to drag myself out of a bog of self-pity. I was in no mood for a grand buffet ball.

Men had worked for days clearing the saloon for dancing, polishing the floor, erecting buffet tables and fitting candles in the chandeliers. Now more people arranged flowers and set out chairs, while in the kitchens a small army of women prepared food. Grandmother, Vicky and Anderson went about with lists, checking every detail, while I stayed on hand to help with flowers and carry messages between saloon and kitchen, library, supper room or cloak rooms.

The party would mark Grandmother's return to a full social life after a year of mourning; it would celebrate Emmet's gaining his degree; and, with senior personnel from Chef Foods and Thorne-Thomas Engineering among the guests, the evening would also launch him on the ladder that would lift him, some day, to the board of the engineering firm. He was the obvious one to assume his father's mantle. It should have been John, but John was gone; Harry was already in charge of Chef Foods; Frank had never shown any inclination for business; so Emmet, considered the brightest of them all, was the chosen heir apparent at Thorne-Thomas.

217

The Lord Lieutenant had accepted his invitation, as had half the gentry of the county, including the Chief Constable. Oliver Wells was also expected, as Vicky informed me with ill-concealed malice. She evidently felt that, Oliver and I being at odds, her own star was rising again.

I decided to put Philip from my mind, if I could, at least for that evening. Saffron was right – the world was full of young men, and I was on the verge of womanhood. Dressed for the ball, I surveyed my reflection with approval. Current fashion style suited the slender figure nature had given me. The green silk had a cunningly draped bodice with tiny slit sleeves, a long slim skirt, split to the knee at the sides and trimmed with heavy fringeing that swirled with me as I moved, and I wore high-heeled slippers dyed the same green. The mirror told me I looked good, as did the eyes of all the men at the party. That night, I almost believed it myself. If only Philip had been there . . .

My partners included the Lacey boys, James and David, and my uncles Harry, Frank and Emmet. Poor Tom spent most of the evening gazing on, wide-eyed, or raiding the buffet, with the outdoor man, Garret, under orders to look after him. When I found a gap on my card I asked Tom if he would like to partner me and we made a few turns around the floor. He didn't so much dance as galumph, but it made us both laugh even if Grandmother did look a bit pot-faced about it.

Dancing with Oliver Wells, I was disconcerted to discover how well we moved together. He felt it, too, complimenting me on my lightness of foot, though the merit was his – it's easy to follow a man who moves with grace, holds one firmly and leads with assurance. Gazing over his shoulder, I tried not to think of our more intimate encounters, but memory was a force between us, if dimmed, for me, by more kindling memories of Philip.

After a while, he leaned back to regard me with concern. 'You're not looking very happy tonight, Kate. Is something wrong?'

'What could be wrong?'

'That's what I should like to know. You're putting on a brave face, but I can see the shadows in your eyes. I hope I didn't put them there by engaging you for this dance.'

'Of course not.' Disconcerted by his perception, I turned my head away to prevent him from reading anything else in my face. Even so, I was touched by his solicitude.

Drawing me back to his shoulder, he executed a fancy turn and I felt his enjoyment of the way I followed him. 'You didn't reply to my letter,' he murmured in my ear. 'Am I forgiven?'

A sigh escaped me. 'There's nothing to forgive. No, really, Oliver. You said you wanted us to be friends. I should like that, too.'

He didn't answer in words, but drew me closer. We concentrated on the steps, moving smoothly together. If only he had been Philip! I closed my eyes and let myself enjoy being held in strong arms, imagining . . .

When the music ended he engaged me for another dance after supper. Writing his name with the little pencil, he glanced at the others on the list. 'James Lacey? *Four* times?'

'James is shy – terrified of dancing with someone he doesn't know.'

The dark eyes lifted to mine, drenching me in their sensuality. 'If you believe that, Kate . . .'

'It's the truth.'

'More fool James Lacey, then.' His glance flickered over me, making me aware of my body under the light evening gown. 'A year has wrought wonders in you. I brought a schoolgirl back from Europe, or so I thought.'

I pulled a face, hoping he couldn't see how he disturbed me. 'Mother always made me dress like a ten-year-old.'

'I expect she couldn't stand the competition,' Oliver said with a wry smile. 'Growing older herself, while you turned into a woman. She should see you now. If I didn't know better, I'd say you were twenty-one, at least. Everyone's asking who the lovely girl in green can be.'

'Now you're flattering me.'

The smile in his eyes reached his mouth, widening into soft laughter. 'That's what I like about you, Kate. No nonsense. Ironic, don't you think? Vicky will believe the most blatant flattery. *You* mistrust me even when I'm sincere.'

'Wise girl, my niece.' Uncle Frank materialized beside us, resplendent in white tie and tails with his dark-gold locks brushing his starched white collar. He was smiling at Oliver, but his smile lied. 'Have you seen that pub by the south gate in Lynn, Kate? The Honest Lawyer – he doesn't have a head! My dance, I think. You'll excuse us, Wells.'

And he whisked me away.

Having allowed James Lacey to claim the supper dance, I escaped with him to the terrace, where a mild September breeze blew softly and the moon played peep-bo among drifting clouds. An ebullient Emmet and a group of his friends were taking the air after the heat in the saloon, talking eagerly about the troubles in Ulster, and the war in the Balkans. What seemed to be a small local problem could easily flare into something worse, they agreed, with Russia on one side and Austro-Hungary on the other, along with their ally Germany. England could get dragged in, as it had in the Crimean War.

'The Kaiser wants a through route to the Middle East,'

Emmet was saying. 'Always had ambitions there. The man's a jolly old megalomaniac if you ask me. But if he tries to . . . Oh, hello, Kate. Sorry, we were just—'

'I heard,' I said flatly, feeling chilled despite the mild night. 'Haven't you anything else to gossip about?' I couldn't betray my distant family and friends by joining in anti-German talk.

Vicky's arrival broke the moment. Dressed in a soft lilac that went well with her strawberry-blond hair, she had come to fetch Emmet away. I didn't hear exactly what she said to him, but when he demurred she scolded, 'But you must! Your whole future lies at Thorne-Thomas. You must at least look a little interested.' Taking his arm, she drew him away, pausing to say sweetly to me, 'You look awfully nice tonight, Kate.'

'Thank you. So do you,' I responded with equal insincerity.

Affording James Lacey a gracious smile – in gratitude to him for keeping me away from Oliver, I guessed – she swept on, a reluctant Emmet with her. She was taking him to the supper room, where Grandmother was holding court among Thorne-Thomas directors and shareholders, with the solicitor at her elbow.

After supper, I danced with George Chorley, under-manager at Chef Foods; he was rather portly, soon sweating from the exertion after eating too much and not sorry to relinquish my company when the butler, Billing, caught my eye and beckoned me aside.

'Excuse me, Miss Brand. There's a lady in the retiring room having some difficulty. Would you mind . . . ?'

I followed him towards the lobby, but, when we reached a spot away from other ears, he paused and confided, 'I fear, miss, I told you an untruth – for discretion, you understand. The fact is, there's a gentleman asking to see you. Wants you to meet him out by the tennis courts.'

'What gentleman?' My imagination leapt from James to David, to Oliver Wells, to Emmet . . . even, inevitably, to Philip, though *he* wouldn't dare to come to Denes Hill, much as I wanted him. 'One of the guests?'

'I assume so, miss. I didn't see him myself. It was one of the kitchen boys brought the message. Anyway, I'll leave it with you, miss. If you'd excuse me . . .'

I had no intention of going out into the garden. Certainly not! But curiosity drew me through the house to the south wing, where a family sitting room had an enormous bay window fitted with french doors. The room lay in darkness, misty moonlight glowing just bright enough for me to see where the furniture was as I made my way across. On such occasions, moving in semi-darkness at Denes Hill, I felt myself surrounded by presences; they whispered just beyond hearing, brushed against my senses. John was never far away. I felt him that night. Waiting . . .

'What do you want with me?' I asked aloud. No one answered, not in words, but a warm feeling of protective affection flowed along my nerves.

The french doors opened on to a small crazy-paved terrace. Beyond it the ground dropped away, rose gardens edged with cushion plants, built in widening terraces intertwined with uneven steps which led down to the croquet lawn. Off to the right, beside the walled gardens, the tennis court lay empty in the moonlight, surrounded by dark woods.

Was that a figure by the wall? As I glimpsed it another cloud drew a veil over the moon and swamped everything in shadows. I stood at the top of the steps, peering into the darkness. If someone was down there, I couldn't see him.

A shiver tingled down my spine. Not fear, exactly, nor

warning of a ghostly presence. Spirits never frightened me, but living people did. Had the summons been a joke of Emmet's? Was Oliver hoping to press further attentions upon me?

Then a stone gritted behind me. As I turned in alarm, a huge figure loomed out of the shadows, reaching for me. All I really saw was the shape of a hat – a military hat, with a badge on it. Carl-Heinz? Willi? A shriek escaped me, dying in a gasp as he hauled me to him and clamped his mouth over mine. Beer fumes assailed me. Sharp teeth, hot lips, a probing tongue, arms like iron bands around me . . .

Terror lent me strength. I twisted and fought, pushing at a hard body clad in thick twill. My fierce resistance seemed to surprise him. He let me go. Then, as I opened my mouth to scream, he grabbed my shoulders in hard hands, gasping, 'Don't shout! It's me! Philip.'

And I hit him.

I heard the splat of flesh on flesh, saw him reel away, a hand to his face. And then the jar of it reached my wrist and made me hug my arm, my palm singing from the blow, my heart unsteady. The moon flitted among the clouds, but I still couldn't see him clearly. I hadn't meant to hit him, but in that uniform he might as well have been a stranger.

After a moment, he said bitterly, 'I suppose I deserved that.'

'You did!' I was too shaken to be other than angry after the fright he had given me. 'How dare you come here and—'

'Thank you,' the mutter came through clenched teeth. 'Thanks a lot, Kate. At last I know where I really stand. I should have listened to Dad.' And he was gone.

Still dazed and breathless with shock, I stood clutching

my wrist, gazing helplessly after him as he headed off down the steep steps, taking them two at a time, to run across the lawn and into the woods.

THIRTEEN

I couldn't go back to the party. Instead, I went up to my room and, not bothering to light the lamp, stripped off the lovely green dress and left it lying in a heap. Wrapped in the familiar comfort of an old dressing gown, I stood staring out of the window feeling at once sick and empty. Faint moonlight slanted mistily across the distant sea, but closer at hand the woods were black, echoing the darkness in my heart.

I shouldn't have let Philip go like that. I should have stopped him and explained: *You startled me. You frightened me. How was I to know?* . . . But why should I explain? The fault was his. Why had he come up to Denes Hill in that uncouth way, drunk and aggressive, to accost me? What had he meant about listening to his father? And why, oh why, had he been wearing that fearful uniform?

As a new school year began at the LSE, I applied myself to my studies with grim determination, trying to shut out both my unhappiness and the still-simmering rumours of invasion and war. I also became more involved with social work.

Visits to the East End revealed the horror of the lot of some women and children, working in awful conditions for a few shillings a week. Through the agency of the East London Federation of Suffragettes, led by Sylvia Pankhurst, these women were being encouraged to band together and

225

fight for their rights. Though I never entirely agreed with some of Sylvia's more strident supporters – including Hermione Harmistead – the work they were doing for the poor seemed to me eminently worthwhile. I spent much of my free time in Bow, manning the shop, or fund-raising, or visiting homes to explain our aims; I even went on one or two marches, and wrote angry articles and speeches. These activities brought me closer to Miss H, but drove widening wedges in my friendship with Win Leeming.

Win didn't approve of marching, heckling and banner-waving. She said I would also be drawn into stone-throwing and fire-raising if I were not careful; surely we could make our point without forgetting we were ladies? In her opinion the Pankhursts were becoming dangerously militant, damaging the cause.

Another area of disagreement between us was her continuing allegiance to spiritualism. She regularly attended Mrs Bly's seances, but since she knew how Miss H and I felt about those gatherings she didn't talk about them. Miss H and I agreed that Win was being deceived, but there our concord faltered: Hermione Harmistead didn't believe in an afterlife of any kind.

'When you're dead, you're dead,' she grunted in her brusque way as we sat one evening over a jigsaw puzzle of ballet dancers amid a strong aroma of ashtray that clung to her clothes and hair.

'Then isn't life a little pointless?' I asked.

'Of course! We're a biological accident. Microbes on the face of the globe. Doesn't have to be a *point*, does there? Doesn't have to be a *reason*?' Placing a piece of a dancer's tutu, she gave a little 'hah' of satisfaction, and looked up. 'Do you go along with the heaven and hell nonsense?'

'I don't know. But I'm sure there's something. If I told

you I had seen spirits of the dead—'

She screwed up her face in disgust. 'Delusions, dear child. Delusions of the mind and eye, that's all. Far better to concentrate on the living. By Jove, look at the time. I'm off to my room for a gasper. And I've got to mix some jam and treacle to pour in pillar boxes tomorrow. We'll wear the dastards down somehow.'

At Denes Hill that Christmas, all the family gathered, including Saffron and Harry. Young Eddy, sixteen months old, was an entertainment all by himself, staggering about, clapping his hands with excitement, beaming at the candles and the shining baubles on the tree, tearing at wrapping paper – and trying to eat it – until Grandmother cried, 'Enough!' and Rollins the nursemaid whisked the baby away. I remember Harry's thin face shining with contentment as he relaxed in a big chair by the fire, with Saffron curled on the floor leaning on his knees, Tom playing with a new clockwork train set behind the sofa, Emmet winding up the gramophone to play us his new records, Grandmother plying her crochet hook, Vicky reading in a corner, and Frank . . . Frank that year was subdued, suffering from a cold and headaches that made him complain at every draught and every noise. Nor did he have much appetite for the Christmas fare.

'Chill on the liver,' Grandmother decided, ordering him to dose himself with castor oil and godfreys.

'Yes, Mother,' said Frank, helping himself to his own choice of medicine – more brandy – which, as Harry pointed out with brotherly bluntness, probably caused his headaches rather than cured them.

'Oh – go boil your head,' was Frank's response. No, he was not his usual cheery self.

In church, hearing Philip's voice raised with the rest, I felt frozen, my own voice choked into silence. But I steeled myself not to look at him. It was over. Over. Whatever it had been. Our glances did meet, though just once, for a fleeting second, as I was leaving the church with my family around me – but it was enough to sear me to the soul. Afterwards I wondered at the unhappiness I had read in those green eyes. Was he as miserable as I was? Oh, Philip! Perhaps I should . . . *You should do no such thing!* my bitter self replied. *Didn't you act the fool by chasing after Carl-Heinz? And look what became of that. Stop reaching beyond your grasp. Find a man who's attainable.*

The rising tide of international unrest subsided once more. The nations in dispute over the Balkans met in London that winter and signed treaties, Britain acting as peace-broker. Newspapers declared that Britain was interested only in peace, while between the lines – and often more openly – they implied that Germany was spoiling for war. But in Berlin, I recalled, the press had accused Britain, and France and Russia, of trying to cage the German eagle, forcing him into a corner where he would have to fight to secure his rights to a share in world trade and growing empires.

Which was I supposed to believe?

The answer came clearer when, early in March, I had a worrying letter from Mother. She asked anxiously after my health, saying she hoped I was taking good care of myself, then, almost as an afterthought to the usual chitchat about everyday matters, the last hurriedly scrawled lines read: *'Pa invited some colleagues to dine last night and, by chance, I overheard some of the conversation. They say that the Kaiser was furious over what Lord Haldane said. Von Moltke advocated immediate mobilization. Now the*

*government has levied a huge new tax. The men say it's to
fund a massive war effort. I don't pretend to understand
what it means but thank God you are safe in England. Stay
there, my dear. Yr very loving, Mother.'*

I didn't pretend to understand it, either.

Not wanting to raise unnecessary alarums, I told no one
about the letter until Uncle Frank came up to town, as he
sometimes did, and treated me to dinner and the theatre.
He was still not well, though he made light of it and brushed
off my concern – 'Just my digestion playing up.'

When I showed him Mother's letter, he read it in silence,
his face still. Then he said, 'The Kaiser's an embittered
man, Kate. He takes offence at the slightest thing. It'll all
blow over.'

But we both knew he didn't believe it any more than I
did. Especially when he tore the letter across, twice, before
handing it back to me. 'Throw it away, girl. Forget about
it. Let's not run after trouble – it might turn and meet us
halfway.'

'But—'

'For your mother's sake, Kate,' Frank said, his slate-
blue eyes sharp with warning. 'She was fearfully indiscreet
to put such things on paper. If anyone found out – even
your stepfather . . .'

I did as he suggested – I burned the letter.

My unease increased when, a couple of weeks later, I
had a brief note from Pa, written in German, curtly telling
me that Mother would not write again until the tension eased.
It was diplomatically awkward, at this time, for him to have
his wife communicating with England. The politics of it all
was beyond me. Or had he – awful thought – discovered
that Mother was gossiping state secrets in her letters?

My own letters went out to her, as usual, at least once a

week. I asked her just to let me know, somehow, that she was well – a postcard, that anyone could read, would be enough. But no reply came. On the other hand, no war started, either. Perhaps it *had* been just another scare.

I did hear from Saffron, though, gossipy letters about Eddy and Harry and her friends in Lynn, her suffrage meetings, and Harry's concern about disputes at Chef Foods: the workers were threatening to strike. Saffron thought it a symptom of the general mood of discontent that seemed to have infected all the working men of the country and all the women who were fighting for the vote. '*Harry says we all need something else to think about. He gets quite snappy at times,*' she wrote.

In reply, I sent her first-hand news of our troubles with rowdies at WSPU gatherings, which became so bad that in April the authorities banned our meetings. They also stopped publication of *The Suffragette*, which infuriated me and made me more fervent in the Cause. Not that opposition stopped us – we continued to hold meetings, especially on Sundays in Hyde Park, and we organized a successful May Day procession, despite the young roughs and idle dockers drafted in by our enemies to make trouble.

My birthday fell on a Saturday that year. Uncle Frank had promised to come up to town for the weekend and take me out to celebrate my being an old lady of twenty. But on the night before he was due I had a strange dream: I was wading frantically into the sea, fully clothed and surrounded by clinging grey mist, with someone I cared about in desperate danger, out of my sight in the waves. I had to reach him! To save him!

My subconscious must have remembered the day John drowned, I reasoned. But instinct told me the danger was more immediate, though what form it would take, and who it threatened, I couldn't guess. When I woke, most of the details fled like mist before sunrise. All the dream had done was leave me with dregs of fear forcing my heart to pump at twice its normal speed. It also brought on one of the blinding headaches that sometimes afflicted me.

The morning post, bringing birthday greetings from friends and family, included an envelope postmarked Berlin and addressed in Mother's writing. At last! After all these weeks . . . But as I went to open it I saw that it had already been torn open and clumsily resealed – the sight increased both my fear *and* my headache. The card bore a sentimental verse, in German, signed with love from Mother, from Rudger, Pieter and Hansi, and from Pa and Fritzi – she had added those last two from habit. Usually she enclosed a letter with her cards, but this time there was nothing. Had Pa, or some officious official at the post office, tampered with the envelope, deliberately preventing Mother from communicating with me?

Was it Mother who was in danger?

Unable to settle to anything, I made my way across town to Liverpool Street station, hoping to meet Frank. I had no idea which train he might arrive on, but the earliest one was due just before eleven.

Inevitably, the train having been on time, the platform was almost empty when I arrived ten minutes after the hour. Only a few stragglers remained, under wrought-iron spaces echoing with the rattle of trolleys and the noisy sighing of engines getting steam up. Either I had missed Frank or he would be on the next train, which wouldn't arrive for a couple of hours. Or had something happened to him? Was that what my dream had meant? I could hardly think for the pain in my head.

And then, as I hovered in muzzy indecision amid the

sighing of steam, the clamour of clashing doors and the stench of old stale smoke, everything faded as a man emerged from the left luggage office: tall, lean, wearing a brown tweed suit and a big cap, with polished brown boots. Through a haze of pain, I stared in disbelief. Philip . . . ?

He had paused to wait for a baggage-laden trolley to clatter by. Across the pile of strapped cases and trunks our eyes met and held, each of us equally startled. Then he snatched off his cap and, as he strode towards me, I reached out instinctively and found his hands waiting for mine, to squeeze so tightly it hurt. Sweet pain.

He said, 'Hello, Kate.'

I stared at him in dazed wonder, oblivious to everything but the message of gladness in his eyes and the vibrance of that rich dark voice. Despite my head's thumping, my heart was suddenly singing. *He's here. Philip is here.*

'What . . .' I managed, and he said, 'How did you . . .' and we both stopped, and laughed a little. 'You first,' he offered.

'I don't know where to start. You . . . what are you doing here?'

'I was on my way to see you,' was the incredible answer. 'How did you know I was coming?'

'I didn't! I was hoping to meet Uncle Frank. He wasn't on your train, was he? I never expected . . . How would you have found me?'

'Care of Mrs Armes, Fourteen Lincoln Square.' Bright green eyes regarded me ruefully as he explained: 'I bribed one of the Denes Hill lads – the one who takes the letters to the post – to copy down your address for me next time someone wrote to you. Well, I had to do *something*. I was beginning to think I might never see you again.'

My initial delight was seeping away as I remembered

the way we had parted. Eight long months ago. I eased my hands free. 'I thought that was what you wanted. Last time we met, you said—'

'I know what I said! But surely—' A train whistle shrieked, drowning his words. He glanced about the station at the passing people, waiting for the noise to die. 'We can't talk here. Can we go somewhere?'

Hurt pride told me I should refuse. But I needed to know why he had behaved as he had. Most of all I needed just to be with him again.

We found a tea shop, not a very smart place. The tablecloths could have been cleaner, but the waitress smiled obligingly, hot scones dripped golden butter, and the tea was hot and strong.

'I want you to know,' Philip said, staring down into his cup, 'that I'm desperately ashamed of that night at Denes Hill. I know I behaved like a madman. But when I saw you with that chap Wells—'

'You saw us? How?'

His head came up slowly, his mouth twisting. 'Through a window. From the terrace.'

'Grief! You were taking a risk. What if you'd been seen?'

'Well, what was I supposed to do? I wrote to you and you didn't answer. You couldn't even be bothered to write a letter!'

'I'd been away!' I cried. 'I was going to write as soon as . . .' Pressing my fingers to my temple, I stopped myself, saying wearily, 'I don't understand you, Philip. Why have you come?'

He sighed. 'I've tried writing letters. But I've torn them all up. I'm hopeless with words. Kate . . .' His face twisted as he sought the right phrase. 'I'm not seeing Lou Roughton any more.' Before I could answer, he reached for my hand

and held it tightly between his own, saying frankly and passionately, 'It's *you* I want to see, whatever my father says. Or your family, or the whole bally world. I don't care about any of them. It's *you* . . .' He couldn't finish the sentence, but he didn't need to.

Staring at him with aching eyes, I couldn't speak. I knew I looked a fright, pale and heavy-eyed. My head throbbed spitefully; crockery clattered around us, other customers chatted loudly, and a scent of burned toast wafted from the kitchen. Hardly a romantic setting. But all I could think was that Philip cared for me. Not knowing whether to laugh or cry, I simply sat there like a fool, feeling the beat of his pulse against mine and letting myself drink in the sight of him. How I wanted to touch him, to explore the texture of his thick hazelnut curls, stroke the planes of his face, kiss his eyes, his mouth, feel his body against me . . .

Staring down at our joined hands, work-hardened thumbs brushing my skin, he gritted his teeth, making the muscle jump in his jaw before he said, 'I wanted to rush into that ballroom and throttle that blasted lawyer. I felt like pounding on the glass and yelling to be let in, or else. I'd been thinking about you all week, wondering why you hadn't turned up to meet me. I'd had my heart set on seeing you that Friday. It . . . it was my birthday. September the twentieth. I was twenty-five.'

'Oh, Philip . . .'

His head came up, green eyes sparking with remembered resentment. 'I'd spent the whole week hoping for a letter that might explain why you hadn't been able to meet me. When nothing came, I felt so bad that, straight after parade that Saturday, I went up to the Black Horse with some of the chaps, to drown my sorrows. I'd had a few beers when someone said there was a big party up at Denes Hill and . . .

Katie, I'm sorry. I shouldn't have . . .'

'No, you shouldn't. You scared me half to death! In the darkness. And in that uniform . . .' The implications were so awful I had to joke: 'I thought for a minute you'd joined the Foreign Legion.'

A slow, rueful smile tugged at his mouth. 'Didn't I tell you I was in the Territorial Army? Second Lieutenant Farcroft, Norfolk Yeomanry.'

Yes, he had told me, I just hadn't registered its meaning. 'Is it like conscription? In Germany the young men have to serve for two years.'

'We don't have conscription here. Don't need it. Our professional army does the job, when it's needed. The Terriers are a part-time volunteer force, just for home defence. We train at weekends, and there's an annual camp in July. But . . . this year we're being called for extra training. They want us well prepared.'

He didn't say prepared for what. He didn't need to.

Hating the thought of it, I said thickly, 'What will happen if . . .'

'If the balloon goes up? We'll be defending our bit of the coast, I expect. But don't worry, Denes Hill is pretty safe. They'll never get past our navy. Britannia still rules the waves, however many ships the Kaiser may have built.' Realizing what he was saying, he squeezed my hand reassuringly. 'Don't worry your head about it. Our chaps are taking precautions, that's all. What with the Balkans, and Ulster . . . It's wise to be ready. It doesn't mean it will happen.'

'I suppose not.' But I preferred not to think about it. 'Will you have some more tea?'

While I poured, he told me how, having discovered my address in London, he had come up to town by the first train that morning. 'It's your birthday, isn't it?' he added, reaching into an inner pocket for a small package which he awkwardly presented to me. 'Happy birthday, Katie.'

The gift was a silk scarf, in a lovely shade of blue. Too choked to speak, I held its softness to my cheek, loving the special way he called me 'Katie'. 'Oh, Philip . . . How sweet of you to remember. It's lovely. Thank you. But . . .'

'No buts,' he said, capturing my hand again, more firmly. 'Let's just enjoy today, while we have it. I had to come, Katie. I couldn't go on without seeing you. I've been so . . .'

'Me, too.' My fingers answered his, stroking and caressing.

'I wanted to speak to you at Christmas,' he confessed, 'but you seemed so remote I didn't dare. I hoped I might see you at Easter, but you didn't come home. So this weekend, when I got the chance—'

'I'm *glad* you came,' I told him. 'It's a *lovely* birthday surprise. The best ever. When I saw you standing there . . .' But the expression of chagrin on his face gave me pause. 'What's wrong?'

'Nothing. Except . . .' He sighed heavily. 'I've got a confession – I had to come to London anyway. It was just, when I realized what date it would be, I decided to take an early train and try to see you. I wasn't even sure I'd have the courage to come calling so, when I saw you there waiting . . . it seemed like fate.'

'It *was* fate,' I said, clinging to his hand and gazing into his dear face. I was sure now – we were soul-mates, bound by old, old ties that stretched from the far past into the far future, linking us for ever. We had known each other, and loved each other, before, and would do so again. I felt that deep in my bones. But I knew better than to tell him so: it would have troubled him. In this life he didn't share my far sight. He would have thought me fey.

'Of course it was,' he agreed, tender eyes smiling indulgently at me. 'It's given us more time together, anyway. But we've only got a few hours. I have to catch another train this afternoon. Four fifteen special, from Paddington.'

I stared at him over the blue of the scarf he had given me, head aching, heart suddenly sick. The chill I felt was more of the spirit than the body. 'Where are you going?'

'Gun practice. With the Field Artillery. On Salisbury Plain.' His eyes gleamed. Obviously he relished the prospect.

'I see,' I said, my head numb. Who was he going to be shooting, if and when trouble came? Fritzi? Carl-Heinz? And they wouldn't be sitting idle – they'd be shooting back.

Hoping that some fresh air might help my head, we decided to take a walk, though first we called at Lincoln Square, where Philip waited on the corner while I went to the house. I asked Mrs Armes to tell Uncle Frank, when he arrived, that I was 'out with friends' but would be home in time to get ready for whatever he had planned for the evening.

'Always assuming he does come,' I added when I told Philip about it as we walked hand in hand along the streets.

'I thought you said he'd promised he would.'

'He did, but . . .' A shiver of apprehension ran through me. 'You'll think I'm silly, but I have the strangest feeling there's something wrong. This morning . . .'

The story poured out of me – the dream, the card with no letter, my fears for Mother . . . He comforted me, sweetly reasoned and gently teased me out of my fears. No wonder I had nightmares, he said; my head was full of funny notions, though he wouldn't change me for worlds. Couldn't there be some innocuous explanation for the opened envelope of

Mother's card? As for Frank, why, he'd be there later, large as life. He'd bet a week's pay on it.

Darling, darling Philip. Walking in the park with him, my fingers intertwined with his, watching his mobile face and expressive green eyes, listening to the deep, caressing voice that sent shivers down my spine, how could I cling to my 'funny notions'? I was risking my reputation being seen alone with him, but in London who noticed one couple among many? For all passing strangers knew, we might be engaged; we might even be married. At the very least Philip would be taken for my best boy. Which he was. And I his best girl. I didn't care who saw us. If one day was all we had then I planned to make the most of it.

By mutual, unspoken consent, in Kensington Gardens we found ourselves in a secluded corner among shrubs, where we paused and looked at each other shyly, nervously. Neither of us could deny the longing that surged between us, or memories of a passionate embrace accompanied by thunder and lightning and drowning rain. It had been so long! Even so, when he reached for me I braced my hands against his chest, afraid of my own feelings. If we began, would we be able to stop? And then I saw the uncertainty in his eyes and was sorry. He had made the first move, coming all this way to see me. Now it was my turn.

'Philip,' I breathed and, like one mesmerized, tipped up my face.

The force of that first tentative kiss wrenched me to the soul, twisting sweet pain inside me. Then he lifted his head to look at me with anxious eyes. 'Is it all right?'

'Yes. Oh, yes!' Against my palms the muscles in his arms felt firm under the tweed of his jacket. How strong he was. How fine! I said hoarsely, 'Please . . . hold me!'

He drew me to him, pulling me ever closer. And oh! he

was warm and strong and wonderful to lean on. I gave myself to the delight of being with him. Nothing else existed. Only Philip and the swooping joy that filled me. If only we had been alone! But not far away people strolled by the Round Pond, children squealed with laughter as they played. A sudden flutter in the trees made us break apart guiltily, only to see a pigeon launch itself away, startled to find us there. In its wake, we looked at each other and laughed, and held each other again, tucked up warm and close and contented.

'Do you miss me?' he asked.

'Every day! Terribly!'

'Even when you're with your other friends?'

Lifting my head to look at him, I said laughingly, 'Other friends? You mean, like Win Leeming?'

'I meant . . . other men.'

My fingers combed through his crisp hair, tracing the shape of his ear. 'There aren't any other men, Philip. Not like you.'

'There might be.' His touch had altered subtly, caressing through my clothes. Strong fingers smoothed my back and shoulders, his darkened gaze sending shivers through me, setting my body alight. 'When I remember how you looked in that ball dress . . .' he said fiercely. 'When I think of that lawyer with his arms round you—'

'Hush!' I silenced him with fingers across his lips, letting my nerve ends feel the shape of his mouth. 'There's no one else.'

'Swear it!'

'I swear.'

Watching his lean brown face and those bright, devouring eyes, I felt a wild need build in both of us. My body was alert, responding to his nearness in ways that had no connection with my conscious mind. Disturbed by the force of those feelings, I said, 'Anyway, what about you? You and Lou Roughton?'

'I told you – that's over.'

'Did you give her up because of me?'

He hesitated, then gruffly said, 'Yes.'

Fierce joy soared through me. 'Mrs Gaywood will be disappointed. She said you'd marry Lou Roughton if you knew what was good for you.'

'Blast Mrs Gaywood!' He bent to kiss me again, crushing me against him, his body telling me he felt the same instinctive hunger that I did; then he pulled my head to his shoulder, where I could hear the lovely rhythm of his heart thudding as he muttered against my hair, 'I love you, Katie Brand. I love you so much I could explode.'

Oh, Philip! As a knot of joy unravelled inside me, I clenched my lips, and my eyes. I couldn't speak. For long moments I stood pressing my face against him, trying to control the emotion that raged through me.

'Katie? Did you hear what I said?'

I lifted my head, showing him my happy tears before I surged up to find his mouth and give him the answer silently, with all the passion in my bruised, lonely soul.

Never have hours passed so swiftly. We even forgot to have lunch. I wanted to stay with him until he caught the train at Paddington, but he said he didn't want to trail me around London – he had to go back to Liverpool Street to get his kit bag, and he'd probably be meeting his friends from the West Norfolk Yeomanry, who'd be arriving about that time. No, he'd see me safely back to Lincoln Square – I had to get ready for my birthday treat with Uncle Frank. He hated goodbyes, anyway.

What he meant, I deduced, was that he didn't want to risk having his friends see him with a girl. But, 'At least we can now write to each other,' he promised me as we clung achingly close. 'There's no hurry, is there? We have all the time in the world.'

It did seem that way. We were young, and we loved each other. Our feelings wouldn't change, however long we waited. We assured each other of that as we parted with tears and sweetly aching kisses, on my twentieth birthday, that year of 1913.

And then he was gone and I trailed up to the house, disconsolate. Even the prospect of an evening with Frank didn't make up for Philip's leaving. But at least I had some memories to dream on, and the summer to look forward to.

Mrs Armes must have been peering out from her curtains, watching for me. She opened the door as I climbed the steps.

'Is my uncle here?' I asked, before I clearly saw her face – she looked troubled.

'No, dear. No, he didn't come.' Drawing me inside the hall, she closed the door and handed me a small envelope. 'But there's this. It came for you three hours ago.'

A telegram . . .

The envelope held bad news: I could feel the vibrations crackling against my flesh. Each of the people I most cared about flashed in my thoughts as my fumbling fingers tore the paper. Mother? Frank? Tom? . . .

The telegram said: '*Harry died this morning STOP Please come Hawthorn House STOP Frank.*'

FOURTEEN

The numbing news gave me just time to catch the late afternoon train to Norfolk. Its wheels sang a mournful song: Harry was dead, Saffron alone, Eddy left fatherless . . . The brightness of the evening sun, as it sank to its setting in a glory of gold and flame, was a mockery, turning my lovely day with Philip to ashes. This, then, was what the warnings had meant.

By the time I reached King's Lynn, only streaks of pinkish light remained in the darkening sky and on the station electric lamps beamed. I had half expected Frank to be waiting for me, but when he wasn't there I took a taxicab to Hawthorn House.

The double-fronted villa stood silent, its curtains firmly drawn to hide its grief. Light showed through the rose-patterned glass in the front door, a gleam falling on the paintwork of Frank's Silver Ghost, which stood in the gravel driveway.

Taking a deep breath, I started down the drive towards familiar brick steps. I felt as if I were sleepwalking, going through motions which, by bright morning, would seem laughable. But this was no joke. Frank's face, when he opened the door, convinced me of that.

'Kate. Thank God. I wasn't sure whether you'd be able to get here tonight.' He took my heavy bag and dumped it by the foot of the stairs. 'She'll be glad to see you.'

'Where is she?'

'Upstairs. The doctor's with her. She's been asking for you.'

A pall of silence lay over the house and, despite the brightness of electric light, shadows shifted just out of sight, beyond open doorways leading to dark rooms. That was odd. I had expected the place to be full of people. 'And the others? Where is everyone?'

'She told them to go away,' Frank said. 'She's not very rational, as you'll discover. Some harsh words have been said. I'm afraid the Mater went back to Denes Hill in a huff.'

He stopped as voices sounded from the hallway above and a man appeared – a doctor, carrying a black bag. Beside him, the maid, Maisie, looked pale, her eyes awash.

'Ah, Mr Rhys-Thomas.' The doctor had seen us. 'And is this Miss Brand? I'm glad to see you, young lady. Your aunt's in need of some feminine company. Why don't you go up and see her? But don't excite her. She needs to be still and quiet. I've given her some medicine that should help.'

I hurried up the stairs and along the hall, to tap on the door of the master bedroom. Saffron's low 'Yes?' beckoned me in.

A cool draught met me. A standard lamp glowed in the corner by the window, which was wide open, drapes drawn back and nets blowing inward. Several moths diced with death, fluttering near the light, and in the high bed Saffron lay flat on her back.

'You'll catch your death!' I exclaimed, hurrying to close the window, only to be stopped by her gasp of, 'No, don't! Leave it, Kate. I need the air. I can't bear to be shut in. I can't breathe! Please . . .'

In the glass, against the darkness outside, I caught a glimpse of my own reflection, and for a second another figure stood beside me: Harry, thin and anxious. His image faded almost at once and with it the breeze died, the nets stopped flapping. As he let go his final earthly ties, I sensed that he was handing over to me, trusting me to care for his wife, and for his son. A shiver ran through me at the thought. It was not a responsibility I wanted. Why me? What could *I* do for them?

'Kate . . .' Saffron's voice made me turn to see her stretching out a hand towards me. She was alone now, with no one left but her small son and a family of in-laws amongst whom she had never felt wanted. If fate had destined me to be her ally, I had to accept the task.

Avoiding zooming moths, I approached the bed where she lay with her hair tangled across white pillows and her cotton-clad arms outside covers pulled up to her breast. Her fingers knotted tightly with mine as I sank down beside her, seeing her hair damp with sweat, her face sallow and blue-shadowed. Hazel eyes stared out from dark, puffy sockets. Tearless. Even calm. No, not calm. Inside, I saw, she was screaming.

Her nails dug into my hand as she said, 'Thank you for coming. It was a rotten birthday present to send you. But Frank said you'd want to know.'

'Of course I did!'

'Eddy will be glad to see you. He's asleep now, but in the morning . . .' Her lips trembled and she lay back, staring up at the ceiling. 'I was horribly rude to the old girl. But she was trying to take over, d'you know what I mean? She insisted we close all the curtains, and I hate feeling shut in. I thought I'd go mad.' Her eyelids squeezed shut, spilling a thin tear down her temple into her hair. 'I know he's her son, but . . .'

Not knowing what to do, or say, I simply sat and held her hand, stroking damp strands of squirrel-red hair away from her brow and watching her struggle with her grief.

Eventually, as if continuing a conversation, she shook her head and looked at me, trying a husky laugh that told of her pain. 'Of course, you know what it is – I just don't believe it's happening. I keep thinking if I lie here and wait long enough he'll just walk in and we'll go on as we always have. Do you know what I mean? He was fine on Friday evening. Just his usual self. We had dinner, and then we both went to look at Eddy, as we often do, and then we sat listening to the gramophone. He read his paper, and I was writing letters – one to you, it's still there waiting for a stamp . . .'

She had to tell it in detail, recounting every last memory of Harry. He had got up early that morning, while she was still asleep. Waking, she had found the place beside her empty, and cold. She had found Harry slumped on the tiled bathroom floor. He too had been cold. She had tried to rouse him, but Eddy's nurse had come and eased her away.

Turning tear-filled eyes on me, she said hoarsely, 'I shall never forgive Oliver Wells! He did it. He killed Harry! As surely as if he'd stabbed a knife into him.'

'Aunt Saffron . . .'

'It's true!' she cried. 'I don't care what Lady Vi says. We all knew Harry's heart wasn't strong. He's never been strong since he came back from the South African war. But lately Oliver's been pressing him to do something about the mutterings at the cannery. Worrying him. Bullying him! And on Friday he went to the office and . . . I don't know what was said. I only know Harry was upset.' Her face contorted into bitterness. 'Oliver's never liked Harry. Never thought he was capable of running the—' She caught her breath, pressing her hands to her stomach, her knees drawing up as she rolled over, away from me, her face contorted in agony.

I jumped up, leaning over her. 'What is it? Are you in pain?'

'It doesn't matter,' she got out.

'Of course it matters! Shall I go and . . . What can I do?'

The spasm must have passed, for she began to relax. 'There's nothing you can do. It's too late. It's already happened.'

Was she talking about Harry's death?

Still lying on her side, her back to me, she added in a small, hollow voice, 'I hadn't told anyone. Only Harry. He knew. But it was too soon to announce it to everyone else. Not quite three months.'

A fist seemed to close round my heart, squeezing. 'Another baby?'

'It would have been. Not now. I've lost it. Miscarried. That's why the doctor . . . He's gone to make arrangements. To get me into hospital. They've got to scrape it all away, haven't they? Get rid of it all. Oh, God. God! Why did this have to . . .' She curled up even more tightly, screwed into a tight ball of despair while helpless sobs shook her; then suddenly she threw herself on to her back to look at me, hatred burning behind drowned eyes. 'He killed my baby, too! Oh, what am I going to do? Help me, Kate. Harry . . . I want Harry . . .'

With Saffron in hospital, resting after her miscarriage, Frank and I helped the nursemaid transfer young Eddy and his belongings to Denes Hill. The tragedy had not been entirely unexpected, but even so its suddenness had been a shock. To Saffron most of all.

Whatever insults her daughter-in-law might have uttered in her extremity, Grandmother decided to set them aside for the sake of family unity. She went about tight-lipped, ashen-faced, but despite her grief she managed to organize everything needful. The house held an air of numbness; none of us could believe Harry was gone. But Eddy was happy toddling about the gardens, or playing in the nursery suite with Rollins, his nurse, and we all took pleasure in his company, especially poor Tom, who became deeply attached to the little boy. Making a pet of Eddy seemed to be Tom's way of compensating for Harry's loss.

Emmet had been summoned from the engineering works at Lincoln. His mother toyed with the idea of putting him in Harry's place at the cannery, but decided Emmet was much too young and inexperienced, especially with the workers agitating for better terms. As a stopgap, Oliver Wells had taken over management of Chef Foods, where, assisted by Harry's deputy, he was handling the strike threat with admirable aplomb.

'Well, he would,' Vicky remarked one evening at dinner. 'Oliver's a born diplomat. If you ask me, he should be appointed permanently.'

'He's a solicitor, not a manager,' Frank reminded her.

'He could do both, couldn't he? George Chorley's quite capable of managing day-to-day affairs. Don't you think so, Mother? Oliver could hold a watching brief, on behalf of the family.'

'He's not family!' Frank snapped.

'Not yet,' Emmet put in with a sly look at his sister.

Hot colour stained her pale cheek, though she ignored the hint. 'Well, who else is there?' she challenged Frank. 'I can't see *you* giving up your life of ease to join Chef Foods.'

'I *work* for my living,' he retorted.

'Enough!' Grandmother's voice cut in. 'Isn't it bad enough that Harry's place is empty, without you quarrelling over it? Let us be thankful that Oliver is willing and able to take over, pro tem.'

'Oh, let's do that, yes,' Frank muttered with an evil glance at Vicky. 'Good old Oliver to the rescue again.'

Tom said, 'He's not!' and leapt up, sending his chair clattering on its back. 'He's not!' he cried again. 'He's not!'

Emmet reached him first, laying a hand on one knotted fist. 'Calm down, it's all right. What's wrong, old man?'

'He's not having Harry's place!' Tom wept.

'No, of course he's not. Nobody said he would. Come on ... Let's go and see if Cook's got any scraps for your menagerie, shall we? Excuse us, everyone.' And he edged his twin out of the room.

In their wake, Grandmother glowered at Frank and Vicky. 'I won't have your petty, childish grievances resurrected over Harry's coffin. He has been living on borrowed time, ever since he was wounded in South Africa. We're all upset about it. Throwing mud at each other won't help.'

'Tell that to Saffron,' Frank muttered.

'Saffron's distraught!' Grandmother replied. 'She doesn't know what she's saying.'

In those days before the funeral, we were all under tension.

One wet afternoon I found myself up in the sanctum, stunned by the news that Emily Davison, an ardent suffragette whom I knew a little, had been killed when she threw herself under the King's horse during the running of the Derby. How unpredictable life was. Life, and death. Staring out of the window through a mist of drizzle towards the Eveningham vale and the Farcroft farm, I wished Philip were there. His humour and good sense would have steadied me.

Uncle John always seemed close to me here in the tower, where his image smiled from the walls. I would have liked to talk with him, too. What did he want with me? Why couldn't he rest? With Harry's death, shadows seemed to gather ever more closely about me: Mother had written of war preparations in Berlin, since when she had been prevented from contacting me. And now Philip was on Salisbury Plain, engaged in artillery training . . .

'Missing your young chap?' Frank asked, and when I jerked round I found him seated across the room, pencil poised over his sketch pad.

'What?'

'Tut, tut. Manners. What would dear Miss Yearling have said? I presume you mean, "I beg your pardon, Uncle Frank, dear"?'

'I'm sorry.'

His smile broadened. 'Good heavens, girl, I'm rotting you. Lost your sense of humour?' But as he watched me his brow furrowed. 'You were miles away. Back in London with, er . . . What's his name, Kate? Isn't it about time you confided in your favourite uncle?'

My scalp seemed to tighten. 'About what? I don't know what you're talking about.' But, as Oliver had observed, I was not a good liar; Frank, who knew me too well, perused my heightened colour with amusement.

'No? Forgotten the young man who, according to my spy, makes you "light up like Christmas"?' He held up a letter which had evidently come that morning. 'Judy saw you coming out of a tea shop last Saturday. Place near Liverpool Street station. She says you were with a young man. Tall chap, broad shoulders, rather good-looking.'

Tossing my head, I turned away in hope of hiding my burning face. 'Judy's a pesky gossip!'

'True!' Frank laughed. 'So who is he? One of your chums from college? Educated fellow, I gather. Polite. Nicely spoken. Held your hand a lot.' In answer to my frown, he added dryly, 'Judy knows the waitress who works there.'

That was too much! 'Did she find out his collar size, too?' I demanded. 'He's just a friend, Uncle Frank.'

'Well, if you say so. I shall have to meet him. We'll go to dinner, next time I'm in town – Judy and I, and you and your school chum.' Thank goodness Judy was such a bad detective! Close as Frank and I were, he would never understand how I felt about Philip Farcroft, the only son of my family's *bête noire*.

'Anyway,' I countered, 'what was Judy Love doing at Liverpool Street last Saturday morning? Or shall I guess? On her way to meet the next train, was she? Hoping to meet *you*?'

A bland smile was the only answer.

Remembering why he had not been on the train as expected, I folded my arms, staring out of the window, trying to get my thoughts back in order. 'Uncle Frank . . . why do you dislike Oliver so much?'

The silence went on for so long that I looked round and saw him glowering. He said, 'I just can't stand the smarmy toad.'

'It's not like you to take against someone without good reason. Wasn't he Uncle John's best friend?'

Again he didn't reply immediately, but watched me under his lashes, his face still. 'What is it you're asking me, Kate? Why this interest in Wells – and John, too? All that was a long time ago.'

'I know, but . . .' I didn't really know the answer. Wrapping my arms about myself, I glanced round the sanctum. 'There's something about this room. Every time I'm here, I think about Uncle John.'

'Not surprising. When he was in the right mood, he liked to be up here with you young ones. Snakes and ladders. Ludo. He made a special favourite of *you*. You loved him, too. I suppose he was a kind of substitute father.'

John's image smiled at me from the wall, telling me nothing. If we had been so close, how could I have forgotten everything about him?

'If I were you,' Frank said, 'I'd let sleeping dogs lie. Look . . .' He showed me his sketch pad, where quick pencil drawings showed identifiable parts of me – my elbow, my hand, my hair and part-profile. 'I've been doodling a few ideas. Can we make a start on this portrait?'

He was changing the subject again. But I let it go. One thing I had learned about Frank – if he decided not to talk about something, he could be just as stubborn as his mother.

'I want you to pose for me out of doors,' he was saying. 'Under that oak tree by the tennis court, you know? With your hair loose, wearing something soft.'

So I indulged him and spent the next few mornings leaning on the oak's gnarled bark, with the breeze playing in my hair. Frank had a charmingly fey image of me, presented on canvas as an elfin princess, long-limbed, poised, slender as a lily in softly clinging cream gown, long flowing hair, white skin and huge, luminous, faraway eyes. The developing picture had a lonely, yearning quality about it – not the way I saw myself. But perhaps Frank's vision was true enough: the portrait is of a woman in love. As I posed for it, my mind was miles away. With Philip.

The family decided that Saffron should not be on her own, for the time being, and when the doctors allowed her to leave hospital I played my part in persuading her to come to Denes Hill. She didn't argue. Her raging grief and bitterness had given way to numb silences, leaving her like a rag doll robbed of its stuffing. The only time I saw her come to life was when she was reunited with Eddy; then she cried and held him too tightly, frightening him.

Two days later, Harry was laid in Eveningham churchyard, beside John.

Grandmother had organized a funeral repast at the house: people seldom missed an excuse to sample Denes Hill hospitality and this occasion would provide good gossip locally. Saffron bore up bravely, head high and back straight, as if determined not to let herself down on that day. She was a fine-looking woman, still young, heavy at the hips, perhaps, but black suited her and the marks of strain on her face paid tribute to her love for Harry. All the same, I heard someone remark sourly that most likely the widow wouldn't remain a widow for long – well, she hadn't mourned long for John; as soon as Harry had returned from the Boer war she'd latched on to him. Who would be next – Frank?

The speaker was Mrs Tranter, a crony of Grandmother's who had buried her own husband years before and never found another. Catching her eye, I let my expression declare my contempt. She had the grace to look away and change the subject, though no doubt after I moved on she said nasty things about me, too. Mrs Tranter seldom had a good word for anyone.

I didn't actually hear anyone comment on the chill that was apparent between Saffron and Oliver, but I noticed some eloquent looks. Whenever he came near her she cut him dead and pointedly moved away, refusing even to speak to him. Though Oliver tried to maintain an air of insouciance, not even he could entirely hide his discomfort. I saw Vicky complain to Grandmother on his behalf, then Grandmother spoke to Saffron, whose reply caused Grandmother to don her very best frozen-dragon glare. I was too far away to hear what was said, but a moment later Saffron had turned on her heel and, in tears, forced her way between groups of the company, turning heads and causing more speculation as she fled for the stairs.

Going after her, I found her lying across her bed, every muscle in knots of fury and despair. No, she didn't need anything. No, there was nothing I could do. She knew I meant it kindly, but would I please go away? I was much too young. I couldn't possibly understand. Why had *that man* been here, on this day of all days? Didn't he have any feelings, any sense of shame? Oh, she hated being in this house. She was going back to Lynn just as soon as she could. And she was going to take her son with her. Lady Vi wasn't going to rob her of Eddy!

Worried, I left her alone and went to see my godson, who was screaming his lungs out, refusing to go down for his afternoon nap. Rollins was fretful, too. 'He's been like this for over an hour. I don't know what's wrong with him, Miss Brand. It's as if he knew . . .'

'Let me take him for some air.' Wondering if little ones could sense vibrations around them, I carried Eddy down to where his perambulator was kept in the lower lobby. The journey down the back stairs silenced his screams, but his little body shook with silent misery. He didn't want to lie down, so I let him sit up and wheeled him out into the garden, first to see Tom, who was with his birds, and then round the flower garden and the croquet lawn, singing to him. He watched me with huge, miserable blue eyes, lids slowly beginning to droop, until at last he lay down and went off to sleep.

I tucked his blanket round him, thinking how sweet and peaceful he looked, unaware of the traumas battering round him. He wouldn't even remember Harry, and that was sad, but we would make sure he knew how much his father had loved him.

Pushing him in front of me, I wandered into the shrubberies, down a grassy pathway which the gardeners mowed regularly. I was still singing under my breath to soothe the baby: ' "I'll be your sweetheart, If you will be mine . . ." ' and thinking of a shady nook in Kensington Gardens, where strong arms had held me close while warm lips caressed my throat. But my song broke off as I caught a whiff of cigar smoke and found myself near the folly, a mock Roman temple that made a kind of summerhouse, half hidden in flowering shrubs. Granite pillars framed the entrance, above a flight of shallow steps, and trees reached out their branches as if to guard the roof. The place appeared to be empty. Yet the scent of cigar smoke was unmistakable.

Nerves tingling, I peered at the growth around me – dark foliage of rhododendron thick with purple flowers, azaleas flaming, trees forming a canopy above, ground ivy snaking across the steps at my feet . . . 'Hello?' I called softly. 'Is anyone—'

'Kate,' Oliver's voice answered on a note of relief and, to my astonishment, he appeared in the doorway of the 'temple'. He had been hiding behind a pillar!

His expression derided his own antics, mouth wry beneath the moustache. 'I thought you were Vicky.'

I couldn't help laughing at the thought of him cowering in the summerhouse for fear of a woman. 'Poor man! Were you terrified?'

'It's not funny,' he objected, stepping slowly down to

join me. 'Do you realize I could find myself obliged to
marry her, or facing a breach of promise suit, when I've
never given her the least cause to—'

'You've been kind to her.'

'I don't have much choice. I can't offend her mother
by— Oh, really, Kate!' as I burst into fresh laughter. But
he too could now see the funny side of it and a slow grin
quirked at his mouth. 'Be quiet, you'll wake the baby.'

We both peered into the pram, but Eddy was worlds
away.

Close beside me, Oliver said in a low voice, 'It's good
to hear you laugh, anyway. I suppose I did look a little
foolish. Did you feel the need to escape, too?'

'Something of the kind.' I straightened, putting more
distance between us. 'Eddy was fretful, so I thought a walk
might settle him.' I had started to move on, but stopped as
a thought occurred to me. 'Actually, Oliver, I've been
hoping to have a word with you.'

Dark eyes caressed my face hopefully. 'Have you?'

'About Mother.'

The hope died, leaving him smiling with chagrin. 'Ah.
Yes.'

'I'm worried about her. I haven't heard from her since
early March.' I told him about the worrying letter, and the
note from Pa which had followed it, and the resealed
envelope with my birthday card. To my relief, Oliver
understood my concern.

'Would you like me to write to them? In my official
capacity, I mean? I'm sure I could invent some good reason
for contacting her.'

'Could you?' A load seemed to lift from me. 'Oh, Oliver,
I'd be so grateful. If I could just be sure she's all right.
With all these rumours flying around . . .' Wanting to give

something in return, I added, 'You know, Saffron doesn't mean to be unkind. She just—'

'I know.' He laid a hand beside mine on the pram handle, not quite touching me, helping me push as we strolled on along the path under the trees, going very slowly. 'She's hurting and she needs a target to hit at. But, I should tell you, in all honesty, Harry and I did have words that day – about the strike situation. We both became somewhat heated. Maybe I *was* partially to blame for—'

'You mustn't think that.'

'I can't help it. All the same . . .' He paused in the dappled shade of oak trees, his hand moving warmly to cover mine. 'I'm glad to know *you* don't hold it against me.'

Steeling myself, I tried not to overreact to his touch. After all, if Uncle Frank had laid his hand on mine I would have taken it for a natural, affectionate gesture. Why couldn't I think of Oliver in the same way? I said, 'I just wish I knew why . . .'

'Why Harry hated me?'

It was no good, I couldn't stand there and let him hold my hand – he was *not* Uncle Frank. I eased free and bent over the pram to adjust Eddy's blanket needlessly. ' "Hate" is a strong word. I don't believe Uncle Harry was capable of hating.'

'What would you prefer? Dislike? Distrust?' He swept his hand across his hair, as if to remove the lingering imprint of my flesh. 'Don't forget I was the charity case – the motherless waif whom they allowed to join in their games. And then I grew up. I became useful to their father in ways they could never emulate. Oh, they all tried – except Frank, who always knew he wasn't a businessman – but not one of them was equipped to follow in Sir Lionel's shoes. Not even Emmet, from what I've seen.

He's bright, but he has no business brain. Strangely enough, Vicky's the one with the most organizational ability. Now, if she'd been a boy . . .'

'What about John?'

His eyes glimmered. 'John prospered on charm. Everything came easy to him. It made him lazy. I think that's why we got on so well together – we were opposites, we made a good team. But he was secure in his position as the oldest son, so he didn't feel it demeaned him to be friendly with someone like me. Which gave Harry and Frank even more excuse to hate me. They never did understand why their older brother and I were so close. Oh . . . I don't blame them. In their shoes I might well have felt the same.'

Behind him, a pale face topped by a mass of red-gold hair peered round a tree. Vicky dodged back when she realized I had seen her, but Oliver turned to discover what had caught my eye and, a moment later, my young aunt gave up the pretence and stepped out into full view, wearing on each pale cheek a flag of scarlet above which her blue eyes blazed. Her thin body was rigid, her neck a pale column rising out of deep mourning.

'I see,' was all she said, but the words were thick with disgust and bitterness.

'Eavesdropping?' Oliver taunted.

Temper flared in her eyes, but she controlled herself, hands knotted at her sides as she said quietly, 'You should be ashamed of yourselves. Both of you. How *dare* you gossip behind our backs? Who do you think you are, Kate Brand? As for you, Oliver . . . I thought better of you. I really thought . . . I shall tell Mother.'

'Tell her what?' Oliver enquired. 'Grow up, Vicky.'

Her colour deepened, running down her throat to flush

her swanlike neck. 'Don't speak to me like that! I'm not a child to be silenced.'

'Vicky . . .' He stepped towards her, but she drew back, gasping, 'No, don't touch me. Don't touch me ever again. Stay with *her*. I know that's where you'd rather be. Well . . . have her. You deserve each other.' Darting me a venomous glance, she grabbed a handful of her skirt and turned away, making for the house with as much speed and dignity as her narrow hem would allow.

'Go after her,' I suggested when Oliver stood unmoving, his broad back turned to me. 'She has the wrong impression. You can't let her just—'

'Can't I?' He looked at me along his shoulder, umber eyes burning. 'She doesn't have the wrong impression, Kate, she has it exactly right – I do prefer to be with you.'

'Oliver—'

'It's all right.' A gesture halted my protests. 'You've made it clear you don't return the feeling. I understand that. I respect it. But does that mean I have to latch on to a girl who leaves me utterly cold? What do you take me for – a fortune-hunter? Vicky deserves better than that. Sooner or later, I trust, she'll find someone who will genuinely care for her. While I, for my sins, will never care for anyone but you. Excuse me.'

And he turned on his heel, striding back in the direction from which we had come – the opposite direction to Vicky.

Saffron remained adamant in her decision to go back to Lynn, despite well-meant advice to the contrary. More harsh words were said, I gathered, as a result of which Grandmother summoned me to her private sitting room. She paced restlessly, a thin figure in black, her shoulders slightly bent with age but still imperious, as she instructed me to go with my aunt and spend a few days with her before returning to London.

'We must not allow this to develop into a family rift. Saffron is an excessively stubborn woman. But Eddy is my grandson. I will not be cut off from my own flesh and blood.' She seemed oblivious to the irony in her own words – she hadn't cared about being 'cut off' from me for years, and she'd never even seen my half-brothers. But of course we didn't count – we were not Rhys-Thomases. As for Saffron being stubborn . . .

'I think she just needs time,' I said.

'Of course she does. We all do! But we should share our grief. I'm relying on you to sow the seeds. Eddy belongs here, at Denes Hill. Make her see that.'

Fortunately she was moving away from me and didn't see my face. Did she expect Saffron and Eddy to move to Denes Hill? Saffron would never agree to that.

'And find some way of softening her attitude to Oliver,' came the next order. 'I realize her accusations were a result of overwrought emotion, but it makes things difficult.' The sharp blue eyes spitted me. 'Well? You can do that, can't you? Speak up for Oliver? Vicky certainly appears to believe you're willing to do so.'

I felt as if someone had rammed me in the stomach with an oar. My face was suddenly burning, my throat all but closed. 'I don't know what Vicky told you, but . . .'

'My dear child,' Grandmother replied with a glance that managed both to reprove and to condescend, 'she told me nothing I wasn't already aware of. Now run along and pack.'

What, exactly, did she mean by that enigmatic answer?

With Saffron, amnesty came less easily. She didn't want to hear Oliver's name, or anything about Denes Hill. Back at Hawthorn House she summoned her own friends around her. And all she talked about was Harry. I was not sorry when duty obliged me to return to London and final cramming before the second-year exams.

FIFTEEN

Over the next month, I acquired a growing bundle of letters which I bound in green ribbon. Philip had said he wasn't good with words, but, however stiff his phrases on paper, I preferred them to the glib compliments which had come so easy to Carl-Heinz.

I replied with equal caution, telling him my news, while in a private notebook I poured out my heart in love poems which, one day, perhaps, I would show to him. I sent my letters care of the post office in King's Lynn, where Philip could collect them on market day. The notebook I kept to myself.

The more I learned of him, the more I loved him. Since his older brother had been expected to inherit the farm, Philip had been sent to boarding school to 'make something' of himself. He had dreamed of being an aviator and had hoped to go to university, but Michael's death had altered everything: at the age of sixteen Philip had left school to work on the farm. He was philosophical about it rather than bitter: the farm was where he was needed. He was also anxious for me to understand his father. The old man was embittered, but not wholly bad. Once he knew me, he could not help but love me. So my darling Philip said.

With the added joy of being in communication with him, constantly assured of his feelings for me, I continued my studies, sat my exams and, in early July, like a lark set free from its cage to soar away and find its mate, travelled back to Norfolk. Fellow passengers on the train must have wondered at the smile on my face as I watched the passing scene and heard the wheels chant Philip's name.

Grandmother sent the wagonette, driven by her outdoor man, Garret, to meet me at Eveningham station. Tom came, too, rushing to greet me with beaming smiles and bear hugs.

As he scrambled up to sit opposite me, a movement behind him drew my eyes to where a man in shirtsleeves was leaning on a post, doffing his cap to cuff sweat from his brow while his other hand held the bridle of a chestnut horse tethered beside him. Philip . . . My heart flipped a somersault, bounced off my stomach and set my insides aquiver, for his smile told me he was not there by chance.

As the wagonette set off, Philip eased himself to his feet and leapt up to the saddle of his chestnut hunter – named Troy, short for Troilus, '*because he's faithful*', so he had told me in a letter. He blew me a kiss in sheer exuberance before setting off at a furious gallop, heading down the beach road, while I bit my lip to stop myself from grinning like an idiot. Philip. Oh, Philip, Philip, Philip . . .

Over dinner, Grandmother quizzed me about school and life with Mrs Armes. I had the impression she had heard hints about the 'young chap in London', though I assured her I had met no one special while I had been away. That was, of course, the truth. Just not the whole truth.

Only Grandmother and Vicky were in residence at Denes Hill. Emmet was now based in Lincoln, learning the engineering business, and Frank had gone away again: would his search for inspiration take him to Llandudno, where Judy Love was appearing that summer?

How fortuitous it now seemed that my room lay well away from the others' and that the back stairs led conveniently to the side entrance. That door was never locked – it was the door Tom used for visiting his animals at all hours, and now it provided me with easy means of exit and ingress whenever I chose.

That first evening I crept out to a rendezvous Philip and I had long planned – ten o'clock, on the path that crossed the railway cutting. As I crept through the woods I remembered the warnings that had come from my lost uncle, John, seeming to tell me to beware of involvement with Philip. But that night John remained remote. Perhaps he knew nothing could stop me. When love beckons so strongly, no force on earth can gainsay it – not reason, not common sense, not conscience . . .

A twinkle of light from a torch showed ahead of me. I stopped, briefly nervous. Then the light blinked: once, twice, three times – our agreed signal! My feet took flight, impelling me towards the tall figure that waited in the starlight, arms opening wide . . .

Oliver Wells had said that I was not a good liar, but my talent for deception improved daily. If I had been free to confess my love for Philip I would have done so happily, but his being a Farcroft and my being from the hill complicated matters.

By day, I found books to read, and walks and cycle rides to take. In Hunstanton, Butcher Ehrenfried had become Butcher Enfield, though the change of name hadn't brought back the customers who had deserted him. By boycotting someone they had known and liked for years, the good folk of Huns'ton displayed their patriotism. Other days, I delivered hundreds of 'Votes for Women' leaflets, or accompanied Mrs Lacey on doorstep visits, trying to raise more support. I also wrote – articles for Gudrun in Berlin, essays, stories and, always, poems for my notebook, telling of my deepening love for Philip. Such activities served to pass time, to fill the gaps that yawned between our meetings.

By night, under a sky filled with afterglow, my love and I strolled on the beach or down dark unfrequented lanes, discovering each other's minds and hearts. At times I was sorely tempted to suggest that we might also explore more forbidden delights, but Philip always drew back before we could topple over that slippery brink. For that I loved him the more, and was grateful: his strength and self-control served for us both.

I was able, at last, to tell him about Carl-Heinz. Darling Philip, so upright himself, didn't understand how any man could behave in such an ungallant manner; no gentleman would have done such a thing – no *English* gentleman, anyway. He was glad I had told him – Philip valued honesty. It worried him that, by meeting me in secret, he himself was being less than honourable, but we dared not confess the truth to my family and when he tried talking about me at home Mad Jack refused to listen. My grandfather had denied him his shooting rights; my mother had spurned his older son; he didn't even want to hear my name mentioned.

'He's never been the same since Michael died,' Philip said one evening as we walked hand in hand along the ridge under the stars. 'And losing Mother was another fearful blow. He blamed your family for all of it. But he will come round, Kate. One day, he must.'

As if disturbed by his doubts, he pulled me to him and we stood holding each other in the darkness, trees whispering above us and in the distance the slate-grey gleam of the sea. Rubbing my face softly against the curve of his throat, I let my lips taste his skin, breathing in the scent of him, feeling his body respond as he bent to kiss me. I wrapped my arms about his neck, giving in to the drowning wonder of being near him.

All too soon, he let me go and moved on, walking so swiftly and furiously that I had to trot to keep up, and holding my hand so tightly that it hurt. I couldn't have put a name to what he was enduring. I only knew that I felt the same aching need and that sometimes I wished he would let the tide sweep us both away.

'What's wrong, Philip?'

'Nothing,' came the gruff answer, then, 'There's something I ought to have told you, Katie.'

'Oh?'

'I have to go away.'

What? As the words sank in, I stopped, and since I was holding his hand he had to stop, too, a pace ahead of me. 'Away where?'

'Training camp.' He turned to look at me. 'I told you we had a camp every July, didn't I?' In the darkness I couldn't see his face, but his defensive tone told me he felt guilty. 'It starts tomorrow.'

I could hardly think for a spurt of hot dismay. '*Tomorrow?*'

' 'Fraid so.'

'But . . . why didn't you say? Can't you get out of it? You don't have to go, surely?'

'I can't duck my responsibilities, not even for you. It would mean telling even more lies . . .'

Disappointment made me pull away from him. 'Heaven forfend that you should lie for me! I do it for you all the time!'

'And whose choice is that?' he responded. 'I've never asked you to lie for me. I hate having to do it. Shall we go up to Denes Hill right now and tell them—'

'No!' I moaned.

'No, I thought not.'

'We can't. Not yet. You know that. They'd be sure to find some way of separating us. Oh, Philip!' Hating to be at odds with him, I threw my arms round his neck and huddled against him. 'I'm sorry. Of course you must go to your rotten training camp. But I hate to think of you being a soldier. And it's beastly unfair. I thought we'd have the whole summer together.'

'I'll be back in two weeks.'

Two weeks . . . it seemed like forever.

Though we parted with sweet kisses, neither of us was happy. I felt bitter, cheated. Trailing home along the main coast road, with the moon rising over the woods, I even wondered if he really cared about me. Then I wanted to run back and find him, and tell him I was sorry, that I loved him and would wait for ever if necessary. But, for the first time since my birthday, I felt the cold draught of reality blowing through my dreams. I was horribly afraid there might be no future for Philip and me.

Halfway down the Denes Hill drive, I stepped aside into deep shadow and sat down on a clump of grass at the foot of a tree, arms about my knees, calling up irritation to counter my sadness. I didn't want him to go away. He ought to have warned me earlier! Well, I wasn't going to sit around sighing for him. If he chose to go off playing soldier, then I, too, would go . . . to Lynn, to stay with Saffron and Eddy. Yes, that was it. Go to Lynn. But, two whole weeks without him . . .

A slight sound in the night made me look up to see someone squatting not many feet away, bathed in moonlight with his tousled fair head on one side in an attitude of concern. After a moment of sheer fright, my heart settled to a steady gallop.

'Tom? You startled me!'

'What's wrong, Kate?' he asked, creeping closer.

'Nothing. Nothing at all.'

He came to help me up and draw me out into the moonlight, where he stood rubbing my arm as if to comfort me. 'It was that man, wasn't it?'

Dismayed, I looked into his ingenuous boy's face. 'What man?'

'Young Farcroft.'

My heart paused and then plunged on at a rate that left me breathless. 'You know him?'

' 'Course I do. He comes from the farm. I've seen you with him. Did he hurt you? I don't like it when things get hurt.'

'I know you don't.' I took his arm, turning him towards the house. 'No, he didn't hurt me, Tom, dear. He's my friend. My very good friend. Have you . . . Have you told anyone about my seeing him?'

'No, 'course not,' Tom said at once, and a sly little smile crossed his face. 'I keep lots of secrets.'

'You do? Then will you keep this one for me?'

'Of course I will. You can trust me, Katie B.'

'Katie B' – that was what Emmet sometimes called me, nicer than that other epithet, my initials, C.L.B., used as an insult.

'Will you walk me home?' I asked. 'I'm starving. Shall we raid the larder?'

Poor Tom was easily distracted. On the way to the house we shared a piece of soggy toffee with brown paper sticking to it. Heaven knows how long he'd had it in his pocket.

In Lynn with Saffron and young Eddy, hating being separated from Philip, I must have been sadly unsociable.

But Saffron herself was abstracted, when she wasn't engaged in some frantic activity. She filled her emptiness with charity work and women's causes that kept her from too much thinking, and she still talked about Harry more than I found comfortable – I was too young to know that that is often how people deal with grief.

A message from Oliver requested me to visit him at his office in the town and I went hopefully, thinking he might have heard from Mother. But what he wanted to tell me was that he *hadn't* received a reply from Berlin, though delays were inevitable. He could have told me that by post, I thought.

As I was leaving, he revealed his true purpose in summoning me: he followed me to the door, saying, 'I don't suppose . . . You wouldn't consider having dinner with me this evening, would you? There's a band concert in the Walks. We might have a stroll, take the evening air, and then go for a meal somewhere. The Duke's Head, perhaps.'

The Duke's Head being the most expensive hotel in town, I was tempted – I liked Oliver, thought of him as a kindred spirit in many ways, and I must admit to being annoyed enough with Philip to contemplate, just for a second . . . but only for a second. 'I'm sorry, Oliver, but—'

'That's all right,' he said at once. 'It was just a thought, since you were here in town.'

But despite the brave words he couldn't hide his disappointment, and that made me feel badly. 'There *must* be someone else you can ask! You're a fine-looking man, Oliver. Any woman . . .'

'Any woman except the one I want,' he answered softly, and reached out to touch my cheek before turning away. 'Run along, Kate, before I do something we shall both be sorry for.'

That evening, for the first time since Harry's funeral, Saffron and I talked about Oliver.

'He came to see me and we had a long talk,' she confided. 'I'm not saying I shall ever like him, but at least I now realize he's a human being, d'you know what I mean? He was really very kind. He brought a lovely teddy bear for Eddy. Frank would probably call it bribery, but—'

'Frank would! Poor Oliver can't do anything right for him.'

Saffron regarded me in surprise. ' "Poor Oliver"? Why, Kate . . . don't tell me Vicky was right, after all? She did make some remark about you and Oliver, but I never dreamed . . . I thought you had a young chap in London?'

'Who told you that?' I demanded.

'Frank did. In confidence, of course.'

Much as I adored Uncle Frank, he was turning into as big a gossip as Judy Love.

On my last Saturday in Lynn – when Philip was due home – Grandmother and Vicky came over to attend a suffragette rally. They also brought a letter which had arrived for me, from Mother. 'It will be a comfort to you,' was Grandmother's comment.

I eagerly tore open the envelope. Mother said that she and the *Menschen* were well; she sent a photograph, showing the boys round her knee. How they had grown! They were all staying at the von Wurthe family residence, in East Prussia, '*where it's safer*,' she wrote, though she didn't say safe from what.

Grandmother and Vicky expressed dutiful relief, while Saffron studied the photograph, asking which of the boys was which, and what was the building in the background? I assumed it must be Schloss Lindhafen, where lived Pa's older brother, the present Baron von Wurthe, and his family.

I had met them, from time to time, though I had never been to the ancestral home. Nor did I know its exact location, so I couldn't write to Mother there. In future my only route was via Berlin, where Pa would no doubt vet all correspondence. I suspected he had allowed Mother to write to me only as a result of Oliver's enquiry. Nevertheless, it was good to have heard from her.

On the station platform that sunny evening we encountered a bronzed and smiling Uncle Frank, also on his way home to Denes Hill. He looked fit enough, but he was awfully thin.

'I do wish you would warn us when you're coming!' Grandmother chafed. 'Have you lost weight? Haven't been ill, have you?'

'Been cycling a lot,' he said. 'In France. Paris sends its love.'

Since Emmet had also arrived for the weekend, the family party was complete. We enjoyed a convivial dinner, though I was aware of time passing: I had promised to meet Philip as soon after nine o'clock as I could manage.

It was nearer half past nine before I could safely retire to my room, and then I had to wait to be sure no one was about before I crept down and let myself out by the side door. Late as I was for the rendezvous, our favourite place among the dunes was deserted, so I sat down to watch the sea and wait, growing ever more anxious as the minutes passed.

Mild night breezes wafted tendrils of my hair, under a sky full of stars with the moon waxing towards harvest. Then: *Kate!* The call, rippling along my nerves, brought me to my feet expecting to see Philip nearby. But the dunes were empty, stretching away on either side, greyed by moonlight. Something drew my glance to the sea, where a figure stood knee-deep in the shallows, dark against the glitter of moonlit waves. Was it John? Was he wading towards me? A drift of cloud shut off the light and when the moon cleared again the apparition had gone. The night wind sighed about me, making me shiver. What was he trying to tell me? Some warning connected with Philip? Had something happened to—

'Katie!' This time the voice was real. Philip was coming, on foot along the beach. Weak with relief, I ran to meet him, throwing myself into his arms to kiss him, until he held me away, protesting, 'Slow down, sweetheart. Let me get my breath.'

'I'm so *glad* to see you!' I gasped. 'I've missed you. It seems like two years, not just two weeks. How was the camp?'

'Oh – fine.' He sounded as if he didn't want to discuss it.

'Did you miss me?'

'Of course I did!' he said at once, hugging me closer. 'I'm sorry I'm late. I've been helping Dad clear the barn.'

'It doesn't matter, you're here now.' Laughing a little, breathless with joy, I drew back and smiled up at him. 'Where's Bess tonight?' I missed the dog's friendly fussing.

'I left her at home. We think she's breeding.'

'I wish I could have one of her puppies.'

I hoped he might say he would keep one for me, but his only reply was a tight, abstracted smile.

We strolled on the edge of the sea, hand tightly in hand, close together but not saying much. My mind was half on the ripple of moonlit water where John had appeared. The sea, the beach . . . something of significance lurked in the shadows, refusing to come forward and be recognized.

As the incoming tide covered the sand, we moved up to

the dunes. Philip spread his jacket for me to sit on, settling himself a little apart and sifting sand through his fist. Only then did I fully realize how quiet he had been since we met.

'Is something wrong?' I asked.

'I'm tired, that's all.'

'You work too hard.'

He sent me a tight-lipped glance, saying roughly, 'Every farmer works hard at this time of year. I can't stay out until all hours the way you do. I'm a working man, Kate. I'm sorry if that's a bore.'

Scrambling closer, on my knees, I laid my hand on his arm, trying to read his expression through deceptive moonlight. 'I didn't mean—'

'Didn't you?' He turned his head to look at me, his face all moon-silvered planes and black shadows, gaunt under the crop of ruffled curls.

My heart lurched and twisted with dismay. Why was he angry with me? I smoothed my hand up his shirtsleeve to his shoulder, laying my other palm along his cheek. 'If you want to go home, you've only to say so.'

'That's the trouble,' he said gruffly. 'I don't want to. I know I ought to, but—' And he reached for me, pushing me back to the sand as he bent over me. 'Katie!' the breath came against my lips. 'Oh, Katie, darling!'

When his mouth claimed mine, something fierce and wild jolted me to the soul. Oh, I loved him. The feel of him, the smell of him, the way his eyes lit when he saw me, the texture of his hair and his skin, his hands on me, his body close to mine. I tried to show him how much I cared, kissing his face all over, his throat, and inside the collar of a shirt whose buttons pulled undone at a touch. I had forgotten how white his skin was, soft and warm under my lips and hands, vibrant with the pulse of young blood.

He answered me kiss for kiss, caress for caress, until we reached the moment when he always drew back, when we found something else to talk about, or dissipated our feelings in brisk walking. But that evening something was different. That evening, his lips traced a singing pathway down my throat, while his fingers deftly dealt with the buttons on my blouse and I felt his mouth hot against the swell of my naked breast. My body felt strange, alive with inchoate longings, my breasts on fire, my stomach taut, my loins running molten. My head seemed to swoop as he lifted himself to lie on me and I felt the heat and hunger in him, the strong hard shape of him through our clothes as his tongue plundered my mouth. He wasn't going to stop. Not tonight.

Terrified by my own feelings, I turned my head aside, jack-knifed my legs and thrust him off. 'Philip, no! No!' Panic drove me to my feet, stumbling backwards to sit with a thump on the sandy slope and stare at the sudden stranger who knelt in the hollow, bent double in some extremity I didn't comprehend. My lungs fought for air. My heart thumped erratically in my throat. My body was still on fire with awful need, though it was cooling fast as shame took over. 'Did I hurt you?'

'My fault,' he got out between his teeth. 'Hellfire, Kate! You could geld a man, doing that!'

The words came like a blow. Philip never used bad language. Never! Realizing my blouse was gaping indecently, I pulled the edges together and leapt up, struggling up the slipping sand to the top of the dune. I stood there fumbling to fasten my buttons, staring at the sea. Was this what John had tried to warn me about – my own wanton nature?

Then Philip was beside me, saying anxiously, 'Forgive

me, sweetheart. I've missed you so much I'm all in knots. I should never have—'

'It was my fault. *My* fault! Maybe Carl-Heinz was right. Maybe I *am* wicked and immoral, and—'

'You're not. You're a natural human girl and I love you for it.'

Grateful for that reassurance, I turned to burrow against him, choking, 'Hold me, Philip. I'm so afraid . . .'

'Afraid of what?' he asked, wrapping his arms about me, breathing in the scent of my hair.

'I don't know. I just feel . . . I don't know.'

'It scares me, too,' he murmured against my ear. 'Sometimes I think I may go crazy. I lose sleep through seeing you. But, if I don't see you, I can't sleep for thinking about you. The joke of it is . . .' He hesitated, then hoarsely added, 'If we were married, it would be all right. It would be expected. You could be there in my bed with me.'

Unable to look into his eyes, I stared at the firm shape of his mouth bare inches away, breathing, 'Yes.'

'But until that day comes . . . perhaps we should be more careful.'

Did he blame me for leading him on? 'Yes. I'm sorry,' I sighed, and, after a moment when cold reality sobered me, I eased away, depressed. 'Perhaps we should go.'

'Is that my answer?'

Mystified, I looked round at him. 'To what?'

He studied my upturned face for a silent moment, his own expression indiscernible; then, 'Nothing,' he said shortly. 'Forget it,' and he swung round on his heel, striding off towards the causeway path.

'Philip, please!' I cried after him. 'What did I say? I honestly don't know what you mean. Please . . .'

But his legs were longer than mine and he wasn't

hampered by long skirts and dainty shoes. 'It's not important,' he threw back. 'I was a fool to think . . .' Just before he increased his pace, I heard him mutter, 'I should have listened to Dad.'

Until that day comes . . . Had it been a tentative proposal of marriage? I struggled behind, wishing I had been more sensitive. Or had I chosen not to understand, because I wasn't ready to face the obstacles?

He stayed ahead of me, slowing only as we crossed the railway and climbed the steep path into the Denes Hill woods, when he took out his torch to guide his way. Realizing my difficulties in the darkness, he lent his hand to help me, chivalrous as ever.

'What has your father been saying?' I panted as we gained more level ground.

His hand tightened on mine, until I thought he would break my bones; then just as I was about to protest, the pressure eased. He said, 'He's been under the impression I was walking out with Lou Roughton. Today, he found out he was wrong.'

'I see.'

'No, you don't. If you knew how—' He stopped himself, taking a breath and letting it out in impatience: 'I told him I intended to go on seeing you. He called me a blasted young fool. He said you might condescend to use me as an amusement for a while, but when it came to marriage you'd want one of your own kind. Like your mother did.' He turned to face me, saying savagely, 'And he was right, wasn't he? Michael wasn't good enough for her and I'm not good enough for you. You'll lead me on, get me tied in knots with wanting you, but when it comes right down to it—'

Was it the wind, or the cry of an owl somewhere close

by, that sent a shudder to wake every nerve in my body? Or was it John, whispering in my ear? I felt sick and cold. How could Philip say such hurtful things? In a small, empty voice, I said, 'I thought you cared about me. You said we should wait until—'

'That's not what I mean!' Though I could hardly see him I sensed that he was clenching his teeth in that way he had, taking time to calm his temper before saying bitterly, 'I thought *you* cared about *me*.'

I do, I thought, but I was in no mood to say so. Him and his stiff-necked pride! 'Then maybe we were both wrong.'

Our hands parted by mutual consent. Sudden chasms yawned between us.

In the silence, startling us both, a shotgun spoke.

As I looked towards the sound, another blast rang out, with an orange flash of fire visible among the trees. Pheasants went calling in fright. Then came a hoarse shout, incoherent with rage and anguish, and the distant crashing of undergrowth.

'Don't!' I reached out to detain Philip, but he was already racing away towards the disturbance. I followed, fighting off clawing thorns.

Just ahead of me, Philip's torch wove a silver trail, touching on trees and bushes thick with leaf. Belatedly remembering my own torch, I took it out and went on, trying to keep my eyes on his dark shape in the night. Life stirred around us, creatures disturbed into flight or hiding, my unseen friends hovering anxiously. Something cold touched my soul with dread as I recognized the sounds of a struggle not far away.

Philip had caught his sleeve on a brier. As I came up to him I heard him curse and tear free of the last prickle. His torchlight swung, and transfixed his father in the act of jabbing the butt of his gun down at the ground, where another man lay unmoving.

'Dad!' The shout, and the light, held Mad Jack in thrall, livid face turned towards us, teeth bared in a rictus of hate. He had lost his hat. His hair stood up in grizzled spikes. Blood trickled down his face . . .

'Aaargh!' With a wordless cry, he hurled his shotgun at Philip. Philip threw up his arm to ward off the missile. I heard him catch his breath as it struck him, though the sound was lost in the crash and crackle of growth as Mad Jack made off among the trees.

'Oh, God!' Philip breathed, and then I saw that his light had revealed the identity of the figure who lay crumpled among flattened bracken. A young man, slight of form, with tousled fair hair . . .

'Tom!' I threw myself down beside him, staring at his pallid face and closed eyes. Oh, no. No!

'Is he dead?' Philip's tense voice came from above me.

Beneath my hand I could feel Tom's heart beating, if faintly. 'No.'

'Thank God for that!'

Furious, I looked up at his dark figure, looming featureless behind the light of his torch. Mad Jack had done this. Shot Tom, then hit him with the gun . . . 'It's certainly no thanks to your father! Oh, I *knew* this would happen. If Tom dies—'

'He won't.' Grasping my shoulders, he heaved me aside as he knelt beside Tom, skilful hands examining him, reminding me of the time he had knelt in the same solicitous way over Saffron. Then, he had been only a disturbing stranger: now . . . now, love and mistrust warred inside me. 'I can't find any wounds,' he said. 'I think he's concussed. You'd better go and warn them.'

277

'And what will *you* do?' I cried. 'You can't cover *this* up. This was more than threatening behaviour. Your father tried to murder Tom!'

His face was unreadable, lit from beneath by faint torchlight, but his silence said much. When at last he spoke, deep bitterness laced his voice. 'And do you imagine I'm about to complete the job?'

I didn't know what I thought. Philip was again a stranger. He still looked like the man I loved, but—

'Just go,' he added in disgust, and bent over Tom to lift him.

Letting myself in by the side door, I raced through the quiet house and up to the tower, where Uncle Frank's lamp still burned, a yellow glow under his door. He had fallen asleep while reading in bed, but roused himself when I told him there had been an accident: 'Tom's been hurt. In the woods. Someone's bringing him home.' I didn't specify who the 'someone' was, nor did Frank enquire.

Our voices disturbed Vicky, who came to see what was happening and, before we could stop her, rushed off to wake her mother. Frank made for the back stairs, while I went to Tom's room, where I drew back the covers and lit a lamp.

When I heard them coming I held the lamp to light their way, remaining by the foot of the bed as Philip brought Tom in and laid him down. Tom was still unconscious, but seemed to be breathing steadily as Frank, on the other side of the bed, covered him up and bent anxiously over him. Then Vicky reappeared, twittering worriedly, her hair in a long plait over the shoulder of her wrap. Behind her a velvet-draped Grandmother leaned on a stick, with Anderson at her heels in a mannish dressing gown.

'What's happened?' Grandmother rapped.

'We're not sure,' I said. 'We didn't really see—'

'There was some kind of accident,' Frank cut me off. 'I've sent Garret for the doctor. Tom's bumped his head. But I don't think he's badly hurt.'

Her mind seemed to work slowly. She looked from me to Frank, then to where Philip was standing with his back defiantly stiff and his eyes dark in the lamplight. I saw the muscle in his cheek knot with tension as a bony finger jabbed the air accusingly at him. 'Who's he?'

'Someone we should be grateful to,' Frank said shortly. 'He found Tom and brought him home.'

Vicky muttered something, to which Grandmother snapped, 'What? Speak up, Vicky! Who?'

'Farmer Farcroft's son,' came the agitated answer. 'You must remember, Mother. Philip Farcroft. We've seen him in church.'

If she had announced him as Beelzebub she couldn't have caused more consternation. '*What?* Why—'

With that, a distraught Emmet erupted into the room, pushing between Grandmother and Vicky as he went to throw himself down beside his twin, crying, 'Tom!'

'Be careful, he's hurt his head!' Frank snapped. 'Better not touch him. The doctor's on his way.'

'I know!' Emmet raged. 'We met Garret on the road and he told us. The Laceys and I were on our way back from the village. What happened? Was he shot? Was it that old devil Farcroft? He was in the Black Horse earlier, blind drunk. Damn it, damn it! I always knew we ought to do something about him. I knew something like this would happen.'

'My father never shot anybody!' Philip said, his voice quiet but forceful, making Emmet twist to stare up at him in disbelief.

'*You!* What the devil—'

279

'Your brother's not badly hurt,' Philip said. 'It was my father who was bleeding. Your brother shot him!'

'Liar!' Letting out a howl, Emmet leapt up. His fist jabbed out and struck Philip, who fell back against a chest of drawers, sending books and a candlestick flying. Then Emmet was on him, beating at him. Philip threw up his arms, trying to protect his face. He was much the larger but didn't attempt to retaliate, only defended himself. Then Emmet threw all his weight into a punch under the ribs that doubled Philip over. I cried out in horror, but I was hampered by the lamp I was carrying. Frank thrust me aside and threw his arms round Emmet, pinioning him despite his struggles, while Philip leaned on the chest of drawers, choking with pain as he clutched his middle. Blood dripped from his nose, splattering the front of his shirt and the white runner that lay crooked across the polished oak of the chest. Scaldingly, I remembered how he had writhed with pain in the sand dunes after my knee had found a vulnerable spot. It hardly seemed possible that we had lain close in each other's arms, not an hour ago.

'Farcroft,' Frank gasped, still struggling to contain Emmet's fury. 'You'd better go. Be at the farm. And make sure your father's there, too. The police will want some answers.'

Philip took out a handkerchief, pressing it to his nose as he eased himself upright, wincing from the pain at his midriff.

'Bastard!' Emmet cried. 'If he dies, I'll see your father hanged!'

'I'll meet you in hell first,' Philip returned with a look of loathing that encompassed us all.

As he turned for the door Vicky, Grandmother and Anderson drew back as if he might contaminate them with the draught of his passing. He noted it, derided it, then just for an instant turned his scorching, inimical green gaze on me. 'We were wrong,' he said. 'We *are* on opposite sides, whether we like it or not. Goodbye, Kate.' And he was gone.

And I? I only remember standing there, the lamp-flame trembling and fluttering so wildly it nearly snuffed itself out.

SIXTEEN

I told my story without adornment, while Uncle Frank fielded questions about my, and Philip's, reasons for being in the woods at that hour. Fortunately, in the shock and confusion, Grandmother's main concern was for Tom: she would eventually demand full explanations, I knew, but the doctor's timely arrival drove all else from her mind.

By then Tom was coming back to consciousness, confused and concussed but, incredibly, uninjured apart from a blow to the back of his head. Even that appeared to be a result of misadventure rather than malice: 'Looks as if he fell and hit it on a tree,' the doctor commented. 'Keep him in bed for a day or two, but I don't believe he's taken permanent harm.' Despite these assurances, Emmet insisted on spending the night beside his twin.

The rest of us began to disperse. As Grandmother was stumping wearily away, she stopped and looked round at Frank, saying, 'No police.'

'But Mother—'

She looked very old and very tired, but her eyes glowed sapphire-hard. 'No police, Frank. Not until we know more about it.'

In my room, unable to sleep, I stood in my nightgown staring unseeingly at the starlit night. I had been so happy, looking forward to seeing Philip again. Now, I felt as though

I had been struck senseless, like poor Tom, left in a limbo of hurt and disbelief.

When a light tapping of fingernails came on my door, I guessed my visitor might be Frank, but instead Vicky appeared in the doorway, looking both furtive and excited. 'I saw your light. Can't you sleep? Neither can I.' Like a feline, slinking sly, she came in and closed the door behind her, her mouth edged with malice. 'I can't help but wonder, Kate, just what you were doing out in the woods so late.'

Oh, not now! I thought wearily. 'I was walking. I often do.'

'Don't lie!' she hissed. 'I know what you were up to. I've known ever since we buried poor dear Harry. Even at the funeral you couldn't stay away from your lover. You had to sneak off to meet him at the summerhouse. I saw you, don't you remember?'

I might have laughed if I hadn't felt so drained. 'If you're talking about Oliver—'

'I know you've been meeting him,' she broke in. 'He visits you in London, too, doesn't he? You might have fooled Mother with those rumours of some college boy, but you never fooled me. Never for a minute, Kate Brand.' Her lip curled as she added, 'Or whatever your name should be.'

'It's Brand. I gave up being von Wurthe when—'

'That's not what I meant!' Her voice soared with triumph and spite. 'Clara's misfortune. Clara's unhappy mistake. *That's* who you are – C.L.B. – Clara's Little Bastard!'

The words made me flinch. 'That's a hateful thing to say.'

'It's the truth!' she flung at me. 'You're illegitimate, Kate. Your mother disgraced herself. With a farm labourer!'

I felt only contempt for someone so twisted she could slander her own sister. 'My mother would never have lowered herself to—'

'Then why do you think they sent her away in such a hurry?' she cut me off. 'Why did old man Brand marry her when he was practically on his death-bed? Oh, they conspired to fudge dates and hope nobody enquired too closely, but in the family it's an open secret. Why else were they so relieved when Clara went off to Germany, taking her shame with her? Why else did they try to forget she – and you – even existed? Emmet and I were never told the details, but we know now. Do you want to see the evidence?' She produced a piece of paper which she waved in front of me. 'I found it among father's papers, when I was clearing his desk after he died.'

'I don't believe you.' But her insistence bothered me, and so did the sight of that paper in her hand.

'You can't shut out the truth,' she crowed. 'Oh, you should never have come back to Denes Hill. Father didn't want it. But Mother was afraid you were going the same way Clara went. Down the slippery slope to sin and shame. And she was right, wasn't she? Look how you repay her kindness – by defying her, by siding with Saffron against her. By staying out until all hours with Oliver Wells! Well, don't think he'll marry you. No decent man will want a fatherless brat who—'

'I was not with Oliver!' That, at least, was a lie I could refute.

Mouth open to spit more vitriol, she stopped, her sharp glance darting about my face with a little less confidence than before. 'Then who were you with? I know you've been meeting *someone*.'

What was the point of prevaricating? I felt incredibly calm. Relieved. Even proud to admit, 'After what happened tonight, I thought everyone would have guessed: I've been seeing Philip Farcroft.'

Vicky caught her breath, her eyes dilating. Philip's name seemed to strike her dumb. Whatever she had expected, it was not that.

'And I'm not ashamed of it,' I added. 'It so happens I'm in love with him. When I'm of age, next summer, I shall probably marry him.' I had lived with the dream too long to let it go without a fight.

Vicky's face changed like autumn skies. The end result was a pallor induced by shock, mouth half open, blue eyes staring into mine with demons of increasing horror spitting in their depth.

'Philip Farcroft?' she got out, her voice hardly audible. 'But Kate ... You can't! Not him. You can't ever marry *him*!'

'Why not?'

'Because he's ... You ... Oh, my God, Kate! Look. This letter. Read it. Read it!'

Finding her horror infectious, I snatched the paper from her hand. It was a page torn from an old account book, the message written in ink that had faded over years. I stared down at it, seeing the words jumble and dance before I forced my brain to take in what my eyes were seeing. It had been written in haste, by an untutored hand, but anger and concern spilled from every damning word.

'Dear Sir, Forgive me for taking this liberty of writing to you but I reckon you ort to know as how your girl have been coming here to the farm for some time and make friends with my boy and today I now cort them to gether up in the hay loft and the good Lord only know how long that have been going on but I reckon as how you shd know and put a stop to it as I will do myself with my boy because if that go on only the good Lord know how that might end and we dont want no shame brung on this here house no more dont

you want none in yours Respectfully, Julia Farcroft.'

Julia Farcroft . . .

'There was only one girl in our family then,' Vicky said, 'and that was Clara. And the boy . . . it was Philip's older brother, wasn't it? The one who bled to death under the plough. Clara was caught with him – in the hay loft – doing something so disgraceful that they packed her off to Cumberland, where they found her a man in his dotage to give his name to her child.'

It's not true, my heart said, but my head was busy thinking, reviewing, frantically seeking to prove she was wrong. 'Mother was a child when—'

'She was old enough! Sixteen, seventeen . . .'

'It doesn't say they were actually—'

'What else could it mean?'

What else, indeed? Hadn't I always been told that I looked and behaved older than my years? Hadn't Mother tried desperately to keep me looking younger than I was? And hadn't I always felt myself a burden to her? Exactly *when* had she married William Brand? The details had always been vague. 'Fudging dates', Vicky had called it. I stared at the letter, trying to make it mean something different. But Mrs Farcroft wouldn't have written it if she hadn't been worried witless. Dear God . . . Was this why Uncle John had kept trying to warn me about Philip?

Vicky must have witnessed the moment when I stopped arguing with myself. Guilt and pity softened her eyes. She laid a hand on my arm and I felt her trembling as she said in conciliatory tones, 'It explains why Clara was disowned, doesn't it? And why Father cursed her. You haven't . . . you haven't done the same, have you? You haven't done "it"? Not with *him*?'

'No!' Wanting neither her sympathy nor her prurient

curiosity, I shook free of her touch and turned away, my arms wrapped round myself. No, Philip and I had not become lovers. Not quite. How did I feel? Sick, maybe. Empty, perhaps. Empty, numb, stunned . . . Nothing. That's the truth. I felt nothing. Not then. 'Who else knows about this letter?' I croaked.

'No one but me. Father must have discussed it with Mother, before they sent Clara away, but I'm sure she thinks it was destroyed long ago. I won't say otherwise. You keep it. Burn it, if you like. Kate – honestly – I didn't intend to hurt you. But it's as well that you know, isn't it? I mean to say, you could never have married him. It's not allowed. You're – what's the word? – consanguineous. It's a proscribed relationship. Kate . . . I swear I didn't mean—'

Did she expect forgiveness? 'Leave me alone, Vicky.'

'But . . . what are you going to do? In the morning—'

Would there ever be another bright morning? 'Please! Just go away. I need to think.'

'Will you be all right?'

Unable to take her belated concern, I grabbed her arm and propelled her towards the door, flung it open and thrust her out into the hall. 'Go away, Vicky. Just go away!'

I shut the door and leaned on it, my forehead against the hard wood, my eyes closed. I wanted to scream – with laughter, with rage, or was it despair? As if sleepwalking, I went to throw the window wide and gulp at the night air, seeing the moon slung low in a glistening net of stars. Not long ago I had lain in Philip's arms watching those same stars, thinking how beautiful they were. Now, I saw only their indifference.

'Help me!' I begged the uncaring sky. But the stars glittered on, aloof and cold. There was no help. For if Michael Farcroft had been my father, then his half-brother

287

was my half-uncle, and if Philip was my half-uncle then we could never marry. Never kiss, never touch, never love . . .

I dozed fitfully and, long after dawn, fell into a heavy, dream-haunted sleep from which I woke with an aching head to find someone beside me, shaking my shoulder, saying, 'Kate, wake up.' I had not drawn the curtains the previous night; morning brightness stabbed at my eyes, making me throw my hand to shade them as I blinked blearily up at Frank. He looked worried.

'I'm sorry to disturb you, dear girl, but I thought you ought to know what's happening. I've been down to the farm and—'

'How is he?' I asked dully.

'Mad as blazes, but luckily the shot only nicked him.'

'I meant Tom.'

'Oh, Tom's up and about. Couldn't keep him in bed. Nursing a gorgeous headache, but—'

'And Philip?'

'Ah.' He twitched thoughtfully at his lower lip. 'Much as you'd expect. Bit of a black eye, bruised pride, standing on his dignity. But he'll survive. I deduce you were with him last night.'

'Is that what he said?'

'He said I should ask *you*. But I'm not a fool, Kate. I heard and saw what went on last night. So did the others. It's bound to come out.'

I didn't argue – what was the point? 'Did he say anything? Send any message?'

Eyes cloudy with sympathy, Frank shook his head. 'No. I'm sorry.'

Feeling as if my brain might explode with the weight of misery it was carrying, I burst out, 'Uncle Frank, is it true what Vicky told me? Is it true that I'm . . . that I'm not William Brand's daughter?'

I saw his face change, and I knew – yes, it was true. He knew. Everyone knew. Everyone but me! Unable to bear it, I turned over and covered my head with my arms.

'Kate, my dear—'

'Don't do that! Don't fudge. Oh, why didn't you tell me? I thought you were my friend!'

'I *am*. I always shall be. But you are who you are. Whoever your parents were, you can't change it. It's hardly relevant at present.'

Hardly relevant! How could he say that? It was the most important thing in the world, for me!

'I'm more concerned for poor old Tom,' he said. 'We've got to protect him. Listen, Katie . . . when you heard those shots . . . how many times did the gun go off?'

I had to force my mind back to last night: it seemed like a bad dream. 'Twice.'

'You're sure that was all?'

Heaving round to look at him, I said, 'Wasn't it enough?'

Frank leaned against the dresser, sighing. 'Twice too many, I fear. The thing is, old girl, I went to look at the place by daylight and . . . I found a shotgun lying in the undergrowth.'

'Mad Jack must have dropped it.'

'No, he didn't. It's one of our guns – one that Garret had charge of. The damn fool knows Tom's not allowed access to firearms, but he must have left this one lying about. He denies it, of course, but then he would. I've put it away and locked up the guncases securely now, but that's rather shutting the stable door after the horses are fled. The thing is, Kate, both barrels had been discharged.'

'Does Tom remember using the gun?'

'Sadly, yes, though it was dark and he's not too coherent about it. It looks as though he disturbed Mad Jack, shot at him and hit the dog instead. When Mad Jack went for him, Tom stumbled and his second shot went high as he fell backwards – only a pellet or two found their mark. That's what the old man swears, and the evidence appears to bear him out. Which is, of course, fearfully bad news for Tom.'

'You mean . . .' I breathed, 'all Mr Farcroft did was defend himself?'

'He wasn't even carrying a gun – he was using snares, he claims. They're threatening to prosecute, but I reminded them that the old man was trespassing, poaching. He's been warned more than once . . .' He shook his head, rubbing the back of his neck and pulling at his long dark-gold locks. 'I think they may let discretion rule, this time. Meanwhile, regarding you and young Philip . . . I'm afraid the game's up. I'm beastly sorry about it, old thing, and I'll do my best to pour oil on choppy seas, but I think it might be a jolly idea for you to pack your things and get back to London. Stay there until the dust settles. I mean to say, it's simply not on with you and him, is it?'

'No,' I said dully, lying back and letting my arm cover my eyes. 'I do know right from wrong, Uncle Frank. I'd already decided I would never see Philip again.'

'Right,' he murmured. 'Fine. We'll say no more about it, then.'

I had forgotten his aversion to awkward subjects – his sister's disgrace and now his niece's brush with mortal sin. Of course he hadn't wanted to tell me the truth before now. How do you tell a child she's a bastard whose existence shames the whole family?

As he made for the door, I propped myself up, struck by an anomaly. 'What did you say – about the dog?'

Frank looked round. 'Dog?'

'Tom shot the dog, you said. Which dog? Boss?'

'I didn't hear its name. It was a bitch. Philip's dog.'

'*Bess?*' Oh, no! 'Is she badly hurt?'

' 'Fraid so, old lady. He had to put her down. Did it himself, so he said. She was in pup, too. Bally awful business all round.' And he departed, leaving me feeling sick and cold. Poor Bess. And oh! Philip . . .

I wrote to Philip, using up sheafs of paper in aborted starts before I settled for brevity and candour, expressing my sorrow for his loss of Bess and for his father's injuries, and adding, as gently as I could, that we would be better to forget each other – because of the huge rift between our families. I wished him well, and I signed it, not without a certain ironic bitterness, '*Catherine Louise Brand*'. No, I didn't tell him the real reason we must part. How could I? His own mother had said nothing, not even to her husband – if Mad Jack had suspected the truth he would surely have said something before now. His wife must have thought she had done enough by parting the young pair. Perhaps she herself had never known what consequence had resulted: the Rhys-Thomases had obviously preferred to keep their shame to themselves rather than admit to having a grandchild in common with their deadliest enemies.

I sent the letter to the farm. No reply ever came.

After returning to London, I heard that Tom had recovered and apparently taken no real harm, for which I was thankful. No legal proceedings arose from either side: my family were protecting Tom by keeping silent, and Mad Jack had good reason to avoid courts of law. So the feud remained unresolved, quietly simmering its brew of bitterness.

Meanwhile I went about my life: I worked in the museum,

compiled charts and attended lectures; and I wrote – articles, speeches, pamphlets – anything to stop me from thinking. But beneath the skin of normality my emotions veered from anger to despair, shame to bitterness. I missed Philip so sorely that I imagined I saw him everywhere – a turn of head, a glimpse of profile, the way a stranger walked . . . Each time my heart leapt with gladness, then plummeted back into a pit of despair as I realized that, even if the man had been Philip, our meeting would only bring more pain. He was my uncle, I his niece: the half-blood made no difference.

If only Mother had given me some hint about avoiding the Farcrofts! I blamed her for my unhappiness; I blamed Mad Jack; I blamed poor Tom. I even blamed Philip. But most of all I blamed myself. Had I truly loved Philip? Or had I been drawn to him because I was wilful and disobedient, attracted by the excitement of forbidden fruit? With Mother's example bleak in her mind, Grandmother had had every reason to doubt me, but she had generously accepted my word over Carl-Heinz and given me a chance to prove myself. How cruelly I had repaid her, by betraying her trust, by sneaking out to meet Philip, by telling lies . . . Perhaps, after all, I was exactly like Mother.

Knowing that I deserved no forgiveness, I wrote Grandmother a difficult letter, confessing my sins of dishonesty but vowing that Philip and I had never been lovers – not that I put it that way: I said something like '*if ever I do marry, I shall be able to don pure white without qualms*'. Well, I was young, and had literary pretensions. Grandmother replied thanking me for my letter. However, '*words must be exemplified by deeds*'. I assured myself I would be blameless, from now on: I would never rebel, never stray from the narrow path, never look twice at another man. Vain hope.

Seeking to change my inner self by altering the outer, I had my hair bobbed and clubbed. The fashion was new – outrageous to some – but I told myself it was more in keeping with my new, ascetic lifestyle: long hair took up too much time; it was a vanity, an irrelevance. Cutting it off was, I suppose, a kind of penance. But I soon came to like it. No more curling tongs, no more pins and padding, no more huge hats – outmoded now, anyway. I took to neat cloche hats and tailored suits. I even wore trousers when I felt especially mutinous.

Eschewing more pleasurable pursuits, I spent my free time in the East End with Sylvia Pankhurst and her followers, including Miss H, in a soup kitchen doling out rations to ragged, half-starved creatures who could still laugh at their own troubles: their fortitude tweaked my conscience. I used their needs as an excuse for not going to Norfolk at Christmas. Grandmother didn't argue. She probably feared, as I did, that if I went home no power on earth could have kept me from communicating with Philip.

Gentle Win Leeming questioned my motives for undertaking so much social work. When she said Miss H was leading me astray, we quarrelled over it. But Win may have been right. During a heated discussion about the rights and wrongs of arson, Miss H accused me of being 'damned by your German upbringing. That's the trouble with that nation. Frightened to go against authority, even when it's in the wrong! Even if it leads 'em over a cliff, like lemmings. You're brainwashed, Kate Brand – afraid to stand up and be counted a dissenter.'

'I'm not!' said I hotly. 'And I'll prove it.'

Which is why, one bitter February evening, I found

myself among a crowd of men, women and children, marching with placards and banners, singing as we went, 'See, the light of dawn is breaking . . .' We planned to disrupt a meeting where hostile councillors were speaking against the WSPU.

Beneath my skirts, calico bags full of flints for breaking windows banged against my legs as I walked. Hermione Harmistead had talked me into carrying them, 'to prove yourself a true suffragette'. She strode beside me, her voice loud and clear raising the anthem, but my own throat felt dry, harbinger of a head cold. Ever a reluctant militant, I wished I had stayed indoors by the fire.

As we approached our target, we marched into darkness – the streetlamps in that area had been extinguished. Next moment, mounted police hemmed us in, jostling us against one another, herding us into a cul-de-sac where other policemen waited. We had expected resistance, but not a cowardly ambush. We were crushed together, women screaming, men shouting, squirming bodies, jabbing elbows, stones flying, sticks and truncheons flailing . . . As I fought to protect a smaller colleague from a horse's iron-shod hooves, something struck me on the head. Dazed, I fell, the weight of stones under my skirts pulling me down. Others fell on top of me. I found myself fighting for my life, hardly able to breathe . . .

I came to in a house I did not recognize, among kindly strangers who tended the walking wounded. Children cried pitifully – one little girl had been half blinded by an elbow, a young woman had been trampled by a horse. A token few had been arrested and dragged off – Miss H among them, I learned – the rest had dispersed, many of them bruised and bloodied as we were. Memories of the evening sickened me. Had it been necessary to send mounted men against a crowd made up largely of women and children?

I trailed back to Lincoln Square nursing fresh grievances, bruised all over, head aching and hair still matted with blood around the wound on the side of my head. Mrs Armes took one look at me and put me to bed, where I remained feeling sick, unable to eat, wanting communion with no one.

At my lowest ebb, I huddled by the fire in my room that night, nursing a hot whisky toddy which Mrs Armes had made to soothe my throat. I was about to go to bed when a tap on the door announced the arrival of Win. She stood in the doorway, still wearing her coat and hat, blinking through her gold-rimmed spectacles. We hadn't really spoken since our quarrel.

'You look perfectly frightful,' she informed me.

'Thank you,' said I without rancour. 'I *feel* frightful, so if you've come to lecture me again—'

'As a matter of fact . . . I've been to hear Mrs Bly. I know you don't approve, Kate, but her meetings are a comfort to me, and to my aunt. She's always pleased when I write and tell her Stanton came through.'

Who was I to argue? 'Did he come through tonight?' I asked thickly, blotting my nose on a damp hanky. 'Please – come in and shut the door. There's a terrible draught.'

She came, and stood drawing her gloves through her fingers, watching me with worried mouse-brown eyes. 'Kate . . . Miss Love is here.'

Miss Love? Who? I could hardly think for my thick head. '*Judy* Love? What – here in the house?'

'I asked her to come back with me. I thought you'd want to see her. The thing is, Kate, she was at the meeting tonight. She wanted to ask Black Hawk about a friend who's in hospital.' She paused, chewing her lip.

'And?' I prompted.

'The friend – the one who's ill . . . It's your uncle, Kate. It's Frank. He had an emergency operation this afternoon.'

Deciding that dying could wait, I ran down to the front parlour, where Judy Love sat on the edge of a chair nibbling her thumb. That evening her blond curls trailed over the mole-fur collar of a cheap plum-coloured coat. She overdressed, wore too much powder and lipstick, and I guessed she bleached her hair, but there was no artifice in the wan blue eyes. She had obviously been crying.

'You're ill!' she exclaimed when she saw me.

'Just a cold.'

Her glance questioned that, but she had other things on her mind – she was worried sick about Frank. 'When we were in Llandudno last year, he collapsed and they took him to hospital for tests. I was frantic, but we were just off to Amsterdam and I couldn't stop behind and let the girls down. Lor', was I *glad* to see him when he turned up in Paris.'

'You mean . . .' I couldn't take this in. 'He was travelling with you?'

'Not "with us" exactly, dear.' She gulped back her distress, dabbing at her tears with a wisp of darned lace. 'But he travels about doing his work and he often turns up to see us. We've kept in touch ever since that night you brought him round to the stage door after the show. Didn't you know?'

The medicinal whisky made my thoughts sluggish. 'Well . . . not exactly.'

'Anyway . . .' she went on, 'since Christmas I've been getting really worried. I finally persuaded him to go and see his doctor in Harley Street, and they rushed him into hospital. They were operating this afternoon. I went over there, but the ward sister's a dragon! Wouldn't give me ten seconds with him!' Fresh tears shimmered in her eyes as she blotted her nose. 'I said to Elsie, you'd have thought I wanted to *poison* him or something. I cried all the time I was doing my make-up for the show tonight. I didn't feel like singing and dancing, but you know how it is – the show must go on. I was in a right stew, though. Got my steps all wrong and forgot my words. As soon as we came off, I rushed round to Mrs Bly's – I thought Black Hawk might be able to give me some word of hope. He did say Frank would be all right, but—'

'I'm sure he will,' Win put in. 'The spirits know these things.'

I wanted to believe that, because suddenly I was afraid. Had I been too wrapped up in my own selfish problems to care about my favourite uncle?

The following afternoon, I took care to camouflage my bruises before I went to the hospital, where I waited with other prospective visitors in a draughty corridor, clutching a handkerchief to stifle my sneezes. Banging doors, muted voices and heavy footsteps echoed along a stone floor and winter light through high windows made the chocolate and pea-green decor ever more dreary. At length, the ward doors opened and a severe-faced nurse glared at us. 'Keep your voices down. Do not sit on the beds. And leave as soon as the bell rings.'

Long rows of beds lined the ward, patients swaddled like corpses under green coverlets. And the smell – carbolic soap and antiseptic covering less healthy odours . . . I have always hated hospitals.

Frank looked awful, hardly recognizable as himself, his face thin and yellow against starched pillows, his long hair matted and great hollows under his eyes. As I paused beside the bed, he looked at me with a glimmer of rueful humour.

'Hello, Kate.'

I could hardly speak for concern, resentment, and the cold in my head that had left me with a thumping headache. 'Why didn't you let me know?'

'What could you have done?'

'I could have *been* here!' I was sick with worry. 'Oh, Uncle Frank, why didn't you tell me you were so ill? Does anyone else know?'

They did not, it seemed. He hadn't wanted to worry the family.

'But you could tell Judy Love!' I accused him.

'Judy's a good friend of mine. I thought you liked her. She's very fond of *you*.'

'I do like her. But she's hardly the kind of person—'

'Snobbery, Kate?' His voice was weak, but the gentle reproval in it made me flush. 'You didn't scorn to fall for a farmer, I seem to recall.'

How could he tease me about *that*? A breath caught in my throat and set me coughing. I turned away, bent almost double by the paroxysm, leaning on a windowsill until the fit subsided and I slowly forced my painful lungs to expand again. Before I could properly recover, Judy Love rushed down the ward in a clatter of heels and a cloud of cheap perfume, her arms full of fruit, sweets, even a bunch of tight-budded early daffodils. 'Frank!' She threw her gifts on the bed and herself to her knees beside him. 'How are you, dear? You look terrible. How are you feeling?'

'Better for seeing you,' he replied with a fond smile that included both of us. 'But shouldn't you be on stage about now?'

'They cancelled the matinée. The water pipes froze last night. Floods all over the auditorium. So I said to Elsie, well, that's me off the hook, then, I'm off to see old Frank.

I couldn't wait, dear. What was it, then, what've they done?'

His problem, he said, had finally been diagnosed as an inflamed appendix which might have ruptured and killed him had it not been removed. I didn't follow it in detail, being too blocked up with cold, too worried, and anyway happily ignorant of things medical. Unlike many girls of my acquaintance, I had no secret yen to be a nurse.

'The thought of convalescence is pretty baleful,' he added, 'but my pals in Torquay will harbour me till the worst's over.'

'You ought to be at home – at Denes Hill!' I chafed.

Frank shook his head. 'No, Kate. They'd only fuss. The Mater can't abide anybody to be sick. It makes her angry. Reminds her of her own mortality. No, I won't trouble her. And I'm relying on you not to tell, either. That'll be several secrets you're keeping for me.'

His glance said he included in that his friendship with Judy.

Listening to them, watching her hold his hand so anxiously and tenderly, I felt myself the unwanted third. So I made excuses and left them together.

A freezing mist of ice and smoke hung in the air, grey veils through which noisy motors and clopping horse-drawn traffic vied for space and people hurried with hunched shoulders. Light-headed with fever and thoroughly sorry for myself, I was crossing a busy road junction when a crowded horse-drawn omnibus loomed out of the mist towards me. I seemed to hear someone call my name and when I glanced back I saw a dark, coat-clad figure, collar up and a homburg hat pulled low over his brow. Oliver? Before my fuddled mind could identify him for certain, the blare of a horn made me jump. A motor van came roaring out of the mist towards me. Oliver lunged for me, wrenching me out of the van's way, shouting annoyance at the driver. Then he dragged me with him to the further pavement where I leaned on a railing shaking, coughing, breathless with fright.

'You could get yourself killed stopping in the road like that!' he chafed, dark eyes snapping in the second before he got his first good look at me. 'Kate?' His horrified concern acted like a mirror, making me see the hollow-eyed wraith I had become in the past few months. I turned away, blundering into passersby who sidestepped to avoid me. But Oliver was close behind me, catching my arm. 'For heaven's sake, Kate, what's wrong? Mrs Armes told us you'd been hurt, but this . . .'

I glanced over my shoulder at him, bleary-headed. 'What? Mrs Armes . . . ?'

'Why do you think I'm here? Your grandmother sent me.'

They were using Mrs Armes to spy on me! Tucking my scarf more closely round my mouth, I forged on, dodging a lamppost that seemed to leap from nowhere. 'Why can't people mind their own business!'

'I only wish someone had informed us before now! You didn't get this thin in a few days. And certainly not as a result of one suffragette demonstration.' When I made no reply he caught my arm, stopping me. 'What is it, Kate? Please, talk to me. Are you ill? Mrs Armes says you're not eating.'

'How can I eat,' I cried, 'when my friends are on hunger strike, being tortured in prison, and people everywhere are starving?'

'That's emotional twaddle! What good will it do them if you kill yourself? My dear girl . . .' He moved closer, taking hold of me, the worried note in his voice destroying all my pretensions. 'Kate, my dear . . .'

'Oh, Oliver!' I leaned on him helplessly, because he was there, because he was familiar, because he cared . . .

With an arm about my shoulders, he hailed a passing hackney – one of the old-style horse-drawn cabs – and helped me into it, telling the driver, 'Anywhere,' before climbing in after me and closing the door. The cab smelled of old leather and tobacco smoke. Blinds across the windows cloaked the interior in kindly shadows, shutting out curious eyes, rushing traffic and clinging, choking fog.

When my tears defied all efforts to stem them, Oliver drew me against him and held me as I wept against the astrakhan revers of his coat. Months of grief, knotted into one numb mass, began to unravel. It was the first time I had really cried over losing Philip. Now, as if a dam had burst, I thought the tears might never stop.

After a while, Oliver bent his head over mine, gentle fingers stroking a strand of damp hair from my face. 'Kate,' he murmured. 'Kate, my dear . . . Enough. You'll make yourself ill. Please . . .'

Strong, warm fingers hooked under my chin and I felt his moustache soft against my cheek in the moment before his lips brushed my skin, light as the caress of a falling leaf, tasting my tears. He murmured soothing words, whispering comfort as if I were a child. And I needed comfort. I needed someone to care. I had felt so alone . . .

Responding to the gentle pressure of his hand under my chin, I turned my head and let him kiss me. It began as gratitude, allowing him a moment of intimacy as a reward for his kindness, but when his mouth hardened something jolted inside me and I found myself reaching up to slide my hands round his neck and answer him in kind. But my head was growing lighter, black wings threatening to claim me.

I twisted away, ducked my head and hid my burning face in his black silk scarf. Beneath my ear his heart, too, sounded erratic and he was breathing fast, his arms hard around me. 'Kate . . .' he whispered.

'Did you hear what you told the cabby?' I wheezed. ' "Anywhere." He might be taking us to Land's End. Or John o' Groat's.'

'Shall I tell him Gretna Green? No . . .' as I tried to move, 'stay where you are. Rest, my love. You're not well. I'll take you home.'

I relaxed against him, wishing all this scene unplayed. He was right – I did feel unwell; my lungs struggled for every breath and not only my face but my whole body was burning. My head seemed to be floating, then swooping like a seagull. Standing on the edge of a black pit, I succumbed to growing faintness which took me spiralling down, down, into warm dark clouds of nothingness.

SEVENTEEN

I have Mrs Armes and Win to thank for my care, and possibly my life, for I myself knew little about the next week or two as I fought the effects of pneumonia. When at last I began to take note again, spring had arrived. My convalescence dragged on towards Easter.

Through Judy Love, I heard that Uncle Frank was recovering. He had been annoyed when the family found out about his illness; he had blamed me, until he had discovered that Oliver was responsible. He had also heard that Oliver was now visiting my sickbed. According to Judy, my uncle was 'dreadfully worried about you, dear. Seems to be afraid you're getting too thick with Mr Wells.' I was not sorry when, after Frank departed for Torquay, his girlfriend went on tour again and stopped playing go-between.

During those weeks, Oliver came to London frequently, bringing me snowdrops, violets, and messages of concern from Grandmother. I gathered that if I remained tractable she might be prepared to overlook earlier sins, especially if I were kind to Oliver. What Vicky thought of it all I don't know: she didn't communicate with me. Oliver said that, when business obliged him to call at Denes Hill, she hardly spoke to him.

My two nurses coyly withdrew when he called, evidently considering him a welcome suitor, whose presence could only aid my recovery. They both found him charming – Mrs Armes said he reminded her of her late husband, and Win repeated her assertions that older men were more reliable.

One April weekend, Oliver and I sat quietly in separate chairs either side of the fire in the drawing room of the house on Lincoln Square. I was drifting, cocooned by the warmth from the fire and the soft hug of the shawl Mother had made me. Even so, when Oliver leaned for a fourth time to stir the fire and add another coal, I realized he hadn't spoken for at least ten minutes.

'Oliver . . .' I ventured. 'You know, it's not necessary for you to keep coming every weekend. I'm much better now. I'm even starting to catch up with my studying. If there's something you would rather be doing . . .'

Sombre bark-brown eyes sought to read my soul. 'I thought you looked forward to my visits.'

'I do. You know I do.'

'You also know, do you not, that my feelings for you are unchanged?'

Unable to bear that steady gaze, I glanced at the fire. Of course I knew. But while it went unspoken I could pretend it didn't exist. 'Yes.'

'Then I think I have a right to be told the truth.'

A little ripple of warning stirred at my nape. Oliver was no fool. He had seen how thin and ill grief had made me; he had held me while I wept. 'About what?'

'I think you know about what.'

I got up and, clasping my shawl more closely round my shoulders, went to stare out of the bay window. In the gardens at the heart of the square, birds flitted and buds plumped the end of every branchlet. Sunlight fell bright through lace curtains, drawing attention to the cushion-like cactus which bristled with tiny acid-yellow flowers on a table in the bay.

'Even Giorgio seems to think it's spring,' I remarked.

'Giorgio?'

'The cactus. Mrs Armes calls it Giorgio. This is the first time I've seen it in flower.'

'I believe cacti are rather unpredictable in that respect,' Oliver said, and I heard the cushions whisper as he got up. 'Kate . . . why are we discussing house plants?'

Aware that he was coming closer, I blurted, 'You do know that . . . that I was seeing Philip Farcroft last summer?'

He was silent for what seemed a long time, then answered slowly, 'It . . . has been mentioned.' Of course it had – Grandmother told him everything.

'Did they also mention why I had to stop seeing him?'

'Because of Tom?'

'If only that were all! Oliver . . . Will you tell me something?'

A slight pause, then: 'If I'm able.'

I glanced round, wanting to see his face as I asked 'Did you know that Vicky and Emmet sometimes refer to me as "C.L.B."?'

But Oliver was a lawyer, skilled in hiding his thoughts. 'Those are your initials.'

'They mean something else, too. I'm not William Brand's daughter, am I?' Though his face was still, his silence gave me the answer. 'It's all right, Oliver. Vicky told me.'

'Poisonous brat!' His eyes narrowed as he came and took me firmly by the shoulders. 'You mustn't mind her, Kate.'

'I don't mind. In a way, I'm grateful she showed me the letter.'

'Letter?' Oliver queried.

'A letter from Mrs Farcroft. In which she told Grandfather

that her stepson, Michael, and my mother ... she caught them together. In the hay loft, she said.' My face burned, my head felt tight. 'So they sent Mother away, and found her a suitable husband. Didn't they?'

A long sigh breathed out of him and I saw the sorrow in his dark eyes. 'One heard rumours, naturally, but I have never known who the man was. This explains a great deal.'

'It should also explain why I stopped seeing Philip.'

He took a moment to think about that, no expression on his face. 'He knows about this?'

'No, of course he doesn't! If he had known I was Michael's daughter, he'd have crossed the world to avoid me. How can you even think—'

'I meant now. Did you tell him?'

'No.' Restless, I edged further away, drawn to stare at the glowing fire as I rubbed my cheek on my shawl. 'I ... I wrote and told him we must never meet again, but I didn't say why. I'd hurt him enough. I couldn't spoil his memories of Michael.'

'Oh, my dear ...' He made a move as if to comfort me, but my instinctive stiffening made him stop and, after a moment, he went to stare out through the netted window.

I heard myself say in a small voice, 'I'm sorry, Oliver.'

His hand, against the window frame, knotted into a fist and when he looked round grim lines bracketed his mouth. '*How* did you get involved with Philip Farcroft? How did you ever ...' I saw the memory hit him like a cold sponge. 'Was that him at the library that day? Under the Greyfriars Tower in the rain? Damn! I knew he looked familiar, but I couldn't place ...' Softly on the carpeted floor, he strode back and stood before me, dark eyes intent on my face as he took me by the shoulders, his hands warm and supportive. 'My dear ... You're vulnerable, just as your mother was.

Like her, you yearn for love and security. But you look for it in the wrong places. Forbidden fruit can be sweet, I know. The danger, the excitement, the allure . . .'

'It was more than that!' I protested, hearing him voice my own doubts.

'Was it? Are you sure? And what was it for him – a chance to get back at his father's enemies?'

'No!' I could not believe that. Not of Philip. 'You don't know him, Oliver. He's not like his father. He's straight, and honest, and . . . oh, he has too much mulish pride, at times. But he's a decent man. A good man.'

Oliver regarded me gravely, slowly removing his hands from my shoulders. 'You're still in love with him.'

In the red heart of the fire, a yellow tongue of flame leapt into life. It jumped and wavered through my threatening tears. 'I was.' *Was, am, have been, will be*, I thought hopelessly: *I shall always love him*. 'I'm sorry, Oliver.'

'That's what you always say: "I'm sorry, Oliver." '

Sensing his dejection, I touched his arm. 'You asked for the truth.'

'I know.' Pain lurked in the depths of his dark eyes, but their gaze was clear and steady. His fingers fastened softly round mine and he drew me closer, his glance flicking to my mouth. 'I do understand, my dear. I've felt that same anguish, as you know. So I'm able to tell you, though you may not believe it now, it will pass. You will love again – perhaps not in the same way. But perhaps even more surely. Excitement doesn't last. Friendship does. Security, mutual trust . . .'

Nearness drove his face out of focus and as I closed my eyes I felt his mouth claim mine with a sensual sweetness that stirred me in spite of myself. *Yes*, I thought. *Yes, Oliver!*

Make me forget that you're not the man I want. Make me forget that the man I want is forbidden to me for ever. I liked to be kissed. I needed to be kissed. And he knew how to do it. But when he held me closer, pressing his body to mine, the hardness at his groin startled me and I stiffened, making a little space between us. A pair of dark, dark eyes asked silent questions and gave me frankly sexual answers, while my veins ran with fires I had thought only Philip could wake. The realization shocked me: I was not in love with Oliver, yet my flesh responded to him. As did his body to mine.

He said steadily, 'You know how I feel about you, Kate. That will never change. If ever you need me, I shall be there. But I, too, have my share of pride. I shall not come begging, ever again. Next time, the initiative must come from you.' He leaned to brush his lips against my brow, said, 'Goodbye, my dear,' and, turning lightly on his heel, left the room.

He would come back, I thought, watching the closing door. He wouldn't just go away. He was testing me. But a few moments later I heard the front door open and from the window I saw him leave, pulling on his hat and coat as he took the steps two at a time and strode off down the street without a backward glance.

Nor did he come back. Not that day. Not the next weekend, nor the next . . . He didn't write to me, either. After a while, I realized that he had meant what he said – he would not come back without some clear sign from me that he was wanted.

Lingering debility after my illness gave me an excuse for drifting, not thinking too deeply, as the months passed and spring edged towards summer. Not only was I grieving for

Philip, whom I could never have, but I felt guilty for hurting Oliver, who loved me in spite of my faults.

That May I reached my majority – a singularly cheerless Sunday which was also, sadly, the anniversary of Harry's death. Apart from a few cards and a fruit cake baked by Mrs Armes, my wish for 'no fuss' was granted. My personal darkness must have made me an uncomfortable companion: everyone stepped round me cautiously, as if I were an unexploded bomb.

Having sat my final exams, I let Win persuade me to go with her to the West Country – anything to avoid facing reality.

Safe in Devon, at first I slept – how I slept! Then slowly the good air, the plain food and the lazy pace of life on the edge of Exmoor began their work of spiritual healing.

On a hot, drowsy day in early August, I walked up to what had become a favourite retreat, a secluded fold of the Exmoor hills, where a stream meandered and trees guarded slopes thick with bracken. There I sat with my thoughts, heat soaking through my light summer dress, until the sound of the stream enticed me to take off my shoes and stockings and step into the cooling flow, treading carefully on hard, smooth pebbles. I always loved to paddle; it set my mind free. Sunlight dappled through the straw weave of my hat, glancing bright darts across the ripples, while small fish became visible as they passed beneath my shadow. For the first time in almost a year, friendly thoughts flickered around me, presences elusive as the fish about my feet, but just as real. Just as they had been on a day long ago, on the beach at Eveningham, where my uncle John had been swimming out where the channel ran deep. I had been wading towards him when the sea fret came rolling in—

The clarity of that memory jerked me back to the present, to stare dazedly round at the empty valley, the guardian trees on the hills. For a moment John had been close, his presence stirring the fronds of hair that brushed my cheek as he urged me to remember . . . No, it had gone, for now. But it was coming back. One day I would grasp and hold it. One day soon.

Looking about with awakened eyes, I knew how Persephone must have felt, emerging from the bleak winter of Hades. The past year of my life was a half-remembered nightmare. But I had come through it. Scarred and chastened, perhaps, but ready at last to go on.

A new sound intruded – the putter of a small engine. As I looked round, sunlight semaphored off glass, momentarily dazzling me; a motorcyclist was making up the valley, weaving around ruts and grassy extrusions. The wind flapped in loose sporting clothes – he looked as if he were ready for a set of tennis – and his body hunched over the handlebars of the bumping bike. But it was his long hair, blowing wildly behind him from under the strap of the goggles, that gave me the clue to his identity. Shading my eyes against the glare, I saw that the rider was my uncle Frank.

The set look to his mouth made me aware of the chill of the water, soaking into my feet and up my legs, as he came bumping up to the bank of the stream. There he stopped and let the engine die, long legs braced either side of the machine. In the silence, the stream resumed its chuckling, a sheep bleated from the hillside and a last late cuckoo called its altered note.

'About time!' was his greeting.

'Uncle Frank!' Did I look as stupefied as I felt? 'Where have you come from?'

He answered me literally: 'Torquay, actually. The early

train.' Leaning back, he pushed the goggles up, revealing a tanned face streaked with sweat and dust. 'I hired the bike in the village. Win told me you were up here, but it's taken me an hour to find you.' He leapt off the bike and heaved it on to its stand; then, standing straddled with arms akimbo, he chafed, 'Look at you – paddling like an infant! Fiddling while Rome burns! How much longer do you plan to hide away here licking your wounds?'

That stung. 'I'm not hiding!'

'Then what would you call it? For God's sake, Kate, you can't keep behaving like a blessed ostrich. Not now. It's your world, too. Don't you care that it's going to blazes in a barrel?'

What was he talking about?

'All Europe's mobilizing!' he exclaimed, throwing out his arms in exasperation. 'Germany's on the march. They've declared war on France and Russia. They're already in Luxembourg and moving on Belgium – which means *we* shall be declaring war any hour. It's happening, Kate! The Great War. It's started!'

The Great War . . . The thing we had all feared for so long.

How had it happened so suddenly?

In recent weeks the shadow had loomed no larger than for years past. The fuss over the assassination of the Archduke Franz Ferdinand in Sarajevo had seemed a local problem between Teuton and Slav, which might perhaps draw the Continental powers into conflict. But, last time I had looked at a newspaper, headlines had warned of danger in Ireland, not Europe. I couldn't take it in.

Ignoring possible ruination of his shoes, Frank strode straight into the stream and shook me forcibly, blue eyes blazing. 'Wake up, Kate! We've got to get home. Win's coming back to London with us, but you and I are heading for Denes Hill. The family should be together while we sort out what this will mean to us all.'

The London train was crowded with people returning early from holidays, regular soldiers reporting back to duty, and Territorials heading for their nearest depot. Territorials ... Philip ... Fresh posters screamed the message of mobilization and people stood in animated groups, pouncing on anyone with the latest edition of a newspaper. As we neared London, more passengers crammed in at every stop and the rash of uniforms grew thicker. Rumours abounded, most of them false – the Germans had landed in Kent; Paris had been bombed by Zeppelins; British people in Europe were desperate to get out before they were caught in the fighting, or interned for the duration ...

Hearing that, Frank relieved the speaker of his paper and read the article for himself, his face grim. 'Damn it! Judy's in Strasbourg.' My heart beat erratically, with both apprehension and excitement. It was happening. Really happening.

By the time we arrived in London, Germany had invaded neutral Belgium; Britain had delivered an ultimatum, demanding that Germany withdraw her troops, and now the government awaited a reply before the deadline at midnight, European time. The city thronged with jubilant people clamouring for news, shouting support for Belgium and for our government's stance against the Kaiser.

Having seen Win safely into a taxi, bound for Lincoln Square, Frank and I made our way through the turmoil in the streets to the apartment off Pall Mall, where we dumped our luggage, ate a hasty supper and went out again to see what was happening. We found Westminster and Charing

Cross brightly lit, crammed with people waving Union Jacks and singing 'Rule Britannia'. A mob jostled with police along Carlton House Terrace, hissing and booing, shouting abuse as they fought to get near the German embassy. As we hurried by we heard windows shattering as stones found their mark. Another mass of people moved along the Mall under a velvet-blue dome full of stars, past beds of geraniums blazing scarlet in electric streetlight. It was impossible not to share the excitement.

Outside Buckingham Palace, tension spread among the hushed, expectant mass of humanity as we watched the lighted windows in the great house and waited for the deadline to expire. The Privy Council was in session. We clearly heard Big Ben chiming beyond the dark expanse of St James's Park and, as the clock struck the hour, a man emerged from the palace to pin up a notice. Amid cheers and general excitement, the King and Queen, and the Prince of Wales appeared on the palace balcony. The word spread – Britain was at war.

Along with manic rejoicing, hatred of all things German surfaced among the milling crowds, jeers aimed at 'the Hun', loud boasts of what 'our boys' would do to them. Before Frank and I retreated to the safety of the apartment, we were caught up in the rush to smash a shop window where a tobacconist had on display some Meerschaum pipes which the crowd grabbed and broke and stamped on in glee. The atmosphere of mindless loathing terrified me.

Though I went to bed, I couldn't sleep. At three a.m. I got up and stood in the apartment's main room staring out of the tall window. People still moved about the streets below. Now and then raised voices, or splintering glass, could be heard. Were similar stupidities being enacted in Berlin? What was happening to Mother and the little boys at Lindhafen? For me, one bad dream had flowed straight into another, separated by a brief period of bucolic wool-gathering.

Usually I enjoyed the ultra-modern decor of the flat, but tonight it felt inhumanly ascetic. It was palely bathed in the mellow light from a pink glass lampshade held by the graceful draped figure of a young nymph moulded in bronze – she reminded me of the portrait Frank had painted of me, draped against an oak tree. Inevitably, that reminded me of Philip. Everything that night reminded me of Philip.

'Can't you sleep?' Frank asked as he came in, drawing his dressing gown securely over a pair of scarlet linen pyjamas.

Curtain rings rattled as I pulled the drapes across, shutting out the sight of the street below. The night was warm but I felt cold and wished I had more protection than my nightdress and light wrap. 'No more than you can, apparently. Are you worried about Judy?'

He was lighting a cigarette, squinting against the smoke. 'She'll be all right. Resourceful ladies, the Gala Girls.' But he stopped to consider the glowing end of his cigarette, adding in a different tone, 'Yes, I'm concerned about her. And not only her. It's to be hoped this whole damned show is over before half the world gets tangled up in it. Fancy some tea? Or chocolate?'

'I'd prefer coffee.'

His grin was more wry grimace. 'Now that we're awake, might as well stay awake, eh?' Opening a cupboard in the panelling, he took out the phone to call the night porter.

The coffee arrived, strong and steaming hot, accompanied by a plate of fancy biscuits, all delivered by a uniformed boy. Frank gave him a handsome tip and sent him away, then poured for us both. 'Come and sit down, old girl. Are you cold?' Responding to my shiver, he lit the gas fire and sat crouched on the end of the cushioned fender while I curled in an armchair with my hands wrapped round a coffee cup.

We talked about the war, what it might mean, what might happen . . . Neither of us was equipped to predict the future. No one was. But we foresaw that this war would be worse than any war before it, because of new weaponry – bombs, guns, submarines, airships – even aeroplanes might play a part, not to mention the tanks so horrifically predicted by H. G. Wells and even now being tested at Thorne-Thomas Engineering. Frank said Emmet could win a knighthood because of them; it was a bad joke. I only hoped that popular belief was right, that it would all be over very soon and we could carry on our lives as if nothing had happened. But every train of thought brought me back to the same frightening question . . .

'Why are they calling up the Territorials?'

'I suppose they're mustering all the forces they have.'

'I thought the yeomanry defended their own home area. They won't be sent abroad, will they?'

'I wouldn't know. Judging by the mood today, most of them would be only too glad to have a go at a real live Hun.'

It had seemed that way to me, too. I stared down into my cup, willing myself to be calm. But the coffee rippled as if an earthquake were rocking it as I thought not only of Philip but of all the young men answering the call, eager to offer themselves to the gods of war. Was my stepbrother Fritzi among the soldiers who had marched into Luxembourg? And Carl-Heinz, and Willi? Riding proudly on their chargers with banners flying and drums beating . . . '*You* wouldn't go, would you?'

315

He thought about that, staring down at the carpet for long silent moments, then:'Not to fight, no. I can understand the appeal of it – the romance, the excitement, the pride and patriotism. But when I think about what it actually involves . . . No, Kate, I couldn't do it. I couldn't take a human life.'

'I'm glad.' At least he would be safe, then. But his certainty puzzled me. 'I thought you didn't believe in God.'

'Who mentioned him?' he asked sardonically. 'We're talking morality, not religion. I make choices out of respect for my fellow man – and for myself – not for fear of hell or hope of heaven. What about you?'

My own creed was less easily defined. I found myself confused about many things, my loyalties torn. But of one thing I was sure: 'I want to do *something* useful. But I hate strife. I couldn't even put jam in a post box on behalf of Votes for Women. I . . . I did once go on a protest march, with stones hidden about my person, but I'm not sure I could have thrown them.'

'I heard about that,' he informed me with a glimmer of amusement.

'Miss H called me a "mindless slave of duty" – like that poor idiot Frederick in *The Pirates of Penzance*. It's not that I'm wonderfully good, or wonderfully moral, it's just . . . I was brought up to live by certain rules. Does that make me a fool? Or a coward?'

'Sometimes it takes more courage not to join in with the crowd.'

That was a comforting thought. 'But I shall write about it. "The pen is mightier than the sword." '

'The brush, too,' he added. 'And the camera. I couldn't be a fighting man, but what I *can* do is record it, in all its horror and glory. It might persuade future generations to be more careful.'

'Perhaps.' But it was the present generation that worried me.

'Anyway,' he said bracingly, changing the subject adroitly as always, 'war or no war, life goes on. What do you plan to do, now you've finished college?'

'I really don't know, except that I want to write.'

I was, in fact, blessed with several choices. If I stayed in London, I might follow a career in journalism; the suffragettes might provide a cause, and work with the disadvantaged; and a professor of history had offered me a post as his research assistant. In Norfolk, Grandmother offered the possibility of my taking a job at Chef Foods, and Saffron had intimated that, if I worked in Lynn, I would be welcome to live with her at Hawthorn House – had they, for once, got together and decided it might be wise to distance me from Far Drove Farm?

'Probably,' Frank agreed. 'They also seem determined to throw you at Wells. He's practically taken over at Chef Foods, you know. Oh, George Chorley's nominally manager, but Wells holds a watching brief.'

'H.G.?' I joked.

'I might prefer him as a nephew-in-law,' he said darkly. 'I'd almost prefer young Farcroft to—'

I winced. 'That's not funny, Uncle Frank.'

'No, maybe not. Sorry.'

'I do wish you could like Oliver more,' I sighed. 'I think you misjudge him. Did you know he was in love with Mother once?'

Frank snorted. 'I remember him mooning round after her, along with half the men in the county. Not that she was interested, except that he added to her tally of conquests. So now he latches on to you. Couldn't get Clara, so he'll settle for her daughter.'

'It's not like that!' I objected.

'Isn't it? Well, if you say so. Madly in love with him, are you?'

If anyone else had put the question so bluntly, I might have been affronted, but since it was Frank I tried to answer honestly. 'I'm . . . fond of him. Oh, I know he's older than I am, but I believe he cares for me. I'm sure he'd make a fine husband.'

His whole face sharpened. 'Has he proposed?'

'Not in so many words.'

He shook his head, giving a dry laugh as he unfolded himself stiffly from his seat on the fender. 'Well, I can't advise you, old lady. I'm sadly prejudiced. Besides, when it comes to matters of the heart I've found it wiser to keep out of other people's business. It's hard enough sorting out my own love life.'

'Judy Love?'

Sighing, he pulled a face. 'Can you imagine her at Denes Hill? I adore the girl, but, well . . . while the Mater's there . . .'

'She wouldn't be happy.'

'Neither would Judy.'

'It was Judy I meant.' Imagining Judy Love at Denes Hill was as difficult as imagining myself in Lynn: Mrs Oliver G. Wells, wife of the sturdy, successful – and sensual – solicitor.

Only a year ago, I had seen my future at Far Drove Farm. Making pickles, salting hams, feeding chickens, brewing beer for the harvest supper in the barn, watching Philip stride his broad acres of good English soil and listening to him sing: 'To be a farmer's boy . . .' A year ago, I had felt in my bones that the farm was where I belonged. Perhaps it was. But not because of Philip. Maybe I felt an affinity

with the farm because it was where my natural father had
lived and died.

I caught myself longing for Philip, remembering, aching,
wishing for the impossible, and wondering how, why,
when . . . It was no good: before I could decide which path
to choose for the future, I had to clear the debris of the past.
The only person who could help me was Mother and, since
she didn't – couldn't – answer letters, I must go to see her.
Only she could tell me what I needed to know – how she
had felt; why it had happened. Whether the von Wurthes
liked it or not, tomorrow I would go and arrange to journey
back . . .

But the thought died before it properly formed. I couldn't
go to Germany, could I? The war . . . I had all but forgotten
the war.

EIGHTEEN

Struggling through the teeming city next morning, bound
for Liverpool Street station, Frank and I passed squads of
marching soldiers and sailors and dodged ladders on which
bill-posters poised, slapping glue as they plastered hoardings
with the call to arms. Newsstands echoed headlines telling
of marching armies and refugees; crowds gathered around
food shops in the hunt for supplies which, rumour said, might
soon run short if German submarines laid siege to the British
Isles; and, outside designated 'recruiting stations', men of
all types and ages queued by the hundred to sign on for the
army, eager to fight the dastardly Hun. Every voice had
another slant to the latest rumour, or some cry of aggressive
patriotism. I was inevitably reminded of Miss H and her
calls for violence in another cause – to me, the war talk
seemed equally misguided.

We settled into a first-class compartment, supplied with
a selection of newspapers in which I immersed myself while
my uncle got out his sketch pad and began jotting little
cartoons and ideas. As yet, the news was confusing: no one
knew quite what was happening, what was going to happen,
or how life would be affected in the short while the war
was expected to last. In Germany and Austria, British people
were being arrested, while in Britain anyone with a foreign
background or accent was suddenly suspect: parliament had
introduced new laws for dealing with aliens, especially those

of German blood; they were to be questioned and interned for the duration. 'Just as well you settled for being "Miss Brand",' Frank said when I read out this news in disbelief. 'Otherwise, there might have been awkward questions to answer.'

'How do you think it will affect Mother?' I asked.

'Hardly at all. She's Frau von Wurthe – mother to three little blue-blooded Prussians. That alone should be enough to protect her.'

Hoping he was right, I went back to the papers, which told how an Expeditionary Force of regular soldiers would probably go to Belgium, while Territorials dealt with home defence; reserves and new recruits would be trained and held in readiness – already a stream of them were applying. But the general feeling was that life at home would go on much as usual. The armies of the Triple Alliance – Britain, France and mighty Russia – would very soon knock the Dual Alliance of Germany and Austro-Hungary for six. Not before time; they'd long been asking for it. Well, now they were going to get it, and after a bit of regrettable bloodshed the Kaiser and his ally would be put firmly in their place, our lads would be covered in glory, and perhaps the world could get back to normal.

But normality was a long way off that Wednesday morning.

At King's Lynn, the station hummed with excited suspense. Railway staff directed us out via a side entrance, keeping the platforms clear for the official party which was waiting to see off a special train filled with local troops – which explained the seething mass of spectators outside.

A downpour had left the ground steaming and puddles waited to soak an unwary foot as I hurried to keep up with my uncle's long strides. I lost him in the crush of people and then I saw him swing up to claim a place on the wall near St John's church, along with other men and excited boys who ought to have been in school. They hung from the railing, calling and whistling as they peered down the road for the first sign of the parade. Small children carried flags to wave. Faces were tense but bright. What an adventure it all was! What a show!

Two mounted policemen cleared the main route from the town centre, telling the gaping crowds to keep back. I found myself hemmed in behind an errand boy whose cycle basket was full of parcels of groceries, with other people clustering round me so that I was imprisoned behind the cycle's rear wheel, but with a clear view of the road.

'What's happening?' someone asked.

'That's the Terriers now leaving,' a man replied.

'Leaving for where?'

'For the war! Blast, bor, hen't you heard?'

Territorials . . . Oh, God. Hand to throat, I savoured the texture of the blue silk scarf Philip had given me on my twentieth birthday. Why had I put it on that morning, as a comfort or a torment? Had I hoped to see him? But not like this. Oh, not like this!

In the distance a bugle called, while a drum tapped a quick-march rhythm. The sound caught at my heart, stirring and thrilling it despite my mind's unease, as the parade came into sight, a moving mass in khaki service dress. Two senior officers led a long column of men marching four abreast with rifles shouldered, flanked by junior officers and helmeted constables. Beneath their smart military caps some faces were pale, some tanned, solemn or smiling, but all with sturdy purpose and steady gaze, arms swinging, boots crunching. I saw them through eyes filled with tears. They looked so proud. So fine.

322

Rejecting a thought too fearful to contemplate, I told myself they were not Philip's battalion: the Norfolk Yeomanry wore dark blue, with yellow flashes at revers and cuffs – Philip had been wearing that uniform when he came up to Denes Hill on the night of the ball. So these men couldn't be ... And then I saw him, on the nearside flank. That fine, tall subaltern in proud khaki, puttees making him look more long-legged than ever. He would pass within three feet of me. I might almost touch him.

My heart seemed to beat to the rhythm of marching boots as the column brought him ever closer. My insides seemed to turn over and lie quivering, leaving me dry-mouthed. My heart was unsteady, a vein in my temple pulsating with tension, but outwardly I stood frozen, unable to take my eyes from that lean, brown face. Oh, so familiar. Oh, so dear! I had forgotten how handsome he was. I'd forgotten how much I loved him, how the sight of him could make me want to cheer and weep all at the same time. Not at all the same emotion I felt for Oliver. What I felt for Oliver was darker, a thing of flesh and intellect rather than spirit. With Philip, despite obstacles between us, there had been mutual delight, brightness, rightness, heart and soul, mind and body. Now that I saw him again, the difference was clear. Which made the fate that had bound us too closely by blood all the more cruel.

As he came closer he looked through me, beyond me, then his glance darted back, widening in disbelief. No one else had eyes quite that green. No one else could hurt me so much by regarding me with such cold contempt. Did he recognize the scarf I was wearing like a talisman? Did he think I was there deliberately, to taunt him? I felt that I was drowning – drowning, or melting, or dying – as the advancing column drew him closer, and closer, until the inexorable moment when he was past me and moving away. Then, all I could see was the kit and greatcoat strapped to his back, and the backs of all the others similarly laden, as they rounded the corner and headed away, making for the station where the train hissed, sending up impatient gouts of smoke and steam. A dragon, come to carry all those fine young men away.

I stood transfixed, alone in a bubble of numb disbelief while about me the crowd cheered and waved. I couldn't forget the hard, set expression on Philip's face, or the hatred in his eyes, or the dull flush that had crept up his lean cheek. Two mounted policemen ended the official parade, but behind them came a sad straggle of women, some pushing prams, some with babes in arms, some holding children by the hand; each of them wanting to bid a last farewell to her man. If only I, too, could follow. Just to say goodbye. Just to wish him well. Just to hear his voice one last time . . .

Around me, the crowd began to disperse and a brewer's dray trundled along the road, pulled by two great shire horses. I looked for Frank, and found him threading his way towards me with drawn face and pity in his eyes. He said, 'Is that why you were asking about the Territorials?'

I nodded. I couldn't speak.

'Oh, hell,' said Frank without emphasis. 'I'm sorry, old girl.' Taking my arm, he guided me down a path beside the church, heading for the park where trees flirted their summer finery and the air smelled fresh after heavy rain. It was quiet there, few people about, strange after the crush in the street. We walked in silence, his hand under my arm both propelling and supporting me, but I knew he understood my grief – he just didn't like to talk about such things. We both paused and looked round as faint cheering came on the breeze – it probably followed the mayor's valedictory speech to the troops, as later reported in detail by the local paper.

'They'll be away soon,' Frank said. 'Then our train will be in. It will be good to get home.'

'Yes.' And with Philip far away there would be no danger of our meeting. I ought to be glad about that.

'We can try telephoning to the Mater to let her know what time we shall be there. Did you know she'd agreed to have the telephone installed at last? It has to be kept in a cupboard, according to Emmet, but the Mater's discovering its usefulness, now she knows it doesn't bite.'

We came to a park bench dewed with rain, which he wiped off with his handkerchief before he sat beside me, leaning on his knees. A pair of ducks waddled up, hoping to be fed. When no bread appeared, they pecked disconsolately around us, echoing my mood.

At last a steam whistle screamed and, with much belching and blowing, grinding of metal and clanking of couplings, the troop train moved off. I saw it beyond a screen of trees and heard the cheering that sent it on its way, accompanied by loud explosions that made me wince. We later learned that railwaymen had set fog signals on the line as a kind of salute, but to me they sounded like gunshots, anticipating the future. I was terribly afraid, and lonelier than I had ever been in my life.

Sorrowful though that homecoming was, as our own train rattled across the marsh flats I found myself watching for the first glimpse of the double-headed hill rising against the skyline, and when we entered the Eveningham vale the place seemed to reach out and enfold me. Somehow, whatever joys and sorrows it might hold, it was more home to me than anywhere else I had ever been.

Once again, Tom was at the station to meet us, hopping from foot to foot as he peered anxiously at alighting passengers. Catching sight of me, he shouted my name in a huge voice that turned heads as he came to envelop me in a bear hug that all but suffocated me.

'Let the girl breathe, old man,' Frank objected.

His brother released me, wiping damp eyes and nose on his cuff, before heartily pumping Frank's hand. I wondered what was upsetting him, but he brushed all questions aside in a rush to tell me about his new dog. 'I call him Jim, because he's got short legs – he reminds me of James Lacey.' That made him laugh as we went to the yard, where Garret was waiting with the wagonette.

As we drove, Tom chattered all the time – about small details of his daily life and, naturally, about his animals. He seemed overexcited, like a small boy, endearingly glad to have me home. I found it difficult to picture him taking a gun and shooting at a dog – and not only a dog: only luck had prevented him from killing Jack Farcroft. But poor Tom appeared to have forgotten all about that.

For me, memories lay everywhere, like sharp stones waiting to trip me. Here Philip had stood with Troy, the last time I came home; in the lane was the spot where I had nearly knocked him down with Frank's car, the first time I laid eyes on him, and where one moonlit night he had claimed a kiss 'as compensation'; the ridge where we had walked formed a skyline, and on its slopes stood the church where we had first really talked, and the lane where he had rescued me from the flood, and . . . and now the vale might as well have been deserted. For Philip was gone. But gone where? *Where?*

Garret turned on to the short-cut lane, beyond whose tall hedge I could see the sway-roofed farmhouse in its hollow, behind its trees, its barns and its pond, surrounded by harvest-rich fields. The farm, where once a wilful girl had defied her family to play promiscuous games with the farmer's older son. Had she not done so, I would not be here, I thought. At that moment I hated Mother for what she had done to me.

A gang of weeders hoed among green tops and corn stood tall, rippling dusty-gold under the breeze. In a fallow field a couple of shire horses grazed, and near them Philip's own Troy, but Mad Jack himself did not appear. Had he given up trying to prevent us from using the farm track?

A young woman was coming from the farm, making across the fallow for the gate which connected with the lane we were on. She wore a shady hat and loose linen jacket with her long skirt, but instinct told me who she was, even before we drew near enough for me to see her clearly. As we passed, she came through the gate and I saw that she had been crying. Then she recognized me and her face changed, hardening. The red-rimmed eyes glared hatred at me.

'He's gone!' she yelled. 'You're too late. He's gone away to the war. And if he get killed I hope he'll come and haunt you, blast your eyes!'

'Who's that?' Frank muttered as the wagonette carried us on.

'Philip's girl,' I managed, though the words all but choked me. Was she Philip's girl again? Had he turned to her for consolation? I stared at her receding figure, wondering what Philip had told her. How I envied her the right to weep for his absence.

At Denes Hill, Grandmother and Vicky had kept a late, cold lunch for us. Vicky put on a show of welcome that disguised whatever she was feeling, but the warmth of Grandmother's greeting seemed designed to assure me that, whatever had happened a year ago, we should put it behind us now.

'I'm glad to see you're both looking well,' she said, surveying both her son and me with sharply observant blue eyes. 'From what Oliver told me, Catherine, I feared you had become a sickly waif.'

'Devon did me the world of good,' I replied. 'I'm sorry if—'

But she cut me off with a gesture. 'No apologies. No looking back. You're here. And we need you. Let us go in to lunch.' Like Frank, she believed that in times of national crisis a family should stick together. Family skeletons, of whatever nature, were best left to moulder in firmly locked cupboards.

Inevitably, we discussed the news. Frank told of the queues of men we had seen outside recruiting stations and his mother applauded their patriotism. 'We may need a few extra men if we're to get through this trouble in short order. But I don't foresee general conscription, do you?'

'Not unless there's a real threat of invasion,' Frank replied. 'In Torquay, they—'

'Oh, there won't be any invasion,' she broke in with an airy gesture. 'Their naval strength is far inferior. And, if a few ships were to get through, our coastal defences will stop them. Plans are already in hand, you know. I think it will be good for the country. It will be a cleansing – we've got too many men chasing too few jobs. If some of them disappear in a good cause it will be all to the good in the end.'

I exclaimed, 'You're talking about human lives, Grandmother!'

Uncle Frank echoed me and for a while a heated argument raged, Vicky adding her two penn'orth with the opinion that to die for one's country was a wonderful thing – all the poets said so. Tom listened, open-mouthed, occasionally crying, 'Yes! Fight!' in support of his mother and sister.

'Sometimes a few must be sacrificed for the good of the majority,' Grandmother insisted. 'Theirs will be the glory. But we shall not be idle. We shall work to support the troops, and help the wounded – and their families. It's never easy for those who have to stay behind. We shall have the worst of it, waiting and worrying. I know. You forget that one of my own sons shed his blood in his country's cause – and died for it, subsequently. I know about sacrifice.'

Which was all very fine and noble when none of the people she cared about was in danger. As yet.

The conversation veered to other aspects of the war. Like a true capitalist, Grandmother foresaw profit for both Thorne-Thomas, making munitions and engines, and for Chef Foods, where the factory would be on full production. In the current crisis, she predicted, the country would need all the food it could get. However, 'Oliver can't be there all the time and, though I trust George Chorley to a point, he's not family.'

'Is Oliver?' Frank put in.

'Oliver is a trusted friend,' his mother responded. 'Don't be churlish, Frank, you know very well what I mean. So, Catherine, you see, a family eye on affairs is what we require at Chef Foods. With your typewriting and shorthand skills, you will be of invaluable use to Mr Chorley.'

'Oh, but—' I began, but she cut me off.

'I'm conscious that you may have had other thoughts in mind. However . . .' She drew herself up, stretching her long neck and dabbing elegantly at a corner of her mouth with a napkin. 'Now that the war is upon us we must all modify our plans. Later, when this emergency is over, you may wish to rethink your career. But in the meantime, Catherine, we need you. The family needs you. *I* need you.'

Perhaps it was better, for now, to remain in familiar places and do what I could to help people I cared about. I might, too, glean news of Philip now and then. Was it so wrong to care about him? After all, he was as closely related to me as Frank or Tom or Emmet, and no one forbade me to care for *them*. His father, too – that horrible, hate-riddled, pathetic old man – was my grandfather. And he was all alone now. How did he feel, with his only remaining son off to the war?

My dreams that night were troubled, nightmares that shocked me awake to lie staring into darkness waiting for my heart to slow down. Philip, blood, land ironclads, Philip marching away from me, Tom lying dead in the woods, John drowning, Philip . . . a tangle of terror. I was thankful when morning came.

Next day, under a bright sun, everything looked so peaceful and normal that it was hard to believe men were fighting, killing and dying, not many miles away across the blue North Sea. But the news of the war continued, affecting us even at Denes Hill. Frank took himself off in his motor to record activities at the docks, along the coast and at Thetford where the Territorials were gathering horses; he told us to expect him when we saw him. Grandmother, Vicky and I all started knitting socks and scarves in spare moments: their Red Cross committee was collecting clothes and necessaries for Belgian refugees: the new telephone was in constant use.

Tom seemed restless, anxious for company. He showed

me where, up against one of the garden walls, he and Garret had built a new, larger aviary for the birds – the mynah had its own small section while the rest was filled with budgerigars flitting their bright wings in the sunlight. In another pen a pair of golden pheasant strutted with four well-grown chicks. The new dog, Jim, proved to be a lively terrier cross, mainly white but patched with black, a friendly little soul with whom I struck up an instant rapport. It was a pity that Grandmother didn't like animals in the house. Jim would have been a merry companion.

Around us, everything swung into a new gear. Men in uniform appeared in Hunstanton and the nearby villages, and in one of Jack Farcroft's meadows hammering sounded as soldiers erected tents, fences for horse paddocks, and canvas screens to hide latrines and protect cooking stoves. Men from Worcestershire and Gloucestershire arrived to stand as home defence for west Norfolk, stringing barbed wire along the beaches and building defences around gun batteries in strategic spots. Our Norfolk Territorials had, I was relieved to hear, gone to perform similar duties in Suffolk. They were not going to the front. Thank God. Thank God!

To Grandmother's dismay, a requisition officer came to Denes Hill and commandeered her carriage horses for use in war work. Her head groom and one of the gardeners took that as their cue to go off and sign up for the army; several young men of the village were planning to do the same once the harvest was over.

'And so they should,' she said at dinner. 'We must all do what we can to support the war effort, and to aid the refugees. The Red Cross committee is meeting again tomorrow, at Mrs Lacey's. I want you to join us, Kate. I'm sure there'll be something you can do.'

'They shouldn't have taken the horses!' Tom cried, banging his spoon on the table with such a crack that we all jumped. 'They're *our* horses.'

'England needs them, dear,' his mother said, as if Tom could comprehend such an answer. I wasn't sure that I did.

Vicky, pinch-faced and pale, argued, 'They needn't have taken them all, need they? How are we to get about?'

'There are bicycles,' said Grandmother, who had never been known to mount one of those wobbling machines. 'And we have the dogcart. They left us Willow, didn't they, Tom?'

'That old hack!' Vicky objected. 'Is she fit to pull the dogcart?'

'I'm sure Tom will look into that for us. Won't you, Tom?'

The prospect of a useful job cheered Tom up, though he resented having old Willow called a hack: she had served him and Emmet well when they were younger.

We were still discussing the transport problem when Billing arrived, his usual imperturbability so ruffled that he was almost wringing his hands. 'I'm sorry to bother you, milady, but some police officers have called. They're asking for Miss Kate.'

Grandmother flicked me a narrow look, but said calmly enough, 'Did they give any reason, Billing?'

'No, milady.'

'Catherine?'

'I've no idea,' I said, puzzled. 'Unless something's happened to . . .' Was it Mother?

As I got to my feet, Grandmother gave an audible sigh. 'Why is Frank never here when we need him?'

'We don't need Frank,' Vicky said. 'I'm sure Kate can handle it, whatever it is. We're three grown women, Mother. We're not helpless just because we've no man here.'

'*I'm* here,' Tom protested, but by then I was leaving the room, wondering what the policemen could want.

Billing had shown them into the saloon, where a lamp or two shed pools of light, enough to let me see four uniformed figures at the far side of the vast shadowed darkness. As I crossed the room, I discerned that the two by the door were not policemen but soldiers, armed with rifles. The others were a tall, thin inspector of police and his burly sergeant, whom I recognized by sight.

'Good evening, miss.' The inspector, a lanky man with a heavy black moustache dividing his lugubrious upper face from a triangle of chin, stepped forward. 'Would you be Miss Kate Brand? Otherwise known as Catherine von Wurthe?'

My heart seemed to twist and sink. This *was* about Mother. But, did it take four men to bring bad news? 'That's right. Wha . . . ?'

'Would you be so good as to get your hat and coat, miss? I need you to come with me back to the station.'

When I hesitated, more out of bewilderment than a reluctance to obey, the two soldiers stepped forward, holding their rifles as if prepared to use them.

'For goodness' sake!' Grandmother's imperious voice cut the shadows behind me, her stick making dull thumping sounds on the Persian carpet. 'What is this? Do I know you, Inspector . . . ?'

He straightened himself. 'Jarvis, ma'am. Inspector Jarvis of the King's Lynn force.'

'And Sergeant Playford of Hunstanton,' she observed.

Her tone made the thickset sergeant look sheepish as he saluted her. 'Good evening, Lady Rhys-Thomas. I'm sorry if that's an inconvenience, but they asked me to come along and assist Mr Jarvis. They now want Miss Brand to go along to Lynn, to answer some questions.'

'In regard to what?'

Jarvis replied, 'In regard to the new law on undesirable aliens.'

'Aliens?' she scoffed. 'This young lady is as British as you are, Inspector. She happens to be my granddaughter.'

'I'm aware of that, ma'am.'

'Are you also aware that the Chief Constable is a personal friend of mine?' She was at her disdainful best, managing to look down her nose at him though he was a good foot taller than she. 'I'm quite sure that if he knew of this—'

Without even blinking, and with the utmost courtesy, the inspector said, 'The Chief Constable asked me to say, ma'am, that the allegations are too grave to be ignored. To do with the defence of the realm. I have orders to take Miss Brand back to Lynn with me at once.'

'Very well.' Her voice turned frosty. 'But you may tell Mr Payne that I hold him personally responsible for my granddaughter's safety. I shall expect a full explanation of this outrage.'

They had brought with them a closed carriage. One soldier rode shotgun, alongside the driver, while I, feeling like a desperado, was put inside, facing Inspector Jarvis and the other soldier. Sergeant Playford started back to Hunstanton on his bicycle. My armed guard wore the Worcestershire Yeomanry flash on his shoulder; he kept looking at me sidelong, clutching his rifle as if he expected me to sprout horns and leap to disembowel him with my talons – after all, I was a German spy. It was pure farce.

The joke turned sour, however, when I found myself incarcerated in a tiny cell under the Town Hall. The stench of vomit and urine emanated from a filthy bucket in the corner. A single candle fluttered and smoked, sending

shadows looming round damp-streaked walls, showing me
the high barred window and the wooden bench with a plank
for a pillow, where lay a rough-looking woman, very drunk
and singing raucously to herself. The song broke off as I
stepped inside and the metal door closed with a clang that
sent a chill through me even before the key grated, locking
me in.

My companion threatened to be overfriendly until she
divined what charge had brought me there, when she spat
at me and called me a filthy murdering Hun. Then, while I
wiped spittle from my face, she lay back on the bench and
sang herself to sleep bawling, 'Just a song at twilight . . .'
Afterwards, I never heard the song without remembering
that night, and her snores.

What seemed like hours but, according to my watch,
was forty-five minutes later, I heard boots treading along
the flagged passageway. With a jangle of keys, my lock
turned and the opening door showed me a grizzled constable,
who gave me a baleful stare and bade me come with him.
He said I was lucky – the Chief Constable himself was going
to speak to me. Come straight from a civic dinner, he had.
Didn't usually take such trouble over female felons.

'I am not a felon!' I exclaimed. But I was grateful to
hear that I would soon be seeing the genial Mr Payne.

As the constable ushered me into a cluttered, oak-
panelled office, the first person I saw was Inspector Jarvis.
But my glance went to the man behind the desk – a slight,
middle-aged man: not Mr Payne. He was in evening dress:
a black, silk-lined cape lay folded on a cabinet, with a top
hat and white gloves. But if his evening had so far been
convivial his pale face had now settled into stern lines.

'Sit down, Miss Brand. Or is it Fraulein von Wurthe?'

Apprehensive, though keeping my chin up, I slid on to

the hard chair. 'Von Wurthe is my stepfather's name. I used it for convenience, when I lived in Berlin.' Glancing at the lanky, mustachioed inspector, I added, 'I understood I was to see the Chief Constable.'

'You are seeing him, miss,' Jarvis replied.

'Mr Payne retired last year,' the other informed me with a glimmer of what might have been satisfaction. 'My name is Hunt. Charles William Hunt. And if I consider you to be a danger to this country, Miss Brand, I shall have you interned, whatever your lady grandmother may say.' His tone said he was not amused by Grandmother's attempts to apply pressure. 'You don't deny being in regular communication with Berlin, then?'

What was this nonsense? 'Why should I? My family are there. My mother, and—'

'We know that, Miss Brand. Your letters go out regularly. But your family don't seem to reply. Is it your family you write to?'

'And one or two friends. I have a problem with my stepfather. I think he prevents Mother from writing to me.' Even to my own ears it sounded a feeble excuse, but before I could amplify with details, he said:

'Does the name Gudrun Thunissen mean anything?'

He mispronounced it, but that he knew her name at all was disquieting. 'She's a friend,' I said, beginning to wonder how all this evidence had been collected. What twisted mind had reported me to the police?

'You've been sending her packages.'

'Articles for a magazine! I'm a writer, you know.'

But, as the questions went on, my apprehension grew. He knew all about me – it was written down on a sheet in front of him, to which he referred now and then. He knew I had been involved with Sylvia Pankhurst and the WSPU;

he knew I was friendly with, and had conversed in German with, Harald Ehrenfried, the inoffensive Hunstanton butcher – who had, my inquisitor informed me to my horror, been interned for the duration. Mr Hunt even accused me of 'loose talk in railway carriages' – by which, I deduced, he meant my talking with Uncle Frank about land ironclads. Dear God, Frank had said he could be dragged to the tower for mentioning that secret to me!

As I argued that my uncle and I had merely been discussing a piece of fiction, which, far from being a military secret, had been published for anyone to read, raised voices outside made us all pause. The door burst open. The duty constable started to apologize for the intrusion, but he was thrust aside by an imposing figure in tails and blue-lined cape. Thank heaven! My shining knight: 'Oliver!'

I leapt up and almost threw myself into his arms, but with one swift glance he steadied and reassured me. How glad I was to see him! Everything would be all right now. He, too, had been at the civic dinner, it seemed, so he had not received the frantic telephone messages Grandmother had left with his housekeeper until he returned home.

After a fraught half-hour or so, when Oliver employed all his legal expertise to secure my release, we were allowed to leave, with stern warnings about my future behaviour. While the war with Germany continued, it seemed, I would remain under suspicion of being an enemy sympathizer.

All I wanted was to put the awful place behind me. Head down, like a whipped puppy, I trotted beside Oliver's long stride, feeling angry, ashamed and bitter, thinking of all the things I should have said. I hardly noticed where we were going, along narrow cobbled streets with ancient houses crowding. Before long, Oliver opened a small door in a big gate and led me into a carriage court lit by gas lamps, where tall windows peered down on all sides from walls thick with ivy.

A porticoed entrance led into a hall with numbered doors leading off it; up a stairway a further door, blazoned with a brass 7, gave into an apartment that felt cool and airy. As Oliver turned up the gas, pale light disclosed a spacious hallway, empty but for a coat-stand and cheval glass, and then a large drawing room. From above a mantel of grey-veined marble a big framed mirror threw back a reflection of the room, showing me my pale-faced self, dishevelled beside Oliver's elegant evening attire. As if roused from a dream, I blinked at the room, seeing it mainly monochrome – a black leather chesterfield and armchairs on a grey carpet, with polished side tables, on one of which stood a chess set carved of ivory and ebony. The only splashes of colour came from leaded glass shades which adorned four gas wall lamps.

'Where are we?' I asked.

'This is where I live,' Oliver said. 'Merchant's Court. I'd have taken you to Hawthorn House, but I'd rather not disturb your aunt Saffron at this hour . . .' He glanced at a black marble clock on his mantel, which said it was past midnight. 'I told my housekeeper to go to bed,' he added, 'but if you would prefer her to be here—'

I stopped him, a hand on his arm. 'No, don't disturb her. I'm sorry, I'm not thinking. I feel . . . unclean! That horrible cell they put me in.'

'That's easily remedied, if you'd care to use the facilities here . . .'

A short while later I found myself soaking in a hot bath, steam rising in clouds to a high ceiling. Black and white tiles chequered walls and floor and, above a dado rail, condensation dewed large mirrors. Oliver liked mirrors, I thought. Was he vain? Perhaps he had a right to be: he was a good-looking man. And he and I were alone together, but for his sleeping housekeeper. The thought made me climb out of the bath and wrap myself in thick white towels.

He had said I might use his guest room for the night, to which end he had lent me a pair of white silk pyjamas, monogrammed 'O.G.W.' in navy blue on the breast pocket, and a navy silk dressing gown. They were large on me, but covered me securely enough with the waist cords tightly tied. I was itchingly aware that they had been next to Oliver's skin, as they were now next to mine.

I discovered him in his drawing room, wearing a loose quilted jacket over his evening shirt, now collarless and open at the neck. He poured me a large measure of brandy, which I sipped perhaps too eagerly, hoping to calm my nerves, perched on the edge of a low armchair while he relaxed on the chesterfield. One would have thought he drank brandy in his apartment with unsettled, half-clad young ladies in the small hours of every night.

We talked about my arrest and questioning; we discussed the war, and my becoming George Chorley's secretary – everything but our personal lives. The brandy loosened my tongue and relaxed me. When I started yawning, Oliver showed me to his guest room and wished me good night.

'Oliver . . .' I ventured as he turned from the door. 'Are you angry with me? I'm sorry to have been a trouble to you.'

'Not at all. As your grandmother's solicitor, it was my duty to help.' He gave me a slight smile that left his eyes sad. 'Sleep well, Kate.'

He was keeping his vow, I realized guiltily as he walked away: any new overture must come from me. What a cruel creature I was to hurt him so!

NINETEEN

I found Oliver's guest bed hard, the bedding redolent of mothballs. Noises came from the riverside, clattering, clangings and bangings, and then a dog began to bark. When at last I slept I dreamed of being incarcerated in a stinking cell, menaced by huge soldiers with fixed bayonets, while in the distance Philip and his girl laughed at me, and Oliver was smoking a cigar in the summerhouse, and an invasion fleet sailed into the Wash, landing on Eveningham beach, where I paddled with Uncle John, who was dragged away and held under the water by a huge soldier wearing the helmet of the élite Death's Head hussars. Someone was screaming. Maybe it was me.

Shocked awake in pulsing darkness, I wondered where I was. The covers had slipped away, leaving me cold. As I sat up, shivering, reaching for the sheet, hands came on me. I shrieked, and Oliver said anxiously, 'It's me, Kate! Only me. You called out for me.'

Probably I had – he had certainly been in my nightmare somewhere. Its remnants still clung about me as I reached for him. 'Oh . . . Oliver!'

'I'm here.' He sat beside me, folding me in his arms, where I huddled shivering, my tears drying on his pyjamas while he stroked and soothed me. How blessedly warm he was. How strong and sure. I leaned against him, burrowing to his warmth like a child, muttering, 'I'm sorry. I was dreaming. Nightmares. I've always had them, ever since I was a child.'

'I know,' he murmured, his breath scented with cigar and brandy as he held me more closely, curling his arms and body round me. 'My dear, you're so cold! Even your little nose . . .' He warmed it with his lips, and from there ventured to brush tentative kisses over my eyes and down my face, until he found my willing mouth.

After that I stopped thinking. Thinking brought pain, but sensation gave sweet oblivion, blotting out the hurt.

He wooed me with tender stealth, rousing me inch by inch, infinitely patient. His mouth and hands coaxed music from my nerves, singing across my flesh in chords of swelling desire. The night air no longer felt cold: it tingled sensually along my skin as the loose pyjamas fell from me under the caressing of warm, strong hands. And, where his fingers led, his lips followed, tempting and cajoling, making me quiver and shiver, unfurling me like a flower to sunlight as he dared deeper and deeper intimacies. I felt myself reaching, straining, for a goal I had only dimly glimpsed before. It drenched me suddenly, forcing a strangled cry from me as terrible pleasure flooded my being.

As the world resumed its normal shape around me I shook uncontrollably, weeping, but Oliver held me close, kissing me, murmuring reassurance. His voice came soft in my ears like the shush of the ocean. 'Hush, my love. Hush, all's well. I'm here. Rest now. Sleep . . .'

And, incredibly, I did sleep.

His moving disturbed me. I thought he was leaving but, as I sleepily opened my eyes to early morning light through heavy curtains, he slid back beneath the sheet and leaned over me, stroking my hair and face, murmuring, 'Good morning.' As he kissed me, I felt his body brush mine. He was naked – when I woke, rather than leaving the bed, he had been undressing.

Feeling the strange, male shape of him against me, I stiffened in apprehension, making him lift his head to search my face. What he saw made him smile. 'It's all right, Kate. Everything's all right now.'

Whatever he had in mind, it was far too late for me to object. Last night we had crossed a threshold from which no retreat was possible.

'Last night was for you,' he said. 'This morning will be for us both. I love you, Kate.' He bent his head to kiss me tenderly, breathing, 'And you will love me, too. I'm going to make sure of that.'

My mind may have protested, briefly. I may have thought of Philip, for an unguarded second. But Oliver's kisses claimed me and my errant flesh was ready, even eager, for further lessons in love from a masterly tutor. My skin quivered to his touch, my breasts came alive, my belly quaked, my mouth answered his and my loins ran molten for him. And yet he delayed the consummation, held back, until I thought I would go mad for wanting . . .

'Oliver!' It was a prayer, a plea, a demand.

'You want me?' Fierce with satisfaction, hoarse with need. 'Say it!'

I almost hated him for making me plead. 'Yes! Oh, yes. Yes, yes . . .'

The conjoining thrust of his body made me cry out with both fear and delight, but he swallowed the sound in a kiss as his control snapped and he plunged headlong towards his own climax. The drowning, erotic tide swept over me only seconds before he stiffened and moaned and I knew he, too, had found fulfilment. He collapsed beside me, his head on my breast, muttering, 'Thank you. Thank you, my love.'

I stared at the shadowy ceiling, my heart thudding with his, the sweat of our bodies mingling between us. But my thoughts ran cold as I felt his body fluid trickling out of me. So. It was done. I had committed myself irrevocably to Oliver Wells.

Oh, Philip . . . forgive me!

Half an hour later, dressed again in my clothes from the previous night, I opened the bedroom door and heard Oliver's voice from the drawing room. Thinking that he was speaking to his housekeeper, I paused, wondering how he would explain my presence. Then I realized he was using the telephone, talking to Billing, Grandmother's butler, at Denes Hill. Softly, not to interrupt, I crept down the hall.

'I was late coming in and my housekeeper had retired,' he was saying. 'She had left me a note, but unfortunately I didn't see it until this morning, when I went straight to the Town Hall and secured Miss Brand's release. There is no reason for her ladyship to be concerned. Miss Brand is a little tired and distressed, but bearing up bravely. I shall see her to the train as soon as she's rested and refreshed.'

Disconcerted to hear lies flow from him so smoothly, I reached the drawing room doorway. Oliver was putting the phone back into a side cupboard and as he straightened he saw me. 'Ah – there you are, my dear. I've left a message for your grandmother. I, er . . .' A long forefinger smoothed his moustache as his umber eyes gleamed. 'I didn't tell the exact truth, as you may have heard. I felt it politic – for your reputation – that she should believe you were in a police cell all night.'

'Better a criminal than a fallen woman?' said I wryly.

Taking that as a joke, he came to squeeze my shoulders, kiss my brow and look down at me appraisingly. 'You look tired. Pleasantly so, I trust?' When I blushed, his smile deepened and he pulled me closer, adding in an undertone, 'I knew I should enjoy widening your education. You enjoyed it, too. Didn't you?'

'Oliver . . .' I protested, squirming away.

'Mustn't we speak, by daylight, of what we do together by darkness?' he teased. 'Well . . . I'll allow you your maidenly modesty, for now.'

'Your housekeeper might come in.'

'I told her not to disturb us before ten. She'll be up shortly.'

'Up?'

'She has rooms on the ground floor. She takes care of all four apartments in this section of the house.'

What? But surely he had said . . . 'You let me believe your housekeeper was here in the flat! If I had known we were alone . . .'

While silence stretched between us, he concealed his thoughts behind a still face and cool dark eyes. 'Are you accusing me of ravishment?'

'No, of course not, but—'

'Do you deny calling out for me? Do you deny welcoming me into your bed? Do you deny your own willing response to my attentions – both last night *and* this morning?'

'You know I can't deny it! But—'

He cut me off with a gesture. 'Please! Don't insult my intelligence by playing the virgin defiled. It's a trifle late for that. I know I am not the first to have trodden that particular path.'

His face seemed to come and go through clouds of disbelief. What was he implying? Not the first . . . ?

'Perhaps you've forgotten,' he said, 'that it was I who escorted you out of Berlin, at your parents' request, to part you from your young lover, what was his name – the soldier-boy – Carl-Heinz? And wasn't there a young man in London? Not to mention the farmer's lad, Farcroft. You haven't been very discriminating in your choice, my dear. Indeed, I could be forgiven for wondering if those three were all.' But as I stared at him in growing horror his expression softened and he came to touch my cheek. 'Don't look so stricken, Kate. I'm a realist. I love you as you are – warts and all, as Cromwell said.'

Appalled, I slapped his hand away, choking, 'You don't love me! If you did, you wouldn't believe those terrible things. Carl-Heinz *lied* about me, Oliver! And there was *no* young man in London. There was only Philip, and he didn't . . . we didn't . . . I thought a man could tell such things!'

'He can!' he answered passionately, and threw his arms around me to fold me close, wrapping my head to his breast despite my resistance – he was immensely strong. 'But not clearly enough, not when he's sick with jealousy. Forgive me, Kate. I've been so troubled. I needed to hear you deny it. I needed to see your face when I put the question. Now I know for sure. Now I know you're mine. Mine alone.'

I was glad he couldn't see my face at that moment, for I didn't believe him. 'Maybe I should have fought you off last night,' I muttered.

'No!' Laughing fiercely, he drew back to gaze down at me. 'I couldn't have borne that. I had waited too long as it was. I'm glad you enjoy your womanhood, my love – I should hate to be tied to a coy, cold Vestal.' Holding me so that I couldn't escape, he rubbed his body suggestively against mine, his smile turning sensual. 'I confess I haven't been entirely celibate – few men of my age could make such a claim. But I want to make you my wife. From now on we shall cleave only to each other. Ours will be a happy marriage, Kate. A marriage of both mind and body. I promise you that.'

'I think . . .' I said through a thickness in my throat, managing to pull free from his disturbing embrace. 'I think we should not be too hasty.'

'You're not going back on your promise, I hope?'

Why did that sound like a threat? I hadn't made any promises – not in words, anyway. 'I just . . . Everything's unsettled at the moment. I shall be working at Chef Foods, and staying with Aunt Saffron. We can see each other. Get to know each other.' Unnerved by his stillness, I rushed on, 'I'm only asking that we be discreet. For a little while, Oliver. If we suddenly announce our engagement, Grandmother may suspect . . .'

'She will be delighted.' He sounded very sure of that. 'However,' he added indulgently, 'let it not be said that I rushed you into a decision before you were ready. The secret shall be ours alone, for the time being. A delicious secret. I shall enjoy courting you openly, Kate. You may be right, at that. Perhaps we should wait until this wretched war is over. Next spring, perhaps. By then you may be able to invite your mother and stepfather to come for the wedding. You would like that.'

He might like it, too, I thought – having Mother as a witness, reminded of her own lost youth, her own lost chances. Repaying her for rejecting him, perhaps? In these last few hours I had seen glimpses of a deeper, darker man than the one I had known before. What were his motives for wanting to marry me? He desired me, yes, and last night he had enjoyed his consummation. A younger wife always boosted a man's self-esteem. And I was a member of the Rhys-Thomas clan – another feather for his cap. But, love?

He might call it so, but it was not – not the way I understood love, not the way it had been for Philip and me. And yet it blended better with my conscience: my own motives were equivocal. Since I should never love any man as I had loved Philip, I might do worse than settle for security and sexual compatibility.

Oliver saw me to the train and stood waving as it drew away, blowing me a kiss in final salute. As we slid through the suburbs into the countryside, I stared at the passing scene, avoiding the eyes of my fellow passengers, feeling as if my new awareness were emblazoned on my forehead: *fallen woman*. My own body had betrayed me. Like mother, like daughter. Oh, Philip, if only it could have been you!

Though Denes Hill had been informed of the time of my train, no one met me at the station. So I set out to walk, the long way, via village and main coast road, avoiding both the short cut across Far Drove and the track through the woods, which held too many memories of Philip. Soldiers patrolled the beach road beyond the railway; others performed arms drill in the field where their camp was set up. Around them, harvest had begun: men with scythes cut a swathe in a cornfield beside the lane, opening up for the sail reaper which came trundling behind me, drawn by two glossy shires. Its blades gleamed wickedly sharp, filling the narrow lane.

'Mind yourself, girl!' a rough voice shouted and Mad Jack Farcroft glowered at me from a gateway, clad in cord suit and bowler, his face unshaven for days. Meeting my eyes, he deliberately spat into the road, and stepped aside to let the horses and their burden move between us. I hurried on, but the image of three scars, livid red beside his left eye, lingered accusingly in my mind – only luck had saved

Tom from blinding the farmer. Was it any wonder he hated me and mine?

By the time I reached the big house I was tired and depressed – the effects of a sleepless night, and traumas with Oliver, on top of ghastly memories of the police cell and the questioning that had made me feel like a criminal. Still, the treatment of 'undesirable aliens' would give me something to write about. I would go and see Mrs Ehrenfried, the butcher's wife, and add her story to mine. How would she and her children cope, with their breadwinner locked in an internment camp?

Under a sky brushed with high, wind-stretched cloud, Denes Hill looked proud in the sunlight, a beckoning haven of security. The tower reached for heaven, soaring over great bays and gleaming windows. From the long, raised terrace, where Philip had hidden to watch me dance with Oliver, sweeping steps led down to a gravel apron where visitors' carriages and cars could draw up. Today, two horses waited there, one of them a fine chestnut – like Philip's Troy. Oh, why did everything remind me of him?

'Miss Kate!' the cry reached me. To my surprise, the unflappable Billing came racing across the terrace and down the steps to meet me, his morning coat flying open over a stained apron – one he wore when polishing silver. Evidently he had been caught at his chores and had flung on his coat in a hurry.

Grandmother? I thought with a quirk of panic.

'Oh, miss, thank goodness you've come!' the butler gasped, more agitated than I had ever seen him. He had a smear of black on his brow. 'I couldn't stop them. Wanted to see the house, they said. Billeting, they said. For soldiers! They can't do that, can they, miss?'

As we climbed the curving steps, he explained that two

army officers had arrived with orders to check all possible accommodation in the area and allocate billet space. Billing had told them there was no one at home: Grandmother and Vicky had gone out, to Mrs Lacey's at Lenhoe – that was why the dogcart hadn't been there for me. 'Now they've taken the horses, we just can't manage!' he fretted. 'But her ladyship said she'd be home for lunch. She's anxious about you, miss.' The officers had insisted that he himself should show them round the house. 'I tried to stop them, Miss Kate, but they wouldn't take no for an answer. Had to do it now, they said. Didn't I know there was a war on? Then one of them went off through the saloon – he had the effrontery to say he was going to look upstairs. I couldn't split myself in two! And then I saw you coming, miss, and what a relief it was to see someone of the family . . .'

Seeing the french doors open, I hurried along the terrace to intercept these intruders, with Billing twittering at my heels. One of them stood in the ballroom, a khaki-clad subaltern with a wispy blond moustache. He stuttered and stammered, introducing himself as Second Lieutenant Gryce, explaining his errand and apologizing for having to do it, but we were under martial law now, Defence of the Realm, the war . . . But what a fine old house it was. Such elegant proportions.

I was not about to be disarmed by flattery. 'Give Lieutenant Gryce a guided tour, Billing. I'll go and see where the other gentleman might be.' Though they had every right to carry out their orders, their ill-mannered methods annoyed me. No stranger should be snooping around unescorted in a private house full of valuable objects and personal belongings.

Upstairs, the door of Grandmother's private sitting room was open. The second officer stood with his back to me, a tall, broad-shouldered figure in khaki twill and puttees, hair cropped close to his neck below the band of his military cap, long legs straddled, great boots planted on the pale carpet as he perused a portrait of Grandfather. His presence was an affront in that delicate blue and white room, making me exclaim in outrage. As he turned, I saw his lieutenant's insignia and knew he was the senior of the two. Even so—

'How dare you—' I began. And then I saw his face.

It was Philip.

Philip . . . I hung there staring at him in disbelief. Was I pale with shock or scarlet with other emotions? A maelstrom of them. He had been promoted! He was safe, he was here, thank God! And Tom, lying between us. And Mad Jack with blood on his face. And a faithful dog that had had to be put down. And I . . . straight from Oliver's bed, where I had hoped to find a cure for love but discovered only my own shame. Could he read it in my eyes?

I wish I had said something witty – something memorable – but what I actually said was, 'What are you doing here?'

He too was startled, for a moment. Then he straightened himself, donning his official mantle, his face a mask. Unlike Oliver, however, he couldn't control his eyes: his eyes said he hated and despised me even while his deep voice said evenly, 'The official billeting officer was taken ill last night. I was seconded to help Lieutenant Gryce, since I know the district.'

'I meant . . . I thought you'd gone to Suffolk.'

'I've been given leave to help with the harvest.'

I hardly knew whether to laugh or weep. I had been imagining all kinds of horrors, and here he was, back at home again as if he had never left.

'As you may recall,' he added, his voice laced with sarcasm, 'harvest's a busy time. A farmer has to work all hours.'

The memory of last harvest pulsed between us – a moonlit hollow in the dunes, sweet intimacies interrupted, hard words spoken . . . had he meant them? Had I? Oh, if only—

He squared himself, stretching to his full commanding height, very much the officer on duty. 'Our orders are to record all available—'

'I know what your orders are! I've spoken with your colleague.'

'Then I won't waste my breath repeating it all.' And he turned to the inner door. 'You'll excuse me if I get on with—'

'Please!' Dodging past him, I barred the way with widespread arms. 'I can't let you go in there. This is Grandmother's private suite. I'll show you the rest of the house, if you wish, but not this.'

His cheek twitched and his look both mocked and scorched me, but he said, 'Thank you,' and bowed me towards the door. 'After you, Miss Brand.' Because I didn't know what else to do, I led the way along the first floor, opening doors just wide enough to allow glimpses inside: Vicky's room, a bathroom and WC, Emmet's room, Tom's room – at whose door I unwisely met Philip's green glance and saw that he too remembered the way we had parted on this spot a year ago. His mouth hardened, but all he said was, 'And the rest?'

Three guest rooms, another bathroom, Anderson's room, a linen room, a sewing room, further utility areas around the back stairs, and, 'This is *my* room.' I flung the door wide and stepped back, saying flatly, 'You might as well take a look at that, too.'

'Since it's the only chance I shall ever get . . .' he muttered under his breath and strode in, going straight to the window. The room was as I had left it before dinner the

351

previous evening, with day clothes across the bed, hairbrushes untidy on the dressing table with oddments of jewellery, and my personal notebook by the bed, where I wrote down my thoughts and scribbled poems and ideas. Did he guess how often his name was written there? What would I write today, recounting last night: '*I am engaged to Oliver Wells*'? Also in evidence, trailing softly across the night table, was the blue scarf he had given me. I slept with it under my pillow. It was my comfort, all I had left. If he saw it, would he guess . . . ?

'You'll have to move,' he said flatly.

I stared at his rigid back, wondering where my sweetheart had gone to. In his place, this hostile stranger in uniform . . . 'I beg your pardon?'

He swung round, his face in misty shadow with bright sky behind him. 'I can't billet troops up here with you in the middle of them. Damn it—' But he stopped himself, shutting his mouth like a trap, jaw muscle bunching as he clenched his teeth. Whatever he had been going to say, he changed it to, 'Why have they consigned you to the back of the house?'

'It happened that way. I don't mind.' I could not resist adding, 'It was convenient when I needed to sneak out unobserved, wasn't it?'

For answer, he strode for the door and came past me, dull colour across his cheekbone making his eyes look greener than ever. 'Where next?'

'Down the back stairs there are servants' rooms – Billing, Annie and Cook live in. Below that, the kitchens and domestic offices. Up here, there's only the tower.'

'Show me.'

So I took him along to the turret, up to the landing leading to the big rooms that were bedroom and studio for Uncle

Frank, then through the final door that led to the sanctum stairs. As we climbed up into brilliant sunlight, Philip looked round with interest, noting the books, the games, the photographs, the views . . . Again, it was the window that drew him.

'I've often wondered how far you could see from up here,' he said, staring out over the woods towards the hidden farmhouse. When I went to stand at the next window, he flicked me a sidelong look. 'What luck that I had this topping excuse to come poking into your family's privacy – all with the sanction of martial law. Who'd have thought that Jack Farcroft's boy would ever have the nerve to trespass in the *sanctum sanctorum* at Denes Hill?'

'If that's meant to be funny—' I said dully.

'It's what you're thinking, isn't it? Believe me, if I'd had the choice I'd have swum the Channel to get to the war rather than come here. The last thing I ever wanted was to have to—' He stopped himself, grinding his teeth as he glowered at the view. 'No, that's not true, either. I've always wanted to see inside this house. And I wanted to see *you* again, if only to find out if you'd have the nerve to look me in the eye.'

A hiccup of tearful laughter almost choked me. Underneath his anger he was still my Philip, upright and true, and cursed with stubborn pride. 'Dear Philip . . . you always have to be so honest! Even with yourself.'

'I'm glad you still find me amusing!' he said savagely, a red tide scalding his throat and ears. 'Don't patronize me, Kate! And don't ever – ever! – call me your dear, because I'm not, and I never was, and how the blazes I was ever fool enough to believe that I might be has me beat.'

'Please—' As he started for the stairs I reached to stop him, but the look he gave me sliced me to the heart. I snatched my hand back as if he had bitten me, and watched him turn away. But I couldn't let him go like that. 'Philip, please! Philip!'

The thud of his boots paused halfway down the stairs, though he kept his back to me, stiff as a spike, his jaw working. His shaven neck was red with fury. Painfully vulnerable, achingly appealing. How I longed to touch him and tell him . . .

The shaking in my legs had got into my voice. 'I did love you. I loved you terribly, ever since we talked in the church. I never laughed at you. I never meant to patronize. I think I knew it could never be, but that didn't make any difference. You were all I wanted.'

He jerked his head round to glare at me, raging, 'Then why didn't you say so at the time?'

What? Whatever did he mean? Blankly, I breathed, 'I did!'

'Never once. Never!'

'But . . .' I tried to think back, but it was all a blur. 'You *knew* how I felt! It must have been obvious. Surely you knew . . .'

'How, Kate? Telepathy? And if you cared so much—'

Another voice intruded, from the lower hall: Vicky's voice, calling, 'Kate? Kate, are you up there?'

Philip gave me a final searing look, saying through his teeth, 'Even if I believed you – which I don't – it's too late. I don't care any more. I stopped caring a year ago, when I had to shoot Bess. For your information, Miss Brand, I'm going to marry Lou Roughton. Thank you for your time,' and he went on down the stairs, banging the door behind him. I heard him say something to Vicky as he passed her, and then her lighter footsteps came tripping along Frank's landing. She pushed the door open slowly, peering up at me with wide, startled eyes.

'That was *him*! Young Farcroft. What was he doing here?'

'What do you think he was doing here?' I responded in bitter despair. 'He came to carry me off to his hay loft and have his wicked way with me, obviously! Oh . . . it's fate's idea of a joke, Vicky. He's helping the billeting officer.'

'He was wearing a lieutenant's insignia! How can *he* be an officer? He's no gentleman.'

Irritated by her snobbery, I found myself defending Philip: 'He's more of a gentleman born and bred than Grandfather ever was! The Farcrofts have been landowners since the year dot. Compared to that, the Rhys-Thomases are nouveau riche Johnny-come-latelys. Besides which, Philip is . . . is straight and true. He's educated, intelligent . . .' *I don't care any more,* he had said. *For your information, Miss Brand, I'm going to marry Lou Roughton.* 'Oh, God!' I turned away, groping blindly for the nearest seat as grief caught up with me.

Vicky sat beside me, trying to comfort me. She still felt guilty that jealousy had made her reveal secrets I was meant never to know. 'But if you had gone on seeing him, something frightful might have happened. Oh, Kate, don't cry. Please! I thought you'd have got over it by now.'

'I have!' I croaked, and drew a long breath, forcing the tears to stop. Why was I so upset over Philip Farcroft? Many troubles clouded my life: my shame over what I had done with Oliver; my newly acquired 'criminal record'; the war, and Mother . . . Philip had been hateful to me. I ought to hate him, too.

But I didn't. I never could. I knew what was causing my worst anguish: I had hurt Philip badly – and I couldn't tell him why.

'Was it frightful – last night?' Vicky asked in concern.

'Did they lock you up in a cell? You must have been fearfully glad to see Oliver.' Her glance faltered, sliding away. 'I . . . I think I've been rather foolish. I thought if you were out of the way he would turn to me, but I know better now. I'm over him at last.'

'Are you sure of that?'

'Completely sure. I . . .' She flicked me a look under her lashes. 'Shall I tell you a secret? I know I'm over Oliver, because . . . because I'm in love with someone else. Don't ask me who, but I wish you could be as happy as I am, Kate, I really do. You know, Oliver is awfully fond of you.'

How odd that she should confide secrets to me, of all people – and that she should plead Oliver's cause. Whoever her man was, knowing him had changed her. 'I know,' I said. 'I'm fond of him, too. That's why . . .' Quite consciously, I set flaming torch to a metaphorical bridge behind me. 'I'll tell you a secret, too. I've agreed to marry Oliver.' If she couldn't keep the secret, it didn't matter. The more people who knew, the less chance for changing my mind.

Grandmother had guardedly accepted Lieutenant Gryce's reason for being in her home when she arrived back from committeeing with Mrs Lacey. But when Philip Farcroft strode into the grand saloon, large as life and showing no sign of humility, she must have felt her world had overturned. I gathered they were polite, if frostily formal, to each other, before Philip and his colleague took their leave. On his way out, Philip had chalked a large '12' on the front door, much to Billing's annoyance.

'Twelve!' Grandmother exclaimed when she recounted this story over luncheon. 'They said it ought to be more – they said the ballroom alone could sleep a battalion.' Her eyes swung accusingly to me. 'What did he say to you?'

I had no intention of answering *that*. 'He had a job to do, Grandmother. Neither of us relished it, but—'

'He was enjoying it. I could tell he was. Getting his own back.'

'Can you blame him?'

Her face pinched. 'I don't wish to discuss it. I feel quite sick. I shall protest to the authorities. Uncouth yeomanry clomping about the house . . .' She glanced at Tom, who was heaping more potato on to his plate and mashing it with rivers of gravy. 'It could prove a disastrous influence. However . . .' Straightening herself, she visibly shook away that unpleasant subject. 'Tell us about last evening, Catherine. Did you see Mr Payne? I'm appalled that he saw fit to—'

'Mr Payne retired last year,' I said.

'Did he?' Her surprise was more on account of her failed memory than for the fact itself. 'Why . . . why, yes, of course . . . I'd quite forgotten. How stupid of me. I've yet to meet the new man – what's his name? Hunt? He came up through the ranks, I believe. Well, that explains a good deal.'

'He knew all about me. Someone had reported all my doings – even my movements in London.'

She stared at me hawkishly. 'Who?'

'I only wish I knew.' I had been over the possibilities, but could think of no one who fitted the role of informer.

'Farcroft?'

'I doubt it. Farmer Farcroft couldn't possibly know about—'

'I meant the son – Philip. Judging by his behaviour this morning he'd be only too pleased to make difficulties for any of us.' She must have seen that I was about to argue in

Philip's defence, for she silenced me with a gesture. 'Men can be furious at being scorned, too.'

'It wasn't Philip!' Of course it wasn't. Philip would never do such an underhand thing. But maybe his girl, Lou Roughton . . . No, that couldn't be right, either. 'I don't know who it could have been. The plain fact is, they knew everything, and it looked bad. And . . . forgive me, Grandmother, but Mr Hunt wasn't pleased that you had tried to use your influence to protect me. They're going to be keeping a close eye on me. I have to report to a police station once a week, and I'm not supposed to leave the area without permission.'

'That's flagrant harassment! How dare they—' She broke off as something made Tom jerk round, staring at the door. We all followed his gaze, but there was nothing to see, or hear.

'Emmet!' Brightening, he flung down the spoon with which he had been eating his potato, and dashed off, shouting, 'Emmet! Emmet, we're here!'

His volume made Grandmother rub papery fingers against her brow as she considered the potato and gravy spattering the cloth. 'Tom is so noisy! But his hearing is extraordinary. Sometimes I almost believe those two are in psychic communication.'

'It can't be Emmet,' Vicky said. 'What would Emmet be doing home on a Thursday?'

Tom's footsteps returned, racing down the hall. He charged in, braking by means of the doorknob from which he swung for a moment, beaming all over his face, crying, 'It's Emmet! Mater, it's Emmet. Look . . .'

Slower footsteps sounded, muffled on carpet then clumping on parquet as Emmet appeared in the doorway, smiling sheepishly. He was in uniform, an infantryman's khaki with enormous shiny boots, cap tucked under his arm.

'He's a soldier!' Tom chortled. 'Look at him! Isn't he splendid?'

Proudly, Emmet held out his arms, displaying his new finery, then ran a hand over his bright, newly cropped hair. He looked like a mischievous choirboy. 'Well? What do you think of this jolly old outfit then?'

'Emmet!' Vicky was on her feet, breathless with pride as she ran to greet him. 'You've volunteered!'

'So I have,' he agreed with a grin. 'Answered my country's call. The Laceys are going, too.'

The news gave Vicky momentary pause. 'Both of them?'

'Some of our other chums, too,' Emmet replied. 'We've been planning it ever since the news broke. We shall all go together. Topping, isn't it?'

Another hesitation from Vicky made me wonder which one of the Laceys most concerned her. 'I'm so proud of you all,' she said. 'I shall telephone to Mrs Lacey and say so,' and she hurried off, confirming, in my mind, that my guess was correct. But which brother had she fallen for – James, or David?

Grandmother remained seated, face like parchment, eyes dull with shock. She had lost her two oldest sons, and now the darling of her heart had volunteered to fight in what everyone was already calling 'the Great War'.

'I say, don't look like that, Mater,' Emmet protested. 'What was I supposed to do? Moulder away in that office when there's adventure to be had, Huns to shoot and medals to be won? The engineering business was boring the socks off me. I'll give it another go when I've done my bit. But first I'm off to teach Kaiser Bill's lot a thing or two.'

'Emmet,' she managed faintly, fear and pride waging

war in her face as she got to her feet and went to embrace
him. 'Oh, my boy . . .'

TWENTY

As 1914 ground on, my life altered irretrievably. I moved to Lynn, to lodge at Hawthorn House with Saffron and Eddy, and I began work as George Chorley's secretary. Within weeks, the demand for tinned goods tripled: fearing shortages because of the war, people bought and hoarded far more than they needed. Our prices soared accordingly: Chef Foods prospered, as Grandmother had predicted.

The *Lynn News* continued to print lists of visitors to seaside hotels and guest houses, but these slowly gave way to a roll of honour naming all local volunteers. Emmet and the Laceys were pictured there – '*More brave Norfolk sons, bound for the front*'.

Harvest passed and, with autumn gilding the woods, many farm workers volunteered for the army. The newspaper reported the social doings of the Norfolk Yeomanry: during one football match, a certain P. Farcroft scored a goal. So, he had gone back to Suffolk. But no Farcroft-Roughton nuptials had been recorded in the Births, Marriages and Deaths column – I had searched the paper every week. Had they married without announcement? Or were they waiting until the war ended? More and more it became apparent that the trouble would not be 'over by Christmas'.

Uncle Frank, commissioned as a war artist, went regularly to France and returned with sketchbooks full of terrible images, some of which were printed alongside the equally graphic photographs in picture magazines such as *War Illustrated*. He was reticent about his own adventures, but his manner grew graver every time I saw him.

At Denes Hill, Grandmother resented the intrusion of a dozen officers and men of the Gloucestershire Territorials. I think she pulled strings, for after a few weeks the lodgers found other billets and Denes Hill was redesignated as a Red Cross Convalescent Home for Officers. Soon, beds lined the ballroom and saloon, transforming them into wards for the patients. The piano went into the staircase hall and a billiard table appeared at one end of the library. Since the nurses who arrived to staff the hospital slept on the first floor, Tom, the only male member of the family still resident, moved into Uncle Frank's rooms a floor above; Grandmother kept her own suite, with Anderson in the dressing room. She also kept the study for her own use. With Vicky's room next to it, that area at the end of the south wing, with the tower stairs leading off it, became private family quarters.

Vicky, loosening apron strings at long last, undertook a formal three-month nursing course, in Lynn. She even became a member of the Rifle Club, much to her mother's disquiet, and in early December joined the staff at Denes Hill.

Although I did what I could to help refugees, the wounded and those left in trouble at home, in conjunction with the Red Cross and the Work for Women Fund, I remained a passionate pacifist; I became a founder member of the Lynn Peace Association, and began to write material for leaflets and the *Cry Peace* magazine. Oliver didn't share my views but he went along to meetings to indulge me, as he indulged me in a good many things. The family knew we were 'walking out'. Neither Frank nor Saffron was entirely happy about it, but they allowed me to know my own mind.

On Fridays, Oliver accompanied me to the police station to report, after which we went to the cinema to catch up on the latest war news. He managed to acquire a car 'for essential business purposes': we didn't use it about town, petrol being short, but we drove over to Eveningham most Sundays. With my reputation to consider, we visited his flat only when discretion permitted – he said that a man's appetite, once roused, had to be satisfied now and then. Anyway, I enjoyed his lovemaking. It comforted me, provided brief respite from the pressures of the war, and it confirmed the bond between us, even if that bond was mainly physical. However, since neither of us wished to find ourselves in the embarrassing position of having to get married, he practised techniques of birth control and even gave me a copy of a rather scandalous pamphlet on the subject, by Dr Marie Stopes. But he relished the prospect of our enjoying a full married life without need for precautions. Wouldn't I please name a date, or at least let him announce our engagement? He was a patient man but, after all, he was nearing forty.

'We'll tell them at Christmas,' I conceded.

Touchingly delighted, Oliver brought out a Wells family heirloom, a ring with three rubies in a band. It proved too small for my finger, but we took it to a jeweller to be altered.

All too soon, Emmet completed his training and wrote that he was '*going over*'. His next letter assured us it was '*just like a picnic. We can scarcely hear the guns at all.*' Tom loved to have the letters read aloud: they made him laugh. He thought it all a huge adventure and wished he could go, too. He might have been tempted to emulate the soldiers he saw parading around with rifles, but all the guns at Denes Hill had been locked away after the incident with Mad Jack.

Although she worried over Emmet and Frank, Grandmother resigned herself to the new situation, her house made into a hospital, her own meals served in her private sitting room, leaving the dining room for the use of staff and mobile patients. She forbore the loss of Billing and other male staff, who were needed in more useful places, but she was thankful that her familiar Annie and Mrs May, the cook, stayed on to help in house and kitchen. She even took upon herself the role of social organizer for the wounded officers. While the war endured, she would do her bit, though she remained optimistic that it would not last long. No more than a few months, that was all.

In retrospect, those months seem unreal: we inhabited a kind of limbo, almost relishing the novelty and excitement but half believing we would, one day soon, wake up to find everything back to normal.

The illusion died in mid-December, when German ships sneaked up through North Sea mist and bombarded defenceless communities at Hartlepool, Whitby and Scarborough, killing some civilians, wounding others, and destroying property. It made us realize our own vulnerability. How easily it could have been Hunstanton, or Eveningham. Would we be next?

Only two days later came news that Emmet had been wounded. He wrote that he was doing fine, it was just a scratch, he'd arranged it so he could come home for Christmas. He arrived on crutches, obviously in pain, his thigh heavily bandaged, but still with that indomitable good humour – which didn't fool any of us.

Denes Hill being full of convalescing soldiers and medical personnel, Saffron invited Emmet, Tom and

Grandmother – with her shadow, Anderson – to spend Christmas Day at Hawthorn House. We missed both Uncle Frank and Vicky, he in France, she on nursing duty at Denes Hill, but we toasted health to 'absent friends' and wished a swift end to the war. Then Oliver got to his feet, rapped his knife handle on the table to gain everyone's attention, cleared his throat and said, 'We all hoped the war would be over by Christmas. Sadly, we were wrong. Let us hope, then, it may be ended by Easter. But, whether it ends or not, I, personally, anticipate that time with pleasure. Kate has promised to marry me in the spring.'

I had promised no such thing. But my objections died before his proud smile as he opened a small box to show me the ruby ring and place it on my finger. It fitted perfectly. It was beautiful, and it weighed hardly anything – so why did it feel like a ball and chain?

'Thank heaven for some good news, for a change,' Emmet cried, coming to kiss me and shake Oliver's hand.

'I agree,' Grandmother concurred. 'A toast. To Catherine and Oliver.'

Saffron, catching my eye, mouthed, 'Here's luck!' while her expression said I would need it. And Tom, I noticed with a pang, was frowning at Oliver. He didn't understand engagements.

Delicately wiping a happy tear from a corner of her eye, Grandmother said, 'We shall have a party to celebrate – a family dinner at Denes Hill. They can't object to our using the dining room for one evening when we've given up our Christmas. Let's hold it on January the nineteenth – Emmet and Tom's birthday – then it can be a double celebration.'

What nobody mentioned was that it would also be another farewell to Emmet, who expected to be summoned back to the front any day.

* * *

Over Christmas, German aeroplanes made three raids on Dover. Though the bombs did little damage, the attacks were another measure of England's vulnerability – and of Germany's lack of sensitivity in choosing that season to deliver such messages of hate. I no longer wondered which side I was on. H. G. Wells had put it succinctly: *'We are fighting without any hatred of the German people. But we have to destroy an evil system that has taken possession of German life. This is a war to exorcize a world madness. We have to smash Prussian Imperialism. We are fighting a war for peace.'* I knew about Prussian ambition and Prussian hubris – I had suffered because of it. But political necessity, waging war on evil, had a habit of destroying everything in its path, including the innocent on both sides. I remained concerned for family and friends in Germany, especially Mother and the *Menschen*. We heard that our Russian allies were pressing into east Prussia. How I wished I knew exactly where Lindhafen lay.

On the nineteenth of January, the day of the dinner party, I caught the afternoon train to Eveningham and, needing to call on Mrs Lacey, borrowed the dogcart and drove myself to Lenhoe, with old Willow between the shafts clopping gamely along muddy winter lanes. The weather was cold but dry, with a brisk wind that froze my cheeks, not helping the niggling headache that had been with me for several days.

At Lenhoe Manor, the parlourmaid who let me in was red-eyed from weeping, but before I could enquire into her trouble Mrs Lacey herself appeared in the drawing-room doorway, white as death but totally composed. 'My dear,' she greeted me, gliding across the floor to take my arm with fingers that dug painfully into my flesh. 'I've just had a letter from Captain Mears. Bad news, I'm afraid. It's James. He's dead. Killed in action. Trying to save a friend. No – don't say anything. He was fond of you, Kate. And you liked him, too, didn't you? Such a sweet boy. We must be strong for him. He knew what he was doing. He gave his life willingly. Like so many others. Will you tell your grandmother for me, please?'

Her terrible, accepting calm, allied with the hand that still bit into my arm, told me that, beneath her composure, her nerves were in shreds. I led her into her drawing room and did what I could to comfort her, mentioning Vicky's name to see how she would react. But evidently Mrs Lacey knew nothing of Vicky's romance with one of her sons. I stayed with her until her husband returned from his business office in Hunstanton.

As I drove back to Eveningham, in a daze of sadness for the Laceys' grief, sunset spread orange flame across the sky, deepening to a sullen red glow. It lit the underside of black bands of cloud against a backdrop of clear aquamarine, as though the mouth of hell had opened, to cast over the world a malevolent reflection of what was happening on the fields of France and Belgium. James Lacey, 'short, but sweet', was dead. And at Denes Hill they were preparing a party to celebrate my engagement and the twins' twenty-fourth birthday, with Emmet due to report back to his depot at the end of the week. How was I to tell him what had befallen his friend? How was I to tell Vicky? Was it James she loved?

I decided not to tell them. Not until later. My headache had grown so bad that I couldn't think.

The sanctum had become 'my' room when I had occasion to spend a night. Now, besides impressions of childhood, it held bittersweet memories of Philip. This was where I had last seen him, watched him leave, knowing he hated me. I remembered it whenever I slept in the tower – though 'slept' hardly describes nights spent tossing in bad dreams or lying awake with troubled thoughts and feelings swirling thickly about me. Most of the wounded men, resting several floors below, kept a cheerful face by day, but many feared their return to the front. Others had been spared, though maimed for life – men with missing limbs, men blinded or emasculated, men mangled so severely one wondered how they had survived. Their agonies disturbed the ether. At night, for me, the house resounded with anxiety, with bitter regrets and silent wailing.

My spirit friends hovered, too, crowding close to the troubled world. Their concern disturbed my sleep and coloured my waking hours. Among them, I often sensed my drowned uncle, John. But, thin though the veil spread at times, neither John nor I could break through with any clarity. I only knew he was there, anxiously observing, worrying and warning.

By the time I had changed, ready for the party, my headache was a dull, leaden numbness, the worst I had felt since . . . since the day Uncle Harry died, now that I thought about it. Oppression clouded my senses and churned my stomach. The ruby ring seemed heavy and tight on my finger, though it turned easily enough when I fiddled with it, as I often did. I had never felt less like attending a party. Were we mad, to celebrate when young men were dying senselessly? Was someone I cared for in danger?

Frank was still away, though he had sent good wishes. Saffron had decided to stay at home with Eddy, who had a chesty cough. But six of us met for the celebration – Grandmother and Vicky, Emmet and Tom, Oliver and I. I had hoped to speak to Oliver alone, to tell him about James, but he was delayed at the office and didn't arrive until just before we were to eat. Then, he seemed so happy that I forbore to spoil his evening. He looked amazingly fit and handsome in his white tie and tails, and I thought perhaps, after all, we might find a measure of happiness together. I *was* fond of him.

The private dinner culminated in further toasts to our future. Even Vicky was generous in her good wishes: if she harboured a flicker of envy she hid it well – more so than some of the wounded officers, who joined us for drinks later. As we gathered in the staircase hall for a singsong, round the piano in the shade of potted palms, more than one man jokingly mourned the loss of another eligible girl: 'And to a man too old to be a soldier!' a wheelchair-bound twenty-two-year-old exclaimed. 'Change your mind, Kate. Run off with me, instead.' Everyone laughed immoderately at this self-mocking joke: Robbie had no legs to run with.

In the library, some patients played billiards while others played cards. The house rang with laughter and song. Vicky played 'Oh, you beautiful doll', and 'Alexander's Rag-time Band', but when some wag broke into 'Waiting at the church' I shook my head at their foolery and moved away from the group, making for the main stairs, longing for peace and quiet. I kept thinking about James Lacey.

As I reached the foot of the stairs, Oliver slid his hand under my arm, asking, 'What's wrong?'

'I have a terrible headache,' I confessed. 'Would you mind if I went to lie down for half an hour? I'm sorry, but—'

His mouth tightened under the dark line of his moustache, but he said, 'Of course. If you're not feeling well . . .'

'I'll come down again the moment I feel a little better,' I promised and, touching his arm in gratitude, escaped up the main stairs. I knew he would not dare to follow me, not in full view of the others. Why did that make me feel better? With some relief, I gained the head of the stairs and the upper corridor, out of sight of the revellers. Cool air embraced me, while behind me the merriment faded to a murmur.

As I opened the sanctum door and climbed the final flight of stairs, I felt I was truly gaining sanctuary. My head had begun to throb as if a storm threatened, but up here all was quiet and cool. I didn't light the lamp but waded through darkness to the couch-bed, to throw a blanket round my shoulders; then I opened one of the windows and let the cold night air lap in, breathing it deeply, willing it to clear my head. The baleful, coal-red sky of sunset had darkened to black velvet scattered with bright stars. A dark, moonless night. A night when warnings beat in the air, fluttering against my nerves like unseen wings, tightening the band of pain round my head. I stood staring into the darkness, twisting Oliver's ring round and round on my finger, uncertain about the future, grieving for James Lacey, longing for Philip . . .

I had opened only one of the casement windows. Now, as I stood staring out of it, something moved in the next pane to my right. *Kate* . . . The soundless whisper lifted the hairs on my nape and along my arms. 'John?' I murmured in answer, and felt his urgency, his anxiety. He seemed to be standing behind my shoulder. I could feel him there, his presence a chill tingle on my senses, though when I glanced round there was nothing to see. Only his reflection shimmered faintly on the window, a dark figure half seen by starlight. 'I'm trying to hear, John!' I whispered. 'Help me!'

I'm not sure what happened then. Did I close my eyes

for a second? All I remember is seeing with a shock that the image in the window had changed. Someone was standing there. Someone real! I shrieked in alarm, fending him off when he reached for me.

'For heaven's sake!' Oliver's voice came tightly. 'What on earth is wrong with you this evening?'

'You startled me!' I managed, licking dry lips, my heart beating so hard in my throat it almost suffocated me. 'For a moment . . . No, nothing.' For a moment I had been terrified – even after I recognized him. Stupid, Kate. Yes, stupid! He hadn't done it deliberately. Hadn't tried to sneak up on me. Why should I imagine he might do such a thing?

'What were you doing?' he demanded. 'Praying? That's what it sounded like. "Help me", you said. Help you do what? Get out of this engagement?'

'Oliver! What makes you say that?'

'*You* make me say it! You, and all those jokers downstairs. I know what they think – you're wasting yourself on me. I'm too old for you. Too old, too staid. They resent the fact that I'm not in uniform.'

'They were joking. They don't mean—'

' "Many a true word spoken in jest",' he quoted bitterly. 'Maybe you think I'm a coward, too. Believe me, if I were younger I'd have been over there by now, fighting with the rest of them.'

The thought turned me cold and I grasped his arm. 'Don't say that! I don't want you to fight. Don't even think about it!'

'Would you care?'

'Of course I would care! Oliver . . .'

He caught me in his arms, pulling me to him, his mouth finding mine in a savage kiss that told me how jealous he was of those younger men below, heroes bearing wounds that told of their courage, while he had to remain behind. 'Then prove it,' he muttered, holding me tight against his body so that I felt his arousal. 'Let me make love to you. Here. Now.'

'We can't—'

'You must! I want you. I need you.' He was pushing me backwards, his mouth hot on my neck. I felt the edge of the couch-bed behind my legs. I overbalanced, falling on my back with Oliver on top of me. His mouth silenced my protests while his hand raked up my skirt, roughly seeking a way inside my undergarments, fumbling at his buttons to expose himself.

Then a light played round the room. A thin beam. Lightning? No – a torch. Its beam shone full in my eyes, blinding me. 'Katie!' said Tom's worried voice. 'Are you all right?'

With a roar like a wounded bear, Oliver heaved himself off the bed, shouting, 'Thomas, you—— ——' The light caught him, found him with shirt tail out, trying to make himself decent. He leaned over the rail guarding the stairs, grabbing for Tom, who ducked and threw up his arm. I heard the blow as his torch hit Oliver's hand. Oliver roared again, swearing bitterly. The torch clattered to the stairs. Its light winked out, leaving me blind. I heard Tom yell as he ran, while Oliver scrambled for the torch and flung it after the fleeing intruder. I think it hit the door as Tom slammed it shut.

I sat up, breathing hard as if I had been running, blood pounding painfully in my temple as I peered through the darkness to where I could hear his hoarse breathing. 'Oliver?'

'Bloody little peeping Tom!' he grated.

'He didn't intend—'

'Of course he intended it! Or is he in the habit of creeping into your room at night?'

I was so disgusted by the implications of that question that I couldn't think of an immediate reply. Then, in a low, sick voice, I told him, 'That is a foul thing to say.'

'I only meant . . . he might come without your knowing it. While you're asleep. I'm sorry. I'm angry. Do you blame me?'

'Before I go to bed,' I said, 'I always bolt the door. Tom wouldn't hurt me, but he sometimes likes to play jokes.' I had never, ever had reason to fear poor Tom. 'I only wish,' I added, 'that I had bolted my door this evening.'

His silence told me he had taken the point.

Then, in that silence, we both heard a new sound: an engine, low and distant, but distinct. It sounded like a heavy transport wagon such as the military used. But the road was a long way away. Even with the window open we should not have been able to hear—

'It's an aircraft!' Oliver muttered.

Dear God! A bombing raid? I threw myself to my knees on the window seat under the open casement, leaning to push the pane wide as I peered out, searching among the stars for a glimmer of artificial light. I could see nothing, but the noise grew louder, a steady, grinding roar like no aircraft I had ever heard. Oliver also came to the window, opening the next pane, staring at the sky . . .

Suddenly my eyes adjusted and there it was – a vast black shape blotting out the stars. I hadn't seen it because I hadn't been looking for anything of that size. A great ship. An airship.

'It's a Zeppelin!'

As we looked at each other, our hands met and clasped in mutual comfort before we turned again to stare at the sky. We knew of such things, of course. We had been told about them in magazines, seen pictures in illustrated weeklies. But this was different. Real. Menacing. The noise of its engine shook the tower, rattled windows, reverberated in my blood and bones. I saw two white lights and one green, vivid against the enormous black bulk. It swam so low we might have touched it. A great shuddering juggernaut, horribly beautiful, it sailed over the woods gulping up stars and spitting them out behind it. A harbinger of hell.

Neither of us said anything that I remember. We were both caught in helpless awe, like pheasants frozen before an inescapable enemy, simply watching, waiting, hardly breathing.

'Oliver—' But as I spoke there came a long hissing sound, then a strange confused flare of light from beyond the woods, and a deafening, crumping crash that made me throw my hands over my ears, crying out at the pain in my head. When I opened my eyes, everything was still. Except that the Zeppelin droned on, moving away.

It had dropped a bomb. Somewhere near Far Drove Farm. Philip's home.

Philip's father . . .

Not waiting to see more, we ran down to where other occupants of the house had gathered on the terrace in animated groups. In the ballroom, patients craned from their beds. Others hobbled on crutches, or came in wheelchairs, all exclaiming and discussing, not so much afraid as excited over the drama and spectacle. The great black shape in the sky was heading for Sandringham, where the royal family had lately been in residence.

'The first bomb came down beyond the woods,' someone said, pointing.

'*First* bomb?' I heard myself repeat in horror.

'There were two! Didn't you see . . .' Several voices joined in, telling how the second bomb had fallen further away, on the other side of the village. 'But the first flash was quite near – over in that direction. Isn't there a farm down there? Should someone go and see if . . .'

I found myself in the forefront of the group that went looking for torches, lanterns, bicycle lamps. As I raced back into the staircase hall, Oliver grasped my arm, saying, 'You're not to go.'

'Why not?'

'Because I say so. Stay indoors. Let the others—'

'I'm going!' I wrenched free of his grasp, almost hating him. 'Don't you understand? He's my grandfather. Isn't he?'

Oliver went still, as if I had hit him, and I hurried away.

Warmly wrapped against the freezing night, we made through the woods – Emmet in the lead, with one of the doctors, myself, three of the nurses and, hobbling gamely behind, two of the more mobile patients. Oliver had tagged along, too. The woods seemed eerily dark and silent, as if the wildlife had all gone to ground.

Gaining the short-cut lane, we hurried between its tall hedges. Then Emmet let out a yell, 'Hold it!' and beam by beam our lights descried the outlines of a low barrier of earth and broken branches thrown across our path. No, not another obstacle dug by Mad Jack, but the edge of a crater some twenty feet across. We stood on it, probing its dimensions with our lights. The bomb had demolished part of the hedge, gouging a deep hole, leaving only a few feet of grass beside the further hedge. Thank God it was here, not near the farmhouse.

'Who's that?' a voice roared out of the darkness –

unmistakably Mad Jack's voice. He appeared on the far edge of the crater, a shadow with a lantern swinging in his hand and a black dog at heel.

'We're from Denes Hill,' the doctor sang out. 'Anyone hurt? If there's anything we—'

But at the mention of Denes Hill, the old man laughed hoarsely. 'You can go back and tell 'em I'd like to see 'em use this lane now! Blast! That Hun airship done just what I've been a-prayin' for.' Another howl of raucous laughter split the night as he slapped his knee. 'Tell 'em I ordered it, special. Invited them Jerries over, just to dig this great hole! Blast, that'll—' The words choked off. The lantern swung wildly, and dropped, its pale light washing over him as he toppled, sliding down the far side of the crater to lie sprawled on the fresh earth. The dog leapt to the rim and stood there, barking alarm.

Impelled by panic, my thoughts all for Philip, I launched myself down the muddy slope and threw myself to my knees beside him. 'Mr Farcroft!' My torch showed his face yellowy-pale with pain and fear, three-day beard bristling as he muttered curses.

'It's my leg. My blasted leg!'

The doctor joined me, kneeling in the mud to make a swift examination by the light of the torch I held. The others gathered round, and, above us, the dog kept barking. I seem to remember snapping, 'Quiet, Boss!' but it ignored me, subsiding only when the old man snarled, 'Hush up, bor!'

After a while, the doctor said, 'He's torn his calf muscle, quite badly. He won't be able to walk. Is there anyone at the farm?'

'No, there en't,' Mad Jack growled. 'I live alone.'

Didn't Lou Roughton live at the farm? I wondered. Wasn't she now Philip's wife? I wanted to ask, but daren't.

The doctor looked up at the circle of faces round us. 'We need some kind of stretcher.'

'I'll go and see,' Emmet offered. 'Come on, Oliver.' And he set off to climb the crater's slope, tramping and sliding in fresh damp earth. After a moment's hesitation, with a black look for me, Oliver followed. Only then did I realize he had no coat over his dress suit – he had rushed out after me without thought for his own comfort. His glower warned me that I was already showing too much involvement, that this was none of my concern. Oh, but it was, it was! Philip would be so worried, feel so guilty for being away. What would the old man do now?

They brought back a wicker hurdle, on which Mad Jack lay muttering imprecations to himself as the men carried him to the house. One of the wounded officers had lost his right hand but valiantly used his left for carrying the hurdle. His friend, leaning on a crutch with his foot heavily bound, hobbled alongside and opened gates for them, while I took charge of Boss, holding him by the collar, the nurses beside me. We felt caught up in some awful, exciting adventure – the war had that effect on everyone.

At the farm, lamps glowed and the fire blazed brightly in the main room. Philip had grown up here, and Michael, my father. They had probably, each in his turn, climbed on the couch, laboured over books at the big table by the window, lain with the dogs on the hearthrug by the fire. Down those stairs Philip and I had come, hand in hand. Had Mother and Michael done the same, in their time? Too many memories lingered here.

While the nurses helped Mad Jack to his couch, where Saffron had rested with newborn Eddy beside her, I hovered anxiously. He kept looking at me – I suppose I was the only familiar face in the group. I wanted to help him, but Oliver's hand on my arm prevented me. Perhaps he was right – if I made too much fuss, someone might wonder why.

'You stay and assist me, Miss Mulligan,' the doctor instructed one of the nurses. 'The rest of you may as well go, we don't need an audience here. Miss Mulligan and I will manage. Perhaps someone would go for the local doctor – he ought to know about this.'

'I will,' Emmet offered.

'Me, too, old man,' the two wounded officers volunteered in the same breath, eager to be back in action.

The doctor almost denied them, but decided against it with a shake of his head and an understanding grin. 'Which leaves you, Mr Wells, to escort these three ladies back, if you will.'

'My pleasure.' Oliver smiled tightly, his hand insistent on my arm. He couldn't wait to get me away. 'Ladies . . .'

As I left, I saw the old man's expression – anxious and angry at the same time. He hated me, but he wished I wouldn't leave him alone, in pain and with strangers. Would he tell Philip I had abandoned him in his need?

During our walk back, the two nurses chattered excitedly, but Oliver said little. When we reached the lights of Denes Hill, I realized why: his elegant shoes and evening suit were thick with mud, and cobwebs festooned his hair. The rest of us were similarly daubed, but accepted it as a result of our excursion; Oliver evidently blamed me for forcing him into an undignified escapade.

'Don't!' He flinched away when I reached to remove the cobweb. 'If you'll excuse me, I'll go and tidy myself up. And then I shall go home. I've early appointments tomorrow.'

Not wanting the evening to end like that, I went down to

the yard to wait for him near his car. But lanternlight drew me to the stable, where old Willow was now the sole resident. I found Tom in there, huddled shivering in a nest of straw in an empty stall, with the little dog, Jim, cradled in his arms. As the door creaked, Tom looked up, lamplight glinting gold in streaks of tears under his eyes.

'Tom!' I exclaimed in concern, going to bend over him.

'I didn't mean anything!' he wept. 'I didn't, Kate. I wanted to make you jump. And then there was something in the sky, and a big noise. It scared me. Oliver did it. He sent it to get me!'

Impulsively I sank down beside him, cradling his tousled golden head to my shoulder as he sobbed against me like a child. I tried to explain about the Zeppelin and the bombs, but he couldn't seem to grasp the idea of unknown enemies sending war machines to hurt us.

After a while, I heard Oliver cranking his car in the yard.

'No!' Tom cried when I tried to get up, his hands fastening on my coat to hold me down. 'Don't go to him. Let him go. Let him go!'

'It's only Oliver, Tom,' I reasoned. 'I need to talk to him.'

'No! No, I don't want you to. He'll hurt you again! I hate him. I hate him, Kate.'

He wouldn't let me go. He wept and pleaded so urgently that I feared for him. 'All right, Tom.' I settled back in the straw, cradling him in my arms, telling myself I could make my peace with Oliver later. 'But he won't hurt you, you know. He was only angry because you crept up on us.'

'He was hurting you.'

'No, he wasn't.'

'He was! He likes to hurt.'

'You mustn't say things like that,' I chided. Poor Tom,

everything was so immediate with him. Because Oliver had lost his temper in the turret, Tom had decided he must be an ogre. He even imagined that Oliver had summoned the Zeppelin to punish him. Poor Tom.

TWENTY-ONE

I sat comforting Tom until his weight grew heavy across my lap and I realized he was asleep. Reluctant to disturb him, I let him rest, intending to wake him shortly. But the events of the day caught up with me and the next thing I knew I was waking, still in the straw in the stable, with dawn light filtering through high windows.

Voices in the yard had disturbed me. Some of the staff slept in the loft over the stable and others came in from the village; they were arriving for duty, chattering excitedly.

Tom and I went with them and shared a pot of tea, while around us girls began to stoke up fires and cooks prepared early breakfasts, everyone talking about the Zeppelin and the two bombs.

'That nearly killed poor old Mr Farcroft,' one of the girls gossiped. 'He had a heart attack, so I now heard.'

'That was a stroke,' another argued.

Heart attack? Stroke? Dear Lord, was the old man really ill?

'Who'll do for him with Mrs Gaywood not there?' the girl added. 'Well, din't you know that second bomb now blasted a hole in her house? She're in a proper to-do. They took her away to stay with her daughter in Lenhoe.'

A third girl, ruddy-faced with sparkling eyes, laughed, 'Well, that'll give Lou Roughton a good excuse to come a-runnin' over from Heacham, playin' nursemaid. Master

381

Philip'll be wholly grateful to whoever take care of the old bor, and I reckon Lou still have hope in that direction.'

Before I could stop myself, I said, 'I'd heard they were engaged.'

'Engaged?!' They all giggled at that and the ruddy one exclaimed, 'Don't know where you heard that, Miss Kate. 'less you listened in to Lou Roughton's dreams!'

Carrying a tray to the dining room for the nurses' breakfasts, I encountered Vicky on the back stairs, looking fresh and pretty in her starched uniform. Against the ornate white cap her red-blonde hair looked extra bright. She had a glow about her lately. Love had done wonders for her disposition. Sadly, I had to mar her happiness.

'You look as if you've slept in a stable,' she observed, removing a piece of straw from my sleeve and noting the mud on my clothes.

'I've been with Tom. He was really upset last night.'

'Poor Tom.' But she hadn't time to worry about her brother just then. 'Shall I take that tray?'

'Thank you. Vicky . . . I'm afraid I've some bad news. I should have told you last night. I was waiting until after the party, but with the Zeppelin and everything . . . You know I went over to Lenhoe yesterday? There was a telegram. James . . . was killed, two days ago.'

Her eyes dilated, very blue in her pale face. 'Oh, no! What fearful news for Emmet, just as he's going back to the show. Is David all right?'

'As far as they know.' Before I could say more she turned away, taking the tray, saying that she would break the news to Emmet and her mother. The sheen of tears in her eyes made my own throat feel thick.

I went up to the sanctum, washed myself hastily and put on more serviceable clothes. I had an appointment in

Hunstanton with the local organizer of the National Egg Collection, but first . . . I couldn't help myself: an irresistible urge beckoned me back to Far Drove.

In the farmyard, I encountered an elderly worker just leaving the house. He slid me a sidelong look, saying, 'He en't well. You'll have to go in the house and call. And then duck, right smart, afore he throw somethin'.'

But it was Boss who met me as I opened the door and went into the dark front hall. The dog stood in the parlour doorway, barking like a fury.

'Hush up, Boss!' the snarl came from inside the room and, 'Who's that? Show yore face.'

I did so, and found him on his feet. Leaning heavily on a stick, with his left foot held off the ground, he bent over the hearth with a log in one hand, making up the fire from earlier embers.

I had half expected a torrent of abuse as a greeting, but instead, as narrowed eyes registered my identity, he said nothing. The longcase clock in a corner tocked the seconds, and the fire crackled and spat as fresh logs caught, while Philip's father regarded me with hooded, hostile eyes.

'I came to see how you are,' I said.

'Hah!' he snorted. 'Do you care?'

'I just . . . I was concerned about you. With Philip away . . . is it just your leg?'

'En't a gammy leg enough?' he demanded.

So much for kitchen gossip! Still, I was relieved it was not worse.

Moving awkwardly, he pushed the last log on to the fire, then levered himself away from the hearth, limped back to the couch and sat down, reaching for a blanket that lay crumpled there. 'Blast! As if I hen't got trouble enough.

Who's going to do all the work? My men off to the army and Mrs Gaywood now gone to Lenhoe . . .'

'I expect someone from the village will look in on you later.'

'I don't need nobody. But,' he slanted me a dark look under bristling brows, 'since you're here, go fill the kettle and put that on the hob. I'm spittin' feathers.'

In the kitchen, dank and cold with the fire out, I pumped water to fill the kettle and took it back to the main room, setting it on the hob plate and swinging it over the fire. As I straightened, I saw on the mantel two photographs in ornate silver frames, one of Michael Farcroft – my father, I thought with a pang – the other a recent portrait of Philip in his dress uniform, taken in a studio. My heart contracted as I picked up the frame and smoothed my fingers on the glass. Philip looked out beneath the proud peak of his military cap, straight and tall, gloves in one hand, the other resting on the hilt of a sword. His pose echoed that of Carl-Heinz in the photo I had once cherished, except that Carl-Heinz had worn an arrogant sneer and Philip was smiling. Philip . . . Oh, my darling . . .

When Mad Jack spoke from behind me I was so startled I almost dropped the photo. My fingers clutched it, holding it to my heart as I spun round and saw the farmer frowning at me. He said, 'You can put that back where it belong.'

I did so, reluctantly, croaking through stiff lips, 'How is he?'

'Steady,' he said at once with a touch of paternal pride. 'Pleased to be doin' his duty. What'd you expect? He en't breakin' his heart over you, missy. Got more sense than that.'

'I . . .' I cleared the catch from my throat, said, 'I'm glad,' and took myself back to the kitchen where, trembling, I found a tray and laid it with breakfast things. A jug of milk sat under a beaded cloth, on a marble shelf in the larder. I poured some into a glass for the old man.

He drank it gratefully, managing to spill some of it down his front. He allowed me to mop him dry, and as I straightened he cocked a beady eye at me, his face marred by those three red scars. 'What're you doing here, girl? That won't do you no good moonin' after my Philip.'

'I'm not here because of Philip. Not the way you mean.' I stood in front of him, staring at my hands, twisting the ruby ring on my finger. 'I never meant to hurt him. But I had to stop seeing him. You see—'

'I don't want to hear no more. Best you go away. Go away and forget him – the way your mother forgot Michael.'

Stung by that, I looked directly at him, seeing his frown waver through a skim of tears. 'You're wrong, Mr Farcroft – my mother didn't forget about your son. She had good reason to remember him. She had *me*.' I let him think about that for a moment, then, 'I'm your granddaughter, Mr Farcroft. I'm Michael's daughter. Perhaps now you understand why I had to give Philip up – we're too closely related.'

In the silence, I heard the kettle begin to sing faintly under the tock-tick of the old clock. Boss came padding to his master's side and the farmer put out a hand, absently pulling the dog's ear, his eyes intent on my face. I could see him thinking back, making calculations.

After aeons, he said gruffly, 'How'd you make that out?'

'Your wife knew. She wrote to warn my grandfather. I can bring you the letter, if you want to see it. She had caught them together. In the hay loft. I'm sorry. I shouldn't have told you, especially when you're not well. But I can't bear knowing that Philip hates me.'

His eyes had narrowed to slits. 'Blast . . .' he said under his breath. 'I was told there'd been words said. Then Clara was sent away, up north. Best that way, so my old girl reckon. Best off with her own sort, she say – and I reckoned she was right. Never did take to her comin' here, putting notions in my boy's head, making him neglect his work. He missed her, blasted fool. Mooned about like a sick calf. But I had other things on my mind. Bad harvests, falling prices. I had a farm to run, and a family to raise.' He rubbed his left thigh as if it ached. 'Then she come back . . .'

The fire spat; a log shifted and sank, sending a shower of golden sparks up the blackened chimney. The kettle sang more loudly and Jack Farcroft rasped a hand across his stubbled chin, saying, 'That wan't the same. She was then a wealthy widow, with gentry chasing after her. Didn't want to know us Farcrofts no more.' He stared into space, his brow dark as he remembered. 'I didn't know what was afoot. Too busy to see what was going on right under my nose – my boy hoping again, and her . . .'

'Did he know about me? Do you think she told him?'

'I reckon she . . . No.' He shook his head. 'That's no good me making up what I don't know. Fact is, I never did understand what was eating the boy. Thought he'd got slack and lazy. I rode him hard. Too hard, maybe. He 'ouldn't talk to me about feelings. Kept that for his mother. He was soft, that boy. Too easy led. When Clara got wed and went away – right away, abroad – I was glad. But he never got over it.' He stared at the fire, his eyes glistening. 'Got careless, he did. That day he was ploughing . . . They came running for me, but by the time I got there he was sinking, the lifeblood running out of him into the soil. "Don't fret," he say. "Don't fret, Dad. That don't make no nevermind." And he just let go. Died, in my arms.

386

Smiling. Glad to be gone. Blast, girl . . .'

He turned his head away, brushing his sleeve across his eyes. Moved by his grief, I stared at the photos of his two sons on the mantel, seeing the family likeness. But Michael was darker, thinner, almost gaunt – shadowed, perhaps, by his sorrow over the girl he had lost and the child he had never known. Had he guessed I was his daughter?

'I'm sorry,' I breathed. 'I'm desperately sorry. For all of us. I know you don't believe I cared for Philip, but—'

'He never believed it, neither,' the harsh voice informed me. 'He en't soft like Michael was. He have a good head on his shoulders. Good solid sense. He knew it 'ouldn't last. You from the hill and him from the farm? No, maw, that never set fair to come to nothing and Philip knew it. "Let's go tell them," he say, and you say, "We can't." "Let's get wed," he say, and you don't answer.'

I could hardly speak for misery. 'He *told* you about that?'

'We talked.'

'I see.' So Philip hadn't trusted me. Every word I'd spoken to him, every word I'd written to him, every time I'd been in his arms . . . 'He told me he was going to marry Lou Roughton.'

'Did he, now?' He wasn't about to share his son's secrets with me.

Feeling my engagement ring under my fingers, I looked down at it, caught by a heavy sense of finality. Until that moment, I believe I had entertained lingering hopes that the tale of my illegitimacy might be false. Now I knew that it was true, and perhaps he had suspected it, in his heart. So my last tiny hope evaporated. Displaying the ring for the old man to see, I said, 'I'm engaged myself. You might tell Philip that, when you write. I'm going to marry Oliver Wells.'

He might not have heard. He watched me, his face still, intent on his own thoughts. Was he seeking some family resemblance, or—

Outside, footsteps accompanied a murmur of voices, a knock on the door. Boss rushed to confront the intruders, barking loudly until a bass command silenced him. Then a trilling female voice called, 'You now there, Mr Farcroft? That's on'y me – Maisie Pike.' She appeared in the doorway, a skinny woman with a pointed nose like a fox, peering through thick glasses under a large hat. 'I've got my Ruth with me. And we met Sergeant Playford in the lane, a-comin' to see about that— Oh.' She had come far enough into the room to realize, despite her short sight, that the farmer was not alone. Behind her, a girl of about twelve hung back as if scared to enter the ogre's den, while the burly figure of Police Sergeant Playford, from Hunstanton, filled the doorway.

'Well, now,' the sergeant said, his investigator's mind drawing all kinds of wrong conclusions. 'Miss Brand.'

'Good morning, Sergeant,' I greeted as levelly as I could. 'I'm glad you've come. Mr Farcroft is going to need some help and I have work to do. I just called in to see how he was.'

'Good of you, miss,' he said, but I knew he was speculating.

I took my leave, wishing Mad Jack a speedy recovery. His expression said he wished the lot of us to the devil. Mrs Pike was already starting to fuss round, telling him what he needed and what he must do.

In a daze of uncertainty, wondering if I had done the right thing in going to the farm, I completed my errand in Hunstanton and returned to Lynn.

The Zeppelin attack dominated all conversation: enemy airships had sailed down the edge of the Wash, passing over the coastal villages, dropping a few indiscriminate bombs as they went. Minimal damage had been done, until the craft arrived over Lynn. There, two streets lay in ruins; people had been injured by flying fragments, and a woman and a small boy had been killed – shocking confirmation that, in this war, danger threatened us all, even in our own homes.

I tried to phone Oliver from my office at Chef Foods, but his clerk said he was out on business. Then I was called to help when one of our girls cut her hand badly and another fainted at sight of the blood. In the noisy, steamy cannery I was trying to restore calm when George Chorley came puffing up, red-faced, with two sturdy women behind him wearing armbands of the newly formed women's Police Volunteers.

'Are you Catherine Brand?' one of them asked, laying officious hold of my shoulder. 'I have orders to arrest you on suspicion of being an enemy spy.' And right there, in front of half the workforce of Chef Foods, she fastened a pair of handcuffs round my wrists.

On the recreation ground, behind a high fence of barbed wire, temporary wooden huts had been erected to house German internees. As I was bundled up the steps into one of these huts, I saw Harald Ehrenfried's pale, startled face. He called, 'Miss Brand!' but the policewomen thrust me through the door and slammed it behind us. They put me in a side room, empty but for a bench and table, its small window frosted and thickly barred. Better than the cell under the Town Hall, but not much.

With my hands still shackled, I paced the room, letting

my shoes rap loudly on the bare board floor to indicate my fury at the way I had been handled. No one had bothered to inform me what crime I was supposed to have committed. Why, suddenly, was I accused of being a spy?

Two hours later, the policewomen returned and led me to another room, furnished with basic desk, chairs and a row of filing cabinets. On the wall behind the desk hung a picture of the King, and beneath it sat the lugubrious Inspector Jarvis. To my relief, Oliver was there, too.

'Oliver! Thank heaven, I was beginning—'

'Say nothing,' he counselled sharply. 'Inspector, is it really necessary for Miss Brand to be handcuffed?'

Jarvis nodded at one of the policewomen, who came to unlock my bonds. Rubbing my wrists, I sat down on the edge of a hard chair, with Oliver beside me, and the questioning began.

The inspector seemed fascinated by my movements the previous day: he even asked about sleeping arrangements at Denes Hill: 'So you're in the habit of using the top room in the house? . . . Did you go up about nine thirty last evening? . . . How long were you there? . . . Were you alone? . . . What were you doing?'

How could I reveal what had happened in the sanctum last night? 'I had a headache!' I repeated for the tenth time, wondering if my face was as scarlet as it felt.

'You see, the thing is, Miss Brand,' the inspector went on, talking through his black bush of moustache, 'we've had a report of bright lights shining from the top room at Denes Hill last night, just before the German airships came over. At least two people in Eveningham village saw lights flash, as if signalling. And this morning you visited Mr John Farcroft, at his farm, which was also showing lights last night. I understand Mr Farcroft openly boasted of having arranged for the airships to come.'

I stared at him, my mind whirling. Where did these stories begin? As the insane interview went on, I gathered that someone had repeated Mad Jack's ravings of the previous night – probably Emmet, or one of the wounded officers, when they went to find the doctor. Begun as a joke, the story had gathered interest as it spread, until it reached the ears of the police as a clear claim of culpability. And, since I had been found at the farm, by Sergeant Playford of all people . . .

'Only a fool would take Jack Farcroft for a German sympathizer!' I exclaimed.

Not pleased at being called a fool, Jarvis demanded, 'Then why were you there? I understand there's no love lost between your family and the Farcrofts. Or is that just a smokescreen?'

I told what had happened after the bombs dropped. I tried to explain that I had gone back on neighbourly impulse. He didn't believe me. Mad Jack and I had obviously been in league, guiding the Zeppelins towards the King's home at Sandringham. Did I deny showing lights in my room?

'Of course I deny it! How could I have made a bright light when there's neither gas nor electricity at Denes Hill? And, you can't see the house from the village – there are too many trees. So which clairvoyant reported these lights? I didn't even light a lamp.'

'Unfortunately,' he said, 'we have only your word for that.'

'No . . .' Oliver said slowly. 'No, inspector, I can corroborate Miss Brand's story. She was not showing any light whatsoever.'

The inspector surveyed him with interest. 'Go on, Mr Wells.'

'We were together, some while before the Zeppelin went over. We both saw it. We watched the first bomb drop, and saw it explode, after which we went down to join the others – as Miss Brand has explained.'

Jarvis's yardbroom moustache fairly danced on his lip. 'You were together? Just the two of you? In Miss Brand's room? In total darkness? For what purpose, may I ask?'

'What the devil do you think our purpose was, man?' Coldly angry now, Oliver got to his feet, imposing in the tawdry room. 'Miss Brand and I are engaged to be married. We had other things on our minds than signalling to enemy ships! But that is neither here nor there. I very much resent your prurient intrusion into our private affairs. As to these outrageous charges . . . be sure we shall not sit idle under such slander. This is the second time you've seen fit to arrest my fiancée on a flimsy pretext. I suggest you hire yourself a good lawyer.'

Under the Defence of the Realm Act, however, the police had powers to arrest anyone they suspected of enemy activities; so litigation was out of the question. Nor did Oliver's protests have immediate effect – except to annoy Jarvis even further. Though he had no evidence, nothing but gossip and a few wild stories told by hysterical people, he decided to detain me while he made 'further enquiries'.

During the few days while I stayed in the camp, I met many people with little more cause than I to be there. Most of them hated the German régime as much as any Briton. But perhaps their imprisonment, as well as neutralizing possible enemies in our midst, offered them protection: feeling against anyone with German connections ran high and hot in those days, as I was beginning to understand to my cost.

In the wake of the airship raid, the German press claimed

to have attacked 'fortified places'. When the true nature of their targets was revealed, they justified their barbarism by saying they had acted in self-defence, having been fired on by civilians with rifles. In fact, the Zeppelin commanders had been hopelessly lost.

Wild rumour trickled through to us in our incarceration: the Zeppelins had been guided from the ground by spies shining lights from houses and motor vehicles. Two men at a Hunstanton hotel were implicated – they had worn British uniform, but had stood in the dining room with their hands in their pockets and their hats on, and they had shared a double room, with a double bed – obviously they were not British! Witnesses reported seeing the airships pass over arrayed in banks of lights, or black as pitch; people had seen the enemy crew staring down, and heard them converse in their guttural tongue: one old lady had even heard the villains shovelling coal to fuel their engine! Hysteria ruled.

As the initial panic faded, the authorities decided they had no case against me. Since I was indisputably British by blood and birth, as my family vociferously reminded them, they released me.

Once again, Oliver arrived to take me home.

Outside wooden gates strung with barbed wire, I hurled myself into his arms and held him tightly, relief making me laugh and cry at the same time. I felt him return the embrace fiercely. Voice muffled against my coat collar, he said, 'I love you, Kate.'

'Oh, I love you, too,' I wept, and at that moment it was true. I felt in need of a strong refuge. When he kissed me, not caring who saw us there in the chilly dusk by the recreation ground, I felt the deep emotion in him and I let myself believe all might be well for us. I did love him. Not quite the way I loved Philip – I should never love any man as I had loved Philip – but what I felt for Oliver was enough. In this life, anyway.

All solicitous concern, he helped me into his car and tucked a travelling rug round me, then cranked the engine into life and settled beside me, gloved hands on the wheel, staring at the windshield. 'Just one thing I need to know,' he said, and turned clear dark eyes to my face. 'Why did you go to the farm that morning?'

'I was concerned about Mr Farcroft. His housekeeper was hurt by that second bomb. He was all alone. He *is* my grandfather, Oliver.'

'So you keep saying. Did you tell him that? . . . Oh, come, Kate, I can see that you did. With what result?'

'No result,' I sighed, turning my head away as I huddled deeper into the seat and the warmth of the rug. 'I think he half suspected, anyway. Do . . . do you know how he is? They didn't arrest him, did they?'

'I gather not. If they had arrested everyone implicated by every unfounded rumour of recent days, half the county would be in gaol. Kate, my dear . . .' He hesitated so long that I looked at him in puzzlement and saw him flick a shamefaced glance at me. 'I want to apologize for my behaviour that last evening. I'm very conscious of being a good deal older than you are. I'm afraid I let the teasing irritate me. And you seemed strangely withdrawn. Yes,' he added as I opened my mouth. 'Now, belatedly, I understand why. You were burdened by the bad news about James Lacey.'

The reminder made me feel even colder. 'How did Emmet take it?'

'Badly, I think, though he put on a good show. He asked me to give you his love and say he'll see you next time he gets leave.'

'He's gone back?'

'Yesterday.' Taking my hand, he squeezed it in understanding. 'Will you forgive me for my selfishness, my love? I'm ashamed that I lost control. My only excuse is that I love you too well. I was afraid I might be losing you. And . . . I wanted you desperately. I've tried to be patient, but . . .'

'I know. I know.' I wanted to forget about that night. All of it.

'You do realize,' he said, 'that, by giving you an alibi, I irrevocably sullied your reputation? When word gets out, as it will, we shall both be undone. Shall we forestall the gossips? I'll apply for a special licence. We could be married next week. What do you say?'

If I hesitated, it was for only a blink. 'I say yes. Yes, Oliver. The sooner the better.'

And so, Oliver and I stood before the registrar to exchange wedding vows and rings. It was not the way I had dreamed of being married, but dreams had always played me false.

As a honeymoon, we spent three days in the cathedral city of Ely. Our hotel was cosy, our room comfortable, our marital bed a haven for both of us, with no further reason for precautions. I tried not to think of anything else. The pattern of my life was set, for better or worse, until death did us part.

Though Oliver did not object to my continuing to work, after my public arrest in the Chef factory everyone agreed it might be politic for me to find another place of employment. Unfortunately, word of my supposed enemy sympathies went with me, like a brand on my forehead, and more than one employer turned me down. So I followed Saffron's example and allied myself full-time with women's charity groups – the Red Cross and the Women's Volunteer Reserve.

I enjoyed living in Lynn, in Oliver's comfortable flat. His Mrs Petrie declared herself glad to see him married at long last, but she wasn't the gossipy sort. We soon established a routine: he had his work and I mine, but we met over dinner and later, in bed, we regularly employed the 'remedy against sin' for which marriage was secondly ordained.

The war impinged on everyone: the need for blackout curtailed evening life; shops closed early, and some foods, such as sugar, became scarce. Newspapers told of continuing sorrow, of battles fought and young lives lost in the glorious cause, of the valour of the British Tommy, the cowardice of the Hun. The true picture, as many of us knew, was not so black and white. I could not delight in news of bread riots in Berlin, German housewives queuing to buy potato peelings, or the victories of our ally, Russia, on the eastern front – Schloss Lindhafen lay somewhere in the east. But after their initial success the Russians were slowly pushed back and I had every hope that Mother and the *Menschen* were safe, for now.

From Emmet we heard regularly, always requesting some small comfort such as cigarettes, or socks, or chocolate. After James Lacey's death he no longer compared the war to a game of cricket, but he continued to gloss over the real horrors. Anyone with an ounce of imagination knew about them – one had only to scan the picture weeklies, or read between the lines of reports from the front.

Uncle Frank wrote that he was on special assignment and might not be in touch for some time; we were to take no news as good news. I consoled myself that my sixth sense would tell me if anything bad happened to him, though the reality of my married life had distanced me from that unseen other world. My ghosts – even John – had stepped back into the shadows.

That summer, Saffron and I took part in a march of willing women workers, in London, where the WSPU had turned its attention to the war effort. Oliver accompanied us, taking the chance to do some business, but we left young Eddy with his nurse. Since I was obliged to obtain permission to leave Norfolk, we decided to stay for the weekend, using the Mayfair flat as a base – which seemed to please Oliver, who said it made him feel a real part of the family. Some of Frank's possessions remained on view, but, according to the doorman, my uncle had not been seen for months.

That Saturday afternoon, the seventeenth of July, 1915, Saffron and I made our way to the Victoria Embankment, where, despite pouring rain, thousands of women turned out to support 'Women's Right to Serve', calling for more female volunteers to join essential industries, and for improved standards of comfort and cleanliness. One of the main speakers was my old sparring partner, Hermione Harmistead. 'Is that your friend? Goodness!' Saffron was impressed.

Promptly at three thirty we set off, banners and flags waving, and at Downing Street our deputation, led by Mrs Emmeline Pankhurst, presented our petition to the Prime Minister, Mr Lloyd George.

That evening, Oliver took us to dine and dance. Above the hum of a darkened city, blinded windows and blinkered headlamps, searchlights probed the night skies and heavy guns waited, poised for action – the Zepps, having improved their navigation techniques, had begun aerial assaults on London a few weeks before. Even in the West End, the war laid its mark on the gaiety, uniforms much in evidence. But, as Oliver and I danced to a ragtime band, rediscovering the sensual pleasure of moving in unison, he held me close and smiled possessively into my eyes, reminding me of the early days of our courtship.

Later, at the apartment, Saffron and I agreed that we were both drained after an exhilarating and emotional day. I hoped Oliver would take the hint, but I had hardly climbed into bed before he came in, in a wildly lustful mood that made him ignore my protests of tiredness. He opened the blind so that the glow from a nearby searchlight lit the room; then he tore off my nightgown and, without preamble, fell upon me. Afterwards, while he subsided to sleep, I lay feeling used rather than satisfied, wondering what had roused him so – was it the dancing, or the wine? Was it the risk of an air raid, or being in the Mayfair flat for the first time? Or was it Saffron's proximity? Unkind thoughts, but I couldn't help them: something other than I had excited him.

On Sunday morning we attended church and walked in the park, seeing recruits at drill while other troops marched proudly along the roads, on their way to and from the front. Later, Saffron and I paid a visit to Lincoln Square and had tea with Mrs Armes. Oliver said he could better occupy the time by visiting an acquaintance in connection with Freemason matters, but I suspect he didn't want to meet Hermione Harmistead. My aunt, however, declared herself 'thrilled' to discover Miss H at home. Having congratulated her on her speech the previous day, Saffron invited her to come to Lynn, to address our branch of the Women's Volunteer Reserve. Miss H readily agreed. She had lost none of her drive and fire, but like most suffragettes she had turned her energies to war work; our struggle for the vote had taken a back seat for the duration.

'As for you, Kate,' she admonished, 'it's high time you had a real job. We're looking for people to oversee recruitment and welfare of women workers in local areas. You know the sort of thing – making sure they get proper training and decent facilities, finding suitable accommodation . . . Just the ticket for you. I shall put your name before the Central Committee. And if that husband of yours has any objection, tell him to take a running jump. How you could ever marry a man like that . . .' She would never forgive Oliver for denying her a refuge in our taxi that night so long ago.

Since my aunt said her feet were aching, I left her talking while I went to find Win Leeming, who had gone to the park to do some studying in the sunlight. Despite the death and disorder in the world, Win still lived in and for her books. As usual, she had become so absorbed that she had forgotten the time. When she saw me coming she jumped up in consternation.

'Goodness, Kate! Is it three o'clock already?'

'It's nearer four,' I laughed.

We walked back together, past posters showing, 'The Girl Behind the Man Behind the Gun', or demanding, 'Is YOUR "Best Boy" wearing khaki?' Yes, I thought: my own 'best boy' had worn khaki from the beginning.

'You look well,' Win told me. 'Married life must suit you.'

'You always said Oliver would make a good husband,' I reminded her.

'But?'

Had my voice revealed doubt? 'But nothing!' I denied.

'You're happy?'

'No one can claim to be happy all the time. I'm contented enough.'

'That's good.' But mouse-brown eyes behind gold-rimmed specs saw too much. Win hadn't changed. I had a feeling she would go on for years and years, looking the same and following the same habits, avoiding emotional upheaval while too clearly seeing it in others.

Win's perception crystallized an underlying uneasiness that stirred in me whenever I glimpsed that other, harder Oliver. But Saffron had warned me that the first flush of married bliss would wane. Oliver worked long hours, not only for his clients but for the Freemasons, and the Fabian Society. Was it any wonder if at times his energies ebbed and his temper grew short?

TWENTY-TWO

When Saffron and I returned to Mayfair, we found a message from Oliver, saying he would spend the evening with his friends; so we treated ourselves to dinner at the Dorchester. Waitresses outnumbered waiters, making us remark on seeing women workers all over the city – operating elevators, conducting buses, sticking bills – replacing men in many jobs.

'They can't deny us the vote much longer,' I observed over hors-d'oeuvres. 'Not after we've proved our worth. Women are at last taking their rightful place alongside men, in the workplace. It's much more effective than laying firebombs, or breaking windows.'

'I'm not sure your husband agrees,' Saffron commented. 'He tries to be modern, but he still believes a woman's rightful place is in the home.'

'I know,' I smiled. 'But I'm educating him. Slowly.'

She gazed at me over a napkin pressed to her lips, then, 'To be honest, I'm not sorry he found other things to do this evening. However hard I try – and I do try, for your sake, Kate – I can't feel comfortable with him, somehow. D'you know what I mean? I suppose it's because Harry didn't like him. And Frank felt – feels – the same.'

The slip made us both silent for a moment. If only we knew where Frank was! 'That's a hangover from boyhood,' I said. 'They always resented Oliver as the interloper.'

'Yes ... Yes, I know.' But she sounded dubious, her fingers worrying at a jet earring. 'He is good to you, isn't he?'

The concern in her hazel eyes made me wonder whether she had sensed, or heard, something of our violent coupling the previous night. 'He's the perfect huband,' I said.

'No man is perfect,' my aunt rejoined. 'According to Hermione, your particular "perfect husband" is more of a pompous prig.'

'He's not complimentary about her, either,' I said, amused, though my disquiet stirred again. Were my marital troubles really so evident?

Saffron sat up, more animated as she confided, 'Speaking of Miss H, I've been meaning to tell you – while you were out meeting Win, we talked about your difficulties with the police. Mrs Armes said something rather interesting. It seems someone approached her, while you were staying there, asking about your movements, who your friends were and so forth – d'you know what I mean? Mrs Armes thought the man had been sent by Lady Vi! But it must have been the police, don't you think?'

'Possibly.' If my movements had been noted ever since I arrived in England, that explained a lot.

'Did you know Mrs Armes was reporting back to Denes Hill about you?'

'I suspected it, on occasion.'

We took a taxi through the blackout. I don't know what time Oliver came in; I was asleep and he didn't wake me. Next day, on the early train back to Norfolk, he said he was not surprised that I had been watched: Britain had long been paranoid about German spies. 'But I'm sure they know by now that you're no threat, my dear,' he added with an indulgent smile.

He was less pleased to hear that Miss H had offered me a job. 'I hope you won't try to emulate *that* type of woman. While you have the time and the leisure for it, you must, of course, "do your bit". But it's my earnest hope that the time may soon come when you are not so free.' Giving me an intimate, meaningful look, he retreated behind his paper.

Saffron's speculative glance made me flush. Oliver longed for a child, but that was the first time he had hinted at it in public.

As the toll of dead and wounded in the trenches mounted, the flood of eager volunteers faltered. The dreaded word 'conscription' arose from many quarters. When David Lacey was blinded, his sweet, gentle mother – who had never recovered from losing James – organized a group of bloodthirsty Valkyries to send white feathers to men who they considered ought to volunteer. I expected Vicky to join them, but, though the news of David's injury moved her to tears, her grief was no more intense than it had been for James. If ever she had loved one of the Laceys, it must have been a temporary affliction; she seemed content to remain at Denes Hill, nursing convalescent officers, attending the rifle club, and playing the piano for fund-raising concerts organized by her mother.

For me, a new role opened, thanks to Hermione Harmistead. Within a month, I had a new title – inspector for the National Union of Women Workers. It was my job to recruit girls and women to fill places in public services such as munitions factories, road works, the police force, and agriculture, to ensure safe and healthy work conditions, and to organize decent accommodation where needed. At last I had something really useful to keep me occupied.

I was assigned a motorcycle, and one of the local men to

teach me how to ride it. Up and down the riverbank at first, with a few spills, and much sweat when I had to lift the heavy beast upright again. Many times I silently cursed my instructor, but soon I was out on the road, bruises fading as I mastered the machine. For riding I dressed in practical shirts and trousers, heavy boots, long leather coat lined with sheepskin, and a leather helmet and goggles. In fine weather the roads threw up clouds of dust; in wet weather mud spattered freely. I loved it. I grew to adore the freedom it brought – and to enjoy the surprise that resulted when I removed my helmet and goggles and revealed myself as female!

My work took me all over west Norfolk, from aeroplane and munitions works in Lynn and Thetford to tiny fishing villages along the coast and farms lost among gently rolling hills. On heathy tops, with room enough for planes to take off and land, airstrips formed. A field at Sedgeford, only two miles from Denes Hill, had been a night landing station for Royal Naval pilots; it became a training station for the Royal Flying Corps, where young pilots learned aerial fighting, zooming about our skies in daring displays of skill. In wooden huts that sprouted there, I installed some of my girls as clerks and drivers. Every day brought more work, more problems to solve, filling my waking hours.

I loved the work, I loved the people I met, the feeling that I was really being useful, and most of all I loved the freedom. I hardly had time to think, let alone worry about personal problems.

Early in November, when the weather turned wet and foul, my work took me out to a farm near Thornham. One of my land girls had been hurt when an RNAS aeroplane, returning from a mission and unable to make the landing strip at Sedgeford, crashed into the barn where she was working. Having seen that she was well looked after in her lodgings in the village, I battled homeward, fighting to hold the bike steady against a howling gale from the sea. By the time I reached Hunstanton, exhaustion drew me to call at Denes Hill, hoping for a respite. But no respite waited.

'Thank goodness you've come, Mrs Wells,' was the greeting I had from Mrs May, who still acted as head cook in the house. 'Lady Rhys-Thomas is in a right old stew. Mr Tom have now gone missin'.'

Racing up the back stairs, I found Grandmother, and Anderson, in the delicate blue and white sitting room. To my concern, Grandmother was in tears – even her indomitable spirit had cracked under the strain: her home had been invaded; Frank had not been heard from in months; Emmet was in constant danger, and now Tom, the last and most vulnerable of her sons, had vanished.

'He must have gone early this morning,' she told me, blotting her tears on a damp handkerchief. 'They've searched the woods and all his usual haunts, but to no avail. And then we discovered that some of his things are missing from his room. All his favourite treasures, Kate. And Jim's gone, too – his little dog. Oh . . . I should have taken more notice! Lately he's been talking about going to find Emmet. Only yesterday, Vicky and I were discussing the Laceys – how they must be feeling with both their sons dead, and—'

'Both?' I breathed. 'I heard David was only—'

'He died of his wounds. Two days ago.'

Dear God! Poor Mrs Lacey.

'And Tom . . .' Grandmother went on, 'he jumped up and shouted that if only he had a gun, he'd go and kill all the Huns and stop them doing these . . .' As her feelings overwhelmed her, Anderson bent over her solicitously, glancing up at me to add, 'One of the nurses found him trying to break open the gun cabinet. If she hadn't stopped him . . .'

I didn't need it explaining to me. 'Has anybody checked at Far Drove? If Tom's got it into his head that he wants to shoot enemies, he might have headed for the farm. Mr Farcroft has guns.'

'We thought of that,' Grandmother croaked. 'Someone went down to ask. He's not been seen there. He could be anywhere, Kate! He may even have gone to try enlisting in Lynn. I'm sure they wouldn't take him, but he gets confused. He may be wandering about, lost.'

Having grabbed a quick cup of tea, I donned my leather helmet, goggles and coat, wrapped my thick scarf round my neck, and went back into the gale, intending to use the last hour or so of daylight to search the nearby lanes. The local defence forces and the Gloucestershire Yeomanry were patrolling on foot, but I with my motorbike could range further afield. Not that I had much hope of finding one poor lost soul and his dog in all that countryside, but I felt better doing something.

As light waned on that bleak November day, my whole body ached from holding the bike steady against gusting wind and the bucking of a hard, ill-sprung seat. I seemed to have covered miles of rough back lanes fraught with potholes and mud, but with no sign of Tom or Jim. Soon the day would be gone. Already the eastern sky darkened towards night and twilight lurked along my way. I stopped to wipe mud from my lamps and make sure they were lit, and wished I hadn't when my sore muscles protested at being asked to climb aboard my machine again.

Approaching a bend where the lane ran through a copse,

I saw a young lad run into the road ahead, waving his arms to stop me.

'Tree down!' he shouted as I let the engine slow to an idle. 'They're now clearing it. Won't be long.'

Up ahead, an old tree had been felled by the wind, to lie right across the lane. Two farmworkers, working with a single heavy horse, had sawn the tree in half and pulled the top of it aside. Now they were fastening chains to the bottom half, whose huge ball of roots lay still partly fastened in the great hole from which it had been torn by the gale.

I could have turned back and reached Denes Hill by another route, but the prospect of even an extra couple of miles daunted me. I hauled myself off the bike, wheeled it to lean on a tree, and waited, pushing my filthy goggles up my brow as I stretched stiff limbs and watched the two men prepare to clear the obstruction. They worked efficiently, accomplishing their aim with a minimum of words.

One of them called the boy to do something. As he ran off, the man raised a hand to me, calling, 'Sorry! Won't be long.'

Answering words died in my throat as I recognized him, even through the twilight. That deep, resonant voice, allied with a rangy frame clad in corduroys and cap . . . My heart twisted in my breast. Philip was home again.

In the failing light, he probably took me for a man, dressed as I was for bad weather, muffled to the nose with mud caking all but the area round my eyes. Common sense told me I should go before he penetrated my disguise. But I couldn't move. I wanted the pleasure of feasting my eyes on him. Once the tree was moved I could put on my goggles and ride by, lifting a gauntlet in thanks. So long as I didn't speak, he need never suspect even my gender.

The chains were fixed. The boy leapt up on the horse's

huge back. The other man laid a hand to its halter and led it forward, taking up the strain, while Philip came, axe in hand, to chop at the roots that still clung. One by one they gave. Inch by inch the great trunk slewed round. And then, seeing the lane almost clear, Philip strolled over to me, taking off his cap to brush at his cropped hair. Thinner than I remembered. Older, more like Michael. But still himself, so achingly dear . . .

'We thought we'd better clear it before the light went,' he said. 'It would have been a hazard after dark.'

I knew I shouldn't speak. But my silence made him look more closely at me and I saw him start, disbelieving his own sight as he looked me up and down before peering again into my face. 'Kate?'

'Hello, Philip.'

'Good grief . . . It *is* you! What the devil—'

'I've been looking for Tom.'

'What?' Then concern drew a comma between his brows. 'Is he still missing? Someone came to the farm earlier, asking if we'd seen him.' He glanced again at my clothes, and at my machine, as if he still doubted his senses. 'How long have you been riding motorbikes?'

'A few months. I've got a new job.' We chatted as if we were no more than old acquaintances, while stormy undercurrents eddied between us.

'Are you on leave?' I asked.

'Just a few days. We've all been trying to get home for a last spell. We'll be off soon.'

I knew what he meant, but, 'Off?'

'Overseas. I don't know where. I don't care, so long as we get into it at long last. I'm sick of unrolling barbed wire, and doing futile drills, and watching other men go up to have a pot at those arrogant bloody Zepps – sorry. I'm out of the habit of being in polite company.'

'It's the war,' I said ruefully. 'You . . . still want to fly, then?'

'Give me half a chance! If not, I'll settle for the trenches. Just so I'm not sitting idle while it's all happening.'

Since I couldn't bear to think about that, I said, 'How's your father?'

'Older,' he replied. 'Changed, like a lot of us. Aware of his own mortality. But physically he's recovered well, I'm glad to say. It was good of you to go and see him. He told me . . . about us being related.'

'Oh. Yes.' Unable to bear his frank regard, I looked beyond him, to where the lane was now clear, the other man and the boy busy removing the chains from the tree.

'I wish you'd told me,' Philip said softly.

Fighting the sting of tears, I shrugged. 'I couldn't. It took me a long time to accept it myself. You . . .' I peered at his face, wishing I could see him more clearly. 'Are you all right?'

'Top hole. Fighting fit. Listen, Kate . . . I'm sorry about the things I said last time we met. At Denes Hill. You know.'

I forced a smile, though my face felt stretched into it. 'Forget it. It was a strange situation. We were both under a strain.'

'Then . . . will you write to me, while I'm away? We could . . . just write. Couldn't we? There's no law against—'

'It wouldn't be a very good idea, Philip.' How could I sound so collected when I was all in pieces inside?

'Why not? You keep in touch with the rest of your family, don't you?'

'It's not quite the same, is it?'

'Why not?'

'You know why not! How can we ever...' Surely he knew we could never be platonic uncle and niece, or even simple friends. 'Besides, I don't think Oliver would like it.'

'Oliver?'

'My husband.' I saw the word hit him like a slap. 'Didn't your father tell you about that? I asked him to. Maybe he didn't take it in.'

'You mean... Oliver Wells? The lawyer?'

'Yes.'

When he spoke again his voice had changed, tinged with bitterness. 'I thought it might be him in the end. Ever since I saw you dancing together at that ball. I thought then that you made a fine couple.'

I could hardly see him for tears. 'Don't hate me for it, Philip. I needed someone, and since it couldn't ever be you...'

Approaching night turned his green eyes dark in a face all craggy with shadows. He said, 'I hope he'll be good to you,' and held out his hand. 'Goodbye, Kate.'

Pulling off my big driving glove, I laid my hand in his, feeling its cool roughness enfold me. That touch was my undoing. Ripples of despair rushed up my arm, flooding me, and before I could stop myself I grabbed his lapel and reached up to kiss his hard cheek, muttering, 'Be safe. Wherever you go. Whatever you do...'

As I tried to draw back, his arms swept round me, holding me breathlessly tight. 'And you,' he said gruffly, gazing down at me in the gloaming. 'Will you keep in touch with Dad for me? He's got no other family. If anything happens...' We both knew what he meant – *If anything happens to me, he'll need someone.*

'Of course I will!' I managed. 'I shall want to know how

you are, anyway. You could . . . send me messages, in your letters. If you wanted. And I'll tell him all my news, so that . . .'

He was close to me in the dusk, so close I could feel his breath on my face and see the way he was watching my mouth, making my lips tingle as they always did for him, aching for his kisses, knowing that if he wanted me I would lie down with him in the mud and let him—

'Goodbye, Kate,' he said, and let me go.

I watched him return to his companions, watched them all start away. Philip led the horse, slowly walking it into darkness that, eventually, took him completely from sight. For a long time afterwards, my whole body and soul ached for the kiss he had not given me.

I remember nothing about the next fifteen minutes or so. I came to on the road to Lynn, not knowing where I was. Realizing I was instinctively heading home, I stopped the bike and sat trembling. I shouldn't be going home, I should be on my way back to Denes Hill – Tom was still missing.

The extra miles I had ridden had depleted my petrol supply. As I turned and headed back, the bike began to misfire. I nursed it as far as the Denes Hill drive, where it finally died on me, obliging me to push it the rest of the way. Too tired to bother going round to the yards, I propped it against a low wall and made for the steps which led to the side lobby where, to the surprise of all three of us, I interrupted Vicky in the throes of a passionate embrace with an officer in uniform.

'Oh!' she got out as they sprang apart. 'Kate!' She straightened her cap and apron self-consciously. 'We didn't hear you. Oh – Tom is safe, you'll be glad to know. Cavan found him and brought him home. Oh – I don't believe you've met, officially. Cavan Fielding – Kate Wells.'

I had seen Captain Cavan Fielding from time to time; he had been among the Gloucesters who had been billeted, briefly, at Denes Hill. Vicky had, it seemed, met him even before that and taken to him at first sight.

'I can't imagine why you ever thought I'd fall for one of the Laceys,' she said later. 'They were both sweet, but—'

But Tom was safe and Cavan's finding him allowed him an entry into the family circle, where he was soon accepted as Vicky's chap. So at Denes Hill all was well, for the time being, except for the continued absence of Emmet and Frank.

I'm afraid I didn't waste much thought on poor Tom, or his motives for running off the way he had. For me, a far worse anxiety had begun: Philip sailed from Liverpool later that month. It was some while before we learned where he had gone. The name of the place was Gallipoli.

When the Turkish campaign had opened the previous spring, few of us had heard of the Dardanelles. We thought of that theatre of war as a romantic desert sideshow, pennons flying above troops of mounted gallants, well-armed ANZACs against turbanned natives with knives. By the latter stages of 1915 we knew better: Gallipoli had become yet another entrenched campaign, where mud, flies, dysentery and fever slaughtered as many men as did enemy artillery. Though the full extent of the carnage was not revealed until later, what we knew was bad enough. And now Philip was there, too, pinned down on bleak, muddy hillsides under constant bombardment, with bitter winter rains and snows ahead. I scanned the news sheets for every detail, finding little comfort in what I gleaned.

Once again, I practised deception. My freedom to travel

the county gave me ample opportunity for calling at Far Drove Farm, but I made sure the family, and my husband, didn't know.

Mad Jack greeted me warily, both suspicious and curious, but he didn't tell me to stay away. He fretted for Philip, and he was lonely; though he would never openly admit it, I fancied he welcomed my visits. Since Mrs Gaywood had stayed in Lenhoe with her daughter after the Zeppelin raid, the short-sighted Maisie Pike now 'did' for him. I let her believe that my visits were part of my Red Cross work. The farmer grumbled mightily about her, but I think he was grateful for her help.

Philip wrote to his father regularly. He wasn't allowed to mention place names, but he gave us ample hints even if he didn't say much about conditions. Then, in mid-December, the letters stopped. Mad Jack and I agreed that this was no worse than other delays, that three or four would come at once. But the news out of Gallipoli was bad. The year turned. No letters came.

I had been writing pieces for women's magazines, telling of women's experiences, how they coped with the changes in their lives, with food shortages, hard manual work, and being without their menfolk. Philip's silence gave me new insight into how those women were feeling and the true nature of mortal fear came home to me – worse for a loved one than for oneself. I hardly knew how I should bear it. But one cannot live in constant terror; after a while, it retreats to a shadow in the background of one's life, kept at bay by more immediate concerns. It has to be held back. If you don't bury it deep inside, it can destroy you.

I caught myself wanting desperately to talk about him. Once or twice I almost mentioned my visits to the farm to Oliver, just for the pleasure of saying Philip's name aloud.

But Oliver would have known at once where my heart lay: I had never been able to lie convincingly to him. Fortunately, the temptation arose infrequently. Business kept one or both of us absent from home on many evenings, and when we did meet we spoke only of trivia. When he turned to me at night, I welcomed the distraction, but it seemed to me that our marriage had become as much a convenience for him as it was for me. His desire for me had turned into the desire to father a child. But, despite his efforts, I remained unfruitful. Perhaps that was my fault – whenever my husband's body blended hopefully with mine, I made mental love with Philip Farcroft.

Fire in the night. Darkness hanging. Screaming shells. Voices moaning. Cold, so cold. Sudden blinding pain and then – nothing. Unfeeling. Peace. Soundless. Floating. Drifting upward. Looking down on a world of hellish mud, broken trees, blood, bones, putrefaction. Death. This was death . . .

No! As feeling rushed back, I found myself fighting with a monster that sat on me, stopping my breath. Weight pressing me down. A hand over my face. Let me go! Let me breathe!

'For God's sake!'

Oliver's voice came from oceans' depths, calling me back. The world re-formed itself around me. Deepest darkness, the bed hot and disordered, the air in the room cold, around us the flat in Merchant's Court lying silent with midnight . . . Oliver lay half across me, heavy on me as he held me down, one hand clamped over my mouth.

'For God's sake!' he said again, and this time I heard the tremor in his voice. 'Are you awake now? Whatever was

414

it? You were screaming. I couldn't wake you. Are you all right?'

I squirmed under him and, as if realizing he had me pinned, he released my mouth and rolled away, getting off the bed. He struck a match. Its flare dispelled the hovering shadows even before he turned on the gas and set the mantle glowing, turning it low. Soft light spread, letting me see that all was normal in the room. Except that my throat was thick, my heart beating so fast I could hardly breathe. Dregs of terror still clung to my subconscious. Normal? No. The dream was gone, but its message remained. Death. Philip . . .

'Was it a nightmare?' Oliver asked.

'I get them,' I said, and sat up, hugging my knees. Sweat soaked my nightgown but I was cold as Hades. Death . . . 'They haven't been so close lately. At Denes Hill they were there all the time.'

'They?'

I looked at him, seeing a familiar stranger, nothing more. 'Ghosts. Spirits. Whatever you like to call them.'

'Spare me,' Oliver sighed, and climbed back under the covers, wrapping himself well with his back turned to me. 'I've a busy day tomorrow. Or should I say today? It's three a.m., Kate. I need my sleep.'

His breathing slowed to a steady rhythm while I sent my senses out into the void, trying to recapture whatever had brought that dream. Please . . . Tell me clearly. It can't be Philip. Don't let it be Philip.

Cold to the bone, I went into the main room, lit the gas fire and opened the shutters, then curled up in a chair and stared at the stars above the roofline of the court. Another cold, glittering night, much like the night, over a year ago, when the Zepps came. No sound at all from the river or the streets. Of my dream, only the terror remained. But

415

something baneful had happened, somewhere, to someone I cared about. So many of them out there in danger . . . Philip, Frank, Mother, Emmet, Tom . . .

As my mind drifted in his direction it seemed to sharpen and focus. Tom . . . Dear God, something to do with Tom! All alone now. All alone. Terrified. Bereft . . . No words can properly express the clear call that said Tom needed me.

I dressed in the bathroom so as not to disturb Oliver, putting on my riding gear before letting myself quietly out of the flat. My motorbike lived in one of the stables off the court, beside Oliver's car. Hoping my employers would excuse me for using fuel for a private trip to Denes Hill, I wheeled the bike out into streets slick with ice.

A full moon accentuated the hoar frost that hung on every twig and leaf, every roof and gatepost. Town and villages lay silent, not a light showing, hardly a creature stirring, my bike and I the only movement, bearing our noise with us. Freezing air numbed every exposed inch of my face, but I hardly felt the discomfort. The need to answer the call drove me. Hurry, hurry! My senses ached with desolation, a drawn-out, insensate howling of a soul in pain . . . help me! *I'm coming, Tom.*

Did he hear me? I couldn't tell.

Denes Hill hung dark and silent, painted black and silver upon its dark backdrop of moon-iced woods. I drove round to the yards, slewing to a stop on icy cobbles, letting the machine rest against a wall as I ran for the side door. And stopped, hairs on my nape tingling. Had I heard a shot? Yes! There it was again. Strangely muffled. From the garden. Somewhere . . .

I'm not sure whether it was hearing or instinct that took me running to the section of the walled garden where

416

the aviary and its nesting shed had been built. The gate in the wall stood open, the garden beyond it desolate but for a few winter greens. Black shadow covered the aviary, but from inside it came the sound of birds panicking, scrabbling, crying out. Some of them were flying free in the frosty night.

With a jolt of both alarm and pleasure, I saw Emmet watching me, as if he had been waiting for me. He was in uniform, his hair silver-bright, his face seeming to glow in the moonlight. I ran up to him, gasping, 'Emmet! No one told me you were coming home! What's happening? I had a horrible feeling . . .'

Saying nothing, he gestured, gently and sadly, at the nesting house, as if suggesting I should look for myself. The side door was ajar, I now saw. I stepped towards it, seeing the interior black. From that darkness came wild flutterings and mournful chirpings. And someone weeping, muttering. As I stepped inside, pushing the door wider, a bird flew at me, its wing touching my face as it escaped into the night. Something soft cushioned my foot. I drew back, peering down through the shadows, and an edge of faint light showed me the small feathered body lying there, a trickle of black blood congealing around it. The acrid tang of gunsmoke hung on the cold air, along with the stench of blood, and fear, and desperate grief . . .

'Tom?'

He huddled in a corner, curled up in a tight ball, knees raised to chest, arms holding his head. Weeping bitterly. When I touched him, he resisted me, muttering incoherently, 'He can't go! Don't leave, Em . . .'

'It's all right, Tom,' I breathed and, when he still pulled away from my hand, I straightened and went out to ask Emmet what had happened.

Emmet wasn't there. The gardens lay empty and cold under the moon.

And then I understood. Emmet had not been there. Not in the flesh. Not that night. Asleep in Lynn, I had sensed the moment of his passing. And Tom, his twin, had sensed it, too. Their combined agony had called to me.

The telegram came three days later. They never found Emmet's body, but his name is among those carved on the memorial at Verdun.

TWENTY-THREE

Few of Tom's beloved birds escaped the onslaught of his grief. Nor was it only the birds which suffered, as daylight disclosed.

Tom must have woken as I did, feeling as though a chunk of his being had been torn from him. He went down to the stables and, trying to rid himself of the terrible tearing sense of loss, expended his feelings on his rabbits, battering them to death with an axe. Then he turned to the birds. Finding that they evaded him, he went back to the house and used the axe to break into the gun cabinet. Some of the birds that were left died of shock; most of those that got loose vanished, probably dying of cold; three budgerigars, and the mynah bird, remained. The dog, Jim, had disappeared.

Tom withdrew into himself, seeming almost blind and deaf. Only Grandmother's fierce defence of her son prevented the doctor from having him certified. She decided to take Tom away for a while, to the cousins in Wales, where gossip couldn't reach. She said all he needed was to be away from reminders of Emmet, until he forgot. And he would forget, she was sure. Poor Tom's memory had never been long.

I didn't tell anyone that I had seen Emmet in the garden. The fact that Tom and I had both known the moment of his death caused enough speculation and awe. But it was quickly pushed aside and forgotten – most people find such things uncomfortable and prefer rational, if illogical, explanations. Oliver dismissed my dream as coincidence. To his mind, my actions of that night proved beyond doubt that I was hysterical and overimaginative. 'But it's hardly surprising – you have too little to think about, Kate.'

'Too little? I have a highly responsible job!'

Yes, and that irritated him, too. 'Only while the war lasts.' What he meant was that I ought to stop working and start breeding.

On the eve of her departure for Wales, Grandmother invited us to dinner. We ate in her private sitting room, Vicky making up the party. I remember it as an evening of conflicting undercurrents which I sensed but could not fathom.

Over coffee, Grandmother astounded me by saying, 'I hear good things about the work you're doing, Kate.'

'It's a pity her mode of transport is so indecorous,' Vicky commented acidly.

'With a war on,' I said, 'decorum is the last thing anyone cares about. The bike gets me where I need to go, that's all that matters.'

'Indeed,' Grandmother agreed. 'Anyway, I want you to know, Kate, that I'm very proud of you.'

'Why . . . thank you.' I hardly knew how to answer such unexpected praise. It seemed to startle Oliver, too.

But perhaps Grandmother was offering olive branches in order to consolidate what she had left of her family. All of us felt the yawning gaps at the table: Emmet gone, and no word from Frank for almost a year – in our hearts we feared the worst for him. Of the male line, only poor Tom remained. And young Eddy, of course.

'I have stopped trying to reason with Saffron,' Grandmother said with a tight smile that made me think

how thin and cadaverous she had grown. This latest tragedy
had sapped her resources. Even her white hair had thinned
and her face was a network of lines and grooves, her blue
eyes dull with despair. 'Eddy's place is here, on the hill,
but she avoids even visiting me now. She says Denes Hill
is not the same. But nothing has been the same since this
terrible war . . .' Her mouth trembled and tears gathered in
her eyes, but with a visible effort she straightened her back,
coughed away the croak in her voice, and went on, 'Until
Frank returns, I look to you, Oliver, as the man of the
family.'

He paused in the act of reaching for his water glass,
glancing at her with a guarded expression. 'Why, Lady
Rhys-Thomas . . . I hardly know what to say. It's very good
of you to—'

'It's not good of me! It's a plain fact. You're Kate's
husband. You're the only man we have left. And I'm relying
on you – as, indeed, I've relied on you so often – to take
care of family interests while I'm gone. I want you and
Kate to move in here.'

No! I thought, my mind reeling from the very thought.
No, I don't want to come back here. Denes Hill is full of
shadows, lurking and waiting. Yet a cool breeze on my
awareness stirred tiny hairs at my nape and on my arms,
speaking of inevitability. Hadn't I always known my fate
lay here? On the hill, in the valley, at the farm, on the beach,
in the woods, along the lanes . . . Whispers along my nerves
claiming me. Michael, my father, and Philip, my love. And
John's shadow, trying to communicate. Ever since I first
came, I had sensed something here that drew me.

'But surely,' Oliver was saying, 'Vicky will be here.'

Pale to the lips, my young aunt shook her head, folding
her knife and fork over a plate still half full. 'I agree with

Mother. I should be happier knowing you were here, Oliver. You – and Kate.' The glance she sent me struck like ice. Resentment? Lingering jealousy? How odd – I had thought all that was done with. 'As a matter of fact,' she added, 'I'm planning to volunteer for work at the front.'

Grandmother gave a little moan. 'Vicky . . .'

'It's no good, Mother, my mind is made up. I don't intend to discuss it again.' Vicky had taken charge of her own destiny. But why did she hate me for it? 'Cavan has been appointed liaison officer to the general staff in France,' she explained to Oliver, 'and I intend to follow him. We shall probably get married. We would have done so before he left, if it hadn't been for Tom, and everything. So, you see, there'll be no one here of the family. Except you two. And someone ought to be here – if only to make sure the house doesn't get too sadly misused. For Frank's sake.' She added the last firmly, defying fate.

'Well . . . I'm honoured,' Oliver said. But humility was not strong in his nature and I detected a secret gleam of satisfaction in his eye. 'In that case, of course we'll come.'

'It won't be very convenient,' I pointed out. 'You'll have to travel to the office every day – have you thought of that?'

'I'll use the train, and keep the car in town.' As if to forestall any further objections from me, he turned again to Grandmother. 'Of course we'll do it, Lady Rhys-Thomas. You're not to worry about anything here. We shall be pleased to act as your caretakers.'

How could I argue? I had promised to love, honour and obey. Besides . . . in spite of everything I loved Denes Hill. It would suit me to be here again, close to the farm, able to drop in on Jack Farcroft more often, feeling close to Philip. Memories of him lay everywhere, in the views from the windows, even the changing seasons. Philip in sunlight and rain, Philip in snow, storm and golden harvest days, in the church, across the fields . . . Would he ever come home again?

Of course he would come! I told myself sharply. If he were dead, I should know. Of that I was sure. At least . . . ninety per cent of me was sure. The rest was all too fearfully aware that two months had passed since we had heard from him. Our forces had withdrawn from Gallipoli, during a bloody battle when a few had held the rear to protect the retreat. The newspapers spoke of 'much wastage' – which meant many more men had died. Some of them had vanished utterly.

Oliver's hand covered mine, making me jump. As my eyes focused I saw him smiling at me fondly. 'We should be very happy if it were to happen,' he said. 'Shouldn't we, my love?'

'Yes,' I agreed, wondering what I had missed.

Apparently he had remarked to Grandmother, by way of cheering her up, that perhaps her first great-grandchild might be born at Denes Hill.

My life changed yet again as Grandmother and Tom left for Wales, with Anderson in tow, and Oliver and I moved to Denes Hill. We took over Frank's airy bedroom, it being the largest and most congenial, situated at attic level, just below the sanctum. I couldn't have slept in Emmet's bed and the only other vacant rooms were in the private suite at the end of the south wing – the blue and white sitting room, with the master bedroom, dressing room and bathroom beyond it. With Grandmother gone, her suite was closed up, sacrosanct, awaiting her return.

For a week or so, Oliver seemed to enjoy our new abode. He went about whistling, and he made love to me with renewed enthusiasm, as if he were trying to ensure that Grandmother had the great-grandchild he had promised her. But gradually old habits set in and I saw less and less of him. He caught the early train to Lynn every day and often dined in town, too. On occasion he telephoned to say he would sleep at his *pied-à-terre* in Merchant's Court. Or he went to London for a day or two, or to the engineering works in Lincoln. Oliver had always worked hard and the war seemed to bring him plenty of new business, from which I benefited, materially. No, the situation did not distress me. If I was lonely, it was not on Oliver's account. And his absence did give me ample opportunity for visiting Far Drove Farm.

Vicky remained cool, when I saw her, which was usually over the dinner table and in the company of other hospital staff. She had won her place with the Voluntary Aid Detachment and was going to France, bound for a place named Le Treport, somewhere on the coast near Dieppe. As the time for her departure came closer, I sensed she was torn between her desire to be near to Cavan, who had been posted to Paris, and her fear of the unknown: Vicky had seldom been away from home, and never without her mother by her side.

On the morning of the day she was due to leave, having heard a sound overhead as I dressed, I discovered her in the sanctum, gazing out across the view as if trying to memorize it for future reference.

'It never changes, does it?' I said, going to stand beside her. 'It's just the same as when we were children. Looking out at that view, you'd never know there was a war on.'

She continued to stare out of the window, her face set and her arms tightly folded across her VAD uniform. '*Every*thing's changed,' she said flatly. 'Everything's spoiled.'

'Not spoiled – altered,' I argued, trying to comfort her. 'Our memories remain. Our thoughts, our feelings . . . they linger in places we've loved, with people we care about. The earth endures, the seasons come and go. Springtime and harvest. We're a part of that. All of us. You know . . . you shouldn't grieve. They're all very close – Emmet, Harry, John . . .'

China-blue eyes blazed fury at me through a haze of tears. 'Going to lay claim to them, too, are you? Even though they're dead, *you're* in mystic contact with *my* brothers. Oh, I hate you, Kate! You're a jinx. A Judas! Ever since you came, nothing's gone right. You were John's favourite. And Frank's. Even Tom loves you better than me. You've taken everything. *I* should have been Eddy's godmother. *I* should have been Oliver's wife. It should be *me* who's mistress here.'

'I'm not—' I began but she swept on, 'I tried to forgive you. I even felt sorry for you, and guilty for hurting you. But Clara's Little Cuckoo came home to roost and turned all the other nestlings out. Even poor Tom . . . Oh, I can't bear to look at you!' She thrust me aside so violently that I overbalanced and sat down on the window seat as she ran away and slammed the door behind her.

We did not speak privately again before she left, nor did she say goodbye to me: when I came in that evening, my leather coat soaked and my trousers muddied to the knee, Vicky had gone. She hadn't said goodbye to Oliver, either – he was away in Lincoln at the time.

Feeling in need of comfort, I went down through the woods as I had done so many times, with a torch in my hand. The bomb crater had eroded with a year's weather; the short-cut track now had a sharp dip in it, making it impassable to motors. Which pleased Mad Jack, of course

– he disliked cars as much as Grandmother did. As for those newfangled motorized tractors that Thorne-Thomas was pioneering . . . Devil's inventions! Typical of Lionel Rhys-Thomas. The old man still had barbs on his tongue where my family was concerned.

That night, when I knocked at the farm door, two dogs answered from inside the lobby – Boss's note I recognized, but the other was a sharper yapping. 'Who's there?' Mad Jack's bellow came over the racket.

'It's Kate,' I said.

He opened the door just far enough to peer round it with suspicion before turning away, leaving me to let myself in as he turned back to the lamplit inner door, slippers shuffling on quarry tiles, still favouring his left leg. Boss barked again as I stepped inside and his smaller companion imitated him, a pale shape dancing nervously in the shadows.

'Hush up!' the farmer roared, and the dogs fell silent. Boss came to nuzzle my hand, but the little dog cowered, backing away. It was a terrier cross, mainly white but patched with black, limping on one crooked back leg. 'Found him living wild,' Mad Jack told me, seeing me stare in disbelief. 'Timid little thing. Must have got his leg broke at some time, same as me. Gammy left legs we've both now got.'

'That's . . . that's Tom's dog,' I said. 'Jim.'

'Ah.' The old man rasped with blunt brown fingers at his stubbled jaw, meeting my eyes with a narrow look – the story of the dead rabbits and birds had soon spread. 'Well, he's called Titch now. Reckon that explain how his leg got broke, though. And why he's wholly nervous. Blast . . . that boy should've been put away years ago.'

Watching the little dog limp away, I couldn't argue. In my heart I knew Tom wasn't to blame, but my intellect said he could be dangerous, given the right circumstances – or perhaps the *wrong* circumstances, someone leaving a gun carelessly about, or a sudden shock like losing a beloved twin. But, to judge by Grandmother's letters, Tom had calmed down. She was hoping to bring him home before long. Perhaps he would be all right, if we were vigilant. I couldn't believe he had ever meant to harm anyone. He just didn't understand.

In the main room of the farm, velvet curtains blacked out the window. The dogs settled on the pegged hearth-rug, in the glow from a log fire that shed both heat and light across the room. The only other illumination came from a lamp on the table, beneath which lay a scatter of oily rags and cartridge cases, spilling across the newspaper which protected the velvet cloth. A jug of ale stood beside a half-full pewter tankard, foam smeared at its rim. Several guns leaned casually against table and chairs, barrels gleaming.

'Never know when I might need to defend myself,' Mad Jack said dourly. 'Do they Huns come, I'll be ready for 'em. Or anyone else that think I have something they want.' He gestured at the old sofa, saying, 'Sit you down. You want a glass of ale? Or some tea?'

'No, thank you. I don't intend to stay. I just—'

'There en't no news,' he told me flatly, resuming his seat by the table, rubbing at a gun barrel that was already shining. 'Still, you know what they say – no news is good news. That's what his mother used to say. I remember when Philip was a little old bor . . .'

He liked to talk about Philip. And for me it was joy to say that beloved name aloud and hear stories of his childhood. I settled opposite the old man at the table, content to share a companionable few minutes with him. Talking about the happier past kept both of us from dwelling on a present devoid of news.

'You've got the Whitfield eyes,' the old man told me after a while. 'My mother's mother had light eyes like yours. Far-seeing eyes. Witch's eyes, so some reckon.'

'Maybe that's what Lou Roughton meant – she said once that I gave her the shudders.'

Through the pale glow from the lamp, he regarded me steadily. 'That seem as how she had cause. If that han't been for you . . .' Out of his pocket, he suddenly produced a battered envelope, which he slapped on the table in front of me. A slender gold chain showed inside it. 'Look at that.'

The rest of the chain slid out of the envelope, attached to a heavy pendant, gold filigree round a stone of pale ice-blue. It looked like a sapphire.

'That was hers,' he said. 'My mother's mother's. That gets passed on through the female line. Wife, or daughter. I did reckon as how it might go to Lou Roughton, but . . . That's yours now.'

What? I looked up at him, wondering if I had heard right. 'I can't possibly . . .'

'Take it. Don't say nothin', just take it.' He became busy checking the barrels of yet another gun, squinting through them and blowing them clean of dust. 'Lou Roughton got wed, I now hear. Some young chap in the Gloucesters.'

I hardly heard him. My fingers had picked up the pendant, seeing the jewel sparkle in the lamplight. It was a sapphire – a family heirloom: he was accepting me as his blood. Was he also trying to tie me to him, because he feared Philip might not come back?

'Philip could've done a lot worse,' he said. 'She'd have made a good wife. She was a worker, that one.'

The fire dazzled through a mist as I wondered if he was

right. Would Philip have been happier married to his girl from Heacham? Both of us would have been happier if we had never met. But we *had* met. Fate . . . 'He'll find someone else,' I said.

'So he will.' His voice had gone rusty and I saw him absently rubbing the leg whose weakness still plagued him. 'And when he come home, girl, you'll have to stay away. You know that. I 'on't have you comin' here upsettin' him. Had enough o' that with your mother. Blast . . .'

For two pins he would have turned on me and told me, then and there, to keep away, but his own need prevented him. He feared I might be all he had left. That was the only reason he tolerated my visits. By clinging to each other, we somehow held on to Philip.

But I couldn't keep the pendant. I returned it to its envelope and laid it back on the velvet cloth, saying, 'Thank you for this, but I can't take it. It's too valuable. Keep it . . . keep it for the next Farcroft wife.' If I had kept the sapphire, it would have been like admitting that Philip was dead. And he wasn't dead. He wasn't!

I returned to the big house, intending to go straight to bed with a hot drink and console myself by recording feelings in my daily book, where I often wrote down what I could never say to Philip. Some day, perhaps, when we were both old and grey, I might amuse my grandchildren by showing them my youthful ramblings. Or perhaps I wouldn't: did I want my grandchildren to know what a wicked, sinful woman their aged relative had been?

What grandchildren? I wondered, a hand to my stomach, which was as flat now as it had ever been. Perhaps it was my curse to be barren.

Leaving my wet coat and shoes in the side lobby, I went

up the back stairs and along the first-floor hallway, where a lamp or two softly lit my way. As I neared the entry to the tower stairs, something made me glance towards the end of the wing, where an extra wedge of darkness showed – the door to Grandmother's sitting room stood ajar. I went to close it, glancing around the room before I did so, seeing a misty light moving beyond the open door of the bedroom.

Wondering what nosy creature was snooping in forbidden areas – a new recruit to the staff, perhaps? – I went soundlessly across the carpet and gently pushed the door wider.

The 'intruder' was Oliver. He stood with his back to me, a lamp lifted in one hand as he surveyed the room, the four-poster bed with its red hangings loosened, the feather mattress stripped to its ticking with a thin blanket across it. Light glinted in crystal pendants on two glass candlesticks, matching the ornate lamp that hung from the ceiling. The room was darkly reflected in the old mirror over the mantel, where more delicate ornaments stood in a neat line, interspersed with photographs in fancy frames, above the black, cold hearth.

Behind my surprise at Oliver's being there came affront, and then with a jolt of panic I wondered how long he had been home. Did he know I had been out?

'Oliver?'

He looked round calmly. 'Ah, my dear, there you are. I was just coming to find you. I concluded my business in Lincoln in time to catch the last train to Lynn, so I thought I'd drive home and spend the evening with you. I looked in here to make sure all was well – no rain coming in or anything. It seems a great pity for these rooms to be shut up. They're the nicest in the house.'

'That may be so, but—'

'Is there any reason why *we* shouldn't use them?'

An unthinkable idea! 'We can't do that!'

'Why not? It seems an eminently sensible arrangement to me. As soon as we hear that your grandmother is coming home, we can vacate—'

'No, Oliver!' I shivered and rubbed my arms, thinking of the warm fire waiting in Frank's room – our room – above.

'Cold?' he asked.

'It's bitter in here. I don't like it. I've only been in here once, that I remember – the night Grandfather died.'

Scorn twisted his mouth awry under the dark moustache. 'You mean, you sense ghosts in here?'

'I mean it's cold, that's all. Please, can we—'

As I turned to the door, he said, 'Has Vicky gone? Wasn't it today she was leaving?'

'Yes. Yes, she's gone. I saw her, early this morning. She . . .' and I told him what had happened at that unhappy parting.

Oliver snorted. 'Why are you surprised? Vicky has always been jealous of you. She's a spoiled darling – the youngest, the only girl among four older brothers.'

'But why did she say she ought to be mistress here? Frank's the heir now – *his* wife will be mistress of Denes Hill. And if he . . . if he doesn't marry, then Eddy will some day inherit.'

'Perhaps not automatically,' Oliver said. 'After all, *you're* the oldest grandchild. The firstborn – as your mother was.'

That drew a sharp laugh from me. 'I can't see Grandmother leaving anything to me – not while there's a chance of keeping the male line going. Oh . . . I don't understand it. I thought Vicky and I were friends. I thought she was in love with Cavan Fielding.'

'She is.'

'But she said she ought to be *your* wife!'

A slow smile warmed his dark eyes. 'My dear Kate . . . do I detect a hint of jealousy?'

'I only meant, if she harboured some feeling for you, you might have sensed it.'

'And returned it?'

'No! I didn't mean . . .' Was I a little jealous of Vicky? Did I want some reassurance that he loved me?

Laughing, Oliver put the lamp down on the blanket chest at the end of the bed, and came to take me by the shoulders, leaning to kiss me. 'I've missed you, Kate. Been away too long.'

I knew that note in his voice. 'Oliver, please.' But his mouth covered mine, and he guided me backwards to the bed, whispering love words. He was my husband, much stronger than I, overcome with lust and determined to have his way.

But the mood I sensed in him reminded me of that first night in the Mayfair flat and suddenly I felt sick. Revolted by his clumsy haste, I stiffened and fought him off.

'Please, Oliver! Not here!'

Surprised by my vehemence, he desisted, getting to his feet and straightening his clothes, demanding angrily, 'Why not here?'

'I wouldn't feel comfortable.'

'Suppose I told you I don't feel comfortable in Frank's room? I feel as if he's there, watching us, every time I make love to you.'

'That's ridiculous.' Rolling off the bed, I completed my tidying, going to look in the mirror over the hearth.

'You don't think it's ridiculous when *you* sense presences.'

'Spirit presences. Sometimes. But Uncle Frank is still . . .' I stopped myself, staring at my lamplit reflection in old glass darkened by age. In it, Oliver was a vague, shadowy shape behind me, and behind him, even more amorphous, other shapes shifted.

He sneered, 'Are you sure of that? Maybe *I'm* psychic, too.'

'Don't say that!' I spun round, stricken. 'Frank isn't dead. He's not!'

Furious, he threw out his arms, shouting, 'Maybe you'd prefer to go to bed with *him*, then. You do seem to have a fancy for close relatives!' and stormed out of the room.

I felt them around me – familiar ghosts, those I had known and those gone before, clustering to comfort me. Was Frank among them? I couldn't tell: they were a mass of invisible wings, making me feel as if I were suffocating. Aware of a growing chill in the room, I shook them off and fled. It wasn't ghosts I needed, however loving. What I needed was someone warm and alive. Someone who cared. I no longer believed that my husband cared for me. Oh, please! my agonized prayer went out into the void. Just let me hear that Philip is alive and well. Only that. I'll never ask for anything more!

Later, Oliver apologized for his outburst. Of course we wouldn't use the private suite unless I wished to, but it was a shame, it ought not to be left to go cold and damp; Grandmother had asked him to look after the house for her, she trusted him . . . 'Very well, I'll leave it for now. But think about it. And forgive me, please. I didn't mean to be unkind. I'm tired and edgy. And I'm frustrated. The trials at Thorne-Thomas are going slowly and someone else may get there before us if we aren't careful.' He didn't say what trials but I guessed he meant the land ironclads – the tanks

– that would bring more death to the hapless boys at the front, both Tommies and Fritzes.

As the trenches – and disease, and despair – continued to reap their bitter harvest, all single men from eighteen to forty were called to sign up. They left vacant places at work benches, at lathes and behind desks, carting coal, mending roads, digging ditches, tending fields, manning railways and driving vehicles. Trying to fill some of those places, I saw groups of women off on trains, bound for work elsewhere, and I met other groups coming to work in Norfolk – with the Women's National Land Service or the Women's Forage Corps. I matched lists of openings against lists of volunteers, made sure my girls were all properly trained, found billets and answered calls for help over injuries, or unwanted pregnancy, or grief after bad news from the front. I worried about the yellow skin some of my girls developed from working with TNT and put in reports asking whether the staining was injurious or not, but it seemed it was one of the unavoidable hazards of the work.

Momentous events in human lives can happen very quietly. A telegram can destroy a family with bad news; a single word can ruin a reputation. In my case, the harbinger was a young boy with a scrap of paper.

Coming home from a trip to Savage's aeroplane manufactory in Lynn, through a soft evening when spring scented the air and one could feel buds waiting to burst, I was approaching Denes Hill when a lad ran out in front of me, waving his arms. With a sense of *déjà vu*, I stopped the bike. The boy was the same one who had stopped me before, when the tree was down in the lane, the last time I had seen Philip.

'Mrs Wells?' he asked, thrust a scrap of paper at me and ran off.

Philip . . . Oh, God, please . . . My gloves hampered me. I couldn't see for dusty goggles. I pushed them up on to my helmet, sank my teeth into my gauntlet and hauled it off, then straightened the piece of paper with a shaking hand. The note was from Mad Jack. '*Philip safe*' was all it said. Two words. Just two short words that made me shout aloud, and laugh, and weep, and read them again, and kiss the paper . . . It was all I needed to know. Philip safe. Dear blessed heaven . . . thank you!

As soon as I had the chance, I went to the farm and shared my joy with Jack Farcroft. Three letters had come at once, one delayed from December, two more recent. Philip had been among the last out during the retreat from Gallipoli, which had been '*quite a lively time*'. He had been wounded, '*nothing serious*', but combined with fever and dysentery it had '*knocked me out for a bit*'. He had got a friend to fill in a Field Service Postcard for him, saying he was all right, but a couple of ships had gone down and he feared the card might not have reached us, so he was writing again to say that he was doing fine, safe with his unit in Egypt, bitten to death by sand flies but otherwise top hole. '*Unlike some of the others, I don't amuse myself shooting stray dogs. They're vicious, skinny things. I often think of good old Bess, and the farm, and you, of course, Dad. Do you see Kate at all? I hope she's well and happy. Yr loving son . . .*'

We worried about his continuing illness, which he couldn't seem to shake off. But when we heard that less than half of his battalion had escaped from Gallipoli, we thanked God that Philip had been spared. It was enough.

In May that year, as my twenty-third birthday approached,

another conscription bill demanded a response from married as well as single men under the age of forty-one. Oliver mourned the fact that he was too old – he had turned forty-one the previous February. He was also putting on weight; he blamed the excess pounds on the contentment of married life.

My own figure remained thin, which irked him.

The new expression 'conscientious objector' made me think of Frank. What would he have done if he had been conscripted – gone as an ambulanceman, as some of them did, or refused to serve and be jailed for the duration? I wouldn't have cared, only that he was alive. But we had no news of him.

Some men who objected to bearing arms on religious grounds were denied exemption and were shipped to France, where refusal to obey orders could mean death. Stupidly enough, that event caused a rift between Oliver and me, when I stood up before the Peace Association and gave vent to my disgust. My speech was reported in the *Lynn News*, together with a reminder of my German upbringing – as if that might have swayed my opinion. I was angry, but Oliver was furious. I happened to call in at his office on the morning the paper came out. He said I should have known better; I had shown him up, sullied his respectable name, made him a laughing stock . . .

'I walked out,' I told Saffron over tea in her sunlit garden, with Eddy playing bat and ball nearby. He was almost five, a sturdy, fair-haired boy just like his father. Watching him, I sighed heavily and looked down into my cup. 'Of course, it wasn't really about my speech. Lately he's been using any excuse for an argument. He thinks I'm deliberately preventing myself from having his child.'

'By what means?'

'Witchcraft, probably. He caught me drinking camomile tea one day.' I made it a joke, though Oliver's reaction had not been funny.

'You do, er . . .' Saffron felt impelled to ask the indelicate question, 'Live as man and wife?'

'You mean, bicker whenever we meet?' I said lightly, and sighed, 'Of course we do. I'm beginning to think I'm barren.'

'Nonsense, Kate.' She reached and took the tea cup out of my hand, upturning it on its saucer, then held it between her palms and gazed into its depths. 'There – see? A boy-child. A bouncing baby boy. Very soon now. Oh, and . . . yes, there's a happy meeting, too. An old friend . . .' She looked across at me, 'Maybe Frank.'

If only I could believe it. Frank, or Philip . . . 'That's a lovely thought, but you don't really think that tea leaves . . .'

'Why not? You believe in premonitions, don't you?'

'Yes,' I said and, not wanting to get into a discussion about that, stood up and reached for my leather jacket. 'I must go. I only called in to have a moan. I'm due to meet a train at three fifteen. More land girls coming in to help with haysel.'

'Hazel who?'

'Hay-sel,' I laughed. 'Cutting the hay. It's a country expression.'

I had heard the phrase from Jack Farcroft, on whom I intended to billet a couple of my new girls. He needed the help; all he had that year was one old farmhand, plus the boy Dick, and anyone from the village who could spare an hour or two. Philip was still in Alexandria, fit and well, so he said, swimming, relaxing and route-marching amid endless dust and flies. I wished I could tell Saffron about him.

Eddy came running and I swept him up in the air and whirled him round, watching him laugh before I hugged him to me. 'Goodness, Ed, I shan't be able to do that much longer. You're getting as fat as your uncle Oliver.'

Eddy wrinkled his nose at me, gave me a kiss and ran back to his games.

'A boy-child,' Saffron said with a significant look as I took my leave. 'I can feel it in my bones.' Considering she had once predicted that Carl-Heinz would beg me to go back to him, I took this with a pinch of salt.

But, as it happened, Saffron was right in one respect: when the train drew in that afternoon, bringing my new contingent of Land Service volunteers, one face stood out, rounded and bonny, with blue eyes and a mop of butter-blond curls. She stopped and stared, then squealed and came rushing with her arms wide to hug me. 'Kate! Oh, Kate, how lovely . . .'

Judy Love had come to Norfolk.

'Had to come,' she said. 'I couldn't bear not having any news of old Frank. I keep sending letters to that address he left with me, but I never get a reply. So I thought, well, all right, if you won't write to me, I'll jolly well go somewhere where I *know* you'll be keeping in touch. I mean, he doesn't keep his poor old mother waiting in suspenders, does he? How is he, dear? *Where* is he?'

Hardly aware of the other girls, or of the hurrying passengers and the sighing engines, I squeezed the hand that clutched mine. 'I don't know, Judy. We haven't heard a word from him since . . . Well, Grandmother had a very brief postcard, in April last year. Since then . . .'

Watching the light die from eyes that suddenly brimmed with bright tears was a painful experience. 'Fourteen months?'

'I'm afraid so. But we haven't given up hope. I'm sure I should know if anything had happened to him.'

'So would I,' she said stoutly, dashing her tears away and searching for her smile. 'Oh, yes, I'd know. He *is* alive, Kate. Somewhere. And when he comes home I'm going to be here, waiting for him. Now . . . back to business. We're supposed to be met by someone from the NUWW. Probably six feet tall with a face like a horse and a hide like crocodile skin, if the ones I met in London are anything to go by. Seen anybody like that?'

'Not since I last looked in a mirror.' Dear Judy, how glad I was to see her. 'I'm your horse-faced crocodile. And, just for that, I know exactly where I'm going to put you, Judy Love. There's one grumpy old man who is sadly in need of a couple of girls to help around the farm.'

TWENTY-FOUR

Having treated the new intake to tea and plain, war-time cakes at the station buffet, I loaded them into the green NUWW van and set off to distribute them around the farms where they were to work. Seven of them rode in the back, sitting on their luggage, but Judy and a bespectacled girl named Clementina crammed alongside me, peering at the countryside.

Two land girls went to Babbingley, where a woman and her newly widowed daughter were struggling to run a dairy farm and a milk round. Four more, wide-eyed at being near royalty, I dropped off to help on Sandringham acres. And the seventh disembarked at a smallholding in Snettisham, where an elderly couple welcomed her like a long-lost daughter.

With only three of us left in the van, Judy felt able to talk more freely, telling amusing tales of her adventures getting out of France in 1914. The Gala Girls had broken up, after that: most of them joined the war effort. 'And *you* married your handsome solicitor,' she observed with a glance at the gold wedding band on my hand. 'I'm surprised he lets you work, though, dear. Didn't strike me as the type to—'

'He has to put up with it,' I said wryly. 'The war, you know.'

'Oh – the war! We all blame a lot on that. My friend Elsie . . . you remember Elsie?'

'The redhead? Yes, of course.'

'She went solo – took up singing, though she's got a voice like a corncrake. Well, I said to her, that's not for me, dear. I wanted to do something a bit more . . . well, you know – useful. Like Frank. I think that's it. I wanted to be worthy of old Frank. I mean, not that I expect he'll marry me, not really. But maybe if I make an effort his mother might not be quite so sniffy. Is she still there, dear, at the big house? Must be big changes there.'

When I told her how big the changes had been, both to the house and the family, even Judy fell silent for a few minutes. 'Lor' . . .' she said at last, a catch in her voice. 'Poor old Frank. Still, I expect there's some educated, high-class lady waiting anxiously to console him.'

'Not that I'm aware of.'

'Really?' That thought seemed to cheer her. 'Well, I'll let myself dream a bit longer, then. Till he turns up, the old rascal. So, anyway . . . where's this farm you're taking Clem and me to?'

When I told her, she gaped at me. 'Not Mad Jack! Oh, Lor'! Frank told me about him!'

'Don't worry, his bark's worse than his bite. And he does need help. He tried to get a couple of his workers exempted from conscription, but the magistrate was hard on him – they'd crossed swords before, I fancy. Which left Mr Farcroft with just old Wilf and young Dick. At busy times, some of the village women help out. Just take no notice of his griping. He likes to play the miserable old curmudgeon. But underneath he's lonely. He's, um, only got one son now – Philip. He's with the army, in Egypt, somewhere near the Suez Canal. He fought at Gallipoli. He was one of the last to leave. We heard yesterday . . .' I could not keep the pride out of my voice, 'that he's been awarded the

Military Cross, for carrying two injured men to safety. He was badly wounded himself while doing it, though he's recovered now, thank God.'

' "We" heard?' Judy commented.

'Oh, I . . . I drop in, sometimes. One can't help but get involved. Mr Farcroft *is* a neighbour. I feel responsible, somehow.'

'I don't see why. If he's your family's sworn enemy . . .'

'Maybe that's why. My family haven't been exactly fair to him, or to Philip. Oh . . . it's a long, boring story. You'll probably hear it from Mad Jack himself, once he gets to know you.'

Judy and Clem moved into one of the bigger bedrooms at Far Drove, set to the haying with a will and soon started to get the house shipshape, thus putting Maisie Pike's nose somewhat out of joint.

'Don't know what's worse,' the old man grumbled. 'A short-sighted widow woman a-tryin' to reform me, or two silly giggling town girls alluss about the place. What do they know about farming?'

As he discovered, the silly giggling town girls had been well trained in basic skills and were eager to learn the rest.

Having some of my girls at Far Drove gave me a perfect excuse for visiting the farm. I loved the way Judy talked so optimistically about Frank, as if she believed he would turn up safe and sound any day. Philip, too – she encouraged Mad Jack, and me, to believe that his son really would survive the war.

Whenever she had a spare hour or two, she came up to Denes Hill, making the patients laugh with her nonsense, wheeling them about in their chairs, doing impromptu song-and-dance routines on the terrace, or calling numbers for

Lotto. Since organization of social events had largely devolved on me after Grandmother left, I was glad of Judy's help with outings, beetle drives, singsongs and concerts. Oliver thought her a bad influence, but I understood her true worth. I hoped Frank *would* marry her – she'd be a breath of fresh air at Denes Hill.

The girls of the Women's National Land Service cheerfully brushed off the suspicions of local women and the attentions of the few men who remained. Old men, mostly. Old men and young boys. The brightest and best of Britain's blood reddened earth and seas in places whose names soon rang like doom in our consciousness: Verdun, Jutland, the Somme . . .

Among the casualties was Major Keith Rawson, whose physical injuries had been slight but whose nerves had cracked under constant shelling. Sent home on leave, he had caught his wife in bed with another man. Now, convalescing at Denes Hill, he couldn't sleep for fear of bad dreams; he had a habit of staying awake all night and going out by day to sleep in the woods. When I found him dozing in the temple summerhouse one day, I was foolish enough to empathize with him over his nightmares. From that day on, he followed me around like a lost puppy, telling me his troubles over and over again, using exactly the same phrases.

'And when I got home, what do you think? There she was. *In flagrante*. Starkers. Absolutely. With the bloody fucking grocer, wouldn't you know?' Such lapses of language only showed the extent of his mental disturbance: in most respects, Major Rawson was a gentleman of the old school, paying me compliments and bringing me bunches of wild flowers.

Other patients took to teasing me about it, greeting me

by singing, 'K-K-K-Katie, beautiful Katie, you're the only g-g-g-girl that I adore . . .' Major Rawson's devotion to me irritated Oliver until, one evening when we met over a hand of whist, my admirer solemnly informed my husband that he intended to run off with me as soon as the invasion came.

'The man's mad,' Oliver observed later.

'That's why I'm kind to him,' I replied. 'He doesn't mean anything.'

One hot afternoon I arrived at Far Drove to find the harvesters sitting in the shade of a hedge partaking of 'fourses', their teatime snap. The women informed me that Judy had had to go back to the house 'unwell', so I kicked more dust from my bike tyres riding down to see her.

As I walked into the main room, wiping dust and sweat from my face, Judy's shriek of alarm came from somewhere overhead. When she continued to scream, I raced for the stairs and reached the bottom just as a large man, stripped to the waist, started down. I stopped, and he stopped.

I'm not sure which of us was most startled – Philip, or me. After a moment when both of us froze, trying to believe our eyes, he gestured back along the landing. 'I didn't know she was there! For God's sake, what's a half-naked woman doing in bed at Far Drove – at this hour?'

'Clem!' Judy yelled. 'Is that you, Clem?'

'No, it's me – Kate!' I called. 'It's all right, Judy, it's only . . .' Only Philip. What was I saying? It *was* Philip!

He came down the stairs, agile in bare feet, lean as a ferret, brown as a nut, hair bleached into streaks by the Egyptian sun. Still trying to explain himself, highly embarrassed about it, he gestured at his muscled torso, which was dewed with water. 'I just came off the train. I was hot, so I took my shirt off and sluiced myself under the pump.

Came in, sat down on the couch and took my boots off, look – there they still are, on the rug – then went upstairs to get changed. Thought I'd have a look round the old place. I didn't even know she was there until she screamed. Who the devil is she – one of the land girls Dad's been writing about?'

'Judy Love.' My own panic was melting into relief that verged on hysteria, thinking of the absurdity of Philip coming home and finding Judy there, and she imagining him to be an intruder . . . A hiccup of laughter jerked in my chest while tears threatened to choke me. The tears won, impelled by the sight of a dreadful scar spreading half across his chest, where his body had been torn. I stared at it through a haze of distress, lifting a trembling hand to touch the ridged tissue as my head reeled with the knowledge of the pain he must have suffered. Why hadn't he said how bad it had been? Dear God . . . My lips shaped his name . . .

From the landing above us, Judy screeched, 'He was in my room! Monster! Pervert!'

'It's Philip,' I said stupidly, watching his face come and go through mists, his eyes holding mine, sharing my agony. *I love you. Oh, I love you so* . . . I swayed as a wave of nausea caught at me and, as Philip reached to support me, the mist claimed me. I remember the feel of his firm, damp flesh, cool under my burning cheek . . .

When I came to, struggling up through layers of sick dizziness, with my ears buzzing, I was lying on the floor. Philip knelt beside me and Judy was bringing a cup of water. Her voice came as if through cotton wool.

'Here, give her this. Don't look so worried, she's only fainted. This heat is enough to turn anybody queer. She works too hard. And that blessed husband of hers . . .'

I felt Philip lift me, supporting me across his lap while

he held the cup to my lips and let cool water trickle down my throat, sending the clouds further away. I lay quietly, my eyes closed, enjoying the illicit pleasure of being so close to him. Perhaps for the last time . . .

Judy chafed at him, rattled by the fright he had given her. He replied tersely – he'd been reacquainting himself with his own home, that was all. He hadn't expected to find anybody there in the middle of the working day. Wasn't she supposed to be helping on the farm, not lying around in bed? *He* was rattled, too, I could tell by his voice: he was embarrassed, and worried for me. Oh, darling Philip . . .

I bit my lip hard, denying the tears that came flooding as I let my eyelids flicker and reached for the cup he held. He helped me drink some more water, nursing me anxiously, then gave the cup to Judy while he helped me up. I leaned on him, my arm round his waist, my head resting on his shoulder, flesh to flesh, savouring the feel of his skin – oh, I admit it! I wasn't even ashamed of myself, not then, and I could tell by the way he cradled me, his arm tight about me, his body not flinching away but pressing close, that he felt the same. He shared my reluctance to part from him as he let me sit down, after which he was forced to straighten away. Judy ranted on, berating him for walking in on her – she'd been feeling unwell, nearly passed out in the field. 'Don't you tell me I'm a slacker because I'm not. You've only to ask your father . . .'

'Oh, *be quiet*!' Philip snapped, turning on her. 'For heaven's sake, woman, I've said I'm sorry, what more do you want? If you're that concerned, lock your door while I'm around – *not* that you've anything to fear from me. I'm not that hard-up for female company. Kate . . .' He knelt beside me, reaching for my hand, face strained and green eyes anxious. 'Are you all right? I'm sorry, I didn't mean to give you such a shock.'

'I know,' I managed, trying a smile, my fingers twined with his. I could have said more, but if I tried my tears might show. 'It's all right. Not your fault.'

Judy, standing with tight lips and arms folded, told him, 'You might put a shirt on. You're back in civilization now.'

'Is that what you call it?' With one last deep glance for me, he eased himself to his feet and looked her up and down in a way that made her redden. But all he said was, 'Excuse me,' before he strode away and took the stairs two at a time.

'Well, honestly!' Judy muttered. 'No need to ask whose son *he* is! I mean, how long do we have to put up with *him* in the house?'

'He didn't say.' Unable to bear the emotions that were building inside me, I forced myself to my feet and made for the door, wishing I didn't feel so sick. 'I really must go. I have two other calls to make. If you're sure you're all right . . .'

She protested that I was the one who needed rest, but I fended off her concern and went out to my bike, strapped on my helmet, pulled my goggles down over stinging eyes and rode off, spraying stones and dust behind me. I couldn't have stayed. I couldn't bear to be near Philip, especially not with a witness who obliged us to hide our mutual pain. That terrible scar on his body . . . the anguish in his eyes . . . He looked so tired, so strained. Changed. Matured. Hardened and tempered by experiences too terrible for him to have told in letters.

I found myself on the beach, where holidaymakers played and paddled, careful of the barbed wire that strung the dunes like obscene necklaces. I took my bike along one of the marsh tracks, heading for less frequented places where I stopped, out of sight of human eyes. I felt torn in many directions: joy that Philip was home; despair that he must soon leave – no fit man was allowed to remain at home for long; sorrow for his wounds; anguish for the torment he had endured; longing for his arms and his kisses . . . I wallowed in memories of the way he looked, the way he felt, the sound of his voice and the odours of his body, more beautiful for being marred by wounds got for his country. *I'm not that hard-up for female company,* he had said. But what girls had he known? Did he write to any of them? Was someone waiting for him, somewhere?

What a guy I must have looked to him, face streaked with sweat and dust, mannish clothes, lank, straight hair cut short and flattened by the leather helmet. Compared with Judy Love . . . Judy, lying on her bed wearing only flimsy underthings when he opened the door, her pale skin damp with sweat, her fair hair tousled round a pretty face with china-blue eyes set off by angry colour in her cheeks. I had been wrong to think her beauty all artifice; as I now knew, her blond curls owed nothing to chemicals. Even dishevelled and hopping mad she had managed to look feminine, rounded body firm under the thin wrap, eyes sparking, her whole demeanour challenging.

What if she and Philip . . . But I had no right to jealousy. I ought to be happy if Philip could find someone to care for. I had Oliver, after all.

Spurred on by thoughts of my husband, I completed my day's work and returned to Denes Hill in time to take a long, scented bath and wash my hair. Oliver, arriving home relatively early, surveyed my blue silk dress, my shining hair and discreet jewellery with a surprise that turned rapidly to appreciation. 'Special occasion?'

'Your homecoming,' I said.

'Indeed?' His answering smile teased me. 'It wouldn't perhaps be because of a certain Major Rawson?'

'Don't mock,' I sighed. 'Poor man . . . The truth is, I'm tired of being Inspector Kate of the NUWW. I wanted to be simply Mrs Oliver Wells, if only for one night. I thought you might like it, too.'

'I do. Very much.' He started towards me, but paused and surveyed me critically. 'Are you well? You look heavy-eyed.'

'It's the heat,' I lied. 'I turned faint this afternoon. Perhaps I've been overdoing it.'

He stared at me with awful hope, making me wish I hadn't mentioned the fainting. 'You're not—'

'No! At least, I . . .' Could it be true? Was I bearing his child? I almost said, *I hope not*. 'I'm not sure. I don't think so.'

But hope turned him solicitous, like a young lover again as we ate dinner and took a gentle stroll in the gardens to look at the new vegetable patches we had both helped to dig, producing sorely needed extra food. Chickens now scratched behind wire that had once been a barrier for tennis balls, potatoes grew in the croquet lawn, and in the walled gardens edible produce occupied every inch, with no more dahlias or roses or gladioli specially grown for decorating the house.

Strolling hand in hand with my husband I tried – oh, I did try! – to think only of him, to share his hope that we might start a family. But my mind wouldn't obey my will: it kept wandering away to the farm in the valley, where Philip and Judy would be sitting down to supper together in sweet lamplit twilight, with Mad Jack and Clem, and Boss and little Titch, who had once been little Jim.

That night, when Oliver began his overtures of love, I

449

turned away, pleading tiredness, saying I felt queasy. 'I'm sorry, Oliver.'

He curled himself behind me, an arm about me cupping my breast as he nuzzled my neck. 'It's all right, my love. All in a good cause, eh?'

He slept, but I lay awake hating the weight of his arm across me, relieved when he turned over and let me alone with my fresh, bleeding memories and my shameful longing for another man.

To Oliver's renewed disappointment, the passing days proved that I was not pregnant. He seemed to think I had deliberately misled him and once again the rift between us deepened – he stayed late in town, or didn't come home at all. The fault was mine, I knew. Oliver deserved better than me. But how was I supposed to live a lie?

While Philip remained on leave, I avoided Far Drove. But I heard about him from Judy. What a lamb he was, she enthused. The memory of their meeting always made her laugh: they'd got off on the wrong foot good and proper. I resisted my longing to talk about my own feelings for him, fearing that, once begun, I might confess all.

But something puzzled me: while I lay half unconscious, she had said something like, 'that blessed husband of hers . . .' I had always thought Judy admired Oliver. So what had she meant?

'Oh, handsome is as handsome does,' she shrugged when I asked her, one evening as we stood on the terrace at Denes Hill. Most of the patients were bedded down for the night and the house stood dark, shuttered windows gleaming like blind eyes in reflected starlight. 'He doesn't think much of *me. And* makes it obvious.'

'My husband is a snob, I'm afraid,' I sighed.

She gave me a sidelong look, said darkly, 'No, it's not that, dear,' then grimaced and laughed. 'D'you know what this reminds me of? Five years ago – the two of us standing in the moonlight on the Channel steamer. Lor', if we'd known then, eh? What was going to come, I mean. The war. And me falling for your lovely uncle, and coming here chasing after him like a love-struck ninny. If you'd read my fortune and told me this was where I'd be, five years on, I wouldn't have believed it.'

I perched on the broad stone balustrade that edged the terrace. 'Don't change the subject – that's one of Frank's bad habits. You implied that Oliver has some dark reason for disliking you. How could he, when you hardly know each other?'

'No, that's right, dear,' she said with a shrug. 'Take no notice of me. Got an inferiority complex as big as this house. Maybe that's what it is – this house. I mean, the more I come here, the more I think I could never belong, even if old Frank . . .'

As the silence lengthened, I said, 'That's the first time I've heard you say "if" and not "when".'

'I meant "if he proposed to me", not "if he comes home",' she said at once. 'He *will* come, Kate. He's got to.'

'No one would blame you if you looked for someone else. He's been gone an awfully long time.'

Judy stared bleakly into the night. 'That's what Philip said.'

'Philip?' Was there a jealous edge in my voice? 'Have you talked to him about Frank?'

'Oh, yes.' As she glanced at me, moonlight caught in wetness under her eye and when she laughed it sounded husky. 'He's easy to talk to, isn't he? So straight. Makes it all seem so simple. Black and white. Good and bad. No in-between with Philip.' She shook her head at me. 'You were a ruddy fool to let him go, dear.'

In the pause before I gathered my wits to answer, an owl swooped over the heathered hilltop, pale against the black band of the woods. 'I don't know what you mean.'

''Course you do. I saw you with him, remember? I saw the way you looked at each other. I know why you ran away from the farm. I *thought* he looked familiar, but I couldn't place him. Then I remembered – it was in London. That tea shop near Liverpool Street. Lor', dear . . . Even if you *did* have a quarrel – even if your family *had* made a stink – you should never have let him go. He's worth a hundred Oliver Wellses.'

'Don't say that.' I jumped off the balustrade and, wrapping my arms about myself, moved a pace or two away. She and Philip must have had quite a heart-to-heart. 'I don't know how much he told you, Judy, but . . . He obviously hasn't told you everything. Trying to protect my good name, probably – that would be like him.'

'He did say there was a reason, but he wouldn't say what it was. Involved other people, he said.'

'That's right. It involved my mother and his brother. And me.' I looked round at her in the moonlight, saying flatly, 'One and one makes three, Judy, if you're not careful. And when one is a girl from the hill and the other a boy from the farm, and their families hate each other . . .'

Her mouth made a dark O in her pale face. 'Kate! You don't mean—'

'I think,' Oliver's hard voice came out of the blackness round the door, 'that my wife has said quite enough, Miss Love. You'll oblige us both by saying nothing of this to anyone. Do you understand me? Slander is a crime in this country and if I find you've been spreading this tale . . .'

I couldn't look at Judy – I was mesmerized by the sight of my husband materializing from the shadows. But I heard the sudden ice in my friend's voice as she said, 'You ought to know by now that I can keep my mouth shut. I'd never hurt Kate—'

'Neither would I!' he grated, cutting off anything she might have added. Despite his words, he grasped my arm so hard, just above the elbow, that pain shot down to my fingertips. 'Now go away. And don't come back. From now on this house is out of bounds to you.'

She gaped at him. 'You can't tell me—'

'I just did! Lady Rhys-Thomas left me in charge here. When she returns, she won't welcome your sort of person hanging around her house. You're employed at the farm. So stay at the farm.'

Judy returned glare for glare. 'This is a Red Cross hospital. You can't stop me from visiting. All right, I'll go, but only because it's late and I've got work to do tomorrow. Good night, Kate. I shall see you soon.'

As she ran down the steps to the drive, Oliver and I stood in silence. My arm tingled – he was stopping the blood.

'You're hurting me,' I objected.

He let me go, but he didn't apologize. He said, 'So, young Farcroft's home, is he? Since when?'

'About ten days,' I replied, rubbing my arm.

'You've seen him?'

'I went to see Judy. She wasn't well. Philip happened to be there.'

'Convenient.'

'It's the truth. I didn't stay long. And I haven't been back since.'

'Sensible of you,' he said in the expressionless tone he could adopt at will. 'After all, seeing him will do neither of you any good.' He took my arm again, saying softly, 'Shall we go to bed – my love?'

I feared that his jealousy might make him take me in anger, but instead he chose sensuality as his means of revenge, using his skill to arouse me until I quivered under him, begging for release. In the end it was not him I hated but my own body, for betraying me and responding helplessly to his cool cajolings. It had nothing to do with love, neither for me or for him – not any more. Afterwards, he lay stroking me, talking softly, saying that he didn't like my being friendly with Judy Love.

'I hadn't intended to tell you this, but perhaps you should be warned . . . Miss Love may try to poison your mind against me.'

'Why should she do that?'

' "A woman scorned . . ." Need I say more?'

Whatever was he implying?

'You will recall,' he said, 'that, even during our journey from Berlin, she paraded the train displaying herself for my benefit. You yourself drew my attention to it. Then, after we encountered her at that ridiculous seance, or whatever you choose to call those entertainments, she discovered where I was staying and—'

'Oliver!' I breathed. 'That can't be right. She'd met Frank by then.'

'One man is never enough for her type. Obviously Frank was more susceptible than I. He may be genuinely fond of her. And she, no doubt, sees in him a meal-ticket. Why else is she here? She couldn't go on being a dancer for ever. She must be near thirty. Perhaps now you understand why I've tried to discourage your friendship with her. My dear, you're so young. I love you for your trust in people. But it can't go on. We must persuade her to stay away from Denes Hill.

When your grandmother comes home in a few weeks'
time, I—'

'Grandmother? Is she coming? And Tom?' I grasped
eagerly at this news as an antidote to my doubts about Judy.

'I had a letter from her today. Yes, she feels she has
been away long enough. Tom seems to be recovered. And,'
he sounded amused, 'the Welsh cousins are becoming a
little restive over her long stay. It will be good to have her
home, won't it?'

'Yes, it will.' Good to have her there as a buffer between
him and me. 'Shall we go back to Merchant's Court?'

'No, I think not. You like living here, don't you? But I
may ask for a more permanent arrangement. It's time we
had proper quarters of our own.'

So he intended to stay at Denes Hill. That came as a
relief – I had not relished the thought of being alone with
him again at the flat in Lynn. Yet I was puzzled; I had
always thought he would want to get me away from the hill
as soon as he could – away from the farm and the Farcrofts,
and now from Judy. Would I ever understand the man I had
married? Would I ever understand anyone? Even Judy . . .
I didn't want to believe what Oliver had said about Judy.
But why should he lie?

Only two days later, on a wet Sunday afternoon, I walked
disconsolately on the beach, under a large black umbrella.
Oliver had been called out by demanding but wealthy clients
whom he didn't like to put off, even on a Sunday. Heavy
rain had driven the holiday-makers back to their boarding
houses and only seabirds inhabited the shore. I stood staring
at a sea where the swell rolled waveless, dappled with
raindrops, murky grey, while my thoughts shifted, forming
patterns as in a kaleidoscope: Philip . . . Philip and Judy;

Judy and Frank; Judy and Oliver; Oliver and I; Philip and I, and Mad Jack, and Mother and Michael . . .

Katie! The cry came from the sea. I knew I had to help. I dropped my brolly and ran – and only as the water splashed up my skirts did I come to my senses and find that I was standing in six inches of water, still wearing my button-strap shoes. The hem of my dress was soaked. And the grey swell of the Wash spread out towards the Lincolnshire coast, empty. There was no mist, no Uncle John shouting hoarsely for help.

That was what had called me – a memory from fifteen years ago, when I had heard John shout and gone running to . . . gone running to . . . Eyes closed, I willed myself to remember. What next? What next? Had I run into the sea and stopped, because I couldn't swim? Had I been forced to stand helpless and watch, while John—

'I say, Mrs W!' a voice called from behind me. 'You all right?'

Oh, not now. Not my unwanted admirer, poor sad Keith Rawson. I tried to ignore him, tried to hold on . . . But the interruption had disrupted the tenuous thread of lost memory.

As I waded back towards him, Major Rawson regarded me worriedly, pink face with pale, blinking eyes under the brim of a military cap, dark macintosh loose over his hospital blues. He had picked up my umbrella, holding it out to me.

'Thank you.' Shivering, I realized the day had turned cold. Or was it only I who had turned cold now that I was so wet?

'D'you often do that?' he asked. 'Go paddling? With your shoes on?'

'I was deep in thought. Composing poetry.'

'Ah.' He rubbed his nose with a short forefinger – he

found my penchant for poetry intimidating. 'Sorry. Wouldn't have bothered you, only . . . er, husband about, is he?'

I hesitated, wondering why he asked. 'Was it my husband you wanted?'

'Hell, no! Bloody ass. Shouldn't leave you alone. What if the Hun comes? Good beach for landing, this.'

'It's too far from anywhere important,' I reasoned, keeping my patience with difficulty. 'Major Rawson, what is it you want?'

'Ah. Yes.' His pink nose received another polishing. 'Message for you. Rum cove. Bit of a reprobate, shouldn't wonder. Thin chap. One eye. Needs a good wash. Ring any bells?'

What was he talking about? 'Someone with a message for me? Where?'

'That temple place. In the woods. Said he'd wait. Only Mrs Wells, he said. No one else. Not a word. Not another soul. Well. I'd seen you go off. Knew where you were heading. Came after you. Of course, I'll go with you. Can't leave a lady alone. Not with a rum cove like that. Never know what might occur. Can't take risks. Not with you.'

'Did he say what he wanted, or who had sent him?'

The forefinger returned to stroke his nose and smooth the bristly hairs on his top lip. 'Told me to fetch you. Pronto. PDQ. Only you. No one else. Not another soul. I'd seen you go off. Knew where you—'

'Yes, you said,' I interrupted before he could go over it all again. 'Thank you. I'll go and see what he wants.'

'Right with you. Lead the way.'

I might have tried to dissuade him from accompanying me, but I didn't care for the sound of this 'rum cove'.

Through pouring rain, huge drops pattering from the trees

to splatter off my umbrella, with my skirts and feet wet from the sea, we returned along muddy pathways, making round towards the temple-like folly. As we came within sight of mock-Roman columns framing a dark opening beyond a flight of shallow steps, I hesitated. The place appeared deserted. Was this a ruse on Major Rawson's part to get me alone in the summerhouse?

'He was here,' he said. 'Right here. Spoke to the chap. Fetch Mrs Wells, he said. Only Mrs Wells. No one else – ah!'

A figure had appeared from behind one of the columns, leaning on the fluted granite as if reluctant to leave the shadows. Worn clothing hung on an emaciated frame. His hair was cropped short to his skull, and a rough beard masked the lower half of a hollow-cheeked face with one sunken eye. The other eye was covered by a black patch which didn't entirely hide the scar tissue beneath.

I caught my breath, drawing back in instinctive horror. Maybe I blanched. My reaction caused the man a certain bitter amusement. His mouth stretched in a dry, mocking smile.

I think I knew that smile. Even before I recognized his voice. 'Not a pretty sight, eh, old girl?' said my Uncle Frank.

TWENTY-FIVE

'You all right, Mrs W?' Keith Rawson asked. 'I'll hold him off, if—'

I shook my head, still staring at Frank. His one blue eye gleamed ruefully in reply. 'No, it's all right, Major Rawson. I know him. He . . . He's a friend.' And so he was: beneath the scars, the rags, the beard, the dirt – this scarecrow was my darling Uncle Frank.

I threw myself at him and hugged him tightly. What did I care if he smelled like a horse? He was home at last. How happy Judy would be.

'No, girl,' he muttered into my hair as I burst into tears, his arms supporting me. 'No, don't. Damn it, that's why I didn't come. Didn't want to distress you, or anyone. Come on, girl, I need you to be strong. For me. Be strong for me. Hold up. Look at me straight – take a good look. This is the way I am. Can you take it?'

'Yes!' I wept, but my heart sobbed *No!* 'It doesn't matter. You're you. Oh, Uncle Frank . . . Oh, Uncle Frank . . .'

In time I came to see beyond the scars he bore. But on that first day I couldn't look at him without lumps in my throat and hatred in my heart for whoever had done this to him.

When I took notice again, Major Rawson had tactfully vanished.

'Come up to the house,' I begged Frank. 'Please! You

459

need a bath, a shave, a change of clothes.'

'No, Kate.' His hands gripped me strongly – still Frank's fine, long, sensitive hands, though hardened by toil and grimed with dirt – and his single gaze held me with blue intensity. 'No, not yet. I'm not sure I shall ever be ready to—'

'But there's no one else there – no one of the family.'

'I know,' he said. 'I telephoned earlier and got the gist. Do you hear from Vicky? And what of Tom?'

'Vicky's fine. She's married now – to Captain Cavan Fielding. He's a liaison officer with the general staff in France. And Tom's well, too. He and Grandmother are coming home soon. You must be here when—'

'No, girl!' His hands gripped me again, even more forcefully, as he said urgently, 'Mother's not to know. You're not to tell anyone about this. Not *anyone*, understand? I didn't intend to come home at all. Better you thought me dead than see me like this. But I had to see *you*. I had to tell you about Clara. I've seen her, Kate. I saw your mother.'

'Mother?' This news dazed me. For a moment I couldn't think. 'Where? Is she in England? Oh—'

'Kate!' He shook me as if to wake me out of a stupor. 'For heaven's sake, old girl, I haven't much time. Listen!'

We sat on the folly steps, sheltered from the worst of the rain by the overhanging portico and the trees crowding above it, while he hurriedly told me the gist of his story. There was much he left out, even then. Some things he never did tell.

He had been to eastern Prussia, a roundabout trip of voyages in cargo ships, days lying low in varied hiding places and nights stealing through hostile territory. Eventually, he had joined up with some Russians, our allies, who were being driven back to their own borders. He had spent some time with them, recording their activities in the pages of his sketchbook.

When a lull came in the fighting, Frank had 'had an outing' behind enemy lines – he made it sound like a pleasant tootle in his motor. He had reached Schloss Lindhafen, where the von Wurthes lived, and contrived a brief meeting with Mother. She was well, as were my half-brothers, safe in their own home, in their own country. She wouldn't think of leaving. She had called Frank a fool, risking his own life and hers by coming to see her – the encounter had been a stormy one.

Afterwards, he had moved back eastwards, come up with a band of Kossacks and been caught in a skirmish. A shell had exploded among them, killing most of his companions and leaving him half blinded. Captured by the Germans, almost dead of pain and loss of blood, he had found himself in a prison camp hospital, where he remained for months, recovering from the loss of his eye and prey to recurring fever. His captors had thought him a Russian.

'Just as well,' he said with a wry grin. 'If they'd known I was British, they'd have shot me as a spy. So I played dumb and stupid. Until the thaw came. Then, a party of us escaped.'

After more adventures in the snow-bound Carpathian Mountains, he had managed to reach England. He had spent further weeks in a hospital, delirious with blood poisoning, weakened by malnutrition and fever, not wanting us to know he was alive. On being discharged he had taken to the road, doing whatever work came to hand. He had almost decided never to come home.

'Except,' he said gravely, folding my hand between his own filthy paws, 'that I needed to tell you I'd seen Clara. I couldn't let you go on believing . . .'

'Did she ask after me?' I needed to know.

His mouth twisted. 'Eventually. She does care about you, in her own self-absorbed way, but it seems your stepfather ordered her to cut off all associations here and she decided you might be happier without reminders – she's good at persuading herself to believe whatever suits her conscience. She was surprised to hear you had married Oliver, though. Surprised, and a touch miffed, I fancy. Probably hoped he'd be hankering after her until Doomsday. So I told her you had grown into a beauty, with dozens of men falling for you.'

'Oh, Frank!' I choked, grasping at his hands, hardly knowing whether to laugh or cry.

'I also told her,' he added, 'that she should have had the courage to tell you the truth about your origins herself, rather than have you find out from vicious gossip.'

'Oh.' His voice and his expression told me there was more, so I waited, feeling numb. Was I about to find out why she had lied to me? I wasn't sure I wanted to know.

'Kate, my dear.' He touched a finger under my chin, making me look at him. 'She swears you're William Brand's child. There *was* no "other man".'

The stillness about me deepened, so profound that it sang in my ears. No 'other man'? What an odd way to put it, as if his identity was in doubt. Couldn't she admit, even now, to being attracted to Michael Farcroft? 'What else could she say?' I asked dully. 'She wouldn't admit that she'd actually—'

'If she was lying, I'll eat my hat,' my uncle said, regarding me earnestly over our joined hands. 'I know when my sister's adjusting facts to suit her own purposes and this time, I'll swear, she was telling the truth. Her husband,

William Brand, was your father. You were conceived lawfully, inside wedlock. Believe it, Kate.'

I shook my head. The notion was too momentous. A million questions tumbled in my mind. Why, how, when, where . . . Which did one ask first?

Before I could speak, Frank leapt up, startled by a sound in the gardens. A wheelbarrow trundling. Someone coming. 'I must go,' he muttered.

'You can't!' I grasped to stop him, but he evaded me. 'Oh, Uncle Frank, please! Come to the house. Have a bath. Something to eat.'

He shook his head, poised to fly, watching for the oncoming danger in one direction while assessing his escape route in the other. Like a cornered, wounded animal. 'No.'

'Don't you even want to see Judy Love?'

He caught his breath, wincing as if her name had stabbed him. 'Is she here?' Clawing a thin hand through his hair, he edged away. 'She mustn't see me like this. Give me time, girl. Don't tell her. Don't tell anyone. Look . . . I'll let you know where I am. I promise. Maybe in time . . .'

'Oh, please!' I begged. But he was gone, shambling off into woods full of September leaf and golden light.

My head ached with confusion as I returned to the house. Should I have stopped Frank from leaving? Where would he go? How would he live? Like a tramp? Denes Hill was his home, his inheritance. I wished Oliver would come: I needed to talk to someone. But Frank had begged me to say nothing. Should I respect his wish? The problem solved itself when I learned that Oliver had telephoned to say that his clients had received bad news about their only son and needed company. He would dine with them and sleep, later, at the flat – he had early engagements tomorrow.

Totally alone, I couldn't rest. I wandered the private apartments, then climbed to the sanctum and stared unseeingly at the view. Around me the air seemed to vibrate with mingled hope and dread as I faced my own dilemma. Was I really William Brand's child, not Michael Farcroft's? How could I ever know? C.L.B., they had called me. Clara's Little Bastard. How had the mistake been made? Mad Jack believed it. Oliver, too. Grandmother had confirmed it. But if they were wrong? Oh, Philip, if they were wrong . . .

My heart, not my common sense, led me down to the farm in the last of that day's light. The sky hung pale, clear of cloud now, with a trace of orange in the west, and beneath it the world was dissolving into shades of grey and black. No lights showed in the farmhouse, though the curtains were open and the main door stood ajar, letting in the soft evening air. As I approached, I heard Judy giggle, answered by Philip's laugh – the deep, warm note quivered along my nerves. If only . . .

Then sharp-eared Titch came yapping to the door. I bent to pet him, but he backed off, still nervous of being touched, as someone came into the lobby. I knew it was Philip, wearing thick khaki socks and brown corduroys, even before my glance slid up to the grey blur of his shirt.

'Kate?' His soft voice questioned my wisdom in being there; it also said he was glad to see me.

'Hello, Philip.' I forced my unsteady legs to straighten. 'Where's Boss tonight?'

'Gone to the Black Horse with Dad.'

'Oh. Right. Is . . . is Judy here?'

'Who is it, Philip?' Judy appeared, peering round his shoulder. 'Oh – Kate! I didn't expect to see *you* here, dear. Is that husband of yours off on his jaunts again?'

Ignoring this sally, I said, 'I need to talk to you, Judy.'

'And *I* need to talk to *you*, dear,' she answered. 'After the way your blessed husband spoke to me—'

'This isn't about Oliver!' I cried, a hand to my buzzing head.

Philip stepped forward, taking my arm. 'What's wrong, Kate? Come inside and tell us.'

'I can't stay. I didn't intend...' But I let myself be persuaded into the living room, to sit on the sofa with Judy, while Clementina drew the curtains and Philip lit lamps. As light washed over him I opened my senses to the sight of him, the sound of him, the sheer vibrant reality of his presence. How much longer would he be at home? How long before I had to dread every day's post?

As if she read my thoughts, Judy said, 'He's off tomorrow.'

'Tomorrow?' The word half choked me, while Philip's eyes met mine in perfect empathy.

'Only to London,' he said. 'For interviews. I've been accepted by the RFC. Pilot, probably. Or a navigator. I don't care which, so long as I get to fly. Of course, there'll be a few weeks' training first. I... I thought that was maybe why you came. To say goodbye.'

I only stared at him, my head buzzing. If he joined the Royal Flying Corps he'd be going up in those spindly, precarious, frighteningly glorious wood and metal and fabric contraptions that had already killed too many young men. Was he going to be shooting his puny rifle at those huge Zepps, or risking his life over enemy lines? I didn't want him to go. Yet I was glad, for him, that he'd gained his dream. Rather that than endure the trenches yet again.

'She didn't know you were off,' Judy informed him. 'I was going to tell her, but that blasted man interrupted. I told you—'

'Don't talk about Oliver like that!' Feeling as if my head might burst, I pressed my fingers to my temples. 'Judy . . . I've seen Frank. He was here this afternoon.'

A flurry of unguarded emotions silenced her. In that instant she forgot she hated Oliver; she forgot Philip; her whole being centred on Frank and her eyes filled with tears that spilled over to plop down her face on to her shirt. 'He's alive? Where? Can I see him?'

She didn't care about details. He was alive. That was all she could take in, for now. If I had doubted her feelings for Frank, I had been wrong.

A hoarse shout from the yard took Titch scrabbling out again. Mad Jack was back, coming roaring in with Boss at heel, full of some argument he'd had at the Black Horse. 'Blast, that old fool of a Benstead! Hen't got no more sense than a May gosling. Why . . . what's to do here? What's Judy now blahrin' about? Not bad news?'

'No, good news,' Judy wept, smiling through her tears. 'I'm off to bed. I'll talk to you tomorrow, Kate. Good night, Mr Farcroft. Philip . . .' And she ran up the stairs, going to weep out her relief alone.

Clem reappeared from the kitchen, bringing a tray with five mugs of cocoa on it. Leaving one with me, one on the table near Philip and another on the cold hearth for the old man, she took the tray upstairs with her as she, too, tactfully retreated. Philip straddled a wooden chair near the table, arms folded on its back, while the two dogs settled on the hearth-rug. The old man had flopped into an armchair, from where he rumbled on about happenings at the pub. Had I not been hampered by brimming hot cocoa, I might have fled. Or did the cocoa provide a good excuse to stay?

At last the farmer seemed to sense the atmosphere, looking from Philip to me. 'Well? What's to-do?'

'Frank Rhys-Thomas is safe,' Philip said.

'Oh, hum?' His father glowered at me. 'That why she's here, is it – to spread the glad tidings? En't you got the sense to stay away, girl? You're as bad as your mother. Worse. She was no more'n a young 'un. *You're* a married woman.'

The surface of the cocoa rippled in response to my trembling. Unable to face either of them, I stared down at the mug as if it were a crystal ball. 'My uncle has been to Germany. He's seen Mother.'

'So?'

'So, he told her I'd found out about her and Michael. And . . . And she denied the whole thing.'

'Hah!' the old man snorted. 'Squit! Does she reckon my old girl lied, then? What about that letter?'

I looked across at him, though I couldn't see him clearly. 'I don't know! That's why I came, to find out. You're the only one who might know . . . *When* was it? What year? What month?'

'How the hummer should I remember?' he demanded, shifting in his chair. 'That was haying time – that's all I know. As to the year . . . well, how old are you?'

For a moment, I couldn't remember. 'I was born in ninety-three.'

'Then it must have been ninety-two.'

'Haying time?' Philip said sharply. 'Kate's birthday is the last day of May. If Clara was last here a whole year before—'

'Maybe I'm wrong!' the old man broke in, waving a gnarled brown hand. 'Maybe that was harvest – August, or September. A few months is neither here nor there. No—' His eyes narrowed as a thought struck him and he peered at me. 'No, that must have been haysel, because it was afore the fatstock show. I remember now. Our bull won the rosette that year. Best in Show. Blast, yes! And Michael was too busy moping to care. I clipped his ear for him. "Not too old for a good beltin'," I say. "Not yet, you en't, bor, for all you're a great long streak o' pump water. Nineteen's still on'y a boy, far as I'm concerned. You better forget that blasted mawther, right quick. She's turned you shanny." '

'Nineteen? Blast—' Philip leapt up, sending his chair crashing on its back as he swept up the lamp and rushed out, still in his stocking feet, to a yard puddled by the day's rain.

'Where's he now off?' the old man muttered irritably. 'He've gone shanny, too. Blasted women!' The look he speared at me glinted with venom. 'What good'll it do you, even if that do happen to be so? You've got a husband. Philip'll never come between man and wife, that I do know. What're you trying to do, send him addled?'

Shaking so much that I was in danger of spilling the cocoa, I leaned and set the mug down on the floor, saying hoarsely, 'I need to know the truth, that's all. No, I shan't trouble Philip any more. It's too late for us. But I need to know . . .'

The outer door crashed as Philip returned. He had left the lamp behind, but in his hand he held a blue rosette, faded and dusty from being on some shed wall. The look on his face made my whole body jump – bright, elated, fiercely triumphant . . . 'Eighteen ninety-one,' he said, shaking the rosette in the air. 'That's when our bull won Best in Show. You said Michael was nineteen, Dad. That would be right, wouldn't it? Eighteen ninety-one . . .' We gazed at each other wordlessly, both of us thinking the same thought – if Mother had been sent away in June eighteen ninety-one, then she had last seen Michael Farcroft two whole years before my birth. He couldn't possibly have fathered me. And if I wasn't his brother's child, then Philip and I . . .

It made no difference. It couldn't. I was married to Oliver Wells.

Distracted, I jumped up. 'I must go. I shouldn't have come. But I wanted to tell Judy about Frank, and . . .' I glanced back at the old man, who was squinting at me, maybe hiding a touch of regret.

'I din't know,' he muttered. 'I din't give it much thought. You told me that was true and . . .' and he had wanted to believe it, because it gave him back a part of Michael. Oh, yes, I understood. I didn't blame *him*. The one I blamed, with a rising, choking fury of bitterness, was my Grandmother: *she* must have known the truth, but she had allowed me to believe this lie. She had done it to separate me from Philip!

I started for the door. 'Good night, Mr Farcroft. Philip . . . thank you.'

'I'll come—'

'No!' I recoiled from him, holding my hands to ward him off. 'No, don't come. I can find my own way. I have my torch. Good night. Oh, and . . . good luck for the interviews tomorrow.'

He didn't reply, not in words. He didn't need to – green eyes heavy with sorrow told me all that was in his heart.

As I walked unsteadily across the wet meadow to the gate that led out to the short-cut lane, stars glimmered in the damp night and a thin new moon leaned over the sea. Soon, trees thick with leaf hid me from the sky. Where the woods were blackest I stopped and flipped my torch off, letting the night draw closely round me. Despite the mild air, I was shivering, hugging myself both for warmth and for comfort. At the farm I had been so sure, so righteously angry. Now, doubts crept in. The old man's memory might not be reliable. How could I be sure? How could I ever be sure? Why had no one else noticed the two-year gap? *Two years*, not nine months. Oh . . . what did it matter? Even if someone brought proof positive, Philip and I could never—

A sound behind me made me whirl, a hand to my throat. As I fumbled with my torch it slipped out of numb fingers, falling soundlessly on wet grass at my feet. 'Who's there?'

'It's me.' Philip's deep voice came out of the darkness. 'Did you think I could let you go like that? Only I had to get my boots on and . . . Where's your husband? Is he at the house?'

'He's staying in Lynn tonight.'

That made him swear under his breath, then he reached for me, touching my shoulders, cradling my face . . . 'You should never have married him, Katie. You never would if things had been normal. I know you're not happy. How can you be, with a man who—' He bit the word off.

' "A man who" what?' I managed.

'Nothing. I don't know the man, do I?'

'What has Judy been saying?' I asked breathlessly. 'She . . . she may have reasons to want to hurt Oliver. She's always been attracted to him. If she made up to him and he . . .'

'*What?* Judy's not like that!'

His vehemence only confirmed my own feelings. No, Judy was not like that. I had never really believed it. 'But why should Oliver lie?'

'To cover his own guilt, maybe.'

What did that mean? 'Philip!'

'Well, human nature's more suited to sin than sainthood,' he said gruffly. 'Didn't you know that? Oh . . . forget him.

470

Are we going to say goodbye yet again without being honest with each other? This may be our last time, Katie. Our only time.'

'What is there to say?' I croaked.

'Plenty. To begin with – I love you.'

He might as well have stabbed me. 'Don't say that!'

'I've got to.' He moved closer, his warm breath on my face as his hands slid behind my neck and into my hair. 'I love you. I love you. I never stopped loving you. I never stopped praying for a miracle. Now it's happened I'm not going to waste it.'

'We can't be sure it—'

'*I'm* sure.'

'Your father might be wrong. No one else has queried it. How could they make a mistake like that?'

'Easily, when it's twenty years ago! There must have been gossip when your mother went away. Then she marries an old man. She has a child. She stays away several more years. It would all get mixed up, wouldn't it? Who would bother to stop and work it out? Dad didn't. You and I didn't.'

That was true. Mother had been only seventeen when she went to Cumbria. John the same, Oliver a little younger, Frank and Harry younger still – they wouldn't have been told the real story. *Fudging dates* was how Vicky had explained the anomaly.

'Besides,' Philip said, his voice hoarse and savage, 'even if we're wrong, I don't think I care any more. I love you. If you're feeling as bloody as I am, then . . .'

'Philip. Oh . . .' Like one bewitched, I melted into his arms, reaching my hands behind his neck. Oh, so sweet. Oh, so right. Our bodies met and blended, and when he bent his mouth to mine glory shuddered through me, waking every nerve and fibre, making me cling more tightly. Desire washed over us both, claiming us, fuelled by too long a waiting and a love too deep to deny. We needed each other. We belonged to each other. Right or wrong. As it had been from the beginning of all things, because he was he and I was I . . .

We devoured each other with kisses, rediscovering each other, hands stroking and caressing, impatient with the clothing that formed barriers between us, needing the closeness of flesh on flesh. How warm and strong his body felt under my adoring fingers. What joy to have him touch me. At last, at last. Philip. My Philip. Unbearable beauty in his readiness for me and mine for him. 'Come to me. Please! Please!'

A cry escaped me, mingling with his groan as our bodies became one. Philip, my soul, my heart, my joy. We were part of the universe, with all that had gone before and all that was yet to come. A little death. A new beginning. A seal on our belonging.

As I clung round his neck, weeping, I became aware of tree bark digging into my back, dark woods rustling wetly around us, our bodies sticky with sweat, bonded together. 'I love you,' I breathed, and kissed his jaw and his throat, my lips savouring the harshness of stubble on his chin. I could say it now, freely and sincerely. 'Oh, I love you! So very much.'

'And I love you,' he murmured. 'For ever, Katie. Whatever happens, no one can take this away from us. If this is to be all there is—'

I stopped the fearful words with my fingers. 'Don't say that. Don't, darling.' Loving the shape of his mouth, I let my fingers trace his lips, wanting never to let him go. 'We have all our lives before us. You must believe that. Philip . . . Oh, Philip, I love you! I wish—'

But he silenced me with kisses, holding me ever closer. So long we had waited. Now we could never have enough. One night . . . Dear God, let it be more than that! Somehow, let there be a way.

We stayed in the wood until the damp chill reminded us of passing time. Then slowly, reluctantly, we made our way towards the house, arms about each other, pausing every little while to hold each other close again.

'Where will they send you?' I asked. 'Will you write to me? We could use a box number at the post office. You will let me know where you're going to be? Do you think your father suspects you came after me? Philip, how shall we—'

'Don't talk about it.' His voice sounded rough as he pulled me to him and kissed me with savage despair, driving his fingers into my hair. 'I don't care about the future. I'm sick of trying to do the right thing. I love you. And you love me. That's all that matters. No yesterdays, no tomorrows. Not for us. Only here and now. One day at a time. I've watched too many good men die before they had a chance to live. That's not for me. Some day, when this war is over, if we're both spared, then we'll think about the future. For now, just keep loving me. Hold on to that, as I will. You belong to me. You always will, whatever may come.'

'I believe that, too,' I answered unsteadily. 'I've known it ever since we met. Nothing can part us. Not . . . not even death.'

'Amen to that, sweetheart,' he murmured. 'But I don't intend to die, if I can help it. I've got too much to live for.'

The following evening when I arrived home, a note from Judy Love asked me to meet her at the back gate at sunset, if not that evening then the next. As it happened, I was able to go that same day.

Judy looked tired after another day stooking sheaves. They were trying to bring in the harvest before the weather broke. 'I thought you'd want to have this as soon as poss,' she said, handing me an envelope before collapsing on to a tree stump. 'Phew, 'scuse me if I rest my legs, dear.'

The envelope had a single 'K' scribbled on it, by Philip. Caressing it with my fingertips, I put it in my trouser pocket, to read later.

Judy gazed down the short-cut track. 'I only saw him for a minute, but . . . I gather you're not related, after all. Pity you got yourselves into such a tangle. What'll you do?'

'When the right moment comes, I shall ask Oliver for a divorce.'

'Divorce?!' She goggled at me. 'Lor', dear, do you know what you're saying? Let it all come out in court? And then what? Someone like me could brazen it out, maybe, in time. But, I mean, someone like you? No, dear, if I were you I'd keep my mouth shut. Let things ride.'

'You mean . . . deceive Oliver?'

'Well, he's not exactly Galahad the Faithful, is he? Oh, I didn't come to talk about your horrible husband. I want to know about Frank. Tell me about it, dear. Tell me everything.'

I did so, while the gold of the sky turned to flame on duck-egg blue. Asking questions, Judy extracted every detail, disguising her feelings behind a show of levity. 'So! Didn't want to see me, eh? Thinks he can get rid of me. Not likely. Soon's you know where he is, dear, you let me know. I'll sort him out. Run off and hide, will he? Not if I have my way!'

'I agree,' I said. 'He's got to come home. We must make him see that.'

She hesitated, watching me for a long moment, then: 'He won't be very happy if he finds your husband acting like lord of the manor. He always said he had a feeling Oliver intended to take over, by hook or by crook.'

'Did he?' What had Frank meant by that? 'Judy, are you going to tell me what it is with you and Oliver? Is it just because Frank doesn't like him? I know you've talked about it to Philip. You might as well tell me, too.'

'I'd rather not, dear.'

'The other night, he . . . he warned me you might try to make trouble for him. He said you had chased after him, and when he rejected you—'

'He said what? Ruddy liar!' She leapt to her feet, but stopped, groaning, as aching muscles protested, and eased herself upright, arching her back, moaning, 'Lor', I wasn't meant to chuck sheaves about.'

'Please, Judy . . . I think I have a right to know.'

For a while longer she resisted, not looking at me, then she came to lean near me, her back against a tree as she studied her work-scarred hands and split nails. 'Remember when we met after one of Mrs Bly's sessions? You were with Oliver and dear old Win Leeming. And I was with Elsie – Elsie Pratt, you know? My friend? The redhead?'

'Yes.' I didn't follow her drift.

'Did you notice the way Oliver and Elsie clicked? No, I thought not. He gave her the once-over, and got the glad eye back. Next evening, he turns up at the stage door. Takes her out to supper. Doesn't bring her back until after breakfast. That was the start of it.'

Recalling that that had been the evening when I firmly rejected Oliver, I tried to be objective. 'He was a single man then. He's never hidden the fact that he's . . . a man of the world.'

'Of course, dear. That'll be it.'

'There's more, isn't there? Is he still seeing her?'

Judy pushed her hands into her pockets, sighing, 'I wish I could lie to you, dear, but . . . I don't know how often, and he's not the only one by a long chalk – Elsie's pretty free with her favours. But last time I saw her, round last Easter time . . . she was with your Oliver. All dressed up, he was – top hat, cape with a blue lining, big cigar . . . And her clinging to his sleeve like butter. They weren't going to spend the night watching for Zepps.

'When I came here,' she added, 'he didn't seem to connect me with Elsie. But one night . . . I'm sorry to say this, dear, but you may as well know it all – I saw him canoodling with one of the nurses. And he saw me. Waylaid me on my way home one evening. I was scared – I told him I knew about him and Elsie, and that made him really mad. He said if I said anything to you he'd wring my neck. Well! I don't gossip, dear, not usually, and I didn't want to upset you. Mind you, if I'd known before the event that you were going to marry him, I might have said something. But it all happened so quick . . .' She leaned to lay a hand on my arm. 'I'm sorry, dear, but you did ask. And you must have suspected, surely. You don't really believe he spends all those nights away from home going to business meetings, do you?'

'I've never given it much thought.' Now, it all seemed so obvious. Why hadn't I seen it before? Oliver's appetites could never be satisfied by one woman. Oh, it had suited his vanity to marry me, for who I was, and he had no doubt enjoyed chasing, conquering and educating a green girl. But he had soon tired of that and gone back to other, more alluring outlets. To my surprise, I felt slightly affronted – betrayed – which was rich, considering my own recent behaviour. Forcing a laugh, I said, 'Ironic, isn't it? I've been feeling horribly guilty about Philip, and now . . .'

'Well, you're not the first, or the last,' Judy said. 'I mean, this war's made people do all kinds of strange things. Marriage vows don't mean much any more. It's the modern way. Well . . . I'd better go, dear. Got another long day in the corn tomorrow. You be all right, will you?'

'I'm fine,' I lied.

Overhead, the sky had deepened to royal velvet. The stars came out, the moon's sickle a touch wider than the previous night, when Philip had been here with me. *One day at a time*, he had said.

Until we knew what the future held, perhaps it was best to be discreet, best not to tell Oliver anything. Since he didn't really care, I couldn't be hurting him by loving someone else. My hand rested against Philip's letter, savouring the contact, knowing it told me of his love. Where was he tonight? Would he learn to fly in France, or in Kent? When would I see him again?

TWENTY-SIX

To my unbounded relief and joy, Philip was not sent to France – not at once, that is. After winning his wings at Farnborough, he came back to Norfolk, to Sedgeford, only two miles from home, to spend a month learning the skills of aerial battle and reconnaissance. A month . . . an unexpected gift which we both grasped with eager hands. Being billeted at Sedgeford with the other trainees, he could say he was walking over to see his father in the evening, or I could stop off somewhere on my way to or from my various assignments, or go out after dark if Oliver was away. We let ourselves imagine we were back in that lovely summer before it all went wrong, except that this time we were in total harmony. Was it sinful? We didn't even think about it. One brief month was ours.

Frank wrote that he was staying at the Mayfair flat and '*getting myself together*'. I could tell the family he was safe, but not where he was, not yet – he didn't fancy having his mother rush down to London to treat him like an invalid. I wrote to Grandmother to set her mind at rest about him. She replied that that had made up her mind for her – she would be home very soon, to prepare for Frank's return.

'She must be so relieved,' I remarked to Oliver. 'At least one of her sons has been spared.'

'Did he give any hint as to where he has been these eighteen months?'

'Perhaps we shall soon find out,' I replied. 'It will be good to have him home, won't it?'

'Yes, indeed, my dear,' he answered, his face unreadable. 'But the war isn't over yet, for any of us.'

Why did I have the feeling that Oliver didn't welcome the thought of Frank's return?

The oddness of my uncle's odyssey in Germany had struck both Judy and me. Why had he gone to the eastern front? Surely not simply to see Mother, though that was what he had let me believe. How had he blended so easily with the Russians, living and working with them for months? I knew he spoke German, but did he also speak Russian?

'You don't think he's a secret agent, do you?' Judy asked, wide-eyed. 'Lor', dear . . . But, if he was, he'd never let on, would he?'

No, he would not. Not ever. But I couldn't help thinking of his strange comings and goings even before the war. Had they all been on account of his painting?

His letter had asked me not to tell the family where he was, but he hadn't repeated his instructions about not telling Judy. Which, I felt, might indicate that he would like to see her. So I told her he was in London, at the flat, and, after a day or two of indecision, she applied for a few days' leave and a rail ticket.

When I saw her off at Eveningham station, I guessed that her joking, brazen front covered a deal of insecurity.

'D'you think I might get invited up to Denes Hill as a proper guest some day?' she asked. 'Even after the old girl gets back?'

'If Frank invites you, he'll make sure you're made welcome.'

' "If . . ." ' She pulled a face at me. 'Will you be all right, dear?'

'Of course! Do stop worrying about me, Judy. Think about yourself for once. Give Frank my love, won't you? Good luck.'

As I walked back up to the village, I noted that autumn had come. October coloured the trees and hedgerows in vivid shades of gold and red, and berries hung in thick clusters. 'Going to be a hard winter,' Mad Jack observed when I called at the farm. 'Wholly hard. You'll see. First that'll froiz, then that'll snew.'

He was in an odd mood, worried about Philip, who must soon move on to the front line in France and who already talked familiarly about the perils of 'Archie' – the shellfire from anti-aircraft guns – and weather reporting, and wireless communication, and fighting Zepps, and flying reconnaissance missions. Philip was loving every minute. His father and I felt less sanguine. But I tried not to think about that. Today, Philip was still close to me. Tonight, I would see him. Tomorrow . . . No. No tomorrows. Only todays for us. Until the war ended.

Mad Jack's prediction of hard weather ahead seemed to be coming true: for a few nights, frost turned the world silver. Oliver had gone to the engineering works in Lincoln – at least, he said he was going to Lincoln. All I cared was that his absence left me free to meet Philip without fear of discovery.

As I was about to leave the house that evening, one of the nurses came with a message for me to telephone the Mayfair flat. I wondered what was wrong – had Oliver turned up there, not realizing Frank was in residence? Was Frank angry because Judy had arrived? I used the telephone in Grandmother's study, asking the operator to connect me.

'Kate!' Frank's voice came tinnily down the line. 'Girl . . . I should be angry. I asked you not to tell anyone. But the fact is . . . Hey!'

'The fact is,' Judy's merry tones took over, 'he's frightfully glad I'm here. What's more, dear, he can't understand how you ever got the idea you were related to Philip Farcroft.' Frank said something in the background. 'Well, *you* tell her, then,' she answered.

My uncle's voice again: 'Kate, dear girl . . . whatever made you think—'

'*You* did, among others!' I exclaimed. 'I told you about it. You didn't deny it.'

'I didn't realize you meant Michael Farcroft!'

'Then what on earth *did* you think?'

'I thought you'd got wind of the rumour about that young chap in Cumberland – Harry overheard the parents talking about that. Next thing we knew, Clara was married to old man Brand and having you. Oh, she did get into hot water for visiting the farm, but that was earlier – the year I went to Winchester. I remember it clearly: eighteen ninety-one. I'd be twelve, going on thirteen.

'When I arrived home for the vacation, Clara was already gone off to stay with the aunts. There was an awful atmosphere in the house, Father pot-faced and Mother ill – she'd had the twins the previous January, and there was all that bother over poor Tom. The servants were whispering, the villagers looked askance. Harry and I knew it had something to do with the Farcrofts. We spent the summer playing spies, watching the farm, being chased off by the old troll. Kate . . . I blame myself. I've messed up your life. I only wish I'd stepped in before, but I had other things on my mind. I didn't understand about Philip. I thought you'd ended it of your own choice.'

'Don't blame yourself, Uncle Frank,' I broke in. 'You've told me all I needed to know.'

All I needed to know was that he and Judy were happy, and that, some day, I might stand beside Philip and announce our love to the world with equal joy. I didn't think any further than that.

I remember that evening clearly, going to meet Philip by byways and back lanes, hiding my motorbike behind a hedge, walking the last half-mile. Our rendezvous was, ironically, a hay loft, above a barn on the edge of a wood. By the time I arrived, the full moon stared down on a world turned extra silver by frost. A flick of a torch told me Philip was waiting, and moments later his arms reached for me.

As soon as I had breath to speak, the story spilled out of me: 'I've spoken to Uncle Frank. Philip, he said . . .'

'Didn't I tell you?' he answered. 'Katie, darling, I knew it. We couldn't feel the way we do if it wasn't meant to be.'

We held each other, laughing and kissing as we fumbled, numb-fingered, at buttons and laces, shivering with both cold and anticipation, coming together in a fever of impatience. Where Oliver made love with cool control, Philip was all fire and passion, his eagerness for me better than any aphrodisiac. Soon we were both warm, lying together under a blanket in a nest of hay, replete and comfortable, while he told me about his day.

He'd flown over Far Drove, practising taking pictures of the land beneath his wings. He'd seen his father rush out, first shaking his fist and then standing astounded when the pilot of the noisy machine waved and called to him. The memory made him laugh, the sound reverberating in the warm chest beneath my cheek. 'I went over Denes Hill, too. They all came on to the terrace and waved. I didn't see you, though.'

'I've been in Lynn all day. The munitions workers are threatening to strike. Some of my girls are ill. TNT is dangerous stuff.'

'We need it.'

Knowing that we would never agree on that subject, I burrowed close to him. 'I'm so sick of all the killing. When is it going to end?'

'When we've won, darling. We can't stop until we've won. By the way . . . I got my orders today.'

I held on to him, my heart suddenly thunderous. 'When?'

'The twenty-ninth. France.'

France. The Somme. That great slaughter was still going on. I had seen the feature film they had made during its early months. Hideous images, the worse for being silent. 'I see,' was all I said, but every nerve in my body became aware of him, drinking in the way he felt against me, smooth warm flesh over taut muscle, scar tissue on his chest, slight roughness of body hair, memorizing every curve, every line, so that when he was far away I could lie alone and remember . . .

'I'll carry your charm with me everywhere,' he said.

'Charm?'

'The little aeroplane you gave me, remember? I wear it behind my lapel. Where's my jacket? Yes, here – feel it?'

I had all but forgotten the silver aeroplane, the lapel pin I had bought for Carl-Heinz and then given to Philip, in the church that day. So very long ago. What children we had been.

'It's kept me safe so far,' Philip said. 'No reason it shouldn't continue to do so. Please don't worry, sweetheart. I don't. All that ever worried me was losing you.'

I clung to him, letting my nails dig into him until he protested. I wanted to hurt him, because he sounded so complacent. He didn't have to worry about losing me. But *I* worried desperately about losing him. It was right what women said – being left behind, to live every moment in uncertainty and fear, sometimes felt like the worst of the bargain.

'I'll come with you,' I decided. 'Yes, I will. I'll be a driver – I'm a good driver. Or a dispatch rider. I will, Philip. I can't let you go alone. If I could just be somewhere near you—'

'Shut up,' he whispered against my mouth, and silenced me with loving.

My plan to volunteer for France was madness, of course. Even had I been able to persuade the authorities to let me go without my husband's permission, they would have sent me home the moment they realized my condition – I was pregnant. I had wanted to tell Philip about it, but I needed to be sure it wasn't a false alarm because if I was having a child it would change everything. Had I the right to burden Philip with added worries just before he went to France? I wasn't even sure whose child it was – in my bones I felt it was his, but that could have been wishful thinking. Perhaps Oliver's efforts had borne fruit at last. Until the baby came, how could I know? Even then, I might not be sure. Was my own child to be saddled with the same kind of uncertainty that had tormented me?

Waking early, disturbed by my thoughts, I dressed and went out for a walk in the crisp, frosted dawn. I might have gone round through the gardens to the woods, except that I saw Keith Rawson wandering there, so I took another path and came to the front drive in time to meet the postman on his bike.

'Morning, Mrs Wells,' he greeted me. 'Fine morning.

They say this cold spell's going to break today. Good for the sprouts, though. Helps 'em set. Here's some letters for you, ma'am. This one's all the way from Switzerland, see?'

'Switzerland? Good heavens, who ... Thank you.' Not recognizing the writing on the envelope, I turned away, tearing it open, taking out the pages inside. They bore a different hand from the envelope: Mother's writing – she had smuggled the letter out via friends, it seemed.

She wrote confirming what she had told Uncle Frank, adding many long-winded explanations and excuses. Most telling of all, she didn't even mention the Farcrofts.

The young man in Cumbria had been a friend only – the rest was a figment of the aunts' fevered imagination, fuelled by their old-maidish horror at the stories they had heard of her misdemeanours at home: '*If I so much as glanced at a man, they had a fit of the vapours. I might as well have been in prison. Brand offered me an escape route. I was fond of him. And, as he himself said, I could look forward to being a rich widow, free to do as I pleased. My dear Kate, I assure you, you are William Brand's child. If you need further proof, you have only to wait for two more years.*

'*Your father feared fortune-hunters, but since you are safely married to Oliver there is no more need for secrecy. I think I may tell you that, when you are twenty-five, you will inherit quite a substantial fortune. I had use of the interest until I remarried, since when it has been accruing nicely, thanks to Oliver's good management. He came to Berlin that time to discuss investment changes. Among other things, he has acquired large holdings in Thorne-Thomas for you. My father appears to have become lax in his old age. Had it not been for Oliver, control of the works might have gone out of the family. I recommend you continue to rely on your husband's advice.*'

She went on at length, about her deprivations because of the war, and about the boys – Rudger and Pieter were both away at school, leaving her only Hansi, who was now six. Pa kept busy in Berlin; Fritzi was on the Crown Prince's staff; Willi von Sturm, having been decorated for bravery, languished in a prison camp in France, and Carl-Heinz had been reported missing, believed killed, at Verdun. As for my friend Gudrun Thunissen, she was becoming famous as a newspaperwoman, with a rare insight into the British way of thinking.

She enclosed a cutting from the daily paper, which proved that my dear friend Gudrun was plagiarizing the articles I had sent her before the war. At that point, I pushed the papers back into the envelope and walked blindly on with my mind in turmoil. '*A substantial fortune . . . when you are twenty-five . . . thanks to Oliver's good management . . .*'

Had Oliver known about my inheritance all this time? Was that why he had chosen to marry me, rather than Vicky? Oh, surely . . .

'I say, Mrs W!' The voice made me jump. Major Rawson had materialized in front of me on the woodland path. 'You all right?'

'You startled me!' I snapped at him, and was sorry for it when he looked like a whipped puppy. 'Forgive me, I didn't mean . . . I've had some rather disturbing news.'

He glanced at the letters in my hand. 'Ah. Yes. Sorry. Me, too. Going home soon. My parents, you know.'

'Yes, I had heard. They'll be glad to have you back.'

Around us, the woods seemed to shift and crack. The ice was giving, the trees beginning to drip, a mist gathering among the trees.

'Come with me,' he said urgently, his hand on my wrist. 'You're not safe here. Saw him. Saw him with the girl.

Miss L. Sweet girl. Saw him hurt her. In the garden.'

'Please, Major.' The hand on my wrist withdrew at once. 'You saw who?' But I knew who – he had seen Oliver threaten Judy.

'That bastard,' he said. 'Saw him. With the girl. *He* knows. Ask him.' A nod of his head indicated the wood behind me, where a figure stood in the shade of the trees. Dark and indistinct though he was, I saw his face clearly, saw him watching me with a steady intensity. John . . . '*He* knows,' Keith Rawson said again. 'He watches you. Same as I do. Anxious for you. Rum cove, though. There one minute, gone the next. Know him?'

I managed a smile. 'Yes, I do. He's my guardian angel. Major Rawson, will you lend me your arm? It must be nearly breakfast time.'

Somehow, I got through the morning, though I don't recall exactly where my work took me. A mild front had driven the frost away. In the countryside a distant mist enhanced a mellow, golden day, but round the coast a sea fret swirled and clung, lapping half a mile inland. It made driving difficult, so I avoided the coast road until, finding myself near Denes Hill soon after one o'clock, I decided to go home for lunch. The mist covered the hilltop, forcing me to drive slowly as I made round the outhouses and into the yard where, to my surprise, I saw Oliver's car parked.

Did I want to see my husband? Whatever our differences, I had never taken him for a calculating liar, but he had lied about his reasons for caring for me; he had lied about Judy. How could I trust anything he said? Had I too been blinded by good looks and surface charm, in common with all the other women of the family? Frank knew better; so had Harry; Tom disliked Oliver instinctively. Even John, from beyond . . . Of course! The warnings had been about Oliver, not Philip!

Illusions gone, I felt momentarily adrift. Then anger came, hardening my resolve. I would hire a private detective, to have Oliver followed, collect evidence for a divorce: dishonesty, unfaithfulness, deception, greed . . . Grounds enough for any judge. Philip needn't be involved at all, thank God. Yes, this was my way out! When it was all over, Philip and I could be married without fear of gossip or reprisals.

On the steps by the side door, I stopped as other pieces fell into place: Oliver had known all along that I was not Michael Farcroft's child. Like Frank, he must have been aware of the two-year gap. Even if it had escaped him, then surely Grandmother would have . . . Fool, Kate! When Oliver told Grandmother about my misunderstanding, she must have agreed to continue the deception. How could Lady Rhys-Thomas allow her only granddaughter – her heiress granddaughter, with large holdings in Thorne-Thomas – to throw herself away on a hated Farcroft? In order to prevent such a disaster, she had colluded with Oliver to mislead me. No wonder he had been so eager to seduce and marry me before I found out the truth. No wonder he had been anxious when he discovered I had talked to Jack Farcroft about it – he had feared the old man might reveal the truth. Oh . . . so many things now rhymed and chimed.

Mentally chilled, physically depleted, I climbed the back stairs and made for the tower.

A flurry of activity in Grandmother's private apartments drew me to the door, from where I heard Oliver issuing instructions and saw one of the kitchen staff wielding a carpet sweeper while another bent by the grate, cleaning it out. Someone else moved in the bedroom beyond – I could hear a brush knocking; then Oliver appeared in the doorway, stripped to his shirtsleeves – most unusual for him.

'Kate! Thank goodness you've come. Your grandmother's coming home. Today! Didn't you see the letter? For heaven's sake – you left it on the dressing table. Why didn't you read it? I expected more notice than this. She forgets we no longer have the staff. It's fortunate I came home early. Can you do Tom's room? Or perhaps the beds – yes, do the beds.'

Infected by his impatience, I obediently hurried to the warm linen room. I'd seldom seen Oliver in such a mood of haste. But, having left him in charge, Grandmother would expect to find everything just so when she returned. Personally, I didn't much care whether we were ready for her or not. Perhaps she should see Oliver less than perfect, for once.

'There's no coal,' one of the girls was saying as I returned laden with a pile of sheets and blankets over which I could hardly see.

'Well, go and get some,' Oliver ordered.

'That en't my place to carry coal! Shouldn't even be doing grates. And Phyllis there have a bad back.'

Furious, Oliver gave her a tight-lipped glare, blew loudly down his nose and swept up the coal bucket, striding past me to the door. 'Keep them at it,' he said as he passed me. 'Good God, we've given up most of the house for them, can't they co-operate with us once in a while?'

'That en't my place—' the girl appealed to me.

'I know,' I said, edging by her towards the bedroom.

'I'm paid to cook food, not skivvy,' the complaint followed me.

In the bedroom, a girl no more than fifteen was examining one of the crystal-hung candlesticks. She jumped as I pushed open the door, and the candlestick leapt from her hand and smashed on the hearth. I didn't say anything, but my expression made her burst into tears and rush past me.

Hugging the pile of bedding, I stared at the bed – red silk hangings let loose from tasselled cords, thin blanket laid across the feather mattress. In this room my grandfather had died, cursing me because he had thought I was his oldest child. In this room, too, my husband had tried to make ungentle love to me. Now I understood why he had wanted to move into the master suite – he would have enjoyed claiming his marital rights over me, here in this bed, symbolically violating the very heart of Rhys-Thomas territory, like some wild Viking invader, raping and pillaging . . .

Sickened, I dumped the pile of bedding on the bed and as it sprawled untidily I heard an aeroplane overhead. I rushed to the window, but outside the mist clung close, a blank grey wall of nothing. It made me feel shut in, as if I were suffocating. Needing air, I ran out of the private apartments and climbed to the sanctum, where blessed sunlight flowed through the windows. A sky of pure October blue smiled down on a carpet of blazing white, like snow, but piled in amazing, changing shapes. The rest of the house was buried in that whiteness. Only the sanctum lifted into the light. Like my life, darkened by shadows, with Philip the only brightness.

I could still hear the aeroplane, coming close again. I flung open the window, leaning out, seeing the double-winged shape of it come out of the sun. Though I couldn't see the pilot clearly for the light in my eyes, my heart said it was Philip, and if not Philip then one of his friends. He wasn't far away. I would see him later. I needed to see him, to tell him . . . *I love you. Oh, I love you!* I waved, and the machine waggled its wings in greeting as it zoomed by, only yards away, sweeping me with its noise and its draught as it lifted up into the blue and went on its way, the engine's drone fading. Philip. Oh, Philip . . .

Suddenly dejected, I sank down on the window seat, head in hands. Did I have the strength for what lay ahead? Before I could be with my love, I had to deal with my husband.

The door at the foot of the stairs opened. 'Kate?' Oliver called, and his head appeared behind the wooden rail that guarded the stairs as he came up to join me. He had a streak of coal-dust across his shirt. Dishevelled, he looked oddly vulnerable. But his dark eyes snapped at me and the line of his moustache pulled tight across his lip. 'I thought you were going to help with the beds. What's wrong with you today? Aren't you feeling well? Why aren't you working?'

'I am,' I said. 'I just called in to have lunch. Not that I'm very hungry.' How easy it would have been to leave it at that. This was not the right time for arguments, but . . . 'Since you ask – no, I'm not feeling well. Grandmother's wasn't the only letter to come this morning. There was another one – from Mother.'

I saw his surprise, and his sudden wariness, before he smoothed his expression, guarded his eyes, assumed the lawyer's detached demeanour. 'Why has that upset you? Is it bad news?'

'No, all's well with her and the boys, thank God. But I knew that. Frank told me.' I stood up, feeling stronger on my feet. 'He came here a few weeks ago. He'd been to Germany – to the eastern front. He's not quite the effete weakling you seem to think him!'

His eyebrow twitched. 'I?'

'Yes, you!' I turned away, wishing I could contain my feelings the way he did, but I couldn't: I was bitterly angry, hating him. Wrapping my arms round my shoulders, I stared out at the brilliant white mist lapping the bottom of the open window. 'You hoped he'd never come back, didn't you? You'd love to be the only man in the family, apart from poor Tom, who doesn't count. You must have thought you'd won. You even thought you could move into the master suite.'

'What are you saying, Kate? My dear—'

'Don't.' I swung round to face him. Oh, how I detested his ability to show nothing of his feelings! I flung out my hands, crying, 'I can't go on like this, Oliver! You never loved me. You only wanted me because of who I am. And the money, of course. My father's legacy. Yes, Mother told me about that: "We don't need to worry about fortune-hunters now you're married to Oliver." What a joke! You're the biggest fortune-hunter of all. Not only the money, but all of this . . .' My gesture encompassed the house and everything it represented.

'Is that what you believe?'

'Will you deny it?'

He hesitated, then said, 'Has it not occurred to you that I might have good reason for feeling entitled to a share in,' his gesture mimicked mine, ' "all of this"? I'm a Thorne, too, by blood.'

'*You* are?' I flung a hand to my head, not believing a word he said.

'George Thorne, your great-grandfather's partner, was *my* natural grandfather,' he said. 'Which means his daughter, your grandmother, is my great-aunt. What does that make us, Kate – second cousins three times removed?'

How could he joke about it? 'It certainly makes us more closely related than Philip Farcroft and I ever were!'

Oliver had the grace to wince. 'That was a necessary lie,

I'm afraid. Your grandmother thought so, too. Couldn't have you marrying a Farcroft, could we? No. Better to keep it in the family, even if I *am* from the wrong side of the blanket.'

'Are you trying to say that Grandmother knows you're . . .'

'That I'm family? She has known it for longer than I have.' His tone sharpened into bitterness. 'I only learned about it seventeen years ago, when my grandfather was mentioned in George Thorne's will, as his natural son. Acknowledged, after seventy years, with a pocket watch and a small pension – which he enjoyed for just a year before he died. One year, Kate.

'It's for *his* sake I had to redress the balance. I was the only one left to do it. All at once I understood why your grandparents had always been so nice to my family – condescending because of George Thorne's conscience. They gave my father work, and allowed *me* to share their social activities. How very gracious of them!

'Can you blame me for taking advantage of their guilt? They haven't lost by it. I'm good at what I do. I've protected their interests over the years. Latterly, when your grandfather was losing his grip, I began to buy into the business, for myself when I could afford it, at other times for you. Between us, we now own a controlling share in Thorne-Thomas. And,' he added, coming slowly towards me, 'I don't intend to give up the ground that fate has given to me. I hope you're not implying that you want a divorce, Kate, because I shall never let you go. Try it and I'll fight you every inch of the way. I'm a lawyer. I'll win.'

Trying to get away from him, I sat down on the window seat, eyes aching from the brightness of sunlight on mist. Behind that blur, he was a huge, menacing figure, coming for me with hands out. Mist . . . clouds blurring my sight . . . a seagull squawking . . . or was it a voice, calling my name?

Memory came rushing like a tide, sweeping me back to childhood, to that day when the sea fret had caught me alone in the shallows and I had heard Uncle John call, and gone to find him, wading well above my waist. And seen him, in the water where the channel ran deep, struggling with another man. John shouting, choking, gone . . . 'Uncle John!' my small voice screamed. I tried to reach him. The sand fell away under my feet, left me floundering out of my depth. And another man rose from the sea, grabbed me. I'm safe, I thought, and then the water closed over my head and strong hands held me down. Roaring in my ears and blackness . . . Then my lungs dragged at air, choking, spluttering. 'Katie, darling!' Mother cried. 'Oh, Oliver, you saved her! You saved her!'

'But I had to let John go,' he had answered. 'It was her or him. Clara, I'm sorry.'

Of course! That was how it had been. John had been in trouble with cramps and Oliver had gone swimming out to him. But, instead of helping, he had held my uncle under the water. He would have drowned me, too, the only witness. But Mother had come in time, and after that . . . after that, kindly shock had stepped in and erased the terrible memory from my mind, except in nightmares that had terrified me for years.

The vision faded, leaving me unbreathing, head and heart thudding, staring up at the man who was now my husband. 'You killed John!'

'Kate . . .'

'I saw you. I *saw* you! All those nightmares . . . Because of you! That's what John has been trying to tell me all this time, ever since I came back to Denes Hill.'

'John?' His eyes narrowed as he reached for me. 'You're hysterical.'

I fended off his hands, shuddering. 'I saw you, Oliver. You tried to kill me, too, but Mother came. She turned you into a hero. Everyone thought you'd tried to save John, but— Oh, God . . .'

I remembered Saffron, weeping. '*I shall never forgive Oliver Wells. He killed Harry as surely as if he'd stabbed him.*' And Tom: '*I hate him. He likes to hurt.*' They had known instinctively that Oliver was not to be trusted. So had Harry, and Frank. Why hadn't I listened?

His hands fastened on me, shaking me. 'Listen to me, Kate! I didn't intend to hurt John. But he panicked. He lashed out at me, and I lost my temper. He'd been bloody to Clara that day. She told me she wished him dead. She often said she hated him. Before I knew what I was doing . . . You must believe me, Kate. I did it for Clara. In a moment of madness. I didn't intend to hurt him. Or you.'

'You did! You would have killed me, too, if Mother hadn't come.'

'Don't say that!' His face was almost black with fury, as it had been that day, murderous rage blotting out his rational self. 'Don't say that!' Strong hands reached for my throat.

I clawed at them, choking, 'You can't! Oliver, I'm having a child. Your child, Oliver!'

The pressure on my windpipe eased, letting me snatch a breath as he hesitated. In the same moment, a cry from behind made him start to turn. A howling figure launched itself at him, a fist raised with some weapon that caught Oliver across the temple. It made him reel, but as his assailant hit again he threw up his arm, deflecting the blow, coming up under it to charge with all his weight, sending the other man flying. He fell over a footstool, sprawled to the floor, sent the chess set flying . . .

It was Tom! Tom! Scarlet with fear and fury, wailing like a banshee, he lifted his arms to protect his head as Oliver snatched up the footstool, raising it— I launched myself at him. My shoulder caught him in the side, sent him off-balance. He crashed into the slender wooden rail that guarded the stairs. It cracked under his weight, split away from the wall. With a howl of fear, Oliver fell into the stairwell.

Silence.

'Is he dead?' Tom asked.

'Oh, Tom!' Trembling, I stood at the top of the stairs, rubbing my arms helplessly as I stared down at my husband's body. He was horribly still, his head at an impossible angle. 'Oh, Tom!'

'I didn't mean it,' he wept. 'He was hurting you.'

'Yes, he was. You saved me. Oh . . . don't cry, please! You didn't do it. I did. I pushed him down the stairs.'

'No. It was me,' he said, and showed me what he had in his hand – what he had used as a weapon to hit Oliver. It was the ivory king from the chess set. There was blood on its crown.

I found Grandmother with Anderson in the small sitting room, both of them wondering why the place was in such chaos. Grandmother was tired, seeming very old and frail that day. How could I hate her for her part in deceiving me? She had done what she thought best for her family, and she too had been manipulated by Oliver. I found room for pity in my heart, but I knew I should never quite forgive her for what she had done to Philip and me.

There had been an accident, I told them, feeling deadly calm. Would they please telephone to the doctor, and to the police? 'It's Oliver. He fell down the stairs. I think he's dead.'

The next few hours are a blur. I remember only feeling claustrophobic, fighting a desperate urge to get away. When the chance came, I simply walked out by the side door, intending to take a short, calming stroll in the garden. But the mist still clung thickly on the hilltop, filling the yards, making it hard to breathe.

My motorbike waited, offering escape from the shadows of the gloomy, fog-shrouded house. So I kicked the motor into life and set off, going I knew not where.

Within half a mile the mist began to thin. It parted ahead of me and I rode out into golden sunlight, finding myself on a familiar road. Now I knew where I was going. This lane led to Sedgeford. To Philip. If I could see him, just for a few minutes, I knew I would feel able to go back and face what had to be faced.

I heard the aeroplane before I saw it, coming in from the sea, trailing a plume of smoke from its engine like a black smudge against the sky. It looked like the one I had seen over Denes Hill earlier. I stopped to watch, straddled on the bike, my heart unsteady and my mouth dry. Was Philip the pilot?

I could hear the motor misfiring, stuttering. Oh, let him be safe. Let him be safe! I can't lose him now! The aeroplane seemed to lurch as it dipped and rose again, straining to maintain height, to reach the hilltop airstrip. It looked like a wounded bird, fighting valiantly to hold the air. I held my breath, fighting with the pilot, sensing how hard he was trying to bring the machine safely in. It must have been damaged. Had it been in a fight? Was Philip injured, too? Hang on, darling! Hang on!

The engine stopped. The aeroplane seemed to glide

briefly, then pause and hang. In shattering silence and slow, slow motion, its nose lifted, one wing dipped. It tipped over, started to fall, twisting in the air. Choking back nausea, I remembered the silver lapel pin, twisting between my fingers in just that way, that day in the church when Philip and I first talked. A premonition? Had I known then how our story would end?

I didn't see the crash. The aircraft dived behind a stand of shimmering golden beech trees. But I heard the sound as it hit, and saw smoke belch above the trees.

No!

Not Philip. Not Philip! Please God . . .

Sick with terror, I was about to let in my clutch when I saw Philip running towards me along the lane. Thank God! Oh, thank God! He was safe. Safe! I let the bike fall and went to meet him, throwing my arms round him, holding him with all my strength. 'Philip! Darling, I had to come. I needed you. Oliver . . .' I don't remember what I said. It poured out of me incoherently. And Philip soothed me, held me, stroked me, kissed me, told me it was all right.

'It's not all right.' I shuddered in his arms, my head ducked under his chin as I hung on to him. 'But it will be. One day.' No tomorrows, he had said. Only this moment.

I let myself savour his nearness, enjoying it to the full while it lasted. Bad times lay ahead, but beyond them, perhaps . . . 'I'm going to have a baby, Philip. It's your baby. I know it is.'

'Yes, darling.' He sounded sure of it. He sounded calm and infinitely peaceful, and when I looked up I saw him smiling down at me. 'I love you, Kate,' he said. 'But I have to go on ahead, sweetheart. I'm sorry, but I can't stay now. I'll see you . . .'

He was on duty, he meant. He would see me at the airstrip

shortly. I let him go, hauled the bike upright, and climbed aboard, looking back to say goodbye . . . Behind me, and ahead, the lane stretched. Empty.

I think I knew then, but I didn't want to believe.

By the time I reached the airstrip, a little knot of people had gathered by the crumpled biplane, helplessly watching it burn. Such a small, frail thing it looked, flames gulping at its puny, mangled skeleton.

As we later learned, it had joined two other aeroplanes in an action against a Zeppelin, over the Wash. In the fight, its navigator had been killed by rifle fire, its pilot wounded, its engine damaged.

They said Philip had probably been dead before he hit the ground. He wouldn't have known much about it.

This time, dear Maggie, the shadows won. In this life they always do, sooner or later, for this earth is the clouded land and none of us escapes its final darkness. But our heritage is the light, which awaits beyond.

Almost eighty years have passed since Philip 'went on ahead', not long in terms of eternity, but for me it has stretched too far. I have tried to use the time wisely – writing, involving myself in local politics, enjoying my family. Passing time, only waiting.

Naturally, I told them I had killed Oliver – after all it was I who pushed him – but if you consult the archives you'll see that the official verdict was 'misadventure'. All the same, they put poor Tom away in an institution, for he insisted that he had struck the fatal blow. He was happy enough, I suppose; he even started to breed birds again, until he died in the 'flu epidemic of 1918, which killed more people than the war had done. So much death. So much futile waste. How can anyone believe this bitter world is all there is?

My grandmother, Violet Rhys-Thomas, lived on to be eighty-three. She became very fond of the ex-dancer whose arrival as Frank's wife scandalized her at first. But Judy produced four fine grandchildren and so redeemed herself. She made a merry mistress for the old place.

Vicky's husband remained in the army. They lived mostly

in India. Aunt Saffron remarried and also moved away, with young Eddy. Over the years, we lost touch.

I stayed at Denes Hill until after my son was born. My son, the green-eyed boy with nut-brown curls, who became your father. Philip's son, of course, as everyone knows. I could not let the world believe I had borne a child by the sad, flawed man I married. When your father was a few months old, we moved to the farm, to be with Jack Farcroft, and I wore the Farcroft sapphire with pride. Oh, folk gossiped, for a while, as folk will. But the boy brought comfort to his grandfather, and he loved the farm, and finally brought an end to the old feud. The old man left the farm to him, and it was there he took his bride, and saw his daughter born – you, Maggie. You, in turn, will wear the sapphire after I'm gone. Pass it on to your daughter, or to your son's wife.

All this time, Philip has never been far away. I haven't seen him clearly – all my ghosts fled on that last day – but I've felt him there on the other side of silences, breathing behind draughts of air and sudden gleams of sunlight. And his picture has kept me company, smiling from above the hearth. I know he is proud of his son, and of you, Maggie. One day soon, I shall tell him all about you, face to face. With love,

Grandee

My father still farms the broad acres of Far Drove. My husband works with him, and our son has just left agricultural college. So the Farcroft family tradition will continue. At Denes Hill, Frank Rhys-Thomas's son runs art courses and birdwatching weekends. But Grandee, my grandmother, Catherine Louise Brand, Katarin von Wurthe, Kate Wells, or her pen-name, by which she was more commonly known, Kate Farcroft, has now 'gone on ahead', to rejoin all those people of whom she wrote in her story.

Yesterday, I carried out her last wishes and scattered her ashes in the woods, at the place where the boundaries of Far Drove meet those of Denes Hill. It was a gentle evening, soft after rain, golden with late sunlight slanting through the trees. As the last trace of dust spilled from the container, I looked up and saw, watching me, a tall young man in uniform. I knew him at once. His portrait, painted by Frank Rhys-Thomas from a photograph, hangs over the hearth at Far Drove. It has hung there as long as I remember, beside the portrait of my grandmother as a young woman.

Nor was he alone in the sunlit wood. By his side stood a slender young woman with dark hair and pale, luminous eyes. Both of them were smiling as they waved to me. Then, hand in hand, they strolled away, into the bright evening haze.

Maggie C. Mapleby (nee Farcroft)
Far Drove Farm
Eveningham
KING'S LYNN
Norfolk

HARRY BOWLING

Backstreet Child

The new Cockney saga from
the bestselling author of
THE GIRL FROM
COTTON LANE

Carrie Tanner's transport business in Salmon Lane is prospering by 1939 and she has earned the grudging respect of her business rivals, even the Galloways, father and son, who have played such a fateful role in the Tanner family's fortunes. The years have been kind to Carrie and her deep love for Joe Maitland has helped him through the darkest times of prison and his alcoholism. But the scars she bears from the long-running feud with the Galloway family are deepened by her daughter Rachel's blossoming love for Geoffrey Galloway's illegitimate son.

Personal feuds though are overshadowed by the outbreak of the Second World War, which brings the terrors of the Blitz to the Tanners' neighbours: enterprising Maurice Salter, and his three daughters; publican Terry Gordon with his guilty secret and his wife Pat, who has had her eye on Billy Sullivan since his wife and children were evacuated; Josiah Dawson, out from the Moor, and his wife, long-suffering Dolly, and simple son, Wallace.

Drawing on all their reserves of courage and humour the close-knit community is determined to survive the difficulties of poverty, rationing and nightly air raids. Even as, one by one, the men are called up, go missing in action or are killed, and homes are bombed, their extraordinary spirit shines through.

Don't miss Harry Bowling's previous Cockney sagas, THE GIRL FROM COTTON LANE, GASLIGHT IN PAGE STREET, PARAGON PLACE, IRONMONGER'S DAUGHTER, TUPPENCE TO TOOLEY STREET and CONNER STREET'S WAR, also available from Headline.

FICTION/GENERAL   0 7472 4180 5